THE SCOURGE
OF FAERIE

Sam Artisan

For everyone who read the last book. If you hadn't enjoyed A PLAGUE ON NECROMANCY, I wouldn't have written THE SCOURGE OF FAERIE, so all of this is, quite literally, for you.

CONTENTS

PROLOGUE: LONDON, 1705

Lord Fabian stood at his window, the moonlight filtering through the ten foot stretch of crystalline glass and bathing him in hues of blue, silver and palest white. It glittered on the furs about his shoulders. It twinkled in the silver of his rings and necklaces, in his long hair and gilded robes. It danced in the gems, lifeblood-red, encircling his thin neck. There the pale light twisted, spilling out a crimson gleam of a far more corrupted source than the one hovering in the peaceful sky on the other side of the glass.

If he closed his eyes, he could see it still – the red shine of stones exposed in wounded earth, corpses sprawled amongst flowers that blossomed hungrily, ready to devour their bounty of nutrients.

Well, no, that was a fantasy. In truth, when he closed his eyes, he only saw more clearly: saw through *their* eyes, faded, clouded and rotten as they were.

He stood guard at a gateway, spear in one boney hand, shield on the other, watching the few travelers hurry past his empty gaze with bowed heads and quaking shoulders.

He scurried along a wall, his whiskers twitching as he searched for the very best place to burrow, waiting to overhear the plotting of the noblemen on the other side.

He lay on the ground, dead to all appearances, listening as the laughing youths poked his corpse body with a sword and bragged to each other that perhaps Lord Fabian was not so perfect after all. Heh...he sent his will to that corpse, and it lunged up with a roar, grabbing the sword and sending the youth and his friends shrieking and scattering.

Yes. Let them learn. Fear was a good teacher.

The corpse shambled to its feet, and slowly made its way after them.

Not as good a teacher as pain, though. He should know, he thought with a grin as he turned away from the window and towards the table by his bed. He'd been a fast learner himself.

Hunger gnawed at his insides; the magic, his ever present pet, demanding to be fed. He considered a bowl of fresh fruit, replenished every three hours by his servants, and chose a shiny red apple from amongst the plump bounty. The crunch of tight skin and firm flesh between his teeth never failed to please him, even after all these years.

A knock sounded on his door, four and then three. He paused with his bite half taken, and lowered his eyelids with a throaty purr. That was Ruphy's knock. Interesting...

He tore his mouthful free, and closed his eyes, switching to the viewpoint of the serpent coiled on the frame just above his door. Yes, that was Ruphys' cloak, with the hood pulled up. His servant's forked tongue could taste his familiar sweet scent in the air. Feeling shy tonight, was he? How amusing.

As if everyone in the place didn't know how special Ruphy's particular position was, in Fabian's...ah... roster.

Fabian swallowed his juicy morsel, setting aside the apple as a second, warmer hunger displaced the first one, making his blood heat and churn. He remained facing his desk and called, "Enter. And I thought *my* appetite was insatiable, dear one, we already had a lovely morning together~"

The door creaked open, and he turned his greedy, feral smile to welcome his most beloved captain of the guard.

Two things happened at once.

One - some horrible silver creature ripped his serpentine servant off the doorframe, destroying it with a chomp of sharp teeth.

Two - a horrible silver dagger flashed across the room and buried itself in Fabian's thin chest.

Pain blossomed in his core like the cruelest of thorned roses.

No!

He staggered back, knocking the table askew and spilling the fruit to the floor. A voice in his mind shouted, 'I have done so much! I have come so far!' but he made no noise, only gripped the blade in his chest with a shaking, slender hand. He coughed, blood spraying from his lips, staining the glittering embroidery of his robes. He stared up at the figure stalking toward him in Ruphy's cloak - and it was not Ruphy's pale, red-trimmed face that looked back at him. It was a dark face, with black, coiled hair, and eyes glowing softly silver.

Silver like the dagger, sunk in so deeply, making his breath wheeze and his vision darken. Silver like the beast, slipping in behind the stranger, hunting through the room and sniffing out, crunching down, Fabian's other hidden servants. He could feel their bonds snapping from him, one by one. But he had others...others to call...others to warn...

He closed his eyes, sending them all commands. *Run to me. Do not let the intruder escape. Run to me.*

So many of them did not respond. Someone had been

severing the bonds, someone had been helping...someone... had planned this very, very carefully.

"Funny."

Fabian opened his eyes, looking up at the speaker who appeared to be no more than a shadow in the moonlight.

"They told me you'd be more of a challenge."

Fabian laughed. His undead wolves howled in the hall, claws scraping on stone to reach him. Too late - a wolf of silver, huge and ghostly, howled in return. It charged from Fabian's room and barred the way, launching at the approaching undead, filling the hall with battle so nobody could come to his aid.

Where was Ruphys?

A last vision from a servant flashed across his gaze before his thread of control was broken by blood loss. His beloved captain of the guard, lying still on the stones under the stairwell.

"Who else have you killed?" Fabian hissed, making no move to stand. At the corner of his vision, something gleamed a different shade of red. The apple with the bite in it! It had fallen bite side down, it hadn't rolled. It was right by his hand.

The dark figure tilted his head, staring down at Fabian's pathetic thin form. "Even now you pretend you aren't a monster. I killed no humans, abomination. Only you."

The commotion in the hallway was atrocious. The wolves' snarls and death cries filled the air. Undead soldiers marched up the other staircase, but slowly, so slowly. Many of them had dropped already, as Fabian's strength faded.

Not yet, Fabian swore as he drew in another wheezing breath. The pain was excruciating, burning his lungs while his fingertips grew cold, but oh, he'd felt it before.

Not yet.

His hand closed on the apple.

"You'll never make it out alive," he rasped. His blood was warm, seeping down his chest with every beat of his heart and pooling on the floor under him. "Not all my servants are dead."

"Slaves, you mean." The dark figure ripped away Ruphy's cloak, staring into Fabian's face with those pale, pale eyes. His skin was like mahogany, his hair kept back from his face in perfect ropes. He wore huntsman's garb, and smelled like pine and musk. "What thinking, feeling man would serve a monster like you?"

"Wrong question," Fabian whispered. He closed his eyes for a moment, gathering his strength and letting his head slump. He waited for the rustle of clothing as the hunter began to stand again, thinking him dead-

-and then he lunged, throwing the apple. It bounced off the startled hunter's face, and he flinched back, raising an arm in confused defense. Fabian was upon him in a flash, his left hand in the hunter's ropey hair, his right drawing the dagger from his own chest. He sliced the hunter's throat clean through with a single, deep stroke.

The man's cry cut off in a spray of blood. He fell heavily, and Fabian laughed, the room spinning around him as he sank to his own knees. "What thinking...feeling man...." he rasped, blood pouring down his front, "...would do something so stupid...as....to assassinate...."

The floor came up to meet him. He heard howling from outside, but it was not the howl of battle, but a howl of grief. Claws skittered on the floor, and something silver flashed past Fabian, to the man now bleeding out before him. But it was far away, so far away...

"...a necromancer."

Fabian's strength left him. He could do nothing but lie with his face on the stone while he lost everything - every connection to his army and servants. Every piece of his plans, shattered into dust. Every sensation of warm, cold, pain; all fading away into the too-familiar blackness.

He had no strength to curse, or to cry. However with the last beats of his heart, he made a silent, soul-searing vow. He swore that he would find which of his wives, his servants, his friends or his foes had ruined everything.

He would find them.

He would not rest until... he... made them pay...

***

London, 1727

Fabian awoke from their nightmare, gasping and sweating.

Someone had to pay!

Fury and terror boiled in their veins. They plunged their hands into the warm blankets, under their pillow, searching.

Where was their knife? Where were the guards? Blood on the floor - they were dying, they-

Ruphys murmured at their side.

Fabian stilled their frantic search, memory returning at last. Of course...the assassination was a lifetime ago. They'd been born again since then, born and grown to new life and strength. Ruphys, sweet, delicious Ruphys, was here with them, sleeping softly in their bed. Even now he stirred, sensing their turmoil, and without even opening his eyes, reached for them.

"S'alright," he murmured in his sleep, patting their knee. "Safe."

Fabian looked at him.

Part of them wanted to agree. How easy it would be to let go of the dream, slip back into the blankets, curl in his strong arms and bask a moment in their present reality.

The other part of them, however, still screamed in agonized fury.

They slipped out of bed, ignoring Ruphy's plea, and pretending as well not to hear the softer breathing from the neighboring, smaller room.

They could still feel it - the pain in their chest, the life fading from their mind, the floor of their bedroom, cold stone, hot blood. The memory was as real and present as the world around them. Perhaps more so than their own pale face,

XII

haunted and wild eyed, staring back at them from their silver-wrought mirror.

They turned away, slipped into their boots, pulled a black robe over their sleep shirt, and shoved their leather plague-mask over their face. The overwhelming scent of pine needles offered little relief.

At the door they paused long enough to fasten their belt around their waist, counting their daggers to be sure.

Six would have to be enough.

Then they were gone, down the hall, out a servant's entrance, and into the night, every beat of their heart trying to drive away the lingering pain of sharp-edged steel.

Vengeance was a heavy burden and a dangerous gamble, but sometimes the necessity outweighed the risk.

Ruphys would just have to forgive them later.

CHAPTER 1: POOR JUDGMENT

Barty Wayman stared at the troubled reflection in his porcelain teacup and wished the downturned mouth and worried eyes of the face within didn't look quite so childish.

"I know what you're thinking," Dr. Peete said to him from across the desk. The director sipped his tea loudly, perhaps as an attempt to fill Barty's silence. "You're upset."

Barty closed his eyes, trying to shut out his mental self image along with the teacup one. Upset didn't even begin to cover it. He was exhausted - physically, mentally and emotionally. He had faced atrocities that would have broken a lesser man. He had battled endlessly against an unflinchingly deadly variant of the black plague, devouring the citizens of London like a rampaging wildfire. He had befriended a necromancer, accepting their aid even when that aid came in the form of walking corpses, half-rotted rats, and the unrestful royalty of ages long past. He'd even faced the very people he was trying to protect - citizens of London doing their best to stop him, not understanding that all he did was for their sake. Not understanding that even as they shot him down, he would still do everything it took to save them.

"Barty," Peete said, half pleading, half tired. "Be reasonable. Times now are not what they were. It's been a year, for goodness sakes!"

This was his thanks. A public that wanted to forget all those hard-won battles. A supervisor that refused to see that the travesty that was not over. A shoulder had healed, eventually, from the bullet wound, but no longer had full range of motion. Barty was lucky he had strength and control enough to perform his duties as a doctor. His mind had, mostly, adjusted to the idea of having the most infamous necromancer in history as a friend one could take afternoon tea with, but he still struggled to accept the mass amounts of death that even a less-lethal plague inflicted upon the population. In Barty's dreams, he wept over the dead. Barty had, and continued to, shed his own blood to contribute to a magical talisman that worked to keep non-infected citizens free of the slightly weakened version of the plague that lingered still, on the fringes of the London population.

All of these things Barty had faced and overcome. On good days, he told himself he'd become a stronger, better man in the process.

On bad days, he just wanted to lie down and let someone else deal with it all.

He didn't have that luxury.

"I'm sorry," he said, setting aside his cup of warm hibiscus tea and looking across the desk at Director Peete. He pushed down his dread, forced a hopeful smile onto his face. "I must have misheard you, sir. Did you just say they're *selling* the talismans?"

Director Peete, Barty knew, was a good man. He had been one of the few doctors in the entire Royal College of Physicians to remain in London as the plague wreaked havoc on the citizenry. His courage and leadership had saved hundreds, if not thousands, of lives through application and enforcement of quarantine protocols as the city collapsed under the weight of disease and neglect.

Peete was a good, reasonable man. Barty knew it. Peete knew it too, which was why he couldn't meet Barty's eye as he sipped his tea and fumbled for words that sounded exactly like the kind of excuse any good, reasonable man would offer when forced to make a choice he knew was wrong.

"Barty, this entire situation has been difficult for everyone. You of all people understand the magnitude of complexity of getting the merchants and the mages to work together to produce the spells with greatest speed."

"Of course I understand," Barty said, masking dread and numbness as patience. He forced more concern into his voice, trying to impress upon his mentor the gravity of the situation, "but there are so many lives at risk, Dr. Peete, and-"

"The more money we have available to pay for resources, the more talismans we can make." Peete stood, walking around his polished desk to the window and gazing out at the busy street. He folded his soft hands across his stomach, the pale flesh of his fingers contrasting with the floral pattern of his waistcoat. "The more talismans we make, the more lives we save. It's not difficult to understand, Dr. Wayman. Look." He pointed out the window.

Barty stood, coaxed his gloved fists to unclench, and walked to stand next to Peete. Dawn had broken not long ago. On the other side of the glass bustled the population of London, busy at their tasks of buying and selling even at this early hour.

A year ago at this time, the streets had lain bare, but for the plague-ridden corpses waiting to be collected, and the rats and crows feasting on carrion.

"There are thousands and thousands of people out there, Dr. Wayman," the director said. His words were proud, devoid of the exhaustion they had carried when Barty had first met him. Gone, too, were the outward signs of despair - the bags had mostly disappeared from under his eyes, his hair, while still thinning, was well trimmed, and he'd put on enough weight to round out the edges of his face. He was, all told, much improved from their first meeting.

However, he still didn't meet Barty's gaze as he spoke, instead watching the citizenry pass by. "Even if money were not the limiting factor, it would simply be impossible to come up with enough amulets for every single person. As you are well aware, each amulet has to be hand-carved with the proper magical runes. Each amulet has to be cut from the same source quarry, to best connect to the root protection spell. And each amulet..." he finally looked at Barty, his blue eyes conveying sympathy, but not sharing Barty's distress, "...can only protect one person."

"Then we should be protecting those who are most at risk!" Barty demanded. Although the streets were crowded now, he could still see the shadow of the recent past hovering over them. Every curb and corner visible from the window had once held a corpse. The air that carried the scents of a fully-functional bakery, fish market and flower shop had only recently shed the smells of disease and rot, of blood and bodily waste.

The heavy, dark wings of death hovered in his mind, even if the people of the recovering city seemed keen to forget them.

He took a calming breath, trying to balance concern with respectable self control. "It is a sign of strength that so many people are now well enough and secure enough to go back to business outside, sir, but the plague is not gone, as you know, for you are the one that assigned me to continue fighting the pockets that remain. People still die, every day, from the same disease that so many think has passed."

He closed his eyes, fighting back the storm of grief and frustration that boiled in his chest. Not a day went by that he did not find a corpse where yesterday had been a patient. "It is worst in the poorest areas. They don't have the support of reliable food and care that the wealthier classes can afford. If a man earns his bread day by day, a day he is home from work means a day he doesn't eat, sir. As myself and Dr. Buckler have emphasized, proper nutrition increase the chances of survival by-"

Peete sighed. "I know, lad. And you have a good heart, for wanting to help them. But-"

Barty's 'good heart' sank. It was always the same. People told him he had a good heart, a soft heart, a bleeding heart, and always followed it up with a 'but.'

Peete continued, "We have to think practically. We have to work within the system if we want to maximize how many people we can help, and how quickly. So that means, Barty..."

Peete turned full away from the window, now. The light streaming in from the glass lit half his face, exaggerating the tired lines and casting the rest in shadow. "...that as much as you don't like it, we need to sell at least some of our inventory to the wealthier folks who don't want to wait. No, it isn't fair, and yes, I know-" he raised a hand to stall the protests in Barty's open mouth, "...I know those well off are less likely to die because they have food and care readily available. But we must be realistic, Dr. Wayman." He patted Barty's slumped shoulder. "We are prioritizing the doctors first, that's something, isn't it? After all, we care for rich and poor alike. If half our stock goes to those willing to pay heavily for it-"

"Half?!" Barty squeaked.

Peete ignored the interruption. "-then we have that much more money to buy stone and pay mages and merchants to do their jobs."

Barty's chest and throat ached. He was trying so hard, but he couldn't keep the shake from his voice. "Surely Her Majesty has granted more than enough for-"

5

Peete raised his eyebrows. "Her Majesty covered the cost of some, but she has an entire country to assist. She is subsidizing everything from seed for farmers, to silk for the tailors." He paused. "Plus, she has to rebuild her own front door."

They carefully did not meet each other's eyes at that. Peete had decided the best way to deal with Barty's possible/definite fraternization with a necromancer was to pretend that it had never happened and treat Barty like he would any new, young doctor. Barty had decided that his best chance at not being jailed or hung for fraternizing with a necromancer would be to follow the director's lead and play the part of the young, new doctor, and so far, it had worked just fine.

"Regardless," Peete said, going back to his desk, sitting in his chair and reaching once more for his teacup, "we need far more money than she has given us, and so we must work with the resources available to us. I know you still yearn for an ideal world, Dr. Wayman, but despite your disappointment, we are doing the best we can with what we have. We don't have the luxury of fairy-tale wishes when we are dealing with cold, uncaring reality."

He picked up his cup and took a sip. Barty remained standing, looking at the toes of his boots and ignoring his cooled tea. He understood what Peete was saying. He didn't argue the logic of it, nor did he deny that they needed the money. The Royal College of Physicians, like every institution in London over the past two years, had suffered devastating losses during the worst of the infection. It was reasonable to do what they could to better support themselves and the people that depended on them. Barty understood that perfectly, in his head.

But his heart cried out in protest, aching for the people too poor to survive even a curable infection of the Black Plague. There were thousands of citizens still living in disease-stricken areas, and only a few handfuls of doctors brave enough to tend them. There simply was not enough help to go around.

And nothing Barty did or said would change that.

The floor swam before him, his eyes filling with hot tears. Director Peete sighed at his desk. After a year of working together, he knew what Barty's stubborn, aching silence meant.

"My suggestion to you, Dr. Wayman," he said, pulling a stack of reports over and draining his teacup, "is that you simply do the best you can with what you've got. Of all of us, you've had the most practice with that, hmm? Take solace in knowing that you are able to help at all." He scanned the top page, already filing Barty away in his mind like yet another piece of already-read paper. "After all, a year ago, not even that was possible."

Right. Because a year ago, Barty hadn't yet shed his blood, sweat and tears, working long hours into the night with the very necromancer the city had tried to hang, fighting to achieve the miracle that the Physician's college, the merchants and the mages were now selling to the highest bidder.

"Thank you, sir," Barty whispered, turning towards the door before Peete could look up and see the wet trickling down his face. "I'll keep that in mind."

He closed the door behind him, then leaned against it, fighting to keep his breath from catching in his throat, and to stifle any humiliating sobs of frustration.

He would do what Peete said. He would do his best with what he had - tend his patients with a smile, with kindness, and with every assurance he could offer and every technique he could minister to ease their suffering.

And then when the day was done, he was going to get himself a drink.

Maybe two drinks.

Maybe however many drinks it took to soak the pain out of his heart and into oblivion, for at least a little while.

He pushed himself away from the door, straightened his coat, and buckled on his beaked mask.

At least with a mask on there was no need to hide his

expression. The last thing he wanted was to let his own fear, exhaustion or depression infect his ill charges.

Just make it through the day, Dr. Wayman, he told himself. *One more day, like all the rest. We've done hundreds of days before, we can do one more.*

He walked away from the Royal College of Physicians, into the warm, busy streets. The crowds parted around him, whispering and wary, but he paid them no mind. He was well used to the fear the general public held of the handful of dark, masked doctors roaming the streets, keeping them safe.

They didn't need to know what it took for them to keep their luxuries of commerce and freedom of movement.

After all, this what was what Barty had fought for: the right of the people to live in freedom and safety.

He would continue to fight, as long as any piece of the battle remained.

Even if some days his arms were tired of wielding that heavy, bloodied sword.

CHAPTER 2: WORKING LATE

Dr. James Buckler stepped into his office, the sun sinking over the sleepy, stinking city of London behind him.

He hung his coat with the others on the rack, set his bag on his oaken desk, and removed matches from the top drawer to light both his lamps. He wanted to work without stopping, and the setting sun meant that the light had already begun to dim in the well-kept room. Once the flames were steady, he turned to run a critical eye over his workspace.

He still wasn't used to being back here, despite how familiar and inviting the desk, window, chair felt after so long away. He looked up at his hooked plague mask on the shelf. It had been sitting there for over a month, now. A full month had passed since Director Peete had told him they had enough doctors managing the plague situation, and James

Buckler could go back to his own practice. After all, plague or no plague, babies were still being born, and the reality of the medical field was that mothers and soon-to-be mothers needed his specialized skills more than the victims suffering from a now-curable, even preventable plague. James had to admit that deep down inside, he was very, very glad to be working in matters of life again, instead of slogging through the eternal battlefields of death.

Hah. The irony.

He sat at his desk, and pulled his keys from his trouser pocket. He unlocked the drawer at the very bottom left side, pulled it open, then shuffled through his papers and coinage until he found the false bottom. This he pushed up from below, and finally, claimed the single sheet of paper within.

He'd read it already, several times, but after a long day of hard work, bodily fluids, and persistent arguing, he felt he'd earned the little coal of hope lit by the words written in a jagged, slanting hand.

I have not forgotten your condition, James. There has been much on my plate, and I know you have had your own fair share of burdens and responsibilities. My powers, while extensive, deal only with one side of the coin of life. As I told you before, I alone cannot undo what has been done. However, there are others whose control extends further. Others who may be willing, perhaps even eager, to offer their services to you. These services would not be without a price, of course, but then again, nothing in life is free. I will need to chase down a few old contacts of mine and do some careful investigation, but I remain convinced that a solution to your problem is both possible and achievable. Perhaps even two solutions, for if I remember your original request of me correctly, there was more than a simple cure that you were interested in. Again, I restate that nothing is free. It may come down to a choice between which change is more important to you. However, it is not to me that any payment will be owed - for as we both know, I am in your debt, as things stand.

To be frank, you might consider whether or not your current condition is in fact more ideal. After all, think of how many lives you would save, working as you do, unfettered by such silly limitations as a human lifespan.

Mina sends her love.

-F

James snorted and carefully returned the letter to its safe place. He wasn't a man who put much stock in emotion, on a general basis. He preferred logic and rationality, science and mathematics to things as changeable as the human heart and all its whims.

However, he *was* still human, and the warm glow in his chest had nothing to do with the light of the lamps and everything to do with hope.

Hope for a cure. Hope that he could be a living, breathing person again, instead of the walking corpse that couldn't digest anything but meat, and who had nothing to offer his wife but a cold embrace.

She told him she didn't mind. She told him she loved him and would keep him, no matter what condition he was in.

She still shivered at his touch, sometimes. He didn't blame her. The hands of the dead were the hands of the dead, no matter how gently they brushed over your skin. He, of all people, knew what dangers a corpse could pose to a living body in terms of exposure. So, although he could wrap her in his arms again, see her beautiful face, and hear her beloved voice, still he had to hold back. Still, he had to be careful.

As if he needed more reasons to be impatient with his body, after a lifetime of struggle.

His ember of hope faded somewhat at that line of thought. He scowled and pushed his wandering memories aside, instead reaching for his bag and pulling out his notes from the day. From another drawer in his desk he drew his record book - almost every case in it fresh and new, as his former patients had either had their babies and survived or else perished in the plague. A handful were the same - women with chronic conditions or who simply hadn't been able to wait between children, but the vast majority were new faces. New lives, waiting to enter the world with screams and flailing fists.

He chuckled as he spread the books side by side and got out his pen and ink. Some things never changed, plague or no plague.

He'd only been writing for five minutes when a knock came on the door. Sighing, he set aside his quill, pushed himself up, and went to the door. One benefit of being undead - he wasn't the slightest bit sore, despite his long day.

He opened the door a crack, peering out with a stern gaze until he saw it was just the postman. "Oh, good evening, Lawrence."

The sturdy old fellow handed him a small bundle of letters, nodding amiably so that his drooping mustaches fluttered. "Evening, Doctor, evening."

James accepted the letters, regarding the old man with a critical eye. "Thank you. I hope you don't have too much further to go. The daylight is almost gone."

"No, no, heading home soon." Lawrence reached over and tapped the top letter in the pile. "You may need to open this one first, sir; Peete said it was time sensitive."

Peete? James furrowed his brow, but nodded, picking up the indicated envelope. "Thank you," he said again. "Good evening."

"Evening, evening." The postman shuffled off, and James quickly shut the door. Tossing the rest of the pile on his desk, he leaned against the edge, scooped up his letter opener and slashed the paper open.

He scanned the contents of the document, and sighed.

Dr. James Buckler left the mail in a stack on his desk, put his coat back on, and re-donned his hat.

Dousing his two lamps, he cast an irritated look at the work he would have to finish tomorrow instead of tonight and stepped out, locking the door behind him.

Some things just couldn't wait.

***

Fifteen minutes later, James found young Dr. Wayman exactly where he expected to find him - with his curly head on a table at the first alehouse they'd visited together, The Hoop and Grape. James scanned the room as he walked over to Barty's corner, noting how much fuller it was now than it had been a year ago. Back then, perhaps a dozen odd patrons lurked in small groups in a room built for a hundred, and there had been few smiles to be seen. Now the place bustled, full of light and laughter. The smells of food, drink and sweat made a cozy accompaniment to the warm hearth and bright lanterns. James couldn't help but feel a touch of pride at the sight of them all. This was possible because of what he had done. What Fabian had done.

And of course, what Dr. Bartholomew Wayman had done.

He pulled up a chair, and sat himself across from the young doctor, removing his hat and setting it on the table. "Evening, Barty."

Barty had ignored the noise of the chair, but flinched at the familiar voice. He raised his curly head a few inches, gave James a bleary look, then dropped his face back on the table. "I don't want you to see me like this," came the muffled, grief-tousled reply.

James took Barty's tankard and sipped the contents. Hmm, a heavy, rich ale. At least the boy had good taste, though whether or not he *could* still taste his drink at this stage was questionable. "Maybe you shouldn't let yourself get this way, then."

Barty took a shuddering breath. James saw the quiver go through him, even to the tips of his brown curls. Instead of offering any explanation or defense, Barty said, "I'm sorry," in a voice that cracked, despite it being only a whisper.

James paused, then set down the tankard with a sigh.

13

"Come on," he said, standing.

"Just leave me here," Barty said, trying to scrunch himself into a stubborn ball of disobedience.

James, congratulating himself on his unending patience, grabbed Barty by the back of his coat and pulled him up, out of his chair. "I'll carry you if I have to."

"D-don't do that, please-" Lord, the boy was a mess. Eyes red from tears and drink, hair caked down at the sides from sweat, face blotchy and lined from where it had pressed against the grain of the table. He couldn't even keep his feet, swaying despite James' hand holding him like a naughty kitten. James hadn't seen him that bedraggled since he'd been shot.

James picked up Barty's hat from the table and pressed it down over his curls, then slung one of the young doctor's arms around his own shoulders. "We're going."

"Alright, alright, just..." Barty fumbled in his pocket for money, spilling coins onto the table.

James eyed the coinage with a critical gaze, and once he was sure Barty hadn't left more than he should, steered the pickled doctor towards the door. "I'm taking you back to my place to keep you under surveillance."

"Oh, James, don't," Barty sounded even more pained. "Don't, don't. What will Jessica think? Please, James." Despite his protests, he did best to match James' pace, even if his mud-stained feet barely kept him upright.

"She'd be angrier with me if I left you alone like this than if I brought you home for a bit of care, Barty."

They stepped out into the night, the cool evening air brushing away the light and warmth of the tavern. Barty drew in a deep breath, and shivered, and James could hear the sobs coming even before he opened his mouth. "Y-you shouldn't say such nice things to me when...when I'm like this..."

"Oh, yes?" James chuckled, gently steering Barty away from the tavern and towards the home he and Jessica had bought the past year. It was only a few streets down,

14

comfortably closer to James' work in the city. "Or else what, Dr. Wayman?"

"Or else I'll just start sobbing all over again," Barty somehow managed to make it sound like a threat, wobbly voice aside. "I'll embarrass both of us in front of your w-wife."

"I think it would take a lot more than tears shed for a noble cause to give you anything to be embarrassed about in front of her, Barty." James slipped his arm around Barty's waist, confident now that his friend would hang on to his neck of his own accord, and preferring to give him a bit of extra support and guidance.

For a moment, Barty walked in silence, processing James' words. When he next spoke, his voice was an entire octave higher, and quite small. "N...noble cause? So you don't... you don't think I'm being stupid about this?"

"I think you're being stupid to get cup-shot over it," James said frankly. "But no. I don't think it's stupid to see the hypocrisy of selling a cure to the rich when it is the poor who suffer the most. It isn't stupid to be frustrated when men you look up to should be doing better, and aren't."

"Oh, James-" a sob interrupted Barty's words. He stopped walking and covered his overflowing eyes with his free hand, shoulders a-quiver.

James sighed, and halted as well, patting his friend's back. "Chin up, Dr. Wayman," he said. "You have a good heart, but you don't need to throw it against the rocks as much as you do, or else it really will break. And that'd help exactly nobody."

"I know it," Barty choked. "I know it, I'm trying to be better but-"

James pitied the boy. He truly did. He remembered a time in his own youth where he had had similar indignation, similar reactions to the stinging pain of the cruelties that life pelted at him again and again.

He'd learned to be steady in the face of these cruelties. The less time one wasted on grieving, the more energy could be put to a solution.

15

And the safer one was from those who would use such weakness to their own advantage.

"Barty," he said again, "listen a moment."

Barty choked down his sobs, clearly trying to do as he was told, but Buckler could see his lip trembling, even in the darkness that slowly deepened around them with the falling of night, painting the street in heavy, thick shadows.

James got them moving again, pulling the young man along as he spoke. "A big part of what we do - of what any doctor does - is knowing our limits. Yes, I am aware that our situations are far from perfect. We cannot save everyone we wish we could, or even those we feel really, really deserve to be saved."

Barty walked along at his side, silent, tears dripping down his face, but listening.

James continued, "Falling to pieces doesn't help. And drinking to the point where you are going to perform *your* duties poorly tomorrow is irresponsible. Better to just go to bed early, or find someone to talk to to get your thoughts sorted out."

Barty sniffed. "I don't really have anyone to talk to but you, sir. Except-"

James interrupted before he could finish. He knew who else Barty thought he could confide in, and he didn't like it. "Then come talk to me."

Barty heaved a frustrated sigh. "Sir - no offense, but you've got a life now. You have your wife, your practice, and who knows what else. I know you're always busy, and... and, I don't know, it's just-" he rested his head against James' shoulder, his voice going softer. His breath smelled heavily of ale. "I don't want to interrupt."

"Barty," James said, touched despite himself, "it's because of you that I got any piece of my old life back. Please know that I am always there for you, no matter what the situation, and I would much prefer you come to me with your problems than go to Fabian."

Barty flinched and went silent. James let him have that silence, focusing instead on the lights of his home patiently awaiting their arrival. He hadn't wanted to say it flat out - he knew Barty thought his softness for the necromancer well hidden - but James was a good fifteen years older than the young man, and knew all too well the look in Barty's eye whenever he saw Fabian.

"She...they're not so bad," Barty said at last. "If you just gave them a chance-"

"I don't need to give them a chance," James said sternly. He knew Barty liked to use 'they,' claiming it represented the many lives the necromancer had led in the past. He also knew Fabian wasn't picky about manner of address. If James had his own way, he would have preferred to use "him," even though Fabian's body was female, so there would be no pretense of forgetting exactly who Lord Fabian had been in his last life. However, James's own physical condition also made him loath to misgender anyone, so he had, with reluctance, fallen into using Barty's 'they.' "What did they teach you this time? Don't pretend you weren't at the mansion yesterday."

With reluctance, Barty admitted, "How to pick locks."

James sighed. "And when would a doctor need to know how to pick locks?"

Barty tried to straighten up a bit. "W-well, what if the patient has collapsed and can't open the door? Now I can get in to help them even if it's locked-"

"Don't make excuses." James snapped, irritated Barty was right. "This is just a small example of their negative influence over you. I know them well, Barty. We've spent many an hour together this past year. I know enough to judge that they are not what you want them to be, and not good for you and your soft heart."

"Blast my soft heart," Barty grumbled. "I'd be so much better at this if I didn't have it, James."

James noticed that the young man had switched the topic away from the necromancer. Still, he patted Barty's back as they got to the gate of his home. "You wouldn't be half the man you are today without your soft heart, Barty Wayman."

Barty sighed, and let go of James' shoulders so James could open the gate. "I suppose I just have to believe you," he said, his eyes on the windows. It was a cold evening, and the glass was fogged from the heat within, yellow-orange and inviting.

James looked too, admired the silhouette of his wife moving swiftly from kitchen to living room, and took Barty's arm, steering him through and closing the gate. "You'll learn, young Doctor Wayman," he said sagely. "As you spend more time in the field, the suffering of others will become, if not pleasant to bear, at least familiar to work with. It will not always cut you so deeply as it does now."

"I don't know if that's a good thing, " Barty said, his voice surprisingly clear despite his less-than-sober state. "I don't want to become like Director Peete, making decisions just because they look good on paper, and unconcerned with the people being affected."

"If you understand that much, Barty," James said as he led the way up the steps and dug around in his pocket for his key, "then surely you understand that, compared to the numbness Director Peete developed over two years of plague management, someone who has lived who-knows-how-many lives, killed hundreds, if not thousands, and uses the corpses of the very people we try to heal as playthings, probably has *no heart at all-*"

The door opened just as he was about to put his key in the lock. He and Barty both looked up, meeting the steely gaze of Jessica Buckler. "Oh, you're both here! Thank goodness." Some of the steel melted, replaced with relief and worry. "I almost sent someone for you. Are you quite alright, Dr. Wayman?" Her blue eyes flickered from Barty to James, already reaching to help with the young doctor's weight and stability.

"I'm alright, I'm alright-" Barty said hastily, trying his best to stand under his own power, and swaying as he did. "Just had a long day, you know how it is."

"A long day and a bit much to drink," James said, passing his colleague off to his wife, then removing his coat and hat to hang on the wall. "There is no cause for concern, dear. It's nothing a bit of food and rest won't fix. I thought it best not to-"

"If he's alright, then I'll take care of him, dear." She cut James off, already helping Barty out of his coat in a hurry. She steered him to a chair, still speaking to James over her shoulder. "There is another patient here who needs immediate care. I've already set the hot water going and brought out clean rags."

James blinked. "What do you mean, another-"

"She means," hissed a familiar voice from the living room, "that a certain heartless necromancer would like some assistance in not bleeding to death. If it is convenient."

James and Barty both spun about - Barty would have toppled right over if Jessica hadn't grabbed his shoulders. Like a crumpled shadow, Fabian the necromancer half leaned, half lay against the wall of the sitting room. They were bedraggled and bloody, a crimson-stained towel pressed to their side, their face even paler than usual but bearing a gaunt smile. "Evening, boys."

Barty whimpered. James sighed, and shared an 'its just going to be one of those nights' look with his wife. "I assume you-"

"Bandages, needle and thread waiting for you on the table," Jessica said with a nod. "And the water should be boiling by now, I started it as soon as they staggered in, once I was sure they wouldn't bleed out before you got here."

James blessed his wife's intelligence, efficiency and foresight. "Jessica, you are a gem."

She smiled at him. "Anything else I can do?"

James gestured to Barty. "Tea, with nothing stronger in it," he prescribed. "And bring the hot water to the living room when you can, please." He made for his study, already rolling

19

up his sleeves. "I'll fetch my bag."

CHAPTER 3:
SMALL PRICE

Fabian savored moments like these.

They knew what their presence meant to the little family. This home - with its warm yellow lights, soft curtains and neatly-papered walls, was never meant to be a medical space, let alone a treatment room for a heartless necromancer. The pleasantly matched furniture and reasonable, if not lavish decorations were supposed to convey a feeling of safety for Dr. Buckler, his wife, and his guest. The cruelties and filth of a London still struggling to recover from plague and hardship were not meant to pass these walls. A sacred castle, this quaint little home.

And yet here Fabian was, bleeding on the hardwood and grinning up at all the stunned, pale faces; a black, dirty rat that had wiggled its way into the holiest of sanctuaries, shattering all illusions that their problems could be kept on the other side of that sturdy wooden door.

Dr. Buckler was not one to wallow in shock. Barely a breath did he take before he was off, getting his medical tools, leaping into action like the hero he didn't even know he was.

And Barty, sweet Dr. Wayman, simply sank into a chair, trembling and staring.

Fabian managed a velvety chuckle for his sake. "Do not fret, Doctor." They peeled the cloth away from their side, peeked at the oozy, gaping hole underneath, and pressed the cloth back with a grimace. More warm blood trickled down their cold skin. "If you think this looks bad, you should see the other guy."

"Who's the other guy?" the doctor squeaked.

"An old acquaintance of yours," Fabian sneered. "Though I think you met him only twice. You remember Father Besom?"

How comical it was, to watch the emotions race across young Barty's face. Pain, anger, fear, all painted as clearly as a quarantine warning on a plague-stricken home. "You killed a priest?" he gasped. "You came here after killing a priest?"

Fabian gave him a flat look, their carnivorous smile unchanging. "That priest, as you are well aware, was responsible for the deaths of thousands upon thousands of innocent people."

Amusing, to watch the protests die in the young man's throat. Delicious, how he shrank in on himself, the side of him that abhorred death and violence smothered by the other side, the one that craved justice in the world. Justice, and perhaps a little vengeance.

"Yes," Fabian said softly, forcing the young doctor to lean closer, his brown eyes full of helpless horror and fascination. "Yes, I killed him, Dr. Wayman. I am a force of reckoning in this city. Justice, for those who cannot defend themselves. Vengeance, for those who fell when I was not there to protect them."

They held his gaze, knowing how their own red eyes gleamed in contrast to his soft brown, knowing too, that he saw the weight of all their past lives, giving solidity and truth to their words, their convictions. "You can't tell me he deserved any less, Doctor. In fact, perhaps in death, he got off too lightly."

"Perhaps the one who got off lightly was you." James Buckler walked back into the room, medical bag in one hand, paper and pen in the other. "It's unlike you, Fabian, to go after someone yourself, and alone." He settled at Fabian's side, his stern gray eyes stealing Fabian's gaze from Dr. Wayman's. "I assume this," he beckoned at Fabian's bloody side, "was Besom's doing?"

"Alas, you are correct," Fabian sighed, moving their rag so Dr. Buckler could assess the puncture. "He was expecting me. If not today, tomorrow. If not next month, next year." A sinister chuckle bubbled up from their core. "I'd been watching him stew for weeks and weeks. Saving the pleasure for a rainy day- *ah*."

They gave a soft hiss of pain as Buckler spread the gash - checking its depth.

"A knife?" he asked.

Sweat beaded on Fabian's brow. They wheezed out an answer, teeth gritted. "Yes. Kitchen knife, even." Fabian forced a grin. "Had it under his pillow. Caught me by surprise. But, well…" their laugh was dirty, now. "I think I surprised him a bit more, when I slit his throat- OUCH."

Buckler had pinched the wound closed again - far harder than necessary. Fabian growled at him through teeth that were more threat than smile, hot blood trickling down their side. "Careful, Doctor. Keep up that kind of hand-work and I'll have to find more excuses to get those fingers on my perso-"

A smart rap on the head silenced their final word, and, teeth fixed in a rigid grin, they looked up to see Ms. Buckler standing over them, kettle in one hand, empty bowl in the other. It was the bowl that she had used to assault Fabian's skull.

"Apologies, madam," Fabian said, eyes glittering. "But never fear, I know to whom he truly belongs."

She sniffed. "I should hope so." She set the bowl and kettle down at the doctor's side, dumped a stack of rags next to them, then, after giving James a dainty kiss on the side of the head, said, "Anything else, dear?"

James Buckler looked like he was trying not to be flustered or pleased, and wasn't managing to hide either very well. "No, Jessica, thank you so much."

She smiled at him and bustled out of the room, paying no mind to the three sets of eyes following her.

Dr. Buckler chuckled. "Drink your tea, Barty. And close your mouth, you'll catch flies."

Barty did indeed close his mouth, only to open it again to say in a rush, "I can't believe your wife just bonked the most infamous necromancer who ever lived."

Fabian managed a dry smile. "I am the only necromancer who ever lived, Dr. Wayman."

"Is that so?" Dr. Buckler began cleaning the gash in Fabian's side with soap and water. It made it bleed more, of course, and hurt like the devil, but Fabian had had worse. Fairly recently, too.

"Yes," they said, turning their gaze on him. "At least, the only one with my particular brand of talent. All the necromancers you have heard of, and quite a few you haven't, in the last thousand or so years were just me. In different lives, of course, but still me."

"I'm surprised your line was able to continue for so long," Dr. Buckler said, threading his stitching needle, "if you always display such a high degree of recklessness."

Fabian took a deep breath and let it out through their nose, trying to ignore the poke and tug of steel and silk in their flesh. "Well, I am not always so reckless, clearly. One does not conquer England without patience, planning, and plenty of helping hands...living and unliving."

The thread pulled at their side, a sharp bite of reprimand. Stupid, it told them. Stupid.

Dr. Buckler seemed to agree with the thread, though he didn't use the same word. "I would have thought you would be more careful, now," he said calmly, "considering how you are only recently recovering from your last *ordeal*." He paused long enough to glance up at Fabian, his expression softening a fraction. "She is doing well, I hope."

Back at the table, Barty cleared his throat and looked away.

Fabian chuckled, both at Barty and at the question. "Willamina is just fine. She was sleeping when I left, as happy and healthy a little creature as ever I spawned."

Barty choked on his tea, then pushed the cup away, coughing into his arm. James made a face, and went back to his stitchwork. "I hope you don't speak that way around her. Does Ruphys even know you went out this evening?"

"He...might," Fabian wasn't sure how awake he'd really been. "I left in something of a rush." They had left half in the dream, in fact, before the sun had risen. If they closed their eyes now, they could still feel the stone, cold and hard under their face, their lifeblood hot against their skin, the thirst for revenge bitter in their throat. The memory made their insides burn.

"What about Jack?" Barty blurted out. "Couldn't she have come with you?"

Fabian cast him an acidic smile. "Jack has never quite recovered from Ruphys showing up in my life. I imagine Jack is happily in the arms of her new girlfriend somewhere."

An awkward pause followed. Barty shifted in his seat and buried his nose in his teacup, while Dr. Buckler shook his head and tied off his stitchwork. "What is it really, Fabian?" he said. "What is this all about? Why now?"

"Why now..." Fabian didn't expect either of the doctors to understand. The word 'revenge' held too little meaning to them - it didn't encapsulate the need, as painful and twisting as hunger or thirst, lodged deep in their soul. It didn't illustrate the dreams, dreams that they had lived with ever since they could remember, of their past lives and deaths, loves and losses. It didn't encompass the pain of knowing that all their children - children they had treasured, in their own, greedy, calculating way - were murdered by the plague that had slaughtered thousands, all because the current monarchy was jumping at shadows, and the mage's guild wanted to feel important and powerful.

"Well. Now, I have finally recovered enough from my nine-month ordeal to get out a bit, and my knives were so sharp, you see." They grinned, showing all their teeth as they lied through them. "Seemed a shame not to put them to good use."

Barty wouldn't meet their gaze. Dr. Buckler sighed and began to apply bandages to their wound.

Fabian let their gaze linger upon him. "You really think," they said, low and soft, "you wouldn't do the same, Doctor? If I could hand you a knife, and the leash of the man who had you drowned, do you really think you wouldn't find the temptation to kill him yourself more than you could resist?"

"He died of the plague almost immediately after it hit London," Buckler said, glaring back into Fabian's face.

"I see," Fabian said, voice full of laughter. "So you already looked into it. Do you know where he's buried? I could bring him back for you, give you a bit of fun."

"Oh, don't." Barty's soft voice, pleading, interrupted the staring contest between doctor and necromancer. A tinge of green shaded his pale cheeks. "I'm - I'm going to be sick just thinking about that."

Dr. Buckler cast Fabian a last glare, and stood, taking the bowl with now-bloody hot water, rinsing it out in the sink, and setting it before Barty. "You're going to be sick because you drank too much," he said gruffly. "Finish your tea, and I'll set up somewhere for you to sleep."

"No, no, I couldn't impose even more!" Fabian could see

Barty practically writhing with embarrassment. "I can walk home-"

"I could walk him home," Fabian grinned, easing off the floor gingerly. Their side ached, but it was already feeling better with the bandages. With the easing of the pain, too, came the return of their other bodily complaints. By the black books, they were starving. "Between the two of us, we'd make a pretty pair."

"I'm going to send word to Ruphys to come get you," Dr. Buckler said, glaring at Fabian. "I don't want you walking home alone, and I don't want you sleeping in my house."

"So cold, Doctor," Fabian said, feigning a hurt expression. "As if I could ever do anything to harm you, after all you've done for me."

"I did it for Willamina," Dr. Buckler said, turning away, "not for you."

"Oh, well then. Since you put it that way," Fabian steadied themself with a hand on the couch, wiping their blood-and-sweat dampened hair out of their face. "Since you did it for her, and not for me...I guess it is *you* who are in *my* debt."

"What?" spluttered Dr. Buckler.

"Yes," Fabian said, and walked towards him, steps unsteady, smile unwavering. "After all, if it weren't for me, James Buckler, you'd be *properly* dead." They met his gray glare. "Just another fish-eaten corpse, half sunk in the muck and filth of the Thames."

James dropped his gaze, his fists clenched at his sides. Fabian lingered a moment, savoring the sweet moment of victory, before turning on Barty. "Pull me up a chair, Dr. Wayman. I'll wait like a good patient while you send for my escort."

"I - Ah - Oh-" Barty stood, only a little unsteady, offering Fabian his own chair. "O-of course, um, Lord-"

"They aren't a lord," snapped Dr. Buckler, as Fabian sat primly. "They don't rule anyone. Not anymore."

Fabian stole Barty's teacup as well, filling it from the kettle and taking a slow sip. "Such hostility for his own patient. Well, perhaps I needn't wait for my escort. Fetch me a carriage instead, Dr. Wayman. Clearly, I cannot walk home in this condition."

Barty wavered, conflict clear on his wretched face, and then he went to the door, avoiding Dr. Buckler's gaze and murmuring apologies as he slipped out, not even putting on his coat.

Dr. Buckler shot Fabian a glare that could have seared rust off of iron, and hurried after him, grabbing both their coats on the way out.

Fabian closed their eyes after the door slammed, instead taking up the viewpoint of the small mouse that 'lived' under Dr. Buckler's porch. The mouse had been dead a long time, its eyes were little more than light-sensitive orbs, but its hearing was good enough for eavesdropping.

"-let them bully you like that. It just encourages them-"

"She's hurt, James - she...they can't walk, and you won't let them stay-"

"That doesn't mean you should just let them walk all over you."

A pair of frustrated sighs.

A moment of silence.

"I'm sorry," whispered Barty. "It's just one more thing. Maybe I'm not cut out for this line of work, James."

"Don't talk like that. You are. You know you are. In fact-"

The mouse could dimly make out the shorter figure turning towards the taller, putting a hand on his shoulder.

"I'll write to Peete for you. For both of us. Tell him at least that he should change the ratios. Seventy five percent of the amulets should go to the poor, if not more. It'll look better if there are two of us united in this. Maybe the others will agree-"

"Really? You'd do that? J-James-"

Barty's voice broke up again, and Fabian sighed, setting

down their teacup. They instructed the mouse to return to its hidey hole, letting the two men have their privacy.

It almost took all the fun out of bullying the boy, he was so soft and genuine. In another world, another life, Fabian might have tried to protect a creature like him. It was rare for any human to have enough strength of character to retain a soft heart into adulthood.

Unfortunately, Fabian had lived many lives since they were that kind of person. Many hungry, painful, all-too-real lives.

They were still running from the consequences of some of those lives.

A shiver went through them, and they pushed down the thought, memories of cold stone and hot blood once more threatening to overtake their vision. They had hoped that achieving some of their vengeance would distance themselves from their dream, but though the feelings of fear and pain had faded, they were not gone completely. Not even their enjoyment of teasing Dr. Wayment had cleansed them of the lingering sense of urgency pressing against their lungs.

If not for that feeling, they would have enjoyed the little game - enjoyed either standing back and watching the boy crack, or being the one holding the hammer, with arms outstretched to catch him as he crumbled.

But something was wrong. Something they couldn't put a finger on, but that had to do with the dream.

As much as they hated to admit it, they had a sneaking suspicion they would end up needing more help in the future.

They picked up their teacup again, trying to drown the chill that lurked in their belly. Now that their heels were cooling, they knew the dream that had sent them on this path was not a coincidence.

Dr. Buckler was right. They would have to be more careful.

More than careful; they would have to be prepared.

CHAPTER 4: THE MAN ON THE SILVER HORSE

The Huntsman rode his silver horse into Whiston.

The fact that he rode into Whiston was an oddity in itself. Whiston, though a sprawling, handsome town with a healthy population in the hundreds, didn't exist on maps. It didn't exist at all, according to anyone who lived outside of it.

That didn't stop the Huntsman, though. Then again, there weren't many things that could stop him. After all, he was on an errand from the King, and knew his way no matter where it led him.

He rode in from the North, his hood up to protect against the chill that lingered over the moor and forest in the early fall morning. Technically, there weren't supposed to be forests on this part of the Dartmoors anymore, but apparently this ancient, silent clump of moss-covered trees hadn't gotten the message. They clung to its stretch of rock-filled ground with the tenacity that was either blessing or curse to so many of the inhabitants in Whiston.

Neither forest nor rock had deterred the Huntsman or his horse.

The pair ignored the stares from curious locals and made straight for Whiston's only inn: The Sunlit Stones. The locals, however, displayed no such reservation; for although it was unwise to interfere when a Hunt was afoot, tales of beasts slain and towns saved circled about the Huntsman and his silver horse like glittering fish in a deep pool. Curious eyes followed his green-cloaked back as he pulled his mount to a stop in front of The Stones' stables. Curious minds observed the many traps, ropes, chains and bottles dangling from the silver horse's back, and wondered what wonderful, terrible beasts they had been used upon.

The battered sword at his hip discouraged any questions, however. He met no gaze, out of neither arrogance nor shyness. He was simply focused on his purpose.

He was focused on The Hunt.

The Huntsman slid off his horse, gave the beast a stern look, and handed the reins over to the gawking stableboy without a word.

The stable boy, tearing his eyes from the Huntsman's sword, managed to stammer out, "H-how long will you be staying, sir?"

The Huntsman hesitated, looking over the town. Smoke rose from many of the chimneys, people bustled here and there about their morning business, dogs ran through the street, barking, and over it all...

...over it all lay a wariness. An edge. The shoppers moved in groups, their voices hushed even when haggling for wares. Windows and doors remained closed, despite the warm sunlight starting to filter in through the mists. A bell

31

tolled, shockingly loud over the hushed voices, its beats slow, mournful; a funeral procession, made known for all to hear.

The Huntsman met the stableboy's eye and rested a hand on the hilt of his sword. The boy, his face a shade paler but his voice less quavering, seemed to understand. "O-oh. You're here to catch the Raven?"

The Huntsman nodded, now stroking his hand over his horse's silver flank. "I'm here to catch a monster."

He dug in his pocket and tossed a silver coin to the wide-eyed youth. "See that no ill comes to my horse."

The boy caught the coin, wary but gleeful. "Yes sir, Mr. Huntsman, sir! Good luck with your hunt, sir!"

The Huntsman nodded his hooded head, then went towards the door of the inn.

"My horse likes hot oats with apple slices in them."

Both the boy and Huntsman stopped in their tracks. The voice was the same that had boasted about catching a monster, but it hadn't come from the Huntsman.

The Huntsman turned slowly, glaring at the silver horse browsing in the grass by the stable.

The boy looked between them, confused. "M-must have been the wind," he said with a laugh. "For a second I could have swore it was the horse who spoke, instead of you."

The horse said nothing, continuing its innocent snack.

The Huntsman glared a moment longer, then shook his head and turned his back on them both, going up the few steps into the inn.

He stepped across the threshold and took a deep breath, admiring both his surroundings and the lingering scents that accompanied. The inn was a sturdy, cozy place, smelling of tobacco smoke, hearth fire and baking bread. The main entrance led into a sitting area where weary travelers could rest and eat while their rooms were prepared. Perhaps it was because not many travelers came through Whiston that the place could stay so neat, clean and warm, with barely a scuff on the floor or scratch on the heavy wood tables.

Before the Huntsman could avail himself of the warmth and comfort, though, a figure blocked his path; a muscular man almost as tall as himself, with close cut hair and a scar across one eyebrow. The Huntsman paused, meeting the fellow's stern gaze with his own silver one.

"Please identify yourself before you enter," the man said, not impolitely, but with a tone that bore no questioning.

The Huntsman raised an eyebrow. To most folk over the age of twenty, his title was well known. This door-guard had to be younger than he looked. The Huntsman raised his hand, holding the man's gaze, and signed with his dark, calloused fingers, '*I am Jeremiah the Huntsman, and I am here in the name of the King.*' Jeremiah, his common name, and the Huntsman, his given title. No fool gave his full, true name this close to the King's lands.

Of course, the King already had Jeremiah's name, but it was still good practice to be careful.

The bouncer squinted at him, the expression somewhere between confused and belligerent, as if he thought the Huntsman to be mocking him with his strange hand motions. "I don't understand that," he said bluntly, one hand going to a heavy club at his side. "Speak normal."

Jeremiah gave the fellow a cold stare, both because the request was downright rude, and because sometimes unrelenting attention was enough to make men back down - especially men who were new to their positions and unsure about their own authority.

This was Whiston, though, where even the bouncers had the same tenacity as the forest that wasn't supposed to exist. The burly man glared right back, and drew his club from its leather holder. "I'm only gonna ask you once more. Who are you, and-"

Jeremiah pulled his scarf down, away from his neck, and raised his jaw, showing the bouncer the scar that stood out, clear and pale, against the mahogany skin of his throat.

The bouncer stared. "Oh...oh, so you can't... you can't

actually talk."

Jeremiah only looked at him, waiting patiently.

The man grimaced, and sheepishly put the club back in his belt. "Right. Er. Sorry. I'll...I'll just get Ms. Ida for you."

Jeremiah nodded, and folded his arms, showing he was willing to wait.

The bouncer hurried off, moving with speed despite his bulk. Jeremiah supposed that was why Ida had hired him - whatever he lacked in courtesy, he probably made up for in skill in a fight. He was young – perhaps his manners would grow with time.

Before long, two sets of feet could be heard approaching from the hallway. Ida's scolding preceded her into the room, her voice as elegant as her steps. "...know your history, boy? Did your parents never educate you about the Huntsman? I mean, really - I know their love could bring down the tallest mountain, but that is no excuse- Ah, Jeremiah. How good to see you."

Jeremiah allowed himself a small smile as Innkeeper Ida stepped into view. She grinned back at him, leaving her abashed bouncer behind and gliding forwards, taking Jeremiah's arm with the hand not holding the pipe that gleamed with as much polish as her nails. "Come, sit by the fire. Harley will bring you a drink - cider, as usual?"

Jeremiah nodded, letting himself be escorted to the seat closest to the merry flames, marveling, as ever, at how Ms. Ida could combine strength and grace with such natural ease. She was only an inch shorter than himself and probably weighed twenty pounds more, but her movements were as easy and gentle as a lazy river, every motion making the firelight sparkle on the gold threads of floral embroidery in her skirt and blouse, and the gold paint over her eyes.

'You look well,' he signed, allowing himself to be seated and casting an appreciative look around the inn, for Ida's benefit. 'As does your lovely inn. It hasn't changed a bit since my last visit. Beautiful as ever.'

"Flatterer," Ida said, smiling, accepting the compliment as if it belonged to her already, and settling down in the chair across from him. "Meanwhile you've gone fully silver. Ah..." she shook her head, earrings tinkling. "Seems like just yesterday you dragged yourself out of the woods, barely out of your teens and all but torn in half from fighting that basilisk."

'*At least I wasn't stone.*' The basilisk had been one of the more difficult of his hunts - and his first magical one. Who would have guessed that a creature that ate rocks could move so quickly? Jeremiah still had the scars down his chest from that educational experience.

"I suppose by comparison to your other adventures, this one will be simpler" she said with a regretful headshake. "I'm sorry to get to business so quickly, but I assume you know already, or else you wouldn't be here." She gave him a steady look, the smile gone from her face. "Something is wrong in this town - something I'm not able to track down, and you know I usually handle everything myself." She settled her pipe between her teeth, sighing and sending a puff of smoke towards the eaves.

Jeremiah nodded. The bouncer, Harley, brought him a mug of frothy cider. Jeremiah accepted it with a grateful touch to the edge of his hood, and Harley gave him a nervous smile, clearly relieved no grudges were held.

Jeremiah took a long sip, enjoying the crisp tang of apple that tasted fresh from the tree even in a tankard. This moment he would savor - this moment of comradery, rest and sweetness.

But it was only a moment.

He set the tankard aside with regret and faced Ida, settling his expression into something grim. '*I am here on business as well. By order of the King,*' he signed.

Ida frowned, sending another plume of smoke from her pipe. "I guessed as much. More than The Hunt, then?"

Jeremiah nodded, and drew two envelopes from his jerkin. '*I need you to post two letters. I am occupied with my Hunt, and the King wants these moving as soon as possible.'*

Ida's expression remained impassive, the firelight glittering on her golden eyeshadow, golden earrings, and the golden trim of her pipe. "I do not work for the King for free," she said, the underlying warning making her smoke-laden words heavier.

'I understand,' Jeremiah signed, but his eyes lingered on the hand holding the pipe. The skin of that hand was a coppery brown, but, once, a golden wedding had adorned her ring finger. It had been gone so long now that not even a pale ghost remained. *'How long has it been since it disappeared?'.*

Ida grunted. "Twenty years or so. I keep wishing it would appear as easily as it vanished." She leaned closer, her tone confidential. "Marshal doesn't mind, of course. He loves me any way I am. But, you know. I mind. It's been a while since I had any children. I miss the pitter patter of little feet, now and then."

Jeremiah nodded again. *'Marshal has been away for some time, hasn't he?'*

Ida frowned, her gaze intensifying. "He was supposed to be back three weeks ago."

Jeremiah set the letters on the table, and pulled yet another from his jerkin. *'In exchange for delivery, the King has had the foresight to see that this letter from your husband was also delivered safely.'*

Ida's scowl grew thunderous. "The King has no right to intercept mail on this side of the lands-"

Jeremiah kept his expression neutral, signing one handed and keeping the letter in Ida's vision. *'Marshal was not on this side of the lands. He wandered astray, and became lost. Post these letters for the King, and not only will the King's Huntsman,'* he bowed slightly, *'give you your message, but the King himself will tell the roads to be straight again, and deliver Marshal back to you. Two favors, for two favors.'*

Ida growled, low and deep. The sound shook the table, vibrating up through Jeremiah's bones and making his heart race. There was something primal about the noise, something that made him want to go back into the forest, find a deep cave and stay there.

"This is blackmail." Ida leaned closer, her smoky breath wafting over Jeremiah's face. "I will accept this task, but the King should know by now that I do not appreciate my hand being forced in this or in any matter. Nor is it proper payment to return what is being withheld, instead of offering a true gift." Her words took on a bitter edge. "He could have easily given me a new ring."

She stood up, towering over Jeremiah and snatching all three letters from the table and his hand.

Jeremiah did not flinch. *'I'll mention it to him,'* he signed apologetically.

She snorted and left the room.

Only then did Jeremiah wipe the sweat from his brow, and take a drink of cider. The whole inn was warm with the heat of the innkeeper's wrath.

Jeremiah was not comfortable with how the exchange had gone. Ida was correct, of course - the King was not playing fair. But the King never played fair, so that shouldn't have been surprising.

Jeremiah addressed that to himself as much to Ida. And yet, his heart was unhappy with the deed. Hunt or no Hunt, he tried to conduct himself as an honorable man at all times. Only the King ever tried his convictions, and he tried them often.

Still. Jeremiah had met Marshal, a jolly little man with a zest for life, for travel and discovery. To think of Marshal stuck on a wearying, ever-longer road as leverage against Ida left a sour twist in Jeremiah's stomach. He was glad the merchant and his wife would soon be reunited.

Ida returned, wiping her hands on her skirt as if the letters had sullied them, her pipe clenched between her teeth.

Jeremiah drained the last of his cider and stood. *'I will go to my room and prepare for The Hunt,'* he signed. *'I will not disturb your business, but if I were you, I would advise the townsfolk to stay indoors during the evenings until I finish. It should take no more than a few days.'*

Ida sighed, smoke curling upwards. "I will. Thank you, Jeremiah. I am sorry we do not meet under happier terms." She offered him a room key.

'As am I.' He accepted the key, tugged once more on his weathered hood, and made his way to the stairs. Even after all these years, their creaking under his boots was like a familiar welcome.

He opened the door to his room, and found it was not empty.

The window sat open, letting in a lazy breeze that stirred the burgundy curtains. Upon the neatly made bed lay a beast - a sizable lizard, with silver scales, long claws, and spines jutting out ridged back of its neck. Its eyes were closed, ribbed sides moving softly in and out with each breath, for all appearances utterly asleep.

Jeremiah sighed, walked over the lizard, picked it up by the tail and dumped it on the floor. He then sat on the bed and began to remove his boots, pointedly ignoring the lizard's indignant scrambling.

"Heeeeyyyy!" whined the lizard, in a gruff, deep voice that made Jerimiah wince. He had *never* complained that way when that voice belonged to him. "I was comfortable!"

'I told you to stay in the stable, Shilling,' Jeremiah signed at the lizard, his expression stern. *'You even requested extra food, risking giving yourself away to a child who would gossip to the whole town.'*

"I was hungry! Anyway, you already told him why we are here, with your sword thing-"

'You are always hungry. And you should have stayed in the stable - now the stable boy will panic, seeing that my horse is gone.'

Shilling sulked, folding his arms and resting his scaled chin across them. "I don't want to sleep in the stable. It's cold out there."

Jeremiah removed his boots, and swung his legs up on

38

the bed. *'It's far warmer than out in the open, where we usually sleep.'*

"All the times I kept you warm with my fur, and you want me to stay in a drafty wooden box-!"

Shilling stood and stretched. While the motion began with him as a lizard, by the time he finished, he was instead a silver fox, with a dainty pointed muzzle and shining, fluffy pelt. The fox hopped up onto the bed and settled on Jeremiah's chest, looking down his nose at The Huntsman. "We are going out again after sunset anyway, aren't we? The stable boy won't even notice, he's probably working on other chores."

Jeremiah sighed, making Shilling rise and fall with the rhythm of his breathing. *'You may stay until we go out this evening to hunt the Raven,'* he mouthed, silent and slow, since the fox was too close to see his hands, *'but when we return to sleep, you will go back to the stable. Even now, you may only stay on condition of no noise or wriggling, as it will be a long night, and I want to gain what rest I can.'*

"Of course!" Shilling said, standing up, turning in a circle on his chest, and settling down again with his bushy tail over his nose. His brown eyes sparkled at Jeremiah over the layer of gleaming fluff. "You won't even know I'm here."

Jeremiah rolled his eyes. Such was the bond between himself and Shilling that he *always* knew when the changeling was there. But there was no room for regrets; the deal had been made. This was simply his lot in life.

He pulled his hood over his face, let out another deep breath, and forced himself to relax.

I hope you are warm in your nest, Raven, he thought to his prey.

Soon, only cold iron will be your home.

CHAPTER 5:
NEGOTIATIONS

Barty Wayman knocked on the door of the perfumer's shop.

It was early in the morning - it had to be, for Barty to squeeze a visit in before his meeting with Director Peete. It was worth the loss of sleep, though; he had woken with an idea in his head and hope in his heart, and he wanted to do a little investigating before he reported in.

The door opened, the early morning sun illuminating the old Jewish gentleman who peeped out at Barty, his bearded face breaking into a smile the moment he recognized his guest. "Doctor, it is good to see you again," Mr. Blum opened the door wider and beckoned Barty inside. "I have heard a little of all you have accomplished. Please, come in and have some tea."

"Good morning, Mr. Blum, and thank you, but I cannot

stay long." Barty stepped in anyway, removing his hat and peeking around. Mr. Blum's house was far less quiet than at his last visit a year ago. Voices filled the wooden halls; a woman soothing a baby's fussing in the floor above, a couple chatting in the kitchen down the hall, and even someone singing from the back garden. It warmed Barty's heart immensely to know that London was now safe enough for Avram's family to return to their home behind the perfume shop.

Barty wanted that for all of London. That was why he was here.

He took a deep breath, put his hat back on, and said, "Sir - do you remember last time I was here, you told me about the mix you put on Mench's fur to keep the fleas away?"

Mench, hearing her name, poked her whiskered face around the corner. She greeted Barty with a trilling 'meow' and trotted over to rub against his ankles and give his coat a fine layer of gray hair.

Mr. Blum nodded, scooping up the cat and holding her to his chest. She purred, burying her face in his beard with obvious delight. "Yes, of course. Did you get a cat, Dr. Wayman?" His eyes twinkled. "Is your new cat so important that you come to me when the sun is barely awake?"

Barty flushed. "N-no sir! No, I, you see-" He made himself stop, took a deep breath, and resumed speaking, slowly and clearly. "You know about the talismans that protect from plague now, I assume?"

Avram nodded. "Yes, this I know. I have regained many of my clients since they became available."

Barty nodded grimly. It made sense that the kind of people who could afford to buy the amulets were also the kind of people who would frequent a perfumer's shop. "Well, there aren't enough of them to go around. There are limits on production, because of how difficult they are to make and how few mages London has. That means people with more money and less need are buying up the stock. Director Peete must allow it, because we need the finances simply to keep

41

production going."

Anger churned in his stomach just admitting it, but he fought past the ashen taste in his mouth and continued on.

"I was thinking, perhaps there is a cheaper solution? After all, um - now we know the plague spreads by fleas. Herbs are cheaper than stone tokens, and anyone can mix things together, one doesn't have to be a mage. So, um, if we could craft your anti-flea remedy you use for Mench, and make it available to many many people in the poorer districts-"

Avram's eyes lit up. "I see! It would certainly help keep people from becoming infected, if the fleas do not want to bite them. That is very clever, Dr. Wayman. Here."

He held out Mench. Barty accepted the cat with awkward care, hoping the gentle purring meant that she wasn't upset with him.

"I will write down the ingredients, and how to assemble them." Avram moved to the next room, sitting at a table with pen and paper. Beside him, a girl who looked to be about four dutifully chewed her way through a biscuit, her other hand clutching a glass of milk. Her brown eyes lingered on Barty.

Barty gave her a smile before turning back to Avram, stroking the still-purring Mench. "Really? Just like that? I thought - well... most merchants wouldn't want to give away their secret recipes for free, sir."

Avram shook his head, already writing. "I would give it away to save a single person, Doctor, let alone so many. After all, our sages say in the Talmud, "Whoever saves a single life is considered by scripture to have saved the whole world.""

Barty's heart swelled. After the callousness of dealing with the director, the mages and the merchants, being around someone with a generous spirit and value of goodness felt like life-giving rain on his dry soul. "Still," he said, peeking at Avram's careful, clean lettering, "I'll try to make sure that your name never leaves the process - I am sure they will arrange something so that you are paid appropriately for your recipe. Especially since they are paying the mages for their work too." Fabian hadn't been paid for their part in designing the schema, of course, but that was how Fabian wanted it. Barty scowled internally, wondering how anyone could question the necromancer's goodness after such a selfless act.

"Do not fret your head over it," chuckled Avram, signing the name of his shop with a flourish at the bottom of the page: *Blum's Perfumes*. "But, well. I suppose I would not say no, if it brings in more business." He folded the recipe neatly and, taking the cat from Barty's arms with one hand, offered him the paper with the other. "Some time, Doctor, you should come for a meal and not business. I think I could teach you a little more about herbs, and perhaps some other things that would interest you." He gestured to the shelf in the corner that held a few well-used books with Hebrew lettering on their spines.

Barty blushed at the warmth in his words, unable to keep the giddy smile from his face. "Really, sir? I'd like that a lot, sir, I..." he tucked the paper into his pocket, for a moment too happy for speech. "I'll...I'll take a look at my schedule, shall I? And when I return with word from my superiors about the recipe, we can plan something."

Avram deposited his cat into the lap of the now-biscuitless child, who proceeded to carefully wipe her crumb-dusted hands on her dress before stroking the soft gray fur. "I look forward to your return, Doctor," he said with a smile, "and maybe I can interest Rabbi Szalwiski in joining us." He gave Barty a knowing look. "His father knew the Hershel family before their deaths. Are you sure you won't stay for a bit of tea?"

Barty's heart skipped a beat. The Hershel family - nothing was confirmed, but both he and Avram highly suspected that Barty's true parents had been the Hershels. He longed to stay and learn more of what Mr. Blum knew, but he also did not want to further irritate Peete - especially with such an important proposal clenched in his hands. "Yes," he said to Mr. Blum, truly regretful, "I'm so sorry, Mr. Blum, but I must go. I am already risking being late."

Avram patted Barty's shoulder. "Never mind, *Bartele*. Next time."

"Next time!" Barty agreed, beaming at the nickname. He bowed himself out and closed the door behind, feeling better than he had in weeks. He didn't know why he hadn't thought of Avram's anti-flea mix sooner! Even now he could smell it on his hands, from holding Mensch, sweet and a little bitter. He'd have to copy it down in his notebook later - what had been the ingredients? Catmint, nutmeg, alum, garlic...

It was a twenty minute walk to the Royal College of Physicians, but Barty almost floated the entire way. The bitterness growing within him like congealing tallow had melted before the warmth of Avram; his generosity, his kindness, and his home. Barty barely noticed the dirt and grime of the streets, or the smell rising through the fog under the warmth of an early fall sun. Even the corpses waiting for the collection cart on the street corner seemed cheerfully fewer than usual.

His euphoria only increased when he stepped into the College and saw Dr. James Buckler waiting for him in front of Dr. Peete's office. "James!" Barty exclaimed, grinning with delight and pulling the recipe out of his pocket. "I've had the most marvelous idea. I really think this one will work - maybe not as strongly as the amulets, but it's definitely better than nothing, and-!"

He trailed off when he saw the quick, unhappy look James gave him. There was pain in that expression, and anger, but more than that...

Pity.

"Barty-" James began, but Director Peete stepped out of the office and interrupted him. "Dr. Wayman! Just the man we were hoping to see."

"O-oh?" Barty, although shaken by James' face, took hope from Dr. Peete's good spirits. "Have you been talking about the talismans? I was hoping-"

"Come in, come in," Director Peete didn't seem to hear

Barty, just took his arm and drew him into the office. James followed after them, his silence like a stone weighing down Barty's hope and his heart. Director Peete settled Barty in a chair almost by force. "Have you ever been introduced to Ms. Magmaydon, Dr. Wayman?"

Barty blinked, his gaze finally settling on the fourth person in the room. She sat by the window, a steaming cup of tea in her weathered hand, her silver hair held back from her face in a very complicated-looking braid that ringed her head like a crown.

She met Barty's gaze and smiled, and Barty felt himself instantly relax, smiling back. "I do not believe we have been introduced, no," he said with a polite bow, "but I do know your name, madam. Magmaydon, of the mages' guild?"

"The same," she said, setting her cup in a saucer on the windowsill and spreading the skirt of her dress (or was it a robe? She was a mage after all) in a politely informal curtsey. Barty's eyes couldn't help but be drawn to the cloth - it was deep purple, with fiery orange runes embroidered all around the hem, as well as up the sides and neckline. Had he any less experience with magic himself, he would have dismissed it as decoration, but as it was, he thought he could recognize some of the runes.

She cleared her throat, and Barty blushed, realizing he was staring at her person instead of her face. "I beg your pardon," he said, mortified, and instantly met her gaze once more. "I, um, have learned a little more about magic in recent months, and I was distracted by the spellwork on your garment. Is it one of Cassandra and Elizabeth's creations?"

"It is," Magmaydon said, smiling at him. Again, Barty couldn't help but smile back. She reminded him of a wise grandmother, warm and sweet, her skin a pleasant shade of tan that put him in mind of baked goods. Not at all the sort of person he expected to be running the mage's guild - for one, he'd thought someone with the ominous name 'Magmaydon' would be wearing all black, and for another, a sweet old granny did not at all align with the cut-throat image he associated with the mages and their bloody history.

She leaned forward, capturing his gaze with her own hazel one. "And of course I have heard something of you, Dr. Wayman."

"Oh?" Barty replied, faintly flattered, faintly worried. Depending on who she had been speaking to, the accounts would vary greatly. "Nothing too terrible, I hope?"

"And what terrible things would I have to say about you, young man?" Director Peete chuckled, filling more cups with tea and passing them to Barty and James.

"I'm sure you could think of something," Barty said with a weak chuckle. His less than perfect education, for example. Or his mysterious part in finding a way to prevent the plague from spreading, about which he still hadn't told Peete the full truth, for obvious, necromancer-related reasons.

Barty accepted his cup of tea gratefully, tension seeping away from his body with the help of the hot drink in his hands. James did not, however. He only shook his head, still standing by the door, his pale features sunk in a deep scowl directed at the floor.

Barty's gaze lingered on his friend. What was James so upset about? Barty trusted James Buckler unequivocally - if something was so wrong that he was this thunderous-

"There are important events at hand, Dr. Wayman," Magmaydon the mage said, pulling Barty's attention back to herself. She gave him a mysterious, praising smile when he looked at her, as if rewarding him for listening. "Energies are moving in the world, and many of them swirl around you. You are a shaper of fortunes, have you realized that?"

"Oh, oh, I'm not really." Barty blushed, her praise only amplifying his faults in his own mind. "I just tend to stick my nose into trouble even when it's not invited. Um." He sipped his tea, trying to prevent himself from saying anything stupid. Focus, Barty. With these two important people here, now was in fact a good chance to push his own agenda. "Actually -

actually I have very much been wanting to speak to you. Both of you. At the same time."

"Oh?" Magmaydon raised her eyebrows, still dark despite her steel-gray hair. "Then it seems we were both destined for this meeting, for I have long been asking-"

Barty knew what she was going to say. He knew she wanted to ask about the preventative charm, about Fabian, and about what Barty had been doing in the mage's guild a year ago. But Barty didn't want to talk about that, now or ever. He wanted to talk about the people who were still suffering, and who could be helped. "Yes," he said firmly, speaking over her. "Destined. You see I have been listening closely to what Director Peete said about the amulets, their production difficulty, the need to raise funds to support their continual creation-" He knew he was interrupting his betters, but it was for a good cause. He did not want to let the thread of conversation be taken from him - not if he could produce something good from whatever bad was making James scowl so.

Though, when Barty managed to peek his way, he could see a slight smirk on James' face, his eyes still on the floor.

"-and of course the magepower required to allow them to function. Director Peete has been right on so many accounts, I have seen that. So, I have a proposal, an alternative solution."

He set aside his teacup and drew out Mr. Blum's recipe. Catmint, nutmeg, marigold, alum, garlic. Dockleaf to form the base of the poultice. Lavender to mask the smell of garlic. Simple, affordable ingredients. He beamed across the desk at Dr. Peete and Magmaydon, hoping their stunned expressions were a good indicator.

"It isn't magical," he said, smoothing the recipe out on the desk, "but I believe it will be very effective at controlling the spread of fleas, and through the fleas, plague. A simple herbal compound, much cheaper to make, and easy to produce in large batches, that would result in-"

"Dr. Wayman." Magmaydon leaned forward, covering Barty's hand with her own. Barty froze in place, mouth still open, staring at her. Her hand was warm and glittered with rings, some rune-etched, some with stones, one that changed colors, twinkling almost playfully with every shift of her hand. Her fingernails, resting against the skin of his wrist, gleamed in shades of deep purple that matched her dress. "Director Peete told me about the goodness of your heart. What you are doing is endlessly admirable, trying to help those less fortunate than yourself."

Barty managed a weak smile, but it was difficult - both because her contact with his hand was somehow making it hard to remember what he was saying, and because, despite his confusion, he could still sense the usual 'but' that came whenever-

"But what we are here to discuss," she continued, still smiling, "is of a far graver nature than just the few pockets of plague left in London."

"I don't think matters get graver than the lives of hundreds of people, madam," Barty said, but his words felt weak and silly. He hadn't even heard what Magmaydon had to say yet, but it was clearly quite important, if she had come all this way at this early hour.

She squeezed his hand, her nails digging into his skin. "Not even the return of the very same cursed variant that you yourself worked so hard to break, only a year ago?"

Barty's heart turned to ice in his chest. "No!"

"I'm afraid so," Director Peete put in. Barty tore his gaze away from Magmaydon, even though she still had his hand, and Director Peete held up a letter, the smile gone from his face. "I just received news from one of my colleagues down in Devonshire. Not only has Plymouth had an outbreak - one with the exact same symptoms as our own dreadful variant - but their doctor who specialized in plague was recently found murdered in his own home." He shook his head. "Dreadful business. Dreadful."

"Yes," James finally spoke up, his voice as tight as suture thread, "and so you are leaping on this convenient excuse to send away the only two doctors who disagree with your methods of distributing and profiting off of the protective amulets."

Director Peete paled visibly. "I am sending you out of concern for these ill citizens, James Buckler," he said, trying to imitate the heat of James' anger, and not quite managing it.

"Wait - wait," Barty broke in, his voice cracking. "You're sending us away? Out of London?"

"Yes, out of London. To Devonshire, all the way down to Plymouth, with instructions to aid any towns that need our assistance on the way." Buckler cast Director Peete a venomous look. "Convenient, isn't it? Getting rid of two dissenters long enough for you to make your pretty penny while the plague is still hot enough for it to matter."

"That is enough! How dare - of all the atrocious accusations!" Peete spluttered. Barty had never seen him angry before. Now, either so indignant or so ashamed he could barely speak, Director Peete drew himself up and pointed at the door, glaring at James. "Get out of my office," he said, the words shaking. "You WILL go as you are sent, both of you."

"You are, after all, the two most experienced doctors in this matter," Magmaydon added, apparently pretending not to see James storm out of the room. She kept her attention trained on Barty, as if expecting him to understand, to be reasonable. "Who better than you two, to send to end the problem? You have already done it once. It is simple, common sense."

Barty's mind was being pulled in two directions. On the one hand, James was right - they represented a problem to Dr. Peete - an opposition that the director would probably be glad to have out of the way. On the other hand, Magmaydon was also right - if this truly was a similar plague, it made the most sense to send Barty and Buckler. They were the only two doctors who knew what the magical curse behind the lethal variant looked like, and how to end it. Nobody else would stand a chance.

In the end, unfortunately, it didn't matter what Barty thought. He had to obey his superior. "While we are gone," he said, trying to hold their gazes, "please consider working on my proposal." He nudged the recipe forward, but Peete didn't even look at him or the paper.

"While you are gone," Magmaydon said gently, "we will still need your blood, to continue production of the amulets."

Barty blinked at her. "What? More?" He had been giving it every week, as much as he could bear at once. The mages had said several times they would work on an alternative solution, but they had yet to come up with any way of replacing 'blood of a person immune to plague' with something of equal value. There had been some search for other persons with immunity, however, immunity was very difficult to detect, and not worth potentially wasting resources and time on amulets made with blood they were less than 100% positive about.

"We don't know how long you will be gone," Peete said, turning away. Barty heard him fumbling in the cabinet, and a cork being drawn. Apparently the Director's nerves had been more shaken by his argument than he wanted to admit. "Amulet production rates must remain steady. We want to avoid panic if you are delayed in Devonshire."

"Am I likely to be delayed in Devonshire?" Barty asked, heart sinking. He had a feeling he already knew the answer.

"Likely or not, it is best to be prepared," Magmaydon said, squeezing his hand. "Stop by the mages' guild after your rounds tonight. I personally will oversee the draw, we will make it clean and quick." Once more, she smiled, and Barty felt both strangely comforted and a bit foolish.

Only when Barty gave her a weary smile back and said, "I'll be there," did she release her grip on his hand.

"Well then, Director," she said, slinging a handbag over her shoulder and carefully arranging her own amulet around her neck - Barty instantly recognized it as one of the plague-repelling ones - "thank you ever so much for your help in this matter." She went over to Peete and took his hand in both of hers. "It means the world to us that you continue to cooperate and support our guild in these difficult times. I have told you before, but I will say it again: if you or yours are ever in need, you can always turn to the mages' guild for assistance."

Peete's tension melted away under Magmaydon's smile and touch, just as Barty's had done. "Thank you, my dear," he said, leaving a kiss on the back of her ring-adorned hand. "Please let me know if you need anything else from me or any member of our College. I'll be sure the boy keeps his word and shows up, as promised."

Barty felt faintly annoyed at this. He always kept his word. He was a man of honor. He didn't need Director Peete looking over his shoulder as if he were a child. However, he said nothing, just drained his teacup, seeking liquid fortification.

It wasn't as soothing as he wanted it to be. In fact, it was quite bitter.

"I'll be off then," Barty said loudly. "Rounds, you know." He already felt like he'd walked ten miles, but he had a full day's work ahead of him still.

"Tonight, Dr. Wayman," Peete said, watching Barty set his cup aside and stand, re-donning his mask. "Don't forget."

"I won't," said Barty. Where only minutes ago there had been hope, there now throbbed dull disbelief. Sent away to Devonshire. More talismans.

No anti-flea remedy.

He walked past Director Peete and Magmaydon, out the door, and onto the dirty, stinking streets of London, unable to wash away the bitterness that lingered in his mouth, unable to will away the ache that lurked in his heart.

He had a long day ahead of him, and a long night after that. He supposed he would carry on, as he always did.

After all, there was nothing else he could do.

CHAPTER 6: REPORTING FOR DUTY

At 8:00 pm sharp, Bartholomew Wayman, unmasked and in plain-clothes consisting of dark trousers, a white shirt, gray vest and a worn-but-presentable coat, knocked on the door to the mages' guild and tried not to wish he was at home in his own bed.

While it was true that there were far less plague victims now than there had been at this time last year, that also meant that many of the doctors working in the city were now assigned to more normal doctorly tasks like setting bones and treating non-plague illnesses. Barty, low ranking and under-educated as he was by comparison to the others, was one of a handful still on plague duty. Meaning that his day had been full, as usual, of swollen buboes, stinking sweat, puss, blood, and other bodily fluids that he was well used to but still rather wished he could do without.

So it was that he wore a cloak of exhaustion over his normal attire, waiting on the doorstep of the mages' guild, watching his breath fog in the cooling autumn air. Summer was gone and winter fast approaching. How time flew, despite all the suffering the world bore.

The door opened and, of all people, Jack the rat catcher stood in the doorway, grinning at him, her freckled face as cheerful as ever. "Well, well, well!" she said, her smile widening with each repetition. "If it isn't my favorite wet rat. Hi there, Barty boy, how are you?"

She offered her hand and Barty shook it, a smile creeping over his own face. Jack's good spirits were terribly contagious. "Better now that I saw you. You look amazing, Jack! I mean-" He realized that sounded like something other than he meant. "Ah, amazingly healed, that is." She had been one of the first plague victims to actually recover, once they broke the curse.

She laughed at his stammering. "I always look amazing! But, yeah. Good as new, me." She thumped her chest, making the lacy ruffles of her shirt poof about. "Clara mentioned something about the doctor with magic blood stopping by the guild, so I thought I'd pop in and stick my nose where it wasn't wanted." She winked at him.

"Clara...your new girlfriend?" Barty said, putting the pieces together. "And there for a minute I thought that, um, you were sent by someone else." Once upon a time, Jack had been Fabian's envoy. No more, apparently.

"Yeeeah, well," Jack's grin went hard at the edges. "*Someone else* has been a bit too busy for me lately. And yet here I am, running their errands anyway." She reached into her pocket and pulled out a large dead rat. "Special delivery from the boss." She held it out to Barty, dangling by its long, bald tail.

Barty, with great reluctance, accepted the rat. It was a

common black rat, sleek and, thankfully, without any signs of mange or rot. "You shouldn't be too hard on them," he said, feeling a bit guilty himself for Jack's neglect, though it was no fault of his own. "The um. The ordeal-" he sighed, shook his head, and dropped the euphemism. "Listen, from what James said, having a baby is a lot to deal with for anyone."

"Yeah, yeah," Jack waved a dismissive hand. "Ain't denying that, Doc. Neither am I denying that you all saved my life, probably, with everything you did. But, you know. I was..."

She stopped, and sighed.

"I was hoping that someday she would stop seeing me as a useful pet and instead as..."

She fell silent. Barty, all at once, remembered several things - how Jack had always cleaned up her appearance before speaking to Fabian. How Jack had gone so far to give Fabian what they wanted, be it rats or recruitment or anything more. How Jack had been running around, even as she fell sick with plague, helping carry out Fabian's plans and paying no heed to her own suffering.

Barty swallowed hard. Fabian had a magnetic personality, it was true. But now Fabian also had Ruphys, lover of a previous life, and father of their child. It wasn't hard to see how Jack would be feeling more than a little neglected.

Barty very carefully told himself that, luckily for him, he had no such problem on his end. He and Fabian had a business relationship, and the business of plague was a continuing issue.

Still, he quickly changed the subject. "So, um. Clara?"

"Yeah!" Jack brightened, grabbed his arm, and pulled him into the guild. "Absolutely GORGEOUS, mate. Redhead, adorable accent, and you know what? First time I met her? She stole my wallet!" Jack laughed uproariously, and Barty couldn't help but grin as she dragged him along the hall. "Stole my heart right along with it. Never met a feistier gal."

"I hope you two will be very happy," Barty said, feeling a little out of his depth but glad for her anyway. "Um. Did she mention anything else about what I'm doing here?"

"Nah, mate," Jack said. "And put that away, before someone sees. Honestly..."

Barty stuffed the dead rat in his inner coat pocket. "Right, um - so what is it for exactl-AH!"

The rat wriggled to life against him, crawling up his shirt and hiding flat along his shoulder. Barty had to stop and put his hands on his knees, gasping, heart thundering in his chest.

Jack chuckled. "Someone doesn't trust the mages," she said, shaking her head. "Can't imagine why. At least this way you have someone watching your back. Er..."

The rat poked its nose out from Barty's collar, and twitched its whiskers at Jack.

"...your back and your front, I guess." Jack reached forward and flicked the rat's nose. "Get in there, little bugger."

Barty shivered as the rat pulled back in. Its fur was soft, but its claws were sharp and cold on his bare skin.

"Anyway," Jack continued, "I'm spending a nice snug evening with Clara and her sticky fingers tonight." She wiggled her eyebrows just to make Barty blush. "But I'm just down the hall, with another one of these." She patted Barty's shoulder, and the rat hiding under the cloth. "Something goes wrong, I'll know, alright? You ain't alone."

Barty nodded, fighting down his flusterment and managing to find some gratitude underneath it. "Thank you, Jack," he said. "Um, who else knows I'm here?"

Jack grinned at him. "James knows, if that's what you mean."

Barty looked down, abashed. He had, indeed, been hoping his reliable friend was aware of the situation. "Thanks," he said, already feeling a bit better.

Jack chuckled. "Shame he's already married, you two would be great."

Barty flushed even brighter, opening his mouth to protest, but Jack patted his shoulder again. "I'm kidding,

kidding.You boys are brothers in arms, or something. Brothers in beaks." She chuckled. "Boss says James is working late on a case tonight, but I think he intends to get here once he's through and see you're alright after facing whatever horrors Magmaydon intends to throw at you."

"Is she going to throw horrors at me?" Barty asked, hoping very much that she wasn't.

"Well..." Jack pulled him around a corner, her pace matching his perfectly despite the fact that she was a good five inches shorter. "Think about it, Doctor. What do mages seek above all else?"

"Magic?" Barty asked, doubtful.

"Knowledge," Jack corrected. "Knowledge is power, buddy boy. And you know quite a few things they don't, and quite a few things they would prefer you didn't. So, if I were you, little rat, I'd keep my ears perked for what kind of questions are being asked, and my eyes peeled for any kind of magic that makes you squeal."

Barty wilted. He didn't know anything about magic, aside from what he'd scraped together to break a single curse a year ago. He also wasn't very good at standing up for himself, either, especially when it came to figures of authority.

He hoped Ms. Magmaydon wouldn't ask prying questions, but part of him already knew she would.

"I'll do my best," he told Jack, feeling absolutely miserable.

She slapped him on the back. "Chin up, Doc!" she said. "You've faced much worse than an old witch and a bit of bloodshed, aye? Worst comes to worst, she'll turn you into gingerbread, right?"

She cackled at Barty's mortified look. "No, she can't really do that. Come on Barty, you know magic. Charms and amulets, enchanted clothes and so on. This is human magic, not fairytale stuff. Just look sharp, alright?"

"Alright," Barty said, pulling himself together. He tugged at his coat so it fell more naturally over the rat now flattened against his shoulder. Its body was cold, despite the soft fur. "Don't get too distracted, um, with Clara."

"No promises mate," she said, winking at him and steering him to a door at the end of the hallway. "Toodles!"

And there she left him, practically skipping back down the plush purple carpet to cuddle her new mage miss.

Barty stared after her, sighing. He wished he could, for once in his life, forgo difficult things and be a person with someone to cuddle instead. Unfortunately, that did not seem to be in the cards for Dr. Bartholomew Wayman, so instead he smoothed his clothes one last time, straightened his hat, and knocked politely on the heavy wooden door before him. He hoped it was the right one - it bore no title, only a single silver star in the middle.

"Enter," said Magmaydon's voice from within.

Barty waited half a second, hoping the door would magically open itself, but it didn't. Feeling a bit sheepish, he pushed it open and stepped in, holding his breath.

He had expected magic everywhere, maybe lights carved with glowing runes, mysterious spell components hanging from the rafters, and, if he were lucky, perhaps an enchanted painting or two with moving occupants. To his slight disappointment, however, he found that the head of the mage's guild had an office that was, in fact, very normal. She stood up from behind her serviceable, dark desk, set aside a paper full of rows of numbers that looked very much like a sales report, and removed her spectacles to smile at him. Her gray hair now lay loose about her shoulders in soft waves. Dark curtains hung over her windows. The sole element of magic in the room was her desk lamp, an enchantment etched orb that glowed a candle-like pale yellow.

"Thank you so much for coming, Dr. Wayman," Magmaydon said, stepping forwards and taking both his hands in her own. "I know you have had a long, trying day, but it means a great deal to me and to the still at-risk population of London for whom you are making this sacrifice."

He flushed and looked down, unable to meet that smile without feeling self conscious, focusing instead on her rings again. "I-it's really nothing," he said, watching the color changing stone shift from green to yellow. "Plenty of folks have shed blood for the good of the people of England. I am just one of many."

Her hands gave his a warm squeeze. "An honorable spirit as well as a humble one," she said. Her nail polish had changed, Barty noticed. It was now a vibrant orange, instead of purple. She reached for his face, tilting his chin up so she could meet his gaze with her own hazel one. "I am sure you have many admirable qualities, Dr. Wayman," she said, her smile somehow making him feel silly even though she was giving him a compliment. "Here, come take a seat."

Magmaydon led him to a chair by her desk, gesturing for him to sit. "Would you like some tea? This may take a little time, and we have found that drinking something while undergoing such a process leads to less side effects."

"Oh, um-" Barty fought back the question of 'why does the mage's guild have experience draining people's blood?' and instead scrambled to find a reason not to drink anything the guild leader offered him. "N-no, thank you, I just had some- OUCH."

He had almost forgotten about the undead rat hiding in his shirt, but its sharp little teeth latching into his skin reminded him in a hurry. It took all his will to not slap his hand over his shoulder, but it had already moved, scurrying down his shirt to the sleeve of the hand that was still held by the guild leader.

"Are you alright?" she asked, giving him a strange look and drawing closer again, resting her other hand over the back of his. "Is something wrong?"

"N-no!" he gasped, staring at her. "Nothing is-" he cut off, feeling those teeth again on the soft flesh under his wrist. He looked down at the cuff of his sleeve-

-just in time to see one of Magmaydon's nails change

from orange to purple.

She peered at him, her expression somewhere between amused and concerned. "What is the matter, Dr. Wayman?"

"Y-you know, you know what? I think I will have some tea after all," he babbled, his mind racing. He *knew* all her nails were orange moments ago. Why had two of them changed? "Sorry, um, my...my shoulder," he put his free hand on his shoulder, "it still pains me sometimes, um. From my injury."

She gave him a not-quite-believing look, but nodded, her smile humoring. "I see. Well, I am certainly sorry for your pain." She finally let go of his hand and moved to a little silver teapot on her desk.

Barty let out a breath at the sound of tea being poured, and rubbed at his stinging shoulder. Ouch. Did Fabian's rat have to bite so hard? "It's alright, I am greatly recovered. I was quite lucky, in fact. I could have died from such a wound, but James Buckler is a most skillful doctor, even under the greatest pressures."

"So I have heard," Magmaydon said, turning back to him with a smile and two cups of tea. One she gave to him, the other she laid by her own chair. She did not yet sit, instead remaining by his side, looking down at him with that same gentle expression. "May I see your arm, Dr. Wayman?"

"Um-" Barty felt a brief moment of panic, but the rat was already moving, scuttling back up the underside of his sleeve and around the back of his shirt. It took a lot of willpower for him to not squirm at the sensation. "Of course - may I ask why?"

He offered his hand to her, and she gently took it, turning it over, pulling his sleeve back to look at his skin. Barty worried she was looking for rat bites, but rather than focusing on his wrist, she traced the indent of his elbow. Multiple marks from thumb-lancet use were there, some old and mostly healed from his time working with Fabian, some fresh from his donations in more recent weeks.

Her fingers lingered on these older marks. "Who was

the first to do this to you?" she asked, her voice soft and sympathetic.

"Dr. Buckler, of course," Barty, said, because he wasn't about to tell the head of the Mage's Guild that he allowed an infamous necromancer to draw his blood. "James is the most intelligent-"

Magmaydon's grip on his arm tightened a fraction, another of her nails changing from orange to purple. "Dr. Wayman," she said, very softly, forcing him to meet her gaze again, "do not lie to me."

Barty stared, and this time he didn't need the warning of the rat's teeth on the skin of his shoulder to understand what was happening.

Magmaydon's nails changed color every time he lied.

The first one had changed when he said he had already had tea. The second had changed when he said nothing was wrong.

Now this one had changed, when he had lied to cover for Fabian.

He was stuck in this room, with the lives of innocent people resting on his willingness to donate blood for the amulets, with the head of the mages' guild that had hated Fabian for decades, with one of Fabian's own undead rats resting on his shoulder, and he couldn't tell lies.

"I'm sorry," he said, fighting to keep his voice steady. "It's been a very long day and I would like to go home. Can we please get this donation finished?"

"Of course." Magmaydon went to her desk, the straightness of her spine and sharpness of the movement of her hands somehow conveying that she was disappointed in Barty and his untruths. She shifted the papers aside, opened a cabinet, and pulled out a strange contraption of glass, stone and rubber. This she set on the desk before Barty, and gave him a small, less-than-friendly smile. "Do you know what this is?"

Barty peered at the piece. The main body was a round glass vial, with two holes in the top. One hole was attached to a rubber tube which ended in a metal point, the other was open. The base of the thing was stone, with slightly familiar runes etched in it. Barty thought he recognized the rune for 'heat' there. That, connected with the implications of the sharp edge, made something click Barty's head. "Is this something for using a change in temperature to draw out liquid?"

"That is correct," Magmaydon said, her smile slightly less frosty. She tapped the stone base, and explained, "First we heat the air within. Then we put a cork in the open segment. Then, once you yourself are connected, we switch the glass to a cooling setting. The hot air contracts as it cools, drawing your blood through to fill the space. Once there is a steady flow, your beating heart will do the rest of the work."

"A very clever device," Barty said, feeling more than a little uncomfortable but determined not to complain. "Let's get it done, then."

Magmaydon tapped the desk with her nails. "Your arm, please, Doctor."

Barty shrugged out of his coat, rolled the sleeve of his white shirt all the way up, and rested his arm on the table. Magmaydon set to work, switching the device to heat, cleaning the metal mouthpiece, and then finally examining his arm again. "Would you prefer I use one of the old punctures?"

"It doesn't matter to me," Barty said, looking anywhere but the sharp metal that was about to enter his skin. The shelves in this room were full of books, all clean and new. He supposed when an area of study had only become legal within the last hundred years, there were not so many ancient texts on the subject. "May I ask you how you became a mage, Madam?"

She carefully pushed the tube ending into his vein, and he managed not to flinch. "My mother was a witch, and her mother before her," she said. "They had to hide it, of course. People were not always so kind to women with our manner of abilities."

"Yes," Barty said solemnly. He thought of his birth

parents, murdered for their religion and heritage. "I have a bit of that caution in my own history." He tried to watch as his blood began to flow through the tube and drip into the glass bottle, but looking at it for more than a few seconds made his head spin, so he closed his eyes. He'd done plenty of blood drawings in recent months, but somehow seeing his own blood leaving his body in such a neat, calculated way felt like an entirely different experience.

"Your own history?" Magmaydon settled in a chair at his side, resting her fingers on his arm. It would have looked like she was only trying to steady the tube, but Barty rather suspected she needed contact with him for her fingernail-magic to work.

"Yes. I'm a Jew by birth, you see," he said stoutly, keeping his eyes closed. "The Jewish people have been treated rather horribly through the ages. Not many people know that they were often blamed for plagues, and attacked because of that falsehood."

"Ah, of course." She seemed unsure of how to respond to that. She touched his hand, and asked with soft concern. "Are you in pain?"

He opened his eyes, meeting her gaze. "I'm alright. How much will you take?"

"To this mark," she indicated a line etched into the glass of the beaker, about one-third from the bottom. "I could take more without hurting you, but you have a long journey in the coming days."

Barty risked another peek at the glass. His blood trickled merrily into it, already a quarter of the way to the mark. He shifted his gaze back to Magmaydon, though, before he got dizzy again. "I really hope," he said, measuring his words, "that this will go to protecting people who truly need it."

She smiled at him. "I am aware of your concerns, Dr. Wayman. Rest assured, we will not turn *all* the way to callous profiteering the second you leave the city."

Barty would have preferred reassurance that they would

spend more resources on helping the poor, not maintaining the status quo. He opened his mouth to press the argument further, but before he could get a word out, she had her own question for him.

"When was the last time you saw Lord Fabian?" she asked, as calm as if she were asking what he had for dinner yesterday.

His words died in his throat. For a moment he just stared at her, his shock that she would ask so blunt a question warring with a panicked struggle of how to respond. He had to tell the truth, but he had to do it in a way that wouldn't actually betray Fabian to the leader of the very guild that housed someone who had engineered a devastating plague to take down all their extended relatives. "Isn't he dead?" Barty said, focusing very hard on the concept of Fabian's previous iteration, the assassinated tyrant-king. After all, James himself had said that present-day-Fabian was no lord.

Magmaydon gave him a cold smile, holding her silence long enough for them both to note that the pitter-pat of Barty's blood dripping into the glass container had doubled with his increased heart rate. "When," she repeated, "was the last time you saw Lord Fabian?"

"I saw Lord Fabian hung on a gallows last year," Barty said, managing to keep his voice steady. Still speaking a truth, if not necessarily answering her question. "So did over a hundred witnesses."

Magmaydon's eyes flickered down to her nails. Barty shot a glance at them very briefly, then returned his gaze to her face, relieved to see that none of them had changed. He could do this. He could answer with truths, just not the truths she wanted.

She looked back to Barty, her green gaze calculating. "And you have not spoken to Fabian since then?"

Barty gave a weak smile. "Do you spend much time speaking to corpses, madam? I think one would need to be a necromancer to do such a thing."

Her smile was definitely sharper now. She had noticed him answering her question with a question. He would have to be more careful doing that. She leaned closer, resting her warm hand on his exposed arm. "Do you spend time speaking to corpses, Barty Wayman?"

His mind whirled at that. He did, in fact - as James Buckler was a corpse. But that he absolutely could not reveal. He would have rather died first. "T-there are many corpses in my line of work," he said. "Many times I have spoken in apology for failing in my duty."

"How sentimental." She brushed a finger along the rubber tube still connecting his arm to the glass. It was now filled halfway to the mark. He just had to hold out a little longer. "Did you know, Dr. Wayman, that there are rumors of you helping Lord Fabian break into the palace last year? You were seen there by several witnesses, under very suspicious circumstances."

Her fingers rested on the metal head of the tube, still embedded in his arm.

And suddenly, Barty was angry.

He stared into her face, unblinking, unsmiling, his memory full of pain, and angry voices, and spellwork glowing on the wall, warding the door against necromancy.

He asked, "Do you know what your own guild member, Zacharius, was doing at the palace at that same time, Madam?"

She froze at that, but only for a moment. "I have no idea what you're talking about."

One of her nails changed color, right there on his arm. Barty stared at it, then up at her, swallowing down the horror that suddenly lurched through his soul.

She knew. She knew one of her own subordinates was connected to the plague.

She too looked at the nail, and then at him, cold understanding in her expression. The game was entirely up, now.

She rested her thumb on the sharp device still inserted

in Barty's arm, the rainbow ring swirling with her every movement. "Is Fabian alive?"

Barty winced at the sudden increase of pressure, metal digging into his already pierced flesh. Even the minute amount of weight from her thumb on the metallic mouth was noticeably painful. "I saw Fabian hang-"

"Don't avoid the question," she said calmly, pressing harder. He gasped and tried to pull away, but her grip was too strong. His blood welled around the metal piece and pattered faster into the glass container - almost to the line, now. "Is Fabian alive?" There was no hesitation in her voice, no regret in those cold eyes. She wanted information, and she intended to get it. "Tell me the truth, Doctor. Now."

Barty couldn't think - the horror of his situation was too much for him. Pain lanced through his arm, so sharp he was afraid she would sever the vein entirely. He couldn't lie, a lie would just answer as much as the truth. So he told the truth - but not the truth she wanted. "I never had a medical education until this year!" he said, his eyes stinging with tears. "I learned only from books and watching-"

She squeezed the metal into his arm. It was agony, he cried out and squirmed to get away, but her grip was firm and cold - a sharp contrast to the hot blood dripping between her fingers. "Where is Fabian now?" she said, her voice cold.

"I wanted to be a doctor all my life," Barty sobbed, "but my parents spent their money on their natural-born son!"

She leaned forward, her green gaze boring into him. "If you think this is a game-"

Please, Barty begged in his heart. Please, somebody. "I took this mask off the dead body of my mentor!" Somebody help me. Anybody. "I drink myself to sleep on evenings I miss my family!" I don't want to die of blood loss when she makes it go all the way through. "I ran away from the first girl who tried to kiss me because-"

The door slammed open. Magmaydon leapt to her feet, and Barty jerked away from her, ripping the tubing from his arm and retreating away from the desk, gasping and choking on his tears. Hot blood ran down his arm.

James Buckler stood in the doorway, trailed by Jack and a young mage with red braids and dark robes that Barty assumed was Clara. James took one look at the two of them - at Magmaydon standing by her desk, carefully wiping her hands on a handkerchief, and at Barty backed into the corner, shaking and leaking blood between his fingers, and pulled himself up to his full height. Still shorter than Barty, but tall enough that it seemed his gray gaze belonged among the thunderclouds on any dark, stormy night.

He kept that dark glare on Magmaydon, but his words were to Barty. "Wayman," he snapped, "have you finished here?"

"Yes," Barty said weakly. "I-" He shot a terrified look at Magmaydon, but she didn't meet his eye, instead turning her cool gaze on James. "They have enough."

"We're going." James shifted to the side, beckoning Barty to squeeze out past him.

Barty stepped forwards gladly, but Magmaydon moved to intercept him. "On the contrary," she said, with all the calm and professionalism of any standard business person. "I was hoping to speak with Dr. Wayman a little longer-"

She tried to rest a hand on Barty's shoulder, but James caught her wrist before she could touch him. Barty had to stop, their locked grip blocking the door.

The silent tension between the two was palpable, gray and hazel eyes locked in mutual animosity that could only be shared by two deeply insulted professionals. "Unhand me this instant," Magmaydon said, the command so cold Barty could practically feel the frost.

"All in good time," James said, and though his tone was more casual, the easy, effortless way he bent her hand away from the door showed a strength that had nothing to do with force of personality. "Out, Wayman."

Barty slipped out, and was immediately grabbed by the

redheaded mage. "This way, quick," she said, steering him down the hall. "I can help your arm. We'll wait for James."

"That would be wonderful," Barty said weakly. He sparing a glance down at his clenched hand and shuddering at just how much blood flowed through his fingers and onto the carpet. "B-bandages would be a great idea."

"Don't need em, Bartyboy!" Jack said, skipping along at his other side with a wide grin. "Clara's a medical mage. She specializes on matters of the flesh, and is very good at-"

"Hush, you," Clara flashed Jack a glare, steering Barty into another room. Jack only smiled more broadly.

Barty cast a last look over his shoulder where James and Magmaydon, though no longer physically touching, remained locked in a very professional, glacier-esque conversation that involved a lot of grim expressions and folded arms. Then Jack closed and locked the door, and Clara guided him to a chair.

It was good she did, because Barty's knees buckled as he sat. He didn't know how long it would be before he could stand again.

Jack patted his back sympathetically. "Looking a bit green there, Doc."

"I don't feel great," Barty admitted faintly. He felt he should examine the room, but one glance up showed him two of everything, so he closed his eyes, resisting the urge to lay his head on the table. "She...she was..."

He stopped, embarrassed. What would they think of him, if he explained how much she had got to him? He had agreed to come, after all. He had known there would be risks. To complain now, especially after he had needed to be saved, would just make him look more pathetic.

"Oh, Lord," Clara said, peeling his fingers back from his arm and staring at the blood trickling merrily onto the table. Barty peeked just enough to see that there was already bruising spreading from the puncture wound, and a red handprint where he'd tried to stem the flow. "That's...wow. Hey, buddy." Clara gently patted his arm. "I'll fix it in a jiffy, alright? You're safe now."

The sincerity in her voice made him look up. Clara was young, about his own age, with eyes so dark they were almost black and a long scar along one cheek. Despite her youth, the understanding in her gaze spoke of experience beyond her years.

She gave him a smile, once their eyes met, and said, "Hate it when people you think you can trust treat you worse than garbage, eh?"

Barty couldn't help it, his eyes watered again and he looked down. "I had hoped....I had hoped it would be different."

The full weight of it settled on him then - the grief and pain of not just being hurt, but being betrayed by someone he had wanted to trust even against his better judgment. He sniffed hard, hiding his face in his shaking free hand. It smelled of blood.

"Jack warned me you're a bit of a softie," Clara said with a sympathetic smile, "but harder people than you have been manhandled by her and come away in tears." She pulled out a small notebook, tearing free a piece of paper and laying it flat on the table.

"Yeah." Jack pulled up a chair, spun it around, and sat in it backwards, draping her elbows over the edges and resting her chin on her arms. "She's a right old b...witch."

"I almost can't believe it." Barty wiped his eyes on his sleeve, trying to laugh through his tears. "She seemed so kind, like a grandma I always wished I had."

"That's how she got so far in the guild," Clara said. Barty peeked over at her - she was writing carefully on a piece of paper - a circle of runes. "Magmaydon pretends to be kind, or even professional, but she's got a mean streak." She sighed. "Magmaydon says anyone who wants to get far in life has to have one."

"And if it's any consolation, Wayman," Jack said, giving him a significant look, "you aren't the first person in the world to think you could trust someone because of charm and kindness, only to find that they want something from you, and they're willing to hurt you to get it."

Barty looked down. "If I weren't so soft hearted-'

"Being soft hearted has nothing to do with it, Doctor." Clara lifted his arm and slid the paper under it, then used some of his dripping blood to write in a few more runes. "People take advantage to get what they want. Any girl on the street will tell you the same thing, honestly."

Barty blinked at that, a bit taken aback. He hadn't thought to draw a comparison between his situation and the one Clara was implying. But now she'd shown the symmetry, he couldn't ignore it. "This world is so awful sometimes," he said, the words flimsy as paper in his mouth.

"Speaking of girls," Jack said, changing the subject with half a grin. "What was the one you were babbling about before we burst in there?"

"What..?" Barty had to take a moment to remember. Oh, she was talking about what he'd been babbling to keep Magmaydon off the trail. "Ah, that?" He gave a weak laugh. Clara was writing on his arm now, using her forefinger and his blood. He was glad to have a distraction from whatever it was she was doing. "It was true. Becky Fields. She'd actually wanted to kiss my brother, but he wouldn't have her. She only tried to kiss me because she wanted to make him jealous." He shook his head, remembering the old ache. "I don't know. Most lads told me I should have just been happy for the attention. But... well." His face heated and he turned his gaze on Clara's work, suddenly needing a distraction from the distraction. "If I do ever kiss someone, I want them to be kissing me for *me*. Not for someone else."

Clara gave his hand a gentle pat. "You are the most innocent, naive boy I have ever met," she said sweetly. "Don't ever change. I hope you get kissed soon."

Barty blushed more and grumbled crossly, "I know what I am. Just get on with it, please."

She did, resting her fingers on the ring of runes written on the paper, closing her eyes, and focusing. Suddenly, Barty's muscles twitched, and he gasped as, with a brief flash of heat and tingling, his wound sealed itself closed. He bent over his arm, staring in awe, and even dared smear away some of the remaining blood to see for sure.

The wound was entirely gone, with only a faint red line to show where it had been, and a bit of lingering bruising.

"That's amazing," he said, stunned. "Maybe I should have come to you guys for my shoulder."

Clara grinned at him. "If there had been any mage-healers left in the city for it, you should have. But I think almost everyone had left."

"Oh, yeah." Barty peeled his arm off the bloody paper. "What a mess."

"Wayman!" A strong knock on the door. "Time to go!"

Jack bounded over, unlocked it, and threw it open, smiling at James. "Perfect timing, Jimmy! The patient is healed!"

James walked in, looking very cross, and more than a little worried. Ignoring Jack, he went right for Barty. "Are you - ah. I see they've already patched you up. Good."

"Yes, sir," Barty stood, staggered, had to grip the back of his chair to keep himself steady. "S-sorry," he muttered, holding tight as the room settled from its leisurely spin. "Lost a bit too much, I think."

"I should say so!" James put a hand on his shoulder. "Sit right back down, let me look you over."

"N-no, James, really, I'm alright-"

"I said sit."

Barty sat, knowing full well that the undead doctor could make him sit if he so chose, and allowed James his inspection. He could see that his friend was still seething from the encounter, but his care was genuine, and his hands were gentle as he took Barty's pulse and checked his pupils. "Alright. You look fit enough to walk. We'll clean you up when we get home, but I want to get out of here."

"I couldn't agree more, sir," Barty said, standing more slowly this time and managing to keep his feet.

He and James bid farewell to Clara and Jack, and soon enough they were outside, in the cold evening air. At least it was a bit less pungent at this hour. The familiar sights of stonework buildings, flickering oil lamps and yellow-lit windows soothed Barty's soul in a way that felt far more magical than any spellwork.

"Thank you," Barty said, once they'd put space between themselves and the guild, "for coming to find me."

James was quiet a moment, then sighed. "I was only able to find you so quickly because of Fabian."

Barty looked up at him, surprised. "Fabian?"

James nodded, his expression guarded. "They sent one of their rats to hang around, with a note saying where you were. The wretched little beast started kicking up a fuss while I was in the middle of my reporting, so I dropped it all and came as swiftly as I could."

Barty reached for his shoulder, and felt the rat still sitting there. He pulled it out, frowning. "Why didn't you bite her?" he demanded, dangling the beast by its tail.

The rat twitched its whiskers at him, and serenely began to wash its face with its little paws, hanging upside down in the air.

"Think about it," James said, scowling at the rat too. "You really expect Fabian to stick their neck out for you by putting something undead right in Magmaydon's view? It was risky enough with me being there."

"I suppose," Barty said, slipping the rat in his pocket. He felt it curl up there, a cold, furry lump. "I suppose, also, Fabian knew you were on the way already."

"Yeah."

They walked in silence, side by side. Barty wondered if Fabian's rat would have done something, if things had gone any further. He sighed, and resigned himself to never knowing.

Soon, they would be leaving London, the Guild, the College, and Fabian, far behind.

It was best to focus on the future.

CHAPTER 7:
RAVEN HUNT

Dark clouds hung heavy over Whiston. A hungry fog tricked in from the forest, licking at the windows and leaving them damp, submerging the entire town in cold, wet blackness. The people of Whiston were stubborn and persistent - but they were not fools. Fools did not live long, this close to the King's lands. One by one they withdrew, locking their doors and shuttering their windows, prepared to wait out the gloom within the safety of their walls and the warmth of their firelight.

Only a fool would remain out in such darkness. A fool, or someone looking for fools.

The Hunt sang in Jeremiah's veins as he checked his watch, the tarnished silver giving off no sparkle in the light from the tavern window. Within the tavern a man dined - a traveling merchant from a bigger city, though which city he was from changed each time someone asked him. This particular merchant had never passed through Whiston before, but Jeremiah had heard of him in a few other places; in Plymouth, Exeter, and some of the smaller towns scattered here and there. The stories were all the same. The tradesman, Istani, would show up, offering exotic looking silks and other imports from the Turkish empire. He would, as well, distribute samples of a strange dark potion, one that made the drinker feel astounding goodness. He did not mention, however, after people had sampled his wares, felt the euphoria, and bought many bottles, that the mysterious elixir was highly addictive. He did not warn his customers that starting down the road of his magical brew would leave them as needy, begging wretches before they'd gotten to the bottom of their supply, unable to think about anything but acquiring more. From what Jeremiah had been told, Istani had been banned from almost every city and town he'd passed through.

But now Istani was here in Whiston, deciding to try his luck among the folks in a place that technically wasn't supposed to exist. Jeremiah could see him now, through the window, in a flashy red cloak at the inn's best table by the fire. The trader was finishing up his dinner, in warmth and comfort, before he went out into the night to peddle his wares away from the eye of anyone who might object. Jeremiah watched, noting the extra flourish Istani used when wiping his lightly-mustached mouth on a colorful handkerchief. It was a casual display of what he had to offer: the handkerchief, silk and patterned with exotic, colorful flowers, hinted at much more hidden away in his cart of wonders. Jeremiah could see the cleverness of the gesture as easily as he could see the traveler's tan on the man's face and hands, or the sun-bleached tips of hair he wore tied back in a well-tended queue. The man gave every appearance of being a wealthy, self-respecting vendor.

Jeremiah had, however, already sent Shilling to check the man's cart of merchandise. He knew that under a few bundles of silk goods were crates full of little glass bottles brimming with dark liquid.

The man was a nuisance, and had led to the deaths of dozens who didn't know what they were getting into.

He was the perfect target: not for Jeremiah, but for the Raven.

Istani stood up from the table. Jeremiah stepped away from the window, The Hunt burning in his veins like potent drink. Istani's words of thanks to Ida drifted out of the fog; smooth, smiling notes accompanied by the clink of coin. "The meal was excellent," the trader said, his voice tastefully accented with French and Turkish. "Thank you so much for your hospitality. I am going to take a walk to ease my digestion. Will the door be open when I return?"

Ida gave some murmured assurances, and Istani's sharp steps made their way to the door. He slipped out without glancing around, brushing past where Jeremiah lingered in the shadows. He took a single detour - stopping by the stable to remove a clinking satchel from his cart. This he hoisted over his shoulder before continuing down the street towards the loudest and most brightly lit of Whiston's three taverns.

Where better to hook more customers, Jeremiah thought bitterly, than in a place where people are already feeding their addictions?

Jeremiah waited until the gaudy red-patterned cloak was halfway down the street before slipping after him. It was not Istani he watched, though, but the rooftops of the surrounding buildings.

The sky was a black haze, letting no light through the thick, heavy clouds. Not a single star twinkled. The only reason Jeremiah could see at all was thanks to the lit lamps that cast a dim light over the main street.

It was because of those faint, flickering lights that he spotted what he was looking for - barely. Among the shadows on the rooftops moved another shadow, silent and lithe, with nothing to betray his presence but the slight reflection of lamplight on leather, and a brief flash of green through glass.

The Raven was on the hunt.

Jeremiah kept his gaze on that shadowy spot. He didn't need to watch Istani - he already knew where the man was going.

Preparedness was everything, on a Hunt. Jeremiah had prepared, these past few days - prepared in knowing the streets in darkness, prepared in researching the prey The Raven had already taken, the times the deaths had occurred, and the manners of those deaths. He had prepared his own trap as well - several of them, in fact, in case anything went in an unexpected direction. So confident was he in the success of his plan, he had even sent word to the King, requesting that the roads remain open and waiting for him this very evening.

The next few minutes would decide if he had done enough.

Istani turned a corner, disappearing from Jeremiah's sight.

The shadow among shadows moved, pulling a blade that gleamed silver-orange in the lantern-light and dropping down from the roof, graceful as a cat, following after the trader.

Jeremiah left his cover, moving swiftly. Drawing his sword with no more noise than the sighing of the wind, he blessed the fog that hid him further.

A screech broke the night silence.

Jeremiah lunged into a run, following the sound of a blade entering flesh. Istani's scream choked off into a gurgle, but still the stabbing noise continued, accompanied by heavy, sharp panting.

Jeremiah rounded the corner, sword swinging.

Steel met steel in a reverberating clang. The Raven leapt away but did not flee, twirling the bloody dagger into a ready pose, green flashing dangerously in his misted glass lenses.

Jeremiah fell into a ready swordsman's stance, his own

blade clean but for the red smear where it had crossed with The Raven's. He gave his opponent a wolfish smile, and got only an empty, emerald-tinted stare in return while the Raven fixed his top hat back into place.

Jeremiah struck again. The Raven parried effortlessly, more blood splattering from his dagger, onto Jeremiah's blade, his clothes. This time Jeremiah pressed him, careful to keep his strikes clear and strong, stepping around the red-cloaked body that lay cooling in a pool of its own fluids.

The Raven retreated from the onslaught of blows, but with no haste. If anything, his steps were polite. Calculating. He let Jeremiah keep the offensive for a time, countering every slash with inhuman grace and speed. Most men would have surrendered, when armed with a dagger in the face of a sword, but not The Raven. He only defended himself, slowly backing away, the tails of his black coat making the movement of his legs hard to read in the deep darkness, his strange leather mask hiding any hint a human face could give away.

It was terrifying, in a way. Jeremiah had been a huntsman for years, and had plenty of skill with his blade. More than enough skill to best most men in battle

Enough skill to know that, even with a superior weapon, he was hopelessly outmatched.

The Raven saw him falter, and lunged, his knife flashing red. Jeremiah choked in shock, his ribs suddenly burning in pain - but the blow that would normally have eviscerated him had been jarred from its course, blocked by one of the many stones woven into his jerkin. There was no time to bring his sword about to counter - the knife was already drawing back for another blow.

The Huntsman kicked instead, his steel-toed boot connecting with The Raven's leg. The man cursed explosively, staggering back, his expletives muffled by his beaked face covering.

Jeremiah ran.

To catch a predator, one sometimes had to act like prey,

but this time, Jeremiah wasn't acting. He clutched at his bloody side, breath coming in ragged gasps as he fled. The Raven stood in silence a moment, perhaps stunned by the sudden disengagement. Then Jeremiah heard the steps, quick and light, barely twenty paces behind him.

He was fast.

The steps drew closer, perhaps a dozen paces behind.

Too fast.

Jeremiah had to slow him. He couldn't get caught before the second alley. He glanced about, lengthening his stride and breathing hard. There! A clothesline, hanging between buildings up ahead, the sheets ghostly pale. Jeremiah took a deep breath, trying to force the sound of rapidly nearing feet out of his mind. He focused his energy, envisioned his goal, and leapt.

His hand closed on the cloth, and not a second too soon. Steel whistled through the air at his back. Jeremiah spun, twisting both to dodge and to yank the sheet free, throwing it into the Raven's masked face before taking off once more.

Muffled cursing befouled the air behind him. The Raven fought to free himself of the sheet. Ahead, Jeremiah saw the alley he wanted. Closer and closer - his legs burned with effort - he hadn't thought he would have to maintain a full sprint for this long, but The Raven was already closing yet again; masked death hunting him not two yards behind. Jeremiah could hear the furious, hungry panting, muffled through the leather.

Jeremiah turned down the alley just as The Raven's gloved hand closed on his cloak.

The Raven jerked him back, hard, sending him to the ground and raising his bloody dagger.

Jeremiah grabbed at the Raven's legs, trying to throw him off balance and calling to Shilling with all his mental strength.

A great silver wolf appeared in a bellowing rush of sound and movement, leaping upon the shocked Raven with a blood-curdling howl. It locked its jaws on the wrist holding the knife and brought The Raven down, both bodies almost crushing Jeremiah in a furious flurry of conflict.

Jeremiah barely managed to disentangle himself from the snarling, swearing pair. He staggered up and away, gasping and shaking with adrenaline. That had been close, far too close. He had underestimated his opponent severely, and now he bled for it. He could almost feel the blood on his neck, almost see those red, red eyes-

No. That was long ago, this was a different hunt. He tore his hand away from his scarred throat and pressed it to his wounded side instead, forced his mind back to the present, looking back at the battle that still raged on the alley floor.

Shilling was winning, but only by a hair. The enormous wolf kept his fanged grip on the Raven's knife-wielding arm, but the Raven had found a foothold among the refuse littering the floor. The man had already half turned the wolf over, and, with brute strength alone, was forcing Shilling back, gaining the advantage by inches, gaining time and space to reach into his coat. Blood trickled from between the wolf's jaws, but the Raven didn't hesitate, pulling out a second knife and preparing to finish the job-

Jeremiah lunged, flicked off the fellow's tophat, and thunked him on the skull with the hilt of his sword.

The Raven collapsed, the green light fading from his misty glass lenses.

Shilling growled at the prone figure, pawing at his masked face to be sure he was really out, before dropping his arm at last. "He was so strong!" the wolf complained, panting. "People aren't supposed to be that strong!"

'He made a deal for that strength,' Jeremiah signed, kneeling beside the unconscious man and producing a set of iron shackles from his belt. He stripped off the Raven's leather gloves, revealing pale, slender fingers, then shut the manacles around the now-exposed wrists, binding his hands behind his back. 'Judging by his mania, it is clear enough that the cost for it was quite high.'

Shilling growled in morose agreement, shivering and turning his head away from the sight of iron touching flesh. "Such a pity! People need to think through their deals more. Imagine, if only he had known, he could have made a deal with one of my brothers or sisters, and had the most wonderful friend any man could ask for." Silver eyes peeked Jeremiah's way, expecting his agreement.

The Huntsman only snorted, binding the Raven's ankles with more iron.

Shilling's wet, black nose twitched. "You're bleeding."

'I know.'

The wolf's tail wagged twice, and he edged closer. "We have a long ride tonight."

Jeremiah did not meet Shilling's hopeful gaze. *'I know this also.'*

"Let me shift to human form!" Shilling's voice was eager, brown eyes shining. "I have seen you use bandages many times - I can do it for you."

'No.' Jeremiah stood, ignoring the blood trickling down his side.

Shilling whined, the noise a strange balance between wolfish and Jeremiah's own voice. "Why not? I wish to be in your shape! To be-"

'I have told you before. I am most comfortable when you respect my person as my own.'

The wolf laid its ears back, making itself as small and sad as a two hundred pound, fanged creature could. "Come on, if I'm borrowing your shape, it hardly counts as a human companion! It's like looking at your reflection! I wouldn't do anything bad..."

'If it eases your emotions, it is not only you.'

Shilling sighed. "Yes, I know, I know. You do not seek human company, not from women or from men. You walk alone, and are comfortable doing so. You need only The Hunt, the forest and the wind." Shilling looked up at him, canine eyes twinkling with mischief, and wagged his tail, proud of using

Jeremiah's voice to recite his old, often-spoken words back at him. "And me, your best friend." Jeremiah snorted. That part was Shilling's addition. "You are a strange human," the wolf concluded fondly.

'I know.' Jeremiah could not help but smile at the Shilling's theatrics. 'But this is how I am, and how I have always been, even before we met. I need a horse, please'

The wolf shifted, morphing instantly into a great, silver stallion. "I like how you are," said the horse, "even if I complain sometimes."

'I also like how I am, even if you complain sometimes. Now that that's settled...' Jeremiah heaved the unconscious Raven onto the horse's back, tying him on with a length of rope. 'The sooner we get him to the King, the sooner I can take time to heal.'

"And then we're coming back, right?" Shilling bent his forelegs, making it easier for Jeremiah to jump onto his back.

'Yes," Jeremiah signed, holding his hand out for Shilling's side-set horse eye to see. 'We will be back, awaiting our next hunt. Now..."

He nudged Shilling's sides with his heels, and the horse needed no more suggestion. Together they took off, Shilling's hooves pounding the cobble, the two of them flying out of Whiston, saddle-less and bloody. Jeremiah was sure he would soon regret not stopping to patch himself up, but now, with The Hunt singing in his veins and his prey successfully captured, he barely felt a sting.

The clouds parted above them, allowing a dim crescent moon to shine down and light their path.

The King himself was expecting them., but this was not the end of their time in Whiston.

Soon, they would return.

Soon, the real Hunt would begin.

CHAPTER 8: 1337

He'd been doing so well in this lifetime.

He'd set up his life perfectly - married a baroness, had a dozen children, and neatly written his will so that the child born first *after* his death would be the main inheritor of his estate, ensuring that, as long as he timed his passing properly, he would reclaim it all almost the moment he was reborn. He'd even chosen a satisfying name for himself- Farris - making sure he would not be stuck with something ridiculous again.

It would have gone flawlessly if his own son/brother had not inherited his ambition.

But Farris tolerated it. He allowed the young upstart - so like him in temper and cunning - to oust him as inheritor. Why not let the boy make his name and spread his bloodline through England? He had the bountiful resources and insatiable appetites to do it. And anyway, the Church had been eying Farris' herds for too long, suspicious of his animals that never died before their time. As difficult as it was for Farris to abandon his lifetime-spanning fortune, there was a certain satisfaction in leaving the Church and all its covetous bickering behind. He also took some bitter pleasure in relinquishing the problems and responsibilities of estate management to the hands that had so mercilessly fought for his inheritance.

Too bitterly. Several of Farris's children/siblings had already died, for the boy's ambition. Their deaths had been both messy and unnatural. Farris knew where the now-Baron had gotten that level of power. He knew what his obsession meant, what ally he had made to get what he wanted, what creeping shadow waited in every corner, wanting more, more.

The Baron would learn that there was a cost to such deals, and Farris made sure he himself wouldn't be there to see it.

Farris fled England all together, in fact, with not much more than the clothes on his back, the pennies in his pockets, and the knife on his hip. France, he decided, was far enough away that neither Baron, Church, nor other prying influences could reach him. He'd found a sweet old herdsman with not much to his name but his flocks and his daughter, living in a beautiful, remote coastal town. Farris, with sweet words and sweeter lips, charmed his way into their home and into a wedding canopy, and made a new life for himself, starting over again with two children, a loyal, eager wife, and any other curious, eager wives who tired of their husbands' affairs and wanted a bit of revenge. Eventually, too, a few husbands, curious what the fuss was about...

Yes, it had been good, for a time.

Then the English had come to France, hungry for conquest, hungry for blood and spoils and hungry for a hero's welcome home once it had glutted itself.

Farris had thought himself safe, in his quiet little coastal town.

Now the town burned.

He'd made a mistake somewhere, he realized dully, lying on his side with eyes half caked closed with his own blood. He was not in a battlefield, but in a tent, tied hand and foot and left on a sleeping roll. He should have died with the other men slain in the battle. The English did not take prisoners of thin, weather-worn herdsmen. Farris had thought that if he was quiet enough, secret enough, no rumor of his true power would make it across the sea. Nobody would have any reason to suspect that Farris the shepherd had anything to do with Ferdinand, the 30-years-dead Baron with immortal flocks. Someone, Farris realized through his pounding headache, had told his shadow where to find him.

He'd never considered that his shadow cared enough to start a war over it.

He had to get out of here. He had to find Emilee and the children, and take them all away.

His wrists were bound behind his back, but they hadn't done a good job of it; the ropes were almost loose enough to slip free. He dashed the heel of his hand against the ground, drawing blood, welcoming the pain, even as he retched from it. The tears leaking down his face softened the blood caked around his eyes, allowing them to open properly. Blinking into the darkness, he worked his wrists against the rope, using his own blood as a lubricant. Before long he slipped his hands free, and clumsily unbound his ankles as well. Any small noise he made was drowned out by the snores of surrounding soldiers.

Dark outside. Good. It must have been only a few hours since he was captured. He would go to the village, find his family, and they would flee under cover of night.

He opened the flap of the tent half an inch, peering out into the darkness, and froze.

He was not in the British camp that had set itself up across from the town.

He was in the town - right in the middle of it, the burned, blackened walls and roof of what had once been the guest house now reinforced with new planks to keep out the rain pattering down beyond the shelter of his tent.

The village was dead. Gutted. The enemy had moved in instead.

Emilee...

He ran out into the night - forcing back tears that had nothing to do with the pain in his hand. He sprinted through the once-familiar, now filthy roadways; leaping puddles, dodging piles of charred roofing, and ignoring the shout of the single soldier keeping watch.

The old trail flew by under his bare feet, mud splashing up his legs with every step, rain soaking the underclothes that were all the British had left on him. He found his home by the cliffs, the noise of troops rallying themselves a distant, unimportant detail. He stood just outside his front doorway, and stared.

Their house hadn't burned, but the door had been broken in, the windows shattered, and he didn't need the flash of lightning above to see what had happened.

The stench of death wafted out to greet him.

Slowly, he stepped across the threshold, his blurred vision barely taking in Emilee's body on the bed, bloody and stiff. The bundles in the corner, the withered form in the chair...they all smelled of rot. Of decay.

It hadn't been a few hours since Farris been knocked out.

It had been days.

It was too late for him to save them, even with all his powers of necromancy.

The room melted into masses of shadow before him, and he fell to his knees, gasping and heaving. What was the point of all his power, all his concealment, all his...everything...if he could not keep them safe!

For a moment he sobbed, overcome by loss, by pain, by anger and fear.

Then he heard it.

Boots, marching on the path to his home.

And he remembered, in fact, what the point was.

Slowly he stood, his breath steadying. He wiped his eyes, tugged the bloodstained blanket from the bed, and threw it around his thin shoulders.

He strode to the wall of his home and pulled a board free, drawing out a delicate necklace of deep red stones set inside silver stars, tarnished spikes jutting out behind them.

This he fastened around his neck, barely noticing the pain as the spikes drove into his flesh, as power flooded him, making all his other aches seem unimportant, infinitesimal.

The marching of boots stopped outside his door, and a voice shouted at him in butchered, English-accented French, "Get out!"

He ignored the voice, spreading his hands in the brief flash of lightning, calling upon the power that gathered around him like the storm.

Emilee stood up from the bed.

"I'm going to count to three!"

Georges stood.

"One!"

Henri stood.

"Two!"

Isabella stood.

"Three!"

Farris did not turn around as his family rushed the door. He did not turn at the surprised shouts of the British soldiers as one dead woman, two dead children, and a dead old man threw themselves upon the warriors, biting and clawing and ripping with mindless, unholy fury.

Only when the screaming started, did Farris swivel to stand in the doorway.

He watched as four small corpses destroyed a troop of a dozen soldiers, the panicked cries of the English louder than the thunder that rolled around them, the gleaming red eyes of Farris' undead family brighter than the lightning that ripped across the sky.

And when silence fell, when the soldiers lay hot,

eviscerated and broken in the mud, and his family lined up at his side, bloody and obedient, only then did Farris turn away.

He made for the bone pile, where his family had thrown the remains of their flocks for many years.

Raising his hands, he called upon them all - the herds who had served him in life and in death, to serve him a third time, in undeath.

Two dozen hoofed, skeletal beasts rose, shambling into a neat line at his direction, horned heads tossing with eagerness.

Farris faced the burned ruin of his town. Lights flickered to life, and panicked, hoarse orders could barely be heard over the rumbling thunder.

One last time, he rested a hand on Emilee's small shoulder, not looking at her blood-soaked face. His other hand rested on the horned skull of the old ram, Louis, who had died only a fortnight ago.

"No mercy," he said softly.

As one, his servants charged, and once again, screams filled the night.

***

Fabian awoke with a sob.

They pushed themselves up, tearing away their blankets and curling tightly among the pillows, head in their hands.

Just a dream. Just another dream.

They wiped away the tears that burned in wet trails down their face.

Just another memory.

They forced themself to breathe, forced their thundering heart to return to a normal pace. Emilee, Georges, Henri and Isabella had been dead for hundreds of years.

"Fabian...?"

Ruphys stirred in the bed at their side, pushing himself up, blinking sleep away. "What is it?"

Fabian managed a shaky laugh. The sight of his scruffy

face framed by mussed, graying hair brought them a little further back into reality. "Nothing, my sweet," they rasped. "Go back to sleep."

Ruphys settled closer to them in the pillows, curling against their bare form. "Won't you join me..?" he asked, his voice half muffled by the softness of their shared nest.

Part of Fabian ached to give in - the part of them that craved things like being held, safe and warm, by the strong arms of their trusted, skillful lover, the doting father of their child, the man who had proved his bravery and devotion a hundred times over. How easy it would be to let go of the dream and melt into that welcoming, loyal embrace.

But the dream still lingered, cold and aching. Blood and death, mud and screams.

Emilee. The shadow, searching for them, reaching across seas, across lifetimes.

They could not be found again.

They rested a hand on Ruphys' cheek, whispered, "I cannot," and slipped out of bed.

Ruphys sighed and sat up again. "Shall I come with you?"

Fabian pulled on a shirt, sturdy black coat, a pair of trousers, the cloth cool against their bed-warm skin. Leather boots, leather gloves, heavy cloak joined. "I need you to stay and watch over Mina."

"She's fine, she'll be sleeping for hours yet...and Wolfred is always around, too." Ruphys yawned and stretched, then left the bed and slipped up behind Fabian, wrapping his strong arms around them, nesting his face in their hair with a deep, wistful sigh. "She needs you, you know," he murmured of their sleeping daughter. "She notices when you aren't here."

"She will just have to get used to it." Fabian allowed themselves a brief snuggle in his arms, then pulled away, tucking their hair into their cowl and slipping on their beaked mask. Lastly, they buckled on their belt with oh so many knives, and checked that the other blades were safely hidden in boot and sleeve. Unfortunately, the sooner Willamina stopped depending on Fabian, the better off she would be. The life of a necromancer was often short.

Ruphys watched these preparations, his somber eyes full of worry, and Fabian both hated and loved him for not bothering to hide how he ached for them. "Will you come back, after...?"

Fabian paused. They turned their masked face, looking over Ruphys's bare form, his bed-tousled hair, his unblinking eyes that accepted their answer before they gave it.

They could smell him, even through the mask, a smell they associated with many, many enjoyable and pleasant things.

They stepped close to him again, resting their gloved hands on the sides of his neck, letting the beak of their mask touch the tip of his nose. "Wait for me, then."

A smile broke out over Ruphy's face. He covered their gloved hands with his own, then knelt before them, bowing his head and resting it briefly against their stomach. "Yes, my Lord."

Just like old times. Fabian shivered, running their fingers through his graying hair. "Ruphys..."

He looked up at them, silently curious.

"I do not blame you for the deaths of my children."

His expression darkened, and he stood, slowly, not meeting their gaze. "I know. It was the plague, there was nothing I-"

"I do not blame you," they spoke over him, "but I will not forget them, either."

He met their gaze through the red-tinted glass, his green eyes sorrowful. Fabian knew what he wanted. They knew he wished they would leave the past in the past, forget the old injuries and be content with him, and with Mina, and whatever future children they would have. "You cannot move forward, and simply live a new life?"

Blood, mud and screams.

Plague and death.

Silver eyes and cold, marble floor.

Fabian grinned, knowing the smile would color their voice, even if he could not see it, wanting him to hear their hunger and their anger.

"I cannot."

CHAPTER 9: UNEXPECTED COMPANY

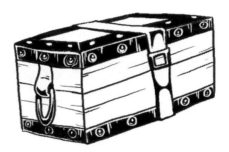

Dr. James Buckler's hired stagecoach rolled up to Barty's rented room. James peered through the window, casting a critical eye over the figure of his associate waiting in the chill London morning. A few wisps of fog blew past the young doctor's dark silhouette, curling about his boots in pale imitation of the brown waves that stuck out from under his hat. Even without his usual beaked mask, it made for an unusually grim picture.

James opened the door of his coach, gave a wave, and asked, "How did you sleep?" He swung down from the coach and approached Barty, hand offered.

"Barely at all, I was so nervous." Despite the early hour and reported lack of sleep, Barty seemed wide awake, giving Buckler's hand a firm shake before sweeping his curls out of his eyes and re-settling his hat to keep them back. "It's been ages since I traveled further than my own feet could take me." Barty peeked past James to the coach. "Did the College really hire this for us?"

"Well…" James turned to peer at the coach as well. It was one of the newer varieties, with glass windows and the improved shocks that made the road bouncing a bit less abysmal. It was also half stuffed with parcels and packages in the back, with minimal seating in front.

James looked back to Barty. "The guild bought us the right to sit inside and ride along with the mail," he said. "The coach was going Southwest anyway. They go as far as Bath, following the turnpikes, but we'll get off at Exeter. To go from there to Plymouth, we'll need to hire a few horses."

He cast a critical eye over Barty's belongings, watching the younger doctor heave his canvas sailor's bag onto his shoulder. "Did you pack cold weather clothing? The nights get pretty chill, with winter coming on."

"I did," Barty slung the bag into the back of the coach, carefully keeping it separate from the other parcels, and went back for his second piece of luggage, a slightly worn sea chest. "And I packed as much medical supplies as I could, too. I don't know how much will be available on the road."

James nodded, stepping over to help Barty with the chest. To him it was light, but his younger, if taller, associate puffed, his face turning red as they heaved it together onto the back of the coach. "You'd better hope a pony can carry that," James said.

"I do hope," Barty said, mopping his brow. "But I wanted something sturdy. The last thing we need is herbs and leeches spilling everywhere because of a few bumps. I haven't used this since my days in the navy." He hesitated, his features crumbling in a moment of grief, then changed the subject. "I packed my mask and coat, as well. I assume we don't need them while we're riding?"

James nodded, curious, but willing to respect the change of subject. "We are merely civilians until we reach Plymouth, though I think having your hat out is a good idea. You are a doctor after all. You deserve the respect that comes with it."

Barty smiled at that, and James felt a touch of amusement that the fellow still, after an entire year, found pleasure in the official title. "I have a few books at hand, too," Barty said, lifting a third, smaller bag and slinging it over his shoulder. "I haven't had much time for extensive study in recent months."

"Study, rest, whatever you need to pass the time." James stepped away from the coach, letting the coachman close the baggage area with a brisk snap. He, personally, planned to spend the time catching up on some of the paperwork he hadn't gotten to, what with his full schedule and dramatic comrades. "As I said, it's going to be a few days of travel."

"Plus we got the other one to pick up," the coachman interjected as he passed.

James grimaced, and didn't meet Barty's confused gaze.

"Other one?" Barty asked the driver.

The coachman ignored him, swinging into the front of the coach and picking up the reins. Barty turned his puppy dog eyes on James instead. "What does he mean?"

James sighed. The echoes of many days of arguments with Director Peete throbbed in his head, and it took an effort of will to keep his temper down enough to not growl his reply. "The mages want someone along with us to assess if the outbreak truly is the same kind of magic-based plague we overcame before, and if it is, to 'oversee' our work with deactivating it."

"What?" Barty said blankly. "They didn't help us before. Why are they trying to do it now?"

James gritted his teeth, and opened the door of the coach, gesturing for Barty to get in. "Officially, their reasoning is for the safety of the patients. They claim anything that goes wrong with the deactivation could affect the afflicted." He waited for Barty to mount the coach, then stepped in after him, slamming the door and settling back onto the thinly upholstered seat. "My guess," he continued, not bothering to hide his bitterness, "is that they don't want us blabbing the secret of the amulet to other mages, when they currently have a monopoly on it."

Barty stared at him, then sat back heavily on his seat, shaking his head. "I hate mages."

"You don't," James said, tiredly. "It was a mage that fixed your arm, wasn't it?"

"Yeah." Barty rubbed at the inside of his elbow. "She was alright I suppose. And Cassie and Liz. And I guess that fellow Fabian brought in for testing the spellwork, but-"

"What you actually hate," James interjected, "is power."

The coach lurched into motion, and Barty put a hand on the wall to steady himself. "Power? What do you mean?"

"These struggles of the mages and the merchants - of rich and poor - it all comes down to power," James explained, looking out the window. He'd spent a good deal of time thinking about this himself; puzzling over why corruption always sang the same tune, even in different circumstances. "Money is power. Authority is power. Knowledge is power. People grab onto such things because they seek control, or because of vanity, or greed, but it all comes down to power."

He looked hard at Barty. "Power corrupts, Wayman. Whether you are the head of a guild, a church, or even a schoolroom. I bet you've met teachers who cared more about enforcing their authority than about teaching."

Barty nodded, removing his hat and settling it on his knees, his expression haunted. "But these things are not inherently bad, are they?" he asked, with his eternal, stubborn optimism. "Money is good when it helps an economy run smoothly. Authority is good when..." he gestured at James, "...when it is wielded by someone who genuinely cares for the wellbeing of the people they control. And knowledge, so much good can be gained from knowledge. It betters everyone's lives."

"All your examples are of those things being used for the sake of others," James said, but he nodded. While Barty was very trusting, and wanted to see the best in every person, he was no fool. "But that is the very issue, Wayman. When you are gathering them for a purpose - to do good, to advance mankind, to fix a problem - you are not focused on yourself. You are focused on others."

He turned his gaze to the population of London rolling by the window. "The line is not easy to see," he continued. "I am sure the mages think their power is for the good of man, and for the good of others like them. But..."

Barty looked grim. "...but Magmaydon, and Peete – they are ignoring those who are most in need, so they can rationalize making money off the talismans."

James nodded. "It is not black and white," he said. "There are some questions that do not have answers that fall neatly into right and wrong. But the moment you stop asking, that is when power corrupts." He looked down at his hands, letting his pupil digest the lesson.

"Has that ever happened to you?" Barty asked softly.

James snorted. "You're asking me if I have ever been corrupted? You *are* a bold one."

"I'm sorry! I didn't mean-"

"It's alright." James sighed. "It's a fair question. And what good would my fifteen years of experience be, if I could not answer it?"

He sat back, folding his arms, thinking. But the answer was before him, staring him in the face with timid brown eyes.

James sighed. "When we first met, I was on the edge."

Barty blinked at that. "What? But-"

"It was a bad time," James continued. "Everyone was dying. Everything was hopeless. My duties were more quarantine enforcement than actual healing. At some point,

I stopped-" he took a deep breath, and let it out. "I stopped checking my choices. I went by the book alone, and closed my eyes to the people before me."

"James..."

James could hear Barty's entire heart in the word. He laced his fingers together, and kept his gaze down, not much wanting to face those eyes while making this small confession. "When you joined... when you cared for every person an individual, instead of as cases..." He glanced to Barty. "I thought you were an idiot."

Barty winced, smiling weakly. "I know."

James allowed himself half a smile in return. "You haven't changed much. But I think I have, a little. You're right. Part of a doctor's job is to make people *feel* cared for, not just to go through the motions of care. I've seen it in my own work; when I am more invested in my patients, they respond better." He tapped the side of his head. "My task is to balance emotional investment in such a way that I neither take on so much that my work suffers, nor allow myself to hide behind pure logic or routine to the degree that I lose the humanity of my care. And that, Barty Wayman, is how you are helping me to be the best doctor I can be, and avoid being corrupted by what little power I have."

Barty laughed, and wiped his eyes. "And my task is to soak up every little thing that you can teach me, sir, for I have never met a wiser person in my life."

James chuckled at that. "You haven't met very many people, then. But, well I suppose this trip will be a start to changing that."

"Well, I've met some! I had my shipmates in the navy, and my fellow students in school, and..."

They talked of such things for a while. Barty told the story of how he and his brother had joined the navy as young men, as their parents had wanted. Barty had spent only a few weeks as a seaman before their commanding officer learned he could read and write and promoted him to ship's clerk, the last one having retired rather suddenly. James, in return, told a few tales of his travels in the army, mostly involving conducting surgery inspections and field medic training. "I once nearly got in a fistfight with a nurse who refused to accept an inspection of her work station," he said with a grimace. "But in general, I learned just as much from the medics as they learned from me. I'm sure there's a saying about that somewhere-"

"Who is wise? He who learns from everyone he meets," Barty quoted, beaming. "That's from a Jewish text called "Ethics of the Fathers." I learned about it from the rabbi I told you about before..." he trailed off, looking around. "We've stopped moving."

James glanced out the window. They had stopped at the westernmost exit of London: Ludgate. "This is where we're meeting the mage."

"Did they tell you who they're sending?" Barty asked, cracking the door open to get a better look at approaching traffic. "I rather hope it's Clara, though I'm sure Jack wouldn't forgive us for taking her away."

"It would be useful to have a healer along," James agreed with a nod, squinting at the crowd. It was a healthy morning bustle, warmly lit by the strengthening rays of sun that pierced the light fog. Gone was the smothering fear of plague, replaced by a healthy, excited hustle and bustle of folk relieved to be out of their homes and conducting business once more.

A figure on horseback turned onto the street, negotiating the crowds with regal assurance that the common folk would get out of the way of their gray horse.

"Oh no," whispered Barty at James's side.

James quite agreed. The figure was hooded, their face hidden in shadow, but he knew that silvery cloak, with the stars embroidered in gold. It could only be one person.

"Of course," James said, through gritted teeth. "Of course they'd send Zacharius. They want to be rid of him just as badly as they want to be rid of us."

Barty looked like he was about to be sick. "We can't

spend days and days sitting in a coach with him," he whispered hoarsely. "We can't. I'll go mad."

James already knew they would have no choice. Every clop of that horse's hooves against stone brought their insufferable doom closer. The very mage whose spellwork had cost the lives of thousands was now to be their officially-designated supervisor, and there was nothing they could do about it.

The horse stopped next to their coach. The hooded figure considered them in a silence that stretched long enough that Barty, unerringly polite, broke it with a forced, "Good morrow, sir."

The mage looked at Barty, lifted a hand, and threw back their hood, revealing the pale, grinning face of Fabian the Necromancer. "Good morrow, gentlemen," they said, clearly relishing the shock that froze James and Barty in their seats. "I am afraid master Zacharius has met with an unfortunate accident. I will be his replacement on this journey."

James recovered from his shock first, blurting out angrily, "What did you do to him?" as if he and Barty had not just been bemoaning the very mage who had, apparently, met with great misfortune that very day.

Fabian cast him a sharp smile, but tossed their reins to the coach driver, pulling their hood back up and alighting easily from the horse. "We can speak at length inside, Doctors," they said. "If you'll assist with my bags."

James glowered at the necromancer. "You can mind your own blasted bags-" but Barty was already slipping out behind him, meekly approaching the horse to help transfer Fabian's many pieces of baggage to the coach.

James scowled at them both, his gaze lingering on the copious bundles that made up the necromancer's luggage. "What on earth do you think you are going to need all that for?"

"Pray you don't have to find out," Fabian said, slipping one of the bundles across their shoulder and stepping into the coach. They closed the door behind them, shutting out the noise, light and bustle of the outside world, and settled back against the wall of the coach. They kept their spangled hood up and their face in shadow, but James could see the glitter of those red eyes observing Barty's struggles with the rest of their gear.

"Why do you do this to him?" James protested bitterly, watching the young doctor stagger under the weight of the many bags. "You take advantage of his good nature, and to my eyes it is only for the sake of cruelty."

"Cruelty," Fabian repeated, not looking at him. "Perhaps it is cruelty. Or perhaps true cruelty would be to pretend to be other than I am." The red gaze slid to meet James' eye. "Perhaps," Fabian said, their voice velvety soft, "true cruelty would be to be gentle with him, to be kind to him... to make him trust me, and long for me. To make him think his attention is changing me to be a better person," a grin stretched across their face, sharp as a knife, "and then to take what pleasure I could from him, before dumping him to wallow in his loss, broken heart, and shattered trust."

They settled back into shadow, leaving James gaping in shock. "Yes," they whispered, "I am, in fact, a being of cruelty, James Buckler. Do not forget it, and do not let him forget, either."

James turned away from the necromancer in puzzlement and disgust. He shoved the door open on the other side and snapped, "Come on, Wayman!" before settling back, not looking at the creature now sitting across from him. Indeed, Fabian had spoken aloud exactly what James feared, but...this assessment seemed less like a statement of evil intent, and more like...

...more like Fabian was claiming that, through their callous treatment of the young doctor, they were protecting him from their own selfish habits.

James snorted under his breath. What terrible, twisted logic.

He watched Barty clamber back into the coach, pulling the door shut behind him and settling into his seat with a breath of relief. "It's all in!" he said happily, smiling at Fabian even as he rubbed his bad shoulder. "I suppose you are very prepared for every possibility! It is good to have foresight."

James glared at Fabian, at the small smile curling their lips, at the eyes that refused to look his way. "Thank you, Doctor," they said to Barty. "Truly, you are a gentleman and a scholar. Perhaps you should have chosen a different life path; your chivalry would have looked well on a knight of old."

Barty beamed, not seeing the mockery in the words. "I-it's nothing," he said, "just common decency."

"Common decency isn't so common," James growled, giving Fabian a pointed look. He folded his arms, settling back against the stiff seat. "I can already see this trip is going to be absolutely insufferable."

"If you've already decided that, Doctor," Fabian said, lacing their fingers over their stomach and closing their eyes with a smile, "who am I to try and change your mind?"

"Did you even think about what we're going to do?" James demanded, ignoring how Barty flinched at his raised voice. "We are going to fight plague, Fabian! We need a mage to make the charms! Undead do not wield magic, and undead do not cure disease! Zacharius was a scoundrel, but he still had the magic to power what we need!"

"And what use is a necromancer in his place, you are asking?" Fabian said with a sneer. "Think, Dr. Buckler, think. The plague you are being sent to fight is the same kind that was after me; and I, James, am the one who told you how to break that curse. I, Doctor, am the one who developed the preventative."

Fabian leaned forward, their smile dangerously white and perfect. "If you really want to stop this new plague, you need someone who understands how it works. Yes, Zacharius was responsible for the old one, but even *he* barely knew what he was doing when he started it. And your true goal IS to stop it entirely, is it not?"

Their gaze slid to Barty. Barty flinched, obviously feeling guilty for overhearing the argument even though he was in the same, very small and confined space as the two arguing parties. "I mean, yes?" he stammered. "Of course we want to stop the plague. And, um, we've been using non-magic methods to cure it for months as well, so..."

James frowned at him, and Barty quailed. "Sorry," he murmured. "M-maybe we can find a mage on the way? Most little villages have some kind of hedge witch, these days."

James sighed, sweeping his hand through his hair and shaking his head. Barty did have a knack for practical thinking, in his own, optimistic way. "I pray for all our sakes that you're right," he said, casting a last glower at Fabian.

The necromancer only smiled and looked out the window.

The coach rumbled out of London, leaving behind the filthy streets, the bustling crowds, the air choked with fog and coal smoke. James looked out the window as well, his temper simmering, and thought bitterly that their going should have been celebrated with music and cheers, for now they were removing the most dangerous person in the entire country from within London's bowels.

He bit his lip to keep from making a wisecrack about an enema aloud, and closed his eyes, blocking out Barty's worried, hopeful face from the corner of his vision. Lessons could wait.

James Buckler needed a moment to cool down, and more than a moment to think about what it meant that Lord Fabian the Necromancer wanted to go with them to Devonshire so badly that they would murder a mage and abandon all their undead helpers as well as their new little family, just to take a stagecoach with the only two living souls who knew Fabian was still alive. James knew it wasn't out of the goodness of their heart - they had practically confessed it. So, whatever it was they wanted, they wanted it so badly they could not wait to organize their own trip, couldn't even wait long enough for travel arrangements that would accommodate any of their undead bodyguards.

James had seen them behaving this way once before. Fairly recently, too.

What Fabian wanted was not the question here, James realized with a small shiver.

Not *what*, but *who*.

Besom was dead, Zacharius too, if Fabian's stolen cloak was any sign.

Who was the next target of the necromancer's blood-thirsty, vengeful blade?

CHAPTER 10:
THE ROAD TO
DEVONSHIRE

The road to Devonshire stretched on, passing through forests, over hills, and seemingly into the infinite horizon.

Barty had thought the trip would be an easy one. After all, not five years ago he'd spent his time in the navy, working first as a seaman scrubbing the deck and hauling rope, then as a clerk, cataloging supplies and recording events as the days passed. The key, he'd learned at sea, was keeping busy while you were awake, and catching up on sleep when you weren't busy.

So he put his experience to work, there in the bouncing jousting confines of the Bath-bound coach. While James rested his eyes and Fabian stared out the window in haughty silence, Barty pulled out his notes and a few blank sheets of paper, and began reviewing, organizing, and re-copying everything he'd learned in his year of treating plague. He'd been recording his progress each day - jotting down observations as to what helped, or didn't help, patients pull through; what symptoms boded death or survival; and even how the patient's social status and income correlated with their survivability. Now, with hours and miles before them, he set about categorizing his findings, doing what he could to condense them down into something easily conveyed to patients and fellow caregivers alike. After all, if they were going into an entirely new part of the country, and if the plague there had even a fraction of the spreading power it had displayed in London, they would need as much assistance as possible. The more prepared they were to train new helpers, the sooner they could get treatment to everyone who needed it.

Assuming, of course, they could stop the curse-part of the plague first.

The more Barty thought about it, the more he had to concede that Fabian was right on that account. Fabian understood magic on a deeper level than Barty or James, even though the necromancer claimed not to be able to do any that was not necromantic in nature. Certainly, having their rat servants around to scope out the town and find the possible locations for such a curse to be carved would be useful. Last time, the spellwork had been chipped into a stone wall behind a bookshelf - there was no denying that extra sets of tiny eyes would be a great help in investigating such hard-to-reach areas.

Barty shivered, suddenly quite certain he knew what was in some of the bundles Fabian had had him load into the back of the coach. He peeked sideways at them, wondering how long they had been planning to come on this trip. Wondering, too, how long Fabian had even known they were going. Barty had only found out yesterday, and had spoken only to James of the venture. And yet, here Fabian was at Ludgate, ready and waiting, their murderous errand already attended to. Barty wondered, too, about Ruphys, and if Fabian had told him they were leaving, or had just gone without a word.

Fabian's gaze slid from the window to Barty, as if they sensed his attention. They gave him a lazy smile, and he looked back down at his work, feeling terribly awkward and making it worse by blushing. "W-what do you see?" he stammered, trying to cover for his gaze. "Out there. Are we being followed?"

"Mmm." Fabian's vision went unfocused for a moment, and Barty had the distinct feeling that they were looking through eyes other than their own. "Not being followed, not yet anyway. Someone has found Zacharius, though, so they know he didn't make it along with you." Fabian gave a dark chuckle. "I imagine I did them a favor, really. Now they don't have to make excuses for him anymore."

Barty fought back a shiver. "Do you think this new plague is connected to the old one?" he asked. "I don't suppose you asked Zacharius where he got that spell, did you? Maybe someone is, um, spreading plague on purpose." He couldn't think why someone would do that. Aside from Fabian, who could use corpses to make an undead army, he couldn't imagine who benefited from killing mass amounts of people with no actual control over who died.

Fabian seemed equally interested in the concept, though. They re-focused on Barty, repeating his words. "Spreading plague on purpose. Yes, it's definitely no coincidence, the same plague popping up so close and so soon." Barty wasn't sure, but to his eyes the necromancer looked almost uncomfortable at the idea. One of their thin hands settled over their other arm - tracing a thin outline under the cloth. Barty would bet his hat it was a concealed knife.

"Plagues often spread along trade routes." James, clearly giving up any pretense of rest, cast Fabian a glare instead.

"Until we get there and see for ourselves, I'm not going to rush to believe the source is another spell. It's entirely possible it just spread out of London, what with the roads opening up again and people traveling further thanks to the turnpikes."

"Entirely possible," Fabian said with a gracious nod. "But in a letter from a mage in Plymouth to Ms. Magmaydon-"

"How do you know what Ms. Magmaydon's letters say?" Barty raised his eyebrows.

Fabian only grinned, and continued, "the letter to Magmaydon said that the affliction came on suddenly, with severe symptoms exactly matching our recent plague. Additionally, the death rate is the same: always fatal after three days. Once we broke the spell on our last plague, the death rate dropped to 60% at worst, 30% in some areas."

"Oh." Barty looked at his notes. None of it would matter, if it truly was the curse-backed plague. People died whether or not they got medical attention, when magic was the cause.

He sighed, and began packing his things away, dread looming up in his chest at the prospect of what they were facing. It had been almost a year since they'd broken the curse. That was a year of hope, of people surviving, of death not being the only answer to disease. To walk back into the hands of the cursed plague was like sitting down at Death's table for another cup of bitterest tea.

Barty could almost hear the rustle of black wings. He shivered, and rubbed his eyes.

"Barty," James said.

Barty looked up at his friend.

James met his gaze, understanding clear in his serious expression. "We're going to help them."

Barty gave a weak smile. "I certainly hope so."

James gave an approving nod. "And until then, we'll make good use of our time. Trips like this are an excellent opportunity to learn; both for your practice, and for your person."

Barty heard the note of speaking-from-experience in

James's voice. "You've done a lot of traveling, then?"

James nodded again. "I was all over the world during my military career. France, Africa, India. Learned a lot, both from my own experience and by talking to local doctors." He sat a bit straighter, held his head higher.

"Is that how you settled on your specialty?" Barty asked with interest. "Through what you saw in the world?"

"Not quite," James said with a grim smile. "I'd known what I was going to focus on before I even went to medical school."

"Really?" Barty knew that James specialized in family medicine - especially in helping a mother through pregnancy, and other related conditions. He admired James both for how important such work was, and for his bravery at...well... studying all the things concerned with the health of the female system.

"It must be, um. A little awkward," Barty said with a sheepish smile. "Meeting new doctors and having to ask them about. Um. How they deal with things. Um. In those regions."

James gave Barty a steady look. "Am I to understand," he said, "that you still have not added things in 'those regions' to your studies?"

Fabian sniggered, and Barty immediately turned crimson. "I - well! There hasn't been time, has there? I've had so much work with the plague, and um, brushing up on the basics." He spoke quickly, both out of personal embarrassment, and because he knew every word he said dug his hole deeper. He shoveled explanations out, hoping to forestall the inevitable. "I didn't go to medical school like you did, sir, and the other doctors who have been overseeing my training usually focus on the most common ailments, like rheumatism and lacerations and infections-"

"Wayman," James said firmly, "half of the world's bloody population is female. I assure you, there are conditions which every female has that a doctor must understand. Signs, that if you truly wish to help people, you must be able to recognize, not only to forestall disaster, but to aid in preserving the pride and maintaining the comfort of your patients."

"Plus," Fabian added, grinning, "there are details it helps to know if you ever plan on spending time with women outside of the medical field."

James shot Fabian a withering look. The necromancer only leered at him and returned their attention to the window, shoulders shaking with silent laughter.

Barty sank down in his seat, his hands over his face. He did not want a lesson in... those things... with Fabian sniggering at him in the background. He was going to die of mortification, and then Fabian would bring him back from the dead just to laugh at him more. "James," he said, without much hope "now is really not a good time."

"Nonsense," James said bracingly, pulling his own bag out and withdrawing a sheath of notes. "Now is the perfect time. In fact, I have long suspected that your education was being neglected in this area, and I have prepared quite a few lessons, since we will be on the road for hours anyway."

When Barty didn't respond, James grabbed his wrist and pulled his hand away from his face. "I became a specialist in these areas, Wayman," he said, a little more gently, "because many men have the same problem you are having. Many men do not want to understand these issues, or don't care that they exist. It leads to a great amount of harm for women and those around them as a result. I know, Barty Wayman, that you are not the kind of man who allows harm to come to others through neglect. If you could face the plague, you can face this."

Barty let out a shuddering sigh. As usual, James was right. If he truly wanted to be a good doctor, which he did, he not only had to know these things, but get over his own hesitation of talking about them.

He supposed James, of all people, would probably be the best teacher he could find. Outside of his worldly experience, he had a unique and very personal perspective on the matter.

Barty wondered if James' 'condition,' the one that he tended with bandages wrapped around his torso every day of his life, had anything to do with why he'd chosen the field to begin with. Barty dared not ask though.

"I...yes. Of course, sir."

He sat up and finished packing away his notes on plague, retaining the blank sheets of paper. He steeled his nerves, firmly kept himself from looking at the necromancer grinning out the window, and said, "I'll do my best."

"That's the spirit," James said, flashing him a grim smile. "Now." He dug in his notes, and pulled out a complex, alien-looking diagram. "Let's review what you know about anatomy."

Barty flushed absolutely scarlet, but nodded, and began writing.

He didn't need to look at Fabian to know they were watching him. He could feel their amusement as a palpable thing, even as he scribbled names and functions and locations to the best of his ability, simultaneously trying to commit them to memory.

This went on for a few hours. Barty did his best, squashing down his self-consciousness and bending the strength of his mind to understanding the complexities and intricacies of Buckler's line of work. Before long, he'd managed to feel almost normal, if not yet comfortable. The reproductive system was, after all, just another set of organs in the body, like the liver or stomach. Certain principles applied to all flesh, and the more he learned, the less embarrassing it all seemed.

Fabian was no help, though, sneaking in snide comments now and then that, unfortunately, were equal parts informative and designed to make Barty blush. He'd pretended to ignore them as best he could, but once in a while, had added some of Fabian's "contributions" to his notes, carefully not meeting Buckler's eye when he did.

Fabian promised to take over the lesson after James had had his say and teach Barty more about the health and hazards of the masculine side of things, claiming they had dozens of lives of study and experience, even if they were not currently equipped with said biological features.

Barty very much wanted to melt into the floor and hide under the floorboards before allowing this to happen. To his surprise and regret, however, James only shrugged in silent agreement.

His studies were interrupted with a sudden jerk as their driver pulled into a tavern to stop for lunch. Their mid-day meal came in the shape of a hearty stew and small loaf of bread that, while clearly nowhere near fresh, was quite tasty when dipped. They also got, at the insistence of their driver, a flagon of ale. "One of the best you'll taste on the road to Devonshire!" their driver proclaimed, filling his own tankard and Barty's with enthusiasm. James forbade any ale entering his glass with a single look, and Fabian only drank from their own flask, which left Barty and the driver to finish the entire flagon together.

With Buckler's lessons behind him and Fabian's looming before him, Barty was all too happy to imbibe.

By the time they got back in the coach, Barty was feeling much better. He hummed an old sea shanty to himself, ignored James' baleful stare, and settled into place, picking up his pen and paper once more and grinning at Fabian. "Alright, most esteemed and educated Lord Necromancer!" he said. "Illuminate me as to the illnesses of mast, sail and anchor!"

"Indeed," Fabian said, raising their eyebrows. "I will tell you all about the ailments of seamen."

Buckler snorted, staring decidedly at the landscape. Barty giggled, blushed and buried himself in his papers. Fabian, mouth twitching to repress a smile, began the next step in Barty's education.

Barty's good mood slowly evaporated, as he learned that there were, in fact, many horrible diseases that afflicted mast, sail and anchor, and while most of them were transmitted on a person-to-person basis, (making him glad for his own restraint in swimming in those deep waters) many, also, sprang up of their own accord, seemingly with no provocation. He scribbled down names, symptoms and treatments, and spent a good amount of sweat trying not to think too hard about just how dangerous it was to own that particular set of tackle.

Their ride was interrupted by a stop at a second tavern, on account of their driver claiming his thirst could only be slaked by the very specific, highly-praised beer that happened to be for sale along the particular road they were traveling. Barty gladly joined the man, who by now he learned was called Paul, for another pint to wash away the stress of his education and the weight of his expanded knowledge.

Neither James nor Fabian joined them this time, however. James, in fact, remarked pointedly that too many stops would add time to their journey, and that lives were at stake.

Barty drowned that thought in his beer as well, but it floated up again in time for him to decline a third round and drag Paul back to his coach before the man could completely pickle himself. Their driver's round face wasn't quite red with drink, but Barty was beginning to suspect that the reason Paul so enjoyed this particular job was that he had memorized the location of every tavern on the road.

Barty's suspicions were confirmed when they stopped three more times that same day, each time with Paul's insistence that they couldn't miss THIS tavern, their cider was remarkable, their whisky was worth dying for, they had the best wine in this part of the country. Barty saw polished wooden floors, walls with animal heads stuffed and mounted with pride, and even an ancient suit of armor, holding not a sword but a huge stone tankard.

He also found, rather quickly, that between his consumption of the various beverages of which Paul spoke so highly and his mentors disapproved, his lessons ground to a halt long before they stopped for the evening.

Neither Fabian nor James had much sympathy for the

headache that had descended upon Barty by the time they stopped at their inn - a cheery little place whose whorled windows shone with a warm yellow light. Its name was "The Cat's Nest," displayed on a lovingly painted sign depicting a tabby cat curled in a nest of straw, clearly stolen from a chicken, if the egg in the cat's painted paws was any indicator.

Barty would have been more endeared to the inn if his head weren't pounding quite so much. As it was, he slumped in behind James and Fabian, trying to put a distance between himself and Paul's cheerful, unapologetic whistling. Embarrassed by his pain, lack of discipline, and the still-lingering lessons of the day, he sank down at their table and wished he could just disappear, leaving James to take care of ordering their food. Paul planted himself at the bar, solidly on the other side of the room from them, and seemed determined to drink himself into a stupor.

The inn was busy, full of people chattering, eating and pushing their bloody chairs around. Barty rubbed his temples and longed for his cool, quiet room back at home, trying to ignore the way Fabian watched him, their hood once more shading their face.

"Uncomfortable, Doctor?" they asked, their concern seemingly genuine.

Barty was too used to their mockery to trust to sound alone, though. He made a face in response and said, "Today has been nothing but discomfort from dawn until dusk."

Fabian gave him a slow blink. "And here I thought you were quite enjoying our little adventure."

Barty cast them a pained look, the memory of their smirks and lessons still uncomfortably fresh in his mind. He couldn't deny they were things he needed to learn, but... "You needn't be quite so smug about it all," he said, knowing he was whining, not knowing how to fix it. "I'm sure back whenever you learned all these things for the first time, it wasn't easy for you either!"

"No," Fabian said with a crooked grin. "Not easy at all.

For many of the ailments both I and dear James spoke of today, I learned through first hand experience, Dr. Wayman."

Barty stared at them, digesting this. The idea of a powerful, legendary necromancer having struggles with venereal diseases in previous lifetimes was at once comedic and mortifying. It certainly put his discomfort into a bit of perspective. "I'm sorry," he said, and meant it.

Fabian shrugged. "That is the price you pay, when trying to...ah...spread one's progeny as far and wide as possible." They tilted their head, surveying the room. "It only took one death in that manner to make me a little more discerning with my choices. Let me tell you, it is an awful way to go."

"I can imagine," Barty said with a shiver. "Well, um. I am glad to hear that you, um. Have learned from your experiences, I suppose."

Fabian cast him a dirty, sharp grin. "Always willing to learn a bit more, Doctor."

The hair prickled on the back of Barty's neck. Before he could reply, however, James came back to their table, bearing a pitcher of water and looking annoyed. "They only have two rooms left for the evening," he said, thunking down a few glasses and filling Barty's before he could ask. "We'll have to double up."

Fabian stirred in their seat, leaning forwards with a grin that made Barty shiver.

"No," James said, before they even opened their mouth. "Barty and Paul will share, and you and I will share."

Barty hid his face in his water glass, but could still hear Fabian sigh and settle back in their chair. "Spoilsport."

James only glared at them, and sat down beside Barty, giving him a steely once-over. "I hope you don't intend to repeat this behavior tomorrow, Wayman."

Barty lowered his glass to the table, shame making his cheeks burn. "I...no, sir," he said softly. "I don't. I'm sorry."

Barty could feel the lecture lurking behind James's closed mouth. But the doctor only nodded and sipped his water, washing away the scolding. "How many treatments do you know for a hangover?" he asked, and Barty could hear the olive branch among the words.

Barty smiled, and recited what he knew from memory until their food arrived. Their dinner certainly lifted his spirits - thick, steaming slices of mutton in a brown gravy, with boiled carrots on the side, and a fat, crisp loaf for them to share. His appetite appreciated the bouquet of smells immensely, and picked up his knife and fork to dig in.

Unfortunately, with the delivery of their meal also came a fiddler - perching his brightly-stockinged form not ten feet from their table, bowing to the room at large, and mercilessly tearing his way into a jolly, window-rattling jig that drove nails into Barty's aching head.

He looked at the plate of food he'd only just received, and wondered just how much more he could eat before he threw it back up onto the table. He gave James a pleading look, but James only shook his head, clearly unsure how to help. "Do you want to eat in your room?"

"Unnecessary," Fabian said. They had, in the few moments their meal had been before them, somehow managed to devour half of it already. They paused now, wiped their mouth on a handkerchief, and stood, rolling their shoulders. "I'll have a word with the merry minstrel," they said. "Drink all your water, Doctor, and taste a bit of salt. That should ease your pain and encourage your appetite."

Barty wasn't sure it would, but he nodded, sipping water and dubiously shaking salt onto his palm while Fabian sauntered over to the minstrel. It was not a fox-like sway of hips that a more feminine person might use to catch attention, nor was it the commanding, bullying stride of a man determined to have his own way. It was something more subtle - a step that spoke both of grace and self control, their long black hair rippling along with their starry silver cloak.

Most of the crowd kept their eyes on their own conversations, but the minstrel himself looked up right away at Fabian's approach, his steady hands fiddling away even as he bent his ear to listen to Fabian's murmured words. The old man's eyebrows raised at whatever the necromancer said to him, but when Fabian held up a coin for him to see, he smiled, nodded, and slowed his fiddling to a leisurely stop.

Fabian left him tucking the coin into his belt and made their way back to the table, more than a few curious eyes on them now.

Barty set aside his empty water glass and leaned forward. "Did he really agree to stop so easily?"

"Oh, he isn't stopping," Fabian said, piling a few more slices of meat onto their plate. "He is just switching songs. My request will be a bit less abrasive than what he was previously playing."

"Is that so?" Barty glanced at the food, already feeling a bit better - at least better enough to cut into his own meat and take a bite. It was surprisingly good, and made his stomach realize just how hungry it was. "What did you ask him to play?"

"A personal favorite of mine," Fabian said, eyes glittering.

Barty nodded, and glanced at James. James, listening, frowning slightly, had nothing to add, keeping his attention on the rest of the room. Probably, Barty thought, making sure nobody was paying their table too much attention.

In fact, most people were looking at the minstrel, wondering why the music had stopped. The minstrel, after tightening his belt, made a great show of adjusting his worn cap and tuning his fiddle. The intensity of his lined face as he tested each string of his instrument quieted the room, dining companions nudging each other, low, murmured questions flickering and dying into silence. It was in this new stillness that the minstrel, his smile almost-but-not-quite hidden by his gray mustache, struck the first chord.

The notes sent a chill down Barty's spine. There was a different feel to this tune from the previous one - it was mournful, secretive, and yet in its own way, just as jolly and upbeat as its predecessor. It felt like turning away from a robin's flight, only to see a carrion crow speeding gracefully in its wake.

Then the minstrel began to sing, his voice rich and sure, and Barty forgot all about his headache as the words tumbled out onto the tavern floor for all to hear.

Oh gather round good people, and I'll tell you a tale,
Of a sight more strange and staggering than any fish or whale
For late last night on me way back home from The Drunken Lancer,
I passed on by the graveyard and saw a necromancer.

At first I didn't believe me eyes, but 'spite the boozy waves
There just was no mistaking him, leaping o'er the graves
He jumped the headstones, row by row, and as he went I heard
Him singing at the corpses, and these were his very words;

'You're sleeping now my beauties, in beds of wood and dirt,
So don't mind me a-passing through, I promise this won't hurt
You might once have been safe from me while breathing in your homes,
How kind of you to now lie still so I can jump your bones!'

The minstrel then continued to sing a list of the graves being jumped, each with a worse double entendre than the last - Poor Donny Brown had been buried face down, sweet Sally Hawk and her rumpled frock, old Mrs. Quip and her broken hip... Barty found himself paying very close attention to his plate so as to not meet Fabian's eye, but he could still hear the necromancer, at first humming along, and then singing every raunchy line as a few voices in the crowd joined in.

Barty glanced around, his curiosity stronger than his embarrassment. Many faces there were confused, some even horrified. In fact, as he looked closer, he noticed everyone singing was of the older generation, men and women with graying hair and lined faces. If he had to judge by their expressions and the slight hesitation at each new verse, he would wager that this song was not common tavern fare now, but had been, once.

"What are you thinking?" James growled. "Asking him to sing a song from your reign of terror? Are you trying to get yourself revealed?"

"Calm down, Doctor," Fabian said. They were grinning – a gleeful, hungry light in their eyes. Barty wondered what memories the song woke in them. "The necromancer in that song is twice dead and buried. There is nothing to fear."

James shook his head and pushed away his empty plate.

Barty looked at his own dinner. It was only half eaten, but his headache was returning with a vengeance. He pushed his plate aside as well.

James looked from Barty's half finished food to Barty, his eyebrows lowering, but before Barty could offer an explanation, Fabian snatched the plate, stacked it on their empty one, and started merrily devouring Barty's leftovers, still humming.

Relieved, Barty stood from the table. "My head still hurts, I do apologize."

James nodded and offered him the room key. "Let me know if you need any help," he said. "My kit isn't far away."

Barty nodded and accepted the key, his gratitude for James' care and friendship feeling far more nourishing than the food sitting in his belly like swallowed stones. "I'll be alright," he said. "I'll just sleep it off."

James nodded again, turning his eyes back to the crowd (now chanting about Mrs. Sally Day, whose bones had been so twisted they'd buried her sideways) "Lock your door."

"But isn't Paul sharing my room?"

"Paul is showing every indication of sleeping on the tavern floor," James said. "I'm glad we only have half a day in his company tomorrow." He let out a disgusted snort. "No wonder the post takes so long, if the drivers are all like him."

When Barty still looked worried, James sighed. "He'll bang on the door if he needs to get in. Lock it. We don't want to take any chances."

Barty nodded, wondering just what chances James was worried about, and left, averting his gaze from the merry singing crowd, and ignoring the necromancer, whose hungry gaze he could feel burning into his back.

It was a relief to close the door on the noise and take a moment just to breathe in the quiet, cool darkness of his room. He didn't bother lighting a candle - there was enough moonlight streaming in from the glass window for him to shed his coat, boots and vest and collapse onto the bed, carefully taking up only half of it in case the driver did make it off the tavern floor.

Sleep pulled at him like an anchor, but his head was still throbbing, keeping him adrift despite his longing to sink. His brain churned with all the lessons, both from Fabian and James, the worries about where they were headed and the ridiculous lyrics of the necromancer song...

He more than half suspected that Fabian had, long ago, written that song themselves. They were sneaky, and clever, full of wit and charm, when they wanted to be. Barty's mind drifted back over their time together the past year. There was much to admire about Fabian; they were full of knowledge they didn't mind sharing, without asking anything of him in return. Full of secrets, and ancient wisdom, and power...

...and that hunger in their crimson gaze, the hunger that never left, that seemed to sear into his soul whenever they looked at him.

A knock sounded at the door. Barty caught his breath

and closed his eyes, knowing it was too early for it to be Paul, knowing James had already said goodnight to him, and it could only be...

"Dr. Wayman," the necromancer's voice was soft, yet clear, despite the wooden barrier between them. "I hope my song did not distress you overly."

Barty swallowed hard, but found his voice. "N-no, um. My distress is of my own making. You don't need to worry about me, madam. Er. Sir. Er-" he had yet to find an appropriate-in-between pronoun for addressing them formally. Even in the darkness, he could feel his face flaming. "Sorry."

A soft chuckle from Fabian. The knob wriggled in the door, but Barty, true to his word, had locked it, and it did not open. "I have told you before, any of them are fine, Doctor." They paused for a moment. Barty found himself remembering, quite vividly, that Fabian had taught him how to pick locks a few weeks ago. If they really wanted to get in, the lock would not stop them.

He didn't think they'd stoop to such a thing, but the thought sent a chill down his spine, nevertheless. What did they want?

"I was wondering, Dr. Wayman," Fabian said, their voice even closer to the door now, "if there is more besides your headache that is bothering you. If there is, perhaps, something I can help you with."

Barty lay stock still in his bed, his heart suddenly racing.

He knew what the necromancer wanted.

"If you are unsure yourself, Doctor, all you need to do is open this door, and we can talk about it. James is keeping an eye on the tavern, and Paul won't be up here for hours yet. There will be...no interruptions."

Barty closed his eyes, a shiver that had nothing to do with temperature going through him. All he had to do was open the door. It would be only to talk. Probably. Even if he did open the door, it didn't mean anything would happen...

...did he want nothing to happen? He wasn't sure.

"Perhaps it is one of your lessons that is bothering you," Fabian continued, their voice as velvety as their favorite cloak. Barty heard them try the knob again. It remained locked. "Perhaps there is something you need...further explained..."

Barty closed his eyes. "Would Ruphys approve of your explanations?" he asked the darkness before him, his voice shaking.

For a moment there was silence. Then Fabian's laugh rippled through the air, sharp and hungry. "Ruphys," they said, "is well used to sharing my time. I had seven wives when I had him first, don't you remember?"

Barty let out a breath. It was a relief to hear that - not because of the permission the necromancer was seeking to grant him, but because he, Barty, knew his own heart. And he, Barty, knew he did not want to be just another corpse jumped in the graveyard.

"I am sorry," he told the darkness, "but I truly think sleep is all I need. It has been a long day, and I hope you will forgive me if I seek wellness in rest."

Another silence, longer than the last. Barty wondered how it felt, to be a necromancer of such power, influence, history and fame, denied by a little upstart of a doctor. Part of him was terrified at his own daring. Part of him was proud of himself, for hearing the soft voice of his soul, and having the strength to listen to it.

"Very well," Fabian said at last. "There will be opportunities in the future, of course, for improving your education."

Barty shivered again, and tried not to think about what those 'opportunities' would entail.

"Sweet dreams, Dr. Wayman."

"Goodnight," he forced out, in barely a whisper.

Light steps strode away from his door. Barty dared to relax, wiping sweat from his brow and feeling both chilled and heated at the same time. His mind was a whirl of emotions -

confusion, pain, along with a little desire he very much didn't want to have, and a feeling of being...well. He'd admired Fabian very much for quite a little while. To possibly be admired back would be-

"No, Barty," he told himself firmly, pulling his blanket tight. "It isn't out of admiration that they do this. It is...it is greed. They simply want everything they can get their hands on. Seven wives, and Ruphys, don't forget."

Still. Part of his mind whispered that Fabian probably knew all sorts of interesting things, from their experiences with seven wives and Ruphys.

With so much in his mind that he was trying desperately not to think about, it took Barty quite a while to fall asleep. Or, perhaps, he didn't want to fall asleep, out of fear of what dreams would be waiting for him.

CHAPTER 11: A LESSON

Light filtered in through the silky curtains, bathing the entire room in a peach early-morning glow she could almost taste.

She drifted in and out of sleep, taking note of every ripple of sensation while her consciousness journeyed from the depths of dreamland to the warm shallows of wakefulness. The sheets against her bare skin were soft as thistledown, the bed holding her shape with perfect gentleness. Even with eyes still closed, she could smell the vine of elderflower trailing over the window, its sweetness only adding to the welcome, lazy breeze that drifted into the room, tempting her to further awakening for the sake of a full, deep breath.

For a moment she savored it, the nest of perfection,

safety, and splendor.

Then *he* stirred in the bed beside her, turning against her, the tinkling sound of his jewels as cold as the stones themselves on her back. He snuggled close, his perfect lips finding her neck.

"And now?" he whispered. She opened her eyes, emotion coiling black and hot in her chest. "Are you satisfied, my sweet pet?"

His hand trailed through the sheets to find hers - she could see it out of the corner of her eye, the rings sparkling in rainbows on his fingers, fingers that even now changed color, shape and length as easily as light shifted in a dewdrop.

"I will never," she hissed, hand turning in his to close on his wrist, "be satisfied."

And he laughed, a sound like golden coins dropping to the floor. His eyes, too, were like gems - every color imaginable, but with no feeling, no soul. Nothing that she could rip from him - or, perhaps something, but too hidden behind the eternal facets for her to catch.

"I know you won't," he said, smiling and hungry, letting her shove him back into the pillows, not even flinching as her nails dug into his ever-shifting skin. "And that is why I will always, always..."

She closed her hands around his neck, breathing hard, trying to stop him from speaking it. Trying to choke the words themselves-

But his perfect lips moved, even as his teeth shifted sharp as a row of brand-new daggers.

"...find you."

**

"Hey - wake UP!"

Fabian gasped, clawing their way back into consciousness. A hand closed on their wrist - strong, too strong for them to jerk free-

"Calm down, Fabian! You're dreaming!"

Fabian blinked. James Buckler's face swam into view,

pale, angry, concerned. "Do you always sleep with a knife under your pillow? Fabian, nobody is attacking you. Wake up!"

Fabian looked around, breathing hard. Wooden walls, warped glass windows. An overcast, gray English day dawning with reluctance outside. They took a deep breath of the chill air, shut away the dream, and forced the breath out slowly, letting the knife fall from their grip. "Relax, Doctor," they rasped, giving him a sardonic smile. "I am awake."

"You're shaking," James said flatly. He let go of their wrist and confiscated the knife before they could pick it up again.

Fabian looked down at their hands – indeed, as the good doctor had observed, their slender fingers had curled themselves into fists, quaking, even now.

They forced their fingers back open and let their hands drop onto the sheets, hiding the red marks left by their fingernails. They couldn't feel a thing.

Cold metal on her bare back.

They curled their lip in disgust, and threw aside the blanket, going to the mirror, pointedly ignoring James' serious, worried look and dragging their fingers through their wild mane of dark hair. "If our driver tries to stop for drinks today," they said, twisting the black locks into a makeshift braid, "I am going to cut his throat myself."

They expected a snort and a wry retort from their companion, but Dr. Buckler held his silence. They could see his reflection in the mirror, already fully dressed and ready for the day, regarding their back with gray, serious eyes.

They twisted to look at him, raising an eyebrow. "If you have something to say, Doctor, you better be sure you actually want to say it."

Irritation clouded James's brow. "Why did you come with us?" he asked, the words extra terse as if to prove he did actually want to say it. "You have everything you want or need, at least according to what you told us your goals are. Why abandon your husband, child and home to risk yourself against another plague?"

Husband indeed; no church had bound their two souls. Fabian snorted and turned back to the mirror, tucking stray strands back into place and trying not to wish Ruphys was here now, to fold them into his strong, warm, familiar embrace. "You know you need my help, Doctor."

"I know you never do things unless they serve some purpose for you," James said acidly. "I know you killed two people before we left-"

"Those people were responsible for the deaths of thousands," Fabian said, pulling down one of their eyelids and checking the color in the mirror. "I expect thanks, not complaints, Doctor."

"And whoever you are chasing now?" James said, folding his arms. "Is he also responsible for the death of thousands?"

Fabian paused.

They kept forgetting that James Buckler was, despite his bluster and state of undead, a very intelligent man.

If they weren't careful, they would give away far more than they wanted him to know.

They undid their braid and picked up their brush, deciding to take the time to tease out the tangles. After all, a gentler approach had its uses, now and then.

Cold stone. Hot blood. He should have been dead, but the contents of that letter...

"Maybe not thousands," they said. "But at least one." Yes, best to hint at the edge of the small issue. Let James sniff around that, and not see the looming shadows that Fabian needed to keep away from Ruphys and Willamina.

The doctor stepped closer, but Fabian didn't turn, keeping up the appearance of focusing on the strokes of their brush.

"If you are driving us into danger," Dr. Buckler said, "if Dr. Wayman comes to grief because of you-" he paused, heaving a breath.

In the mirror, Fabian could see his hands balled into

fists. They fought to keep a curling smile from their face - the doctor was disturbed indeed, if he was breathing for the sake of self control. What a silly, emotional corpse. "Are you threatening me, Doctor?" they said, amused, meeting his eye in the looking glass. "Do I need to express how ridiculous that is for you, personally?"

Dr. Buckler looked away from them, visibly biting his tongue. He knew that Fabian, the necromancer, could do terrible things to his corpse-bound person.

"I will not stand by while you bring him harm," James said through gritted teeth. He glared back into the mirror, the force of his gaze palpable even in the glass. "*Any* harm, Fabian. Don't break his bones, his mind, or his heart."

Fabian twisted their shining hair back into a braid. "I will consider your request, Doctor."

"It isn't a request."

Fabian turned their head ever so slightly, looking at his face out of the corner of their vision. Then they stood, turning to face him, stepping closer with a ripple of their dark sleeping robe. "Not a request?" they repeated, voice velvety soft. "Are you giving me orders now, Doctor?"

"If that's what it takes." James Buckler did not back down, meeting Fabian's stare, his gray eyes like steel.

Fabian smiled at him, and shook their head. "Perhaps you lack imagination after all. You're a scientifically minded man, Dr. Buckler... let's try an experiment."

They took a deep breath, and focused, twitching the threads of power that let the sweet corpse move.

Dr. Buckler dropped to his knees with a gasp, his pose now resembling that of a kneeling soldier awaiting orders. He cursed and struggled against Fabian's compulsion, but Fabian kept him down, kept their sharp smile on their face, looming over him.

"I respect you, James Buckler," they said, running a hand through his neat, sandy hair. "I give you your freedom, both of mind and of body, at all times. But let us be very, very clear, my little corpseling..."

Their grip on his hair tightened, and they pulled his head back. His eyes were so wide the whites showed on all sides. No breath escaped his clenched teeth.

"...I can take it all away just as easily as I gave it," Fabian hissed in his ear. "Do not presume to command me, Doctor. Do not think you understand my intentions. Do not, for your own sake, try to stand between me and what I want." They released his hair and reclaimed their knife from his pocket. "Do I make myself clear, Doctor?"

"Very," he said, and Fabian had to admire the fiery twist of anger in the word. Most men would be terrified at this point. How useful that fierce spirit would be, if Fabian could but turn him in the right direction.

Fabian gestured with their knife like a conductor waving a baton, flexing their power and enjoying the shock in the doctor's face as they pulled him upright once more. "Good man," they said, and turned back to the mirror to check that their hair was still in place. "If you are so concerned with Dr. Wayman's welfare, perhaps you had better make sure he is up and about. I'll find our driver once I'm dressed for the road." They loosed their mental control, letting the threads of magic return to their usual configuration.

James glared at them, but left the room, his stride stiff with dignified outrage.

Fabian watched him exit. They held their silence for a long moment, listening to the creak of his steps vanish down the hallway.

And then they bent their head and rested it on the table, wheezing out laughter at the memory of the shocked, horrified, indignant expression on James' face when they'd dropped him to his knees.

Oh, they would pay for that petty trick later, with nothing but frost and mistrust from him for a day or two. But in their book, it had definitely been worth it.

Anyway, they thought, forcing themselves up with a

giggle and going to dress, it was a far better moment to linger over than any whispered words from dreams. They were relieved, honestly, that James had only stumbled upon half the answer.

Yes, chasing someone, if the man mentioned in the letter was who they thought it was.

But they were also fleeing - running away from where the last rumors of their presence still lingered. Running to protect a family that would be in great danger, if the dreams meant what Fabian thought they meant – if the old shadow was searching for them once more.

They made sure all their knives were sharp. Hunting or fleeing, they would be prepared.

**

Fabian was not one for regret, but as their little group piled into the coach, with a furious Dr. Buckler to one side, and a quietly-focused-only-on-his-notes Barty across from him, they had to admit that the prevailing mood in the vehicle was a bit less cheerful than it had been the day before. They had half an impulse to pester both their traveling companions into conversation, but that seemed like too much of an acknowledgement of their own desire for company, so they kept their mouth closed, focusing on the scenery rolling by while the reluctantly sober driver guided the coach on its bumpy way towards Exeter. Fabian only half saw the gorgeous rolling hills, shining lakes, and cloud-cathedral skies through the veil of their own self reflection.

There were always challenges when in the younger, fresher part of a lifecycle. They knew this - they knew this with every incarnation. Somehow the cold, clear logic gained in older years, the self control, the emotional regulation, even the subconscious insight of a mind well practiced in deliberation and patience, were very difficult to maintain in earlier stages. It was a strange thing indeed, how an intellect full of ancient knowledge and experience could still have impulses and desires more appropriate to their physical age.

Some day Fabian would have to study that in a laboratory setting; to find out why being in a younger body also affected the balance of priorities in the mind. Perhaps it had something to do with patterns of indulgence; perhaps being with Ruphys, and the accompanying safety, warmth, physical and emotional gratification, had somehow imprinted a lack of discipline on their faculties.

A little herd of wild ponies milled in a field heavy with clover and heather. Fabian watched their soft noses munching purple blossoms and sighed internally. No, they had to admit, they hadn't exactly been well behaved in their elder stages either. Seven wives, plus Ruphys on the side...they knew their old habits. They knew they relished indulgence and gratification. They also knew that to gain such privileges, one needed power - and power came through control, through knowledge, through understanding and restraint and patience.

How many rulers of the past had fallen for lack of control over their urges? Countless.

How many times had Fabian themselves died, because of carelessness due to overindulgence? Caving to desire, be it for pleasure or power? More than a handful.

Somewhere there had to be a balance. Somewhere between the cold analysis and the burning hunger.

Fabian watched the fat, shaggy little ponies enjoying their eternal salad, feeling almost envious. How much simpler life seemed, when your only indulgence was grass, and your only enemies were wolves.

Well. The way to strengthen skill with a tool was to practice. Today would be a day of self control.

They turned back to Barty and, ignoring his guilty flinch as he jerked his eyes back to his papers, said to him, "Let's review from yesterday, shall we?"

"Oh! Um. Yes, um..." Barty's worried brown eyes darted from Fabian, to his notes, and back again, pink touching his cheeks as he stumbled over his words. "A-all of it?"

"Let's just stick to diseases and treatments for now," Fabian said, ignoring Dr. Buckler's glare. This was self control, James Buckler, even if Barty seemed sweeter to sample than any sugar-glazed pastry. "Tell me what you have written, and I, or Dr. Buckler," Fabian gave that scowl a calm, controlled smile, "will let you know if you need any corrections."

"Right," Barty said, seeming to relax under Fabian's genuine focus on his education. He cast Dr. Buckler a shaky grin, and returned his eyes to his notes. "Right, um. So. First and most common, syphilis..."

With Barty immersed in his notes, the journey went smoother. First Fabian, and eventually James, helped Barty perfect his documentation and understanding. The miles passed unobserved with all parties focused on medical discussion, and the tensions of before eased into a shared feeling of determination; all three aware of what dangers frail humans faced, and sharing battle tactics for overcoming them. The union was not terribly surprising - Fabian had worked with both doctors before, when facing the magic of the cursed plague - but it felt good to reaffirm that they all shared a purpose in this manner. All three shared the same foes, in this treacherous battlefield.

Funny, Fabian found themselves musing, how such moments were as gratifying as other, more obvious pleasures. Perhaps it was their youth acting up again, but they found the unity as pleasurable as a good meal. Barty's smiles, James' eagerness to share his professional expertise, even Fabian's own accounts of past life experience built something between them all. Perhaps trust would be too strong a word, after Fabian's various oversteps, but...

Well, Fabian already knew their own proclivity for indulgence.

Before long they approached Exeter - heralded by the great orchards of apple trees, standing laden and proud in their responsibility for the region's fine ciders. The trees clustered so close to the road that Fabian was able to crack the door and catch an apple. They split it in half, and, after giving half to Barty, devoured their own piece with noisy relish. The flesh was not terribly sweet, but the crunch in itself was worth it.

Barty timidly suggested that they at least try the famous cider once they drew into town, and Fabian, licking apple juice from their fingers, looked to Dr. Buckler, allowing him the choice.

The doctor shrugged. "We've made good time today, and you have been diligent in your studies," he said. "We can stop in one of the taverns for lunch, before we buy horses and carry on towards Plymouth."

They stopped at The Oxford Inn, in fact, which served cider aplenty. Even Fabian tried it, and found it as pleasant a draft as any they had sampled, crisp and cool and tasting as if the apples had only been plucked from the trees yesterday.

The party said goodbye (and good riddance, under Buckler's breath) to Paul their driver once they finished eating, and acquired two good horses (Fabian still had theirs from before), as well as a baggage pony, in the market. Barty, clearly having enjoyed his cider, wondered aloud if perhaps they should stay the night in the town and leave the next day, but Dr. Buckler told him firmly that they already had a destination to overnight at, and they would have to leave soon if they wished to get to the little village before dark. Barty consoled himself with scratching his new mount under the jaw. The horse leaned into the scratches, his pointed brown ears relaxed, clearly enjoying the attention.

Fabian paid no attention to their own gray mount. Instead, they looked at the ruins of the city walls, and remembered a lifetime long ago, when those barricades had been strong and sturdy enough to keep out hoards of invaders. Now the walls were open, for the hoards were welcome to Exter's bountiful market of fish, fruits and wares, as long as they brought coin. The entire city had grown fat and beautiful with the prosperity of its orchards, fields and fishing. The plague clearly hadn't hit Exeter as hard as it had London.

The doctors loaded up their horses and pony and set off. The autumn sunshine beamed down at them through the trees. The breeze flowed cold and fresh as the cider Barty was so loath to leave. Fabian whistled bits of 'The Leaping Necromancer' and watched the great clouds billow over and through each other. Barty and James rode side by side, and fell into talk of their various military histories. Fabian only half listened, though, to James' tales of different field hospitals and their abysmal conditions, or Barty's story of his vessel spending a week chasing a pirate ship and failing miserably to catch it.

Perhaps it was several lifetimes of having made enemies, but Fabian couldn't shake the feeling that they were being watched. They spent most of their attention scanning the fields, hills and valleys for...

For what?

They didn't know.

The group rode for several hours, the sun lazing its way across the sky and deepening the shadows around them into blue-black. Rolling hills of greenery and sky-blue ponds surrendered to harsher terrain: chunked-up stretches of grass-covered granite interrupted by the occasional bog. Lichens clustered anywhere the grasses hadn't claimed, and with darkness falling, bats and foxes could be seen braving the twilight to search for food.

Before them a dark shadow stretched across the horizon, broken only by a single cluster of lights. To these lights they rode, and soon saw that the stretch of darkness beyond was in fact a massive groove of ancient oak trees. The twinkling gleam emitted from a single, tiny village, ringed round with a low wall of mossy stone. The buildings almost seemed an outcropping of the forest itself, silent and unwelcoming.

A chill breeze wafted towards their group from the village, carrying a heavy scent that, to Fabian, was all too familiar.

Rot. Death. Disease.

Plague.

And, strangely enough, smoke.

"Oh, dear," Barty said, straining his eyes in the darkness. "Do you think there was a wildfire?"

"No," Dr. Buckler said, squinting as well. "We would have seen the smoke rising in the air long before now. It must have been something smaller."

"Smaller," Fabian agreed, taking a deeper breath and catching the scent of roasted meat. "But recent, nevertheless. That generally means one thing, in this particular village."

Dr. Buckler turned a frown in Fabian's direction. "What does it mean? Have you been here before?"

Fabian shook their head. "I have not visited this place myself. When I still wore the crown, there were rumors, however, that they took great issue with, ah...being ruled by sorcery." They gave James a grim smile. "Don't let any of the townies get too close a look at you, Doctor. They might not like what they see, and they express themselves in very *heated* ways."

Dr. Buckler scowled at Fabian and turned away, but Fabian knew he would heed their counsel. James Buckler was not one to let pride get in the way of good advice, as much as it seemed he would like to, at times.

They found the source of the smoky smell a few hundred meters from the village gates. A heavy stake loomed over the road, charred and withered, with the remnants of a great fire about its base. The day before, perhaps, there had been a significant blaze here, for the charcoal smear left by hungry flames stretched a good eight feet up. All that remained now were ashes, a few scorched branch ends, and bones.

Fabian stopped. Dr. Buckler swore. Barty said, very softly, "Oh, no..."

Fabian swung down off their horse and stepped closer, ash puffing up from every pace of their boots.

It was almost a complete skeleton. The fire had not been built well enough to burn very hot, so while all of the flesh, tendons and hair were gone, most of the bones were still in place, even fragments of the smallest finger bones.

"Who could have done this?" Barty whispered, the shock of a good heart clear in his voice. Fabian wondered dryly if his view on the goodness of mankind would change, after this moment.

"Don't you know the saying, boy?" Fabian asked, closing their eyes to push away away dream memories of how it felt to die in such a way, skin crackling and hair sizzling. "'Burn the witch.'"

"But nobody does that anymore," Barty protested, unable to tear his eyes away from the skull nestled in the ash. "It's been illegal for ages."

"Made illegal during *my* reign," Fabian said dryly. "I haven't been around to enforce it in twenty years. And your current monarch," their lip twisted in mockery at the word, "doesn't have time to pay attention to little villages out in the middle of nowhere. Especially in Devonshire, which is already so independent, with the Stannary Convocation attitudes still lingering. They might be part of England, but they have considered themselves separate since 1201. I don't know what it is about tin mining that makes people so uppity..."

Barty furrowed his brow in puzzlement. "But then, doesn't it seem strange that they wrote to us in London, asking for help with plague, instead of managing things themselves?"

Fabian shrugged. "I believe it comes down to the nature of the plague. Again, we are the only ones who have ever defeated an outbreak with a 100% mortality break. Be that as it may..."

They looked back towards the village. Dark had settled completely now, forming a greater contrast to the well-lit windows behind the low wall. Between the windows and themselves, though, were more stakes, and more sets of charred, brittle bones. Fabian knew that ignorant minds turned desperate when faced with crisis. If these people had been burning their own citizens in order to 'cleanse' themselves of witchcraft and be free of the plague...

"Perhaps," Fabian said softly, "we should leave these people to their suffering."

"Absolutely not," Dr. Bucker said. "We have a responsibility both as doctors and as British citizens." He turned his horse towards the village entrance and rode on, leaving no room for argument.

Barty, clearly relieved, followed after him, leaving Fabian standing in the ashes.

Fabian watched them make for the gate, and smiled.

They bent down, patted the ashy skull, and murmured, "Fret not, sweet thing. You'll get your chance."

Then, leaving the finger and leg bones twitching and shifting in the ash, Fabian turned away, going to the next stake.

And after that, the next, and the next...

By the time they caught back up with their doctorly companions, both Barty and Buckler had reached the gates, and were arguing heatedly with the gatekeeper.

"I'm telling you, we are doctors!" Dr. Buckler half-shouted. "We were sent by the Queen herself to provide relief for the people suffering in and around Plymouth!"

"T'was outsiders that brought the plague upon us," said the gatekeeper, a thin, hunched man with a pinched mouth well used to frowning. "People like you caused our suffering. Not letting you in. Stay out there with the other cursed and leave us be."

Fabian looked around. The 'other cursed' were piled up corpses of plague victims, not even wrapped in shrouds to protect them from the elements. Fabian retrieved their mask and gloves from their horse and went to investigate these bodies, still listening to the argument at the gate. The words of the gatekeeper painted a vivid picture when accompanied by the sight of a dozen plague-blackened, bloodied forms, most of which were no more than a day or two dead.

"I have a writ of permission given me by the Royal

College of Physicians and ordered by the queen herself," Dr. Buckler said, pulling the paper out of his coat and showing it to the gatekeeper.

"Can't read it," the gatekeeper said airily. "Won't do you no good here, upstart."

"Then fetch someone who CAN read it!" Dr. Buckler roared.

Fabian had to stifle a laugh, peeling back a bloodied eyelid and checking underneath it. Yes, it was the same plague that the letters had spoken of. The decay of soft tissue was there. It must have spread all the way from Plymouth already.

"Shan't," said the gatekeeper.

"Do you WANT your citizens to keep dying?" Dr. Buckler demanded.

"Better for the unworthy to die, than for us to submit to the unnatural tortures designed by the government!" the gatekeeper snipped back. "But you know what? Fine. I'll show you it's not just me what thinks so. I'll get the mayor hisself, then you'll have to just turn around and leave, won't you?"

"You'd better hope that your mayor isn't half as addle-brained as you," Dr. Buckler snapped, "or none of you will be left alive in three days!"

The gatekeeper pulled a face at Dr. Buckler and, making sure the gate was still locked, shuffled away, coughing and muttering to himself.

"James," Barty said, and Fabian repressed an internal sigh at the pain in the young doctor's voice. Really, the boy had to stop caring so much. "What if they actually won't let us help?"

"Then we'll just have to journey on without helping," Dr. Buckler said grimly. "We can't help people who won't help themselves, Barty. A sad necessity to understand in the medical field. If people die over their own stubbornness, it cannot be blamed on us."

Fabian stared at the piled corpses, but didn't see them.

"It is not the blame I am worrying about." Barty's voice

was soft, yet audible, over the night breeze.

Fabian dusted off their gloves and stood.

"Gentlemen," they said, walking back to the doctors. "We are wasting our time here."

Dr. Buckler pointedly ignored their words, addressing Barty. "Alright, Wayman. Even if the mayor is a fool, it may be that the people themselves are interested in aid. We can at least give them the chance to choose for themselves."

Barty nodded at this, looking relieved. "I like that. Maybe one or two will even be able to tell us how this started."

"Here now, here now, what's all the...what's all this about then, hm?" An officious man with snow white hair, a patchy beard, and eyes with heavy bags strode towards them, a lantern held in one hand. His rank was clear in the fine quality of his vest and coat, as well as the respectful distance the gatekeeper and another official-looking gentleman kept. The gatekeeper's mouth was twisted in a self-satisfied smirk, which Fabian took as a bad sign, and the other gentleman had disapproval stamped all over his thin, judgmental face. "Maurice has already told you we don't want strangers here," the man said. "Especially not such strange strangers." He scowled at Fabian's white, beaked plague mask. "You can clear out and sleep in the road like all vagrants do, you shan't get any shelter here."

"We are doctors, sir," Dr. Buckler said with thinly masked patience. "We are specially trained to fight plague, and are passing on our way to Plymouth, which is also having an outbreak. We only want to help-"

"We have managed just fine without our doctor for weeks," the mayor blustered over him, his darting eyes telling all three strangers that things were anything but fine. "In fact, we are fairly certain that it was *because* of our doctor that we are now cursed with this plague. He was the first to fall ill, and we all know it was because he is being punished for letting his son marry a witch."

"Oh?" Fabian spoke up before Dr. Buckler or Barty could

reply to this. "Congratulations to the son. How long ago was this?"

The mayor looked irritated. "Well, it was - well. It was almost thirty years ago, but still-"

"But seeing as your doctor was the first one to fall ill, the only possible reason you could decide that such a thing would happen was because his son married a witch?"

"Yes! Exactly. Such a grievous sin-"

"Witches are of course legal now, and have been for the past sixty or so years, but regardless." Fabian drew off their mask, shaking out their long, black hair and smiling at the mayor with their white teeth and red, red eyes. "How do you know she was a witch?"

The mayor gaped at Fabian, his eyes going from Fabian's crimson gaze to their gloved hands and pale, beaked mask. "W...witch!" he gasped.

"No," Fabian said patiently. "Answer the question."

"She came from the forest, witches always come from the forest! She came and lured away our doctor's only son." The man wiped his forehead. "The whole village wept for his father's sake, and cursed her name. Some betrayals can never be forgotten!"

Fabian thought of the stakes in front of the villages, and the pile of bodies left to rot in sun and rain. "Yes," they agreed softly, "some betrayals can never be forgotten."

They mounted their horse and turned his gray head away from the gate. "Come on, doctors," they said. "These people are already dead. You cannot save them."

"But-! But we could-" Barty tried to protest.

"Listen to your superior, Doctor," Fabian sneered at him, already riding back down the road. "You cannot help *anyone* who doesn't want to be helped."

But Barty did not turn to follow them. They heard him speaking earnestly to the mayor, "Please, please sir - don't the lives of your citizens mean anything to you? Don't you wish to spare them such suffering? At least tell them we are here and

138

let them choose-"

"Better to save their souls than their flesh," the mayor said. "Leave this place and take your evil with you!"

Fabian slowed their horse, and waited for Barty to remount his own steed and catch up. They gave him a raised-eyebrow look that said 'I told you so,' but he only frowned, his expression determined.

"Before you even think about it, Dr. Wayman," Dr. Buckler said, trotting up on his other side, "if you try to sneak back into that town in the middle of the night, I will catch you and turn you over my knee."

Barty blushed furiously and fastened his gaze on the pommel of his saddle. "I won't, sir," he said.

Fabian grinned, rather hoping he would.

**

The group decided to circle the village entirely and make camp just inside the shelter of the protective oaks of the forest. There was a spacious cleared area not too deep among the bows, with a few stumps here and there that made satisfactory chairs. Barty and Dr. Buckler worked together to build up a fire for heat and light, and Fabian sat on their stump and ate their portion of dried fish and apples, vaguely wishing for fresh rabbit. If they had stumbled across the carcass of any large carnivore during their travels, it could have been arranged, but as all they had found were the corpses back near the town, they had to make do with the scant provisions they'd acquired in the Exeter marketplace.

Hell. They didn't need a large predator.

Fabian went to their luggage and pulled down one of their bundles, aware that Barty and Dr. Buckler had paused their awkward, silent meals to watch.

They unwrapped the cloth, waved a hand over the contents, and half a dozen glowing-eyed rats immediately jumped out and scampered into the forest.

They covered the bundle again and went back to their stump, sitting down in front of it, closing their eyes, and folding their hands on their chest.

The rats hunted, scurrying under leaf and branch, through burrows and tunnels, looking for anything that moved.

"Put another log on the fire," they told Barty. "I'm going to cook something."

"Y-you're hunting with rats?" Barty said, surprise evident in his voice even as Fabian heard him move to do as they commanded.

"Yes," Fabian said. "They have sharp teeth and keen senses of smell. I am going to need a bit of extra food, and it is not wise for me to overly deplete the stores when we have so much further to go tomorrow."

"What do you mean, you are going to need extra food?" Dr. Buckler asked sharply.

But Fabian only smiled, eyes still closed, and said, "Patience, Doctor. Time will answer your question soon enough."

He grumbled, but did not press further. "If you're going to be up anyway, then," he said, "you can at least keep the fire going."

"I will," they said, in answer to both his statements.

The doctors settled down for sleep, with only bedrolls between themselves and the leaf-littered ground, stars twinkling in the open sky above.

Fabian's rats returned with a magnificent pheasant. Fabian sent the rats up the road to keep watch, and had the bird skinned and roasting before the moon rose. They tore into the meat almost before it was cooked, hunger weighing heavily on their limbs, making their hands shake. They ate with their eyes closed, almost not tasting the meat between their teeth. A simple matter of caloric intake - of giving their body fuel enough to conduct the power running through them. Fabian knew what to expect tonight, and had to be ready. Fabian could see them coming, with their torches and pitchforks, rope and anger. Any minute now...any minute...

There. A group of men with muttering voices and heavy farming tools clutched in gloved hands, leaving the gate, seen through the eyes of half a dozen little spies. The group, twenty strong, trudged down the road, thinking to find the band of doctors back the way they had come, just like they had said. Then, finding no camp 'back where you came from,' they circled back, passing the burned stakes and body piles, towards the light of the fire, now visible against the blackness of the forest with their town not in the way.

Fabian smiled, crunched a pheasant bone, sucked out the marrow, and commanded their *other* servants to follow the crowd. Not too quickly, not too slowly. Far enough away to not be seen, near enough that they would arrive on cue when the show started.

"Gentlemen," they spoke aloud, knowing that neither Barty nor Buckler were asleep through the sensory ordeal of a pheasant being skinned, cooked, roasted and devoured, "I suggest you make yourselves presentable. We are about to have company."

Barty sat up, fumbling for his hat and cane. "What do you mean?" he said, getting to his feet and looking around. The glimpse Fabian got of his face was full of unease. "What company?"

"Nothing truly remarkable," Fabian said, licking grease from their fingers. "Only dead men."

"Is that supposed to be funny?" Dr. Buckler demanded. Fabian noted how, despite his anger, he still heeded the warning, rising up and donning his hat and stick as well.

"Everything is funny, if you only know how to look at it," Fabian purred, tossing aside the bone and standing. "Grab the horses, will you? I don't want them scared off."

"Scared off by what-"

But the answer was already upon them, their marching steps audible even over the crackling of the flames.

"See," Fabian hissed, pointing back along the path. "The dead walk, and it is not even my doing, this time."

Barty and Buckler looked.

Two dozen villagers approached, carrying their torches and pitchforks and rope. Two dozen men, and a few women, of varying ages, with hard expressions and angry, loud voices. "There they are!" someone called. "They brought a witch to our land! The plague is here to warn us of them!"

"Don't be idiotic!" Dr. Buckler shouted, stepping forward to address the group. "Your plague was here long before we arrived. We are only passing through and we stopped to offer you help!"

"You brought a witch!" screeched a voice - Fabian recognized the gatekeeper, Maurice, with a flaming torch. "If we kill her, we will purify the land! And rid ourselves of the plague!"

"And how has that worked out for you so far?" Dr. Buckler asked sarcastically. "Did the plague lesson because of the others you murdered? Who was it you killed yesterday? Some poor old grandmother who couldn't care for herself?"

An awkward silence from the crowd.

"It...it is commanded! Thou shalt not permit a witch to live!"

"And what," Fabian said, speaking over the arguing voices, "Is commanded regarding murder?"

Another silence fell. More uncomfortable shifting. The torches flickered in the chill night.

Barty stepped forwards, drawing every eye to himself and spreading his hands in a placating gesture. "Please," he said, "we mean no harm, nor have we done any harm. Please leave us be, and go back to your homes. If you will not accept our help as doctors, shouldn't you at least be spending your energy trying to help each other?"

"How can they, Barty?" hissed Fabian. "How can they turn around, knowing they have killed so many innocents in their quest for salvation? To go back now..." they turned their eyes on the crowd, "...would be to admit their blood. Their guilt. No. These cowards would never be able to accept such enlightenment, no matter how you shove the truth before them like pearls before swine."

More than one face in the crowd flushed in ugly anger. Indignant mutters broke out, and the mayor pushed forwards, pointing a thick finger at Fabian. "We will not be insulted by a witch!" he shouted. "We will cleanse the land of evil, and free ourselves of disease!"

"Yeah!"

"Hand her over," the mayor had to push forward again, the crowd having bustled in front of him, bristling with violence. "Hand her over, boy, and we will let you and your companion go free."

Fabian glanced at Barty, raising an eyebrow, but Barty only shook his head, shifting his stick into both hands and clearly preparing to fight. "I won't!" he said, his voice shaking. "This is wrong! Go home!"

And Fabian laughed, even as the crowd's angry mutters turned to shouts, and shouts turned to thrown stones. The mob pressed forward, almost upon Barty and Buckler. The doctors lashed out at anyone who dared get close, managing to hold their ground with nothing more than canes and determination, but it wouldn't last.

"Fall back, boys," Fabian said, grabbing both doctors by their collars and pulling them out of the firelight, into the shadows of the forest. "Fall back, this is not your fight."

"What do you mean?" Barty shouted, raising his arms to shield himself from further stones. "What-"

"Behold!" Fabian said, their voice ringing clear even over the clamor. "The dead will take their own revenge."

Out from the shadows of the forest, from the very shadows Fabian was dragging Barty and Buckler into, stepped corpses.

Corpses, soft and rotted from plague, and the charred, brittle skeletons, now free of their stake prisons.

Fabian let go of Barty and Buckler, and the slaughter began. Fabian watched, unblinking, grinning, as the victims of abuse and neglect fell upon their abusers, tearing them apart, rending their flesh. Blood poured onto the ground and screams filled the air. Men fought to flee, trampling each other to escape the reaping of what they had sowed.

James Buckler turned away, looking sickened and grim. But Barty...

Barty stared, open mouthed, tears dripping down his face.

"I told you," Fabian said softly. "I told you, they were already dead. Do not grieve for them, Dr. Wayman. They are not worthy of your pity."

The screaming continued, the smell of blood filling the air while men died, while men fled and were pulled down, howling and terrified.

"Make it stop!" Barty grabbed Fabian's shoulder, shaking them. "Stop it! Fabian!"

Fabian sneered at him. "They have earned this, Dr. Wayman. You saw the ashes. You saw how they treat their own."

"They are terrified and ignorant!" Barty shouted, eyes brimming with tears. "Fabian - STOP IT!"

Stillness fell in the clearing as, one and all, the corpses stopped. Fabian wasn't looking at them, however, or at the carnage spilled in the dust and leaf litter. They had eyes only for Barty.

"Your own parents," they told him, "died in a fire set by rabble just like this."

"You think I don't know that!?" Barty's voice cracked, and he shoved Fabian away, stumbling through the blood and death, to where a man lay moaning on the ground. "How... how will the world ever get better," he choked, "if we do not teach people to BE better?"

He kicked a charred skeleton off the body and crouched beside it, sniffing and checking for vital signs.

After a moment, Dr. Buckler followed him, kneeling by another bloodied figure and searching for a pulse.

Fabian stared at them both, hating their defiance, admiring their spirit. These fools...the very people they tried to save would have killed them without hesitation moments ago.

"People," they said aloud, "cannot change, no matter how many stars you wish upon or prayers you send."

"I hope for your own sake that you are wrong, Fabian," Barty said, bitterness and pain making his voice prickle like dried brambles. "Because I still have hope for you. That you will change, from all you have been."

He said this even as the tears continued to drip off his jaw. He said this even as his hands shook, wet and red from the stones thrown by the dead before him. The figure he knelt by let out a last rattling wheeze, and fell still.

Barty stood and moved to the next body, letting out a shaky breath. "Can you bring any of these back?" he asked, still refusing to look at Fabian, kneeling in the dust beside yet another corpse. "You're a necromancer, aren't you?"

Fabian watched him work. "I am a necromancer," they agreed. "I could bring back one to true health, maybe two." Maybe more, if they really put their mind to it.

Barty looked up at them, hope shining in his soft brown eyes.

They grinned at him, equal parts amused and disgusted.

"But I won't," they said.

And they turned away, slipping into the black forest, calling their rats to hunt.

Let the doctors fiddle with the lives of the unworthy, if they were so eager to waste their time and energy.

Fabian was still hungry.

CHAPTER 12: THE THIRD BARGAIN

The Huntsman knelt on the polished marble floor, head bowed, staring at his reflection.

It was far easier to meet his own silver gaze than it was to look into the ever-changing eyes of the King. Far easier to watch the shadows dance, cast by the lights of the evening candles, than to face whatever it was the King wanted from him this time.

"Jeremiah Kelly," the King said, and it made the Huntsman shiver to hear his full, true name being spoken aloud, even if nobody else was around to hear it. "You have done very well."

Jeremiah fought down the unease that the King's praise brought, but it wasn't easy. The King only ever spoke to him when he wanted something, and only ever praised him when he wanted something especially difficult, or something he knew Jeremiah would not wish to do.

Of the three times the King had spoken to him in that tone, Jeremiah had only been able to refuse him once, and that had cost him.

He kept his wits, however, and moved his hands before his head, priding himself on how steady his fingers were, though he trembled in his core. *'I honor my side of our bargain, Majesty.'*

"That you do," the King said. Jeremiah wondered if the King knew that his reflection could be seen on the smooth stone, changing from green to blue as he stepped closer. "That is why I trust you, Mr. Kelly. That is why I task you with only the most important of missions."

Liar, a small voice in Jeremiah's head said. But how could it be a lie? Nobody could lie in this land, not even the King himself.

Or could he?

He wished Shilling was here. Shilling loved to answer such questions, considering the excuse to talk Jeremiah's ear off a fair trade for any information conveyed. Jeremiah's heart squeezed at the thought of his friend, still in the stable because he had been too terrified of the King to accompany Jeremiah into the throneroom, even though he'd very much wanted to. Jeremiah didn't blame him – he'd faced rabid wolves wearing more comfort than he felt now, with those polished, glittering boots coming into his view as the King stopped right in front of him.

"I have another task for you," said the King. The point of his scepter, glass today, with ever-changing gems set in a delicate ring, flicked into Jeremiah's view, touching his bearded chin and tilting his face up. "I believe you already know what it is."

Jeremiah let his head be tilted, but did not meet the King's eye, intentionally keeping his gaze unfocused so he would not look at that shockingly beautiful face. *'I cannot do this thing you ask,'* he signed. *'I hunt only monsters. I have only, ever, hunted monsters.'*

"This is a monster you have hunted once before, Jeremiah Kelly." The King pronounced his name softly, but it felt like he whispered right in Jeremiah's ear, sending a chill through him that he could not quite hide. A reminder that the King did not have to ask nicely.

'Do you suggest that I did not fulfill my duty the first time?' Jeremiah signed, keeping his expression stoic. He would not let the King think he was getting to him. Jeremiah was not one who was ashamed of his emotions, but he wanted to give his creditor no cause for enjoyment in this exchange. There were rules in this land, even if the King knew his name. *'I paid my price for my mistake, but did I not achieve what you asked of me, even so?'*

"Of course you did, my dear Huntsman." The King smiled at Jeremiah. Even with his gaze unfocused, even with unease sinking teeth ever deeper into Jeremaih's chest, the Huntsman could not help but ache in his very soul at the beauty in that smile. He hated it. "I am only telling you that this is a monster that is familiar to you," said the King. "You cannot hide behind your sense of honor, this time."

'It is dishonorable to lead a free person to imprisonment.' Jeremiah signed, his expression unchanging.

The King sighed, his colors rippling to a sulky silver-blue. He turned away from Jeremiah. "You are still brooding over the matter of the Raven."

'Was it not your bargain that drove him to madness?' Jeremiah signed. Even if the king was not looking at him, he knew he would understand the question anyway.

"The Raven had a delicate mind to begin with," said the King, examining the rings on his left hand. His fingers sparkled with gems, all different colors that shifted and changed under King's kaleidoscopic gaze, at least three on each finger. "He was going mad from grief long before he struck a bargain with me. How else do you think he was able to call me at all...? Our lands are not easily found by the sane and rational."

Liar, repeated the small voice in Jeremiah's mind. But he did not press the argument – this was not where he wanted the conversation to go.

"Anyway," The King turned back to Jeremiah, his robes brightening to a hue of vivid, spring-like green, "I will do you a favor, Huntsman. I will make this easier for you."

'*I do not want any favors from you*,' Jeremiah signed flatly, but it was too late.

The King spoke on, as if he hadn't read Jeremiah's words, his voice echoing off the marble pillars, the glittering glass windows, the shining, golden throne behind him. "You do not need to capture them. You do not need to harm them. You don't need to kill anyone at all, in this hunt. All you need to do is get them where I can speak to them. That is not unreasonable, is it?" The King smiled. After all, said that smile, once they are within my grasp, I do not need you, Huntsman. I will catch them myself, with my words and my magic and my power.

It made Jeremiah sick.

The King must have sensed the refusal on his fingertips, for he stepped closer, and rested a hand on Jeremiah's shoulder. "And," he said, ignoring Jeremiah's stiffening of dislike, "this favor means so much to me, Huntsman, that if you accomplish it, I will call us even."

That got Jeremiah's attention. He rose to his feet, signing in earnest. '*Truly even? My debt will be paid, if I do this thing for you?*'

"Yes. Your debt to me will be paid. Shilling will remain your companion, with no further obligation to me on your part, until you have some other favor you seek of me. Your very life, back in your own hands." The fingers on Jeremiah's shoulder tightened.

Jeremiah let out a shuddering breath, and the King

closed his eyes, listening with a perfect, pleased smile. "So," he breathed in Jeremiah's ear, his arm slipping around Jeremiah's shoulders with a tinkle of bracelets. "Do we have a deal?"

Even with his freedom in his reach, Jeremiah could not keep his hands from shakily signing the words, '*Stop... stop touching me.*'

The King sighed, but stood back, resting his scepter on his shoulder, his hand on his hip, and looking down at Jeremiah.

Jeremiah closed his eyes, forcing his thoughts in order. He thought of Ida and her merchant husband – how the man had gotten lost, just in time to get a request from the King that compelled her to do what he wanted. He thought of Shilling, so terrified he wouldn't shift out of his horse's form. He thought of himself, and how he'd been caught by the King so many years ago, first with a bargain for his aid, and then a bargain for his very life as he lay dying...

It was dangerous. It was very dangerous. But being free of the King forever was more than worth whatever small risk there was in this seemingly simple task.

It wouldn't be simple. Jeremiah knew that. There would be complications, but he had faith in himself, and in Shilling, that there was nothing they could not accomplish as a team.

Jeremiah caught his breath, gathered his thoughts, and, once he was sure he was back under control, he nodded.

'*We have a deal,*' he signed.

And the King smiled.

CHAPTER 13: SUSPICIOUS FORTUNE

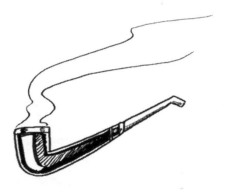

Dr. James Buckler was getting tired of coincidences.

Or maybe he was just tired.

"Bless my good fortune, that you happened to pass by just when I needed help the most!" The merchant in the middle of the road bounced up and down on his toes, beaming at James, Barty, and Fabian on their horses.

James, Barty and Fabian had passed a bleak morning in silence, enjoying neither the chill of the misty, moorish weather nor the chill of the silence between the three of them, a coldness of spirit made of equal parts of Barty's lingering horrified shock, Fabian's aloof refusal to admit any wrongdoing, and James' irritation at Fabian combined with his own helplessness to have prevented the awful situation. James was grateful that Fabian had stepped in to save them all from being burned alive, but it had not escaped his notice that Fabian had goaded the crowd on; as if the necromancer had wanted to prove to both of them that not all humans deserve to be saved - which was completely counterintuitive to everything Barty and James fought for.

And now this. A well dressed, travel-worn little merchant with bright, layered clothes, luxurious whiskers he had a fondness for twirling, and a cart with a broken axle and no working beast in sight.

"I was just heading home – finally, home!" The merchant paused to sigh dramatically and mop his round face with a floral handkerchief. "And then a terrible great wolf came howling down the road! Scared poor Jenny right out of her harness, I tell you. She's a stubborn thing at the best of times, but one look at the teeth on that silver beast and she kicked clean free of the wagon, leaving me here with not a hope in my heart or a prayer in my pocket."

James shook his head, but his companion was of a softer nature.

"That's terrible," Barty said with genuine sympathy. He slid out of his saddle and went over to look at the broken harness straps trailing in the dust. "Are wolves very common in this part of the forest?"

"I don't think so. I mean, I've never had a problem with them before! But then again, it has been a good long while since I passed this way. The road seems to have changed since I left." The merchant laced his fingers over his belly, his eyes drifting from Barty to James to Fabian, who was looking into the shadows of the forest and paying no mind to any of the others. "Where were you folks headed? It wasn't Whiston, by any chance?"

Fabian's head snapped back around at that, but James answered the question. "No, we have been summoned to

Plymouth. We are plague doctors, sir, and by the grace of the Queen, we go where we're needed."

"Plague in Plymouth?" The merchant said doubtfully. He curled his mustache again, and shook his head. "Wasn't any plague when I passed through a fortnight ago. Are you sure you're going to the right place?"

"Of course I'm sure," James said, frowning. "We got a letter from them this week."

"I suppose I am fortunate to have just missed it, then!" said the merchant cheerfully. "Luck can't be bad all the time, I suppose! After all," he laughed, "you all are here to save me in my time of need. And further," he eyed the horses, "Whiston is between here and Plymouth. Not out of your way by any degree. If you don't mind hitching to my wagon for a day, I'd be happy to see to it that you got food, lodging and directions once we get to Whiston."

"Why, that's terribly kind of you!" Barty said, looking up from the straps with an eager smile. "You know James, I think if we tied the axel together with something, and fastened the remains of these straps to one of the horses, we could make it work. Especially if we're allowed to shift some of the baggage to the wagon. How long did you say it is to this Whiston place, Mr...?"

James rolled his eyes. Barty was clearly happier about getting the chance to help someone than he was about the promise of free room and board. Admirable, but lacking in the basic amount of suspicion necessary to survive in the world, in James' opinion.

"Marshal! And no Mr. about it." The merchant extended his hand to Barty, and the two shook with good natured enthusiasm. "It is only a few hours down the road from here. At least, it should be. The roads seem to be getting longer and longer for me, in my old age." He gave a self deprecating sigh. "So it's a deal then? Your transport for a safe bed and a hot meal tonight?"

Barty looked to James, who nodded with some

reluctance. "We do need lodging."

"Out of curiosity," Fabian said, finally tearing their gaze away from the forest so they could pierce the merchant with it, "is it your own home you are proposing to invite three perfect strangers into?"

"You won't be strangers by the time we've spent hours on the road together, madam!" Marshal said with a charming smile. "But no. Not my home, but rather, my wife's beautiful inn!"

Fabian's red eyes widened, and James was amused at how much younger the necromancer looked when surprised. "Your wife's inn? In Whiston?" Fabian considered this a moment. "Are you...married to Ida...?"

The merchant's entire face lit up with an ecstatic, beaming smile. "Yes! Yes, that is right! My beautiful, intelligent, strong, so strong and so beautiful wife! But no, you know her too? Ah! Good fortune indeed! Let me assist you with those straps young man, and we can be on our way at once!" The merchant bustled to help Barty get the wagon ready for travel, producing tools, more straps, and twine from his cart.

"I knew her," Fabian said, though softly enough for only James to hear. "Several lifetimes ago, I knew her."

James turned to regard Fabian in surprise, but answered just as softly, "Several lifetimes? How could she be so old?"

Fabian grinned, watching Barty and Marshal work together on the cart. "She is a very unique individual, on more than one level. I think you will find her interesting, James Buckler. But if Ida is in Whiston, that means we are very close to the edge."

"The edge?" James repeated. "The edge of what?"

"Will you aid us as well, sir?" Marshal called, holding bits of leather straps together in a bundle. "We've almost got it, we just need one more set of hands!"

James nodded, nudging his horse closer, but his gaze remained on Fabian.

Fabian followed. "Do you believe in faeries, Doctor?"

James snorted. "Absolutely not."

Fabian's grin was a brittle, bitter thing. "Men," they said, shaking their head. "You see magic with your own eyes. You are a living, breathing...ah. Well. You are a stark example of the impossible being true, and yet, presented with a new impossible thing, despite a whole wonderful history to draw upon, you call it untrue."

"I am a man of science," James said stiffly. He slipped down off his horse and went over to hold the straps as directed. He spoke his next words loudly enough that Barty would hear, and perhaps learn from, his attitude. "I believe new claims only when they are proven."

"Can you prove magic then, James?" Barty asked innocently, fastening straps to his own horse.

James glared at him. "Magic has real, tangible effects on the world that I can see with my own eyes," he said. "I can observe the effects myself. I can see how words and intent cause physical changes with power that arises from sources accessible to those with the right tools. I have never, once, seen a fairy, or any proof that fairies are more than tales told to children."

"But you see, it is the same thing!" Marshal burst in, his voice full of surprise.

All three turned to look at him. He beamed, bounced once more on his toes, and reached over to tie James' leather straps together. "Magic is the *science* of the faeries. Where our world is run by laws; laws of chemistry, physics, time and space," he nodded grandly to James, as if acknowledging the merit of his side of things, "and magic must be strong to break these laws – the opposite is true in the world of the fae folk! Magic rules there, following no laws but the will of the fairies themselves, and physical laws must work VERY hard to change things in the Fae realm." He chuckled. "Law-gic, if you will."

James shook his head in disgust, but Barty was clearly fascinated. "You speak as if you've seen it! Or even been there, sir!"

"Ah, maybe I have, young man." Marshal gave Barty a very obvious, gleeful wink. "Or maybe I have heard stories from my beautiful wife. Or maybe, I have traveled so many places, and heard so very many stories, that I know better than to doubt something simply because I have not seen it myself, when so many others have seen it!"

"Doubt," Fabian said, speaking softly but cutting through Marshal's jolly words like an iron razor, "is a luxury we cannot afford, if we are going to Whiston." The necromancer looked at James and Barty, their smile unusually grim. "If you value your skins, your minds, and your freedom, humor me, and understand that the place we are going is far too near the realm of the fae for comfort."

James and Barty both stared. James shook his head. "Where is this coming from? You've never spoken of fairies before, not even when we told you where we were going!"

"I assumed this road would lead to Plymouth, not Whiston," Fabian said, eyes glittering. "It is supposed to be impossible to get to Whiston in this day and age. The way has been closed for years and years. But here we are, with a guide and no other road, unless we want to turn around completely." They sat tall in their saddle, drawing their gray hood up to shadow their face. "If you want my advice," they said, nudging their horse to a walk and heading down the road, "you will ask our jolly guide what the customs of the town are, so as to avoid making any irreversible mistakes."

Barty mouthed the words 'irreversible mistakes' and looked at James, worry radiating from him like heat from a forge. James snorted, and said "They are just trying to frighten you, Wayman. Pay them no mind."

"Well..." Marshal clambered into the front seat of his wagon, patted the seat beside him for Barty to join, then gestured for James to begin riding. James did so, leading the baggage pony, and Barty's horse, after a few puzzled steps adjusting to the new weight, tried to follow its companions. The sturdy creature was not used to pulling a wagon, however, and as soon as the big contraption started to follow, it spooked, trying to run away from the burden and sending the entire wagon lurching astray. Only James' quick thinking of moving the other horses to block the brown's escape kept the entire thing from falling off the road. In the end, the harness got very twisted, and the whole group had to stop to straighten things out. Marshal, tisking in sympathy for the wild-eyed horse, took it upon himself to gently lead the brown a few paces until he got used to the burden.

Upon seeing that nothing terrible happened, the brown horse reluctantly settled into a walking rhythm. The wagon, pulled by the makeshift tack and harness, rolled if not gracefully, at least without breaking apart. "Phew!" Marshal clambered back up to his seat. "Your horse is smart, to learn this quickly. As for the customs of the town, hmmm…perhaps your friend is wiser than you give her credit for?" Marshal's eyes lingered on Fabian's slender form. "She feels like one of them, a little."

"One of who?" Barty said, blinking.

"One of the faeries," Marshal chuckled. "Though maybe not! I have never known a faerie to give advice for free. They prefer to make deals, at every possible opportunity."

"Of course," James said, shaking his head at Barty to keep him from asking more questions.

Barty sighed, but shut his mouth, and James turned the conversation back to practical, worldly matters. "How far is it from Whiston to Plymouth then, Mr. Marshal?"

The merchant smiled at him. "Just Marshal, Doctor. And it is a day and a bit, but the weather can add or subtract miles depending on its mood. Ah, it is amazing how the roads change, under the sweet hands of sun and rain, wind and the sky…"

James didn't interrupt, letting the merchant ramble about his travels. He tried to listen, tried to drown out the deep unease that had settled in his chest at Fabian's sudden strange focus on faeries and their ways. James hated to admit it, but he had begun to rely on the necromancer's wisdom. After all, a being of many lifetimes had vast experience and intellect to draw upon. One would have to be a fool to ignore them completely.

James's gaze settled once more on the slight, hooded figure ahead of them.

Was James a fool anyway, for even considering Fabian's fairy tales?

Or would he be an even greater fool to ignore the warnings of the necromancer?

There were too many questions, and James did not yet know how to seek the answers.

He had all day to think about them, though, and he set his mind to work as the little party traveled through the cool forests.

***

They arrived in Whiston just before sunset, with Marshal marveling aloud at how quick their travels had been. "You have good horses!" he said. "Or, someone wants us to be here…"

Fabian gave the merchant a sharp look, but when they caught James watching them, they only smiled, grim and hungry. "We have good horses," they said, "but hold back just a few moments longer, Marshal. I want to give these boys a bit of advice, before we plunge headlong into Whiston."

James rolled his eyes, but he and Barty pulled their horses short, patiently waiting for Fabian to speak.

Fabian, for once, seemed hesitant, choosing their words carefully. "Names," they said at last, "hold power. The closer you get to the border, the more power they hold."

"Fabian," James said tiredly, about to protest, but Barty put a hand on his arm. "Perhaps we should just listen, James?" he suggested, at once apologetic and insistent. "It can't hurt, can it?"

"It's utter nonsense," James grumbled, but he stilled his tongue, ignored Fabian's red, impassive stare, and nodded, showing he would be quiet.

Fabian gave James a mocking bow, and continued. "The safest choice is just to use a piece of your true name, or even your title. Try to refer to each other as 'Doctor' as much as possible, especially in earshot of anyone you suspect to be...unusual. First names hold little power. Nicknames, like Barty..." their gaze rested on James, "...or Jimmy, even less so."

"Don't even think about it," James growled.

"But what about you?" Barty said. "You've been Fabian for two lifetimes! I don't think I even know your surname-"

"You don't," Fabian agreed, eyes glittering, "and I was not named Fabian when I was born in this current life. Plus, I have had so many lives, and names. My true name is far more complicated than any simple mage could understand. I am confident that even a faerie spellcaster would be unable to bind me with "Fabian". The same goes for you in fact, Doctor," they nodded to Barty, "as you don't yet know your birth name, do you?"

Barty nodded, muttering something about meaning to ask the Rabbi when he got back.

Fabian turned their gaze to James. "And you are complicated as well. Your name was not always James, was it? But that was long ago, and everything you are now is under the name James."

James scowled back at the necromancer, trying to ward off this turn of conversation with disapproval alone. He did not like being reminded that Fabian knew he'd once had another name. "My old name," he said stiffly, "means nothing to me."

Fabian smiled, seeming genuinely pleased by this remark. "As long as you believe that," they said, "it will be true. But take care, nonetheless."

With that unsettling advice, they turned, leading the way into the town's main gate.

James shook his head, mentally brushing away the disturbed cobwebs the necromancer had left in his mind, and followed, walking his horse so Barty's cartbound one could keep up.

Whiston's front gate lay ajar, wordlessly inviting the travelers inside. However, the open gate was the only sign of welcome in sight. Instead of the bustling streets full of business like those they had left behind in Exeter, here dwelt a silence, a stillness that seemed an unnatural contrast to the sturdy buildings, well-kept gardens and bright, cheerful sunlight.

They entered the gate, and soon the paradox resolved: some of the closed doors bore an all too familiar warning: "Plague" in red paint, visible even from the street.

Despite the sudden weariness that descended on James' bones, he observed that not every door bore the red declaration, and there were no bodies piled up waiting to be collected, either. If he had to judge, plague had not been long in this town.

"I can't believe it," Barty said, sounding every bit as dispirited as James felt. "Here too? We haven't even gotten to Plymouth yet, and it's already spreading."

"This, this can't be!" Marshal said. He leaned out from his wagon, dismay aging his jolly features. "Please, keep going - my wife's inn, it is just down there, see? The big building, with the many chimneys!"

James pulled his mask out of his bag and slipped it on, the scent of roses and nutmeg overwhelming any stench of plague. Barty did the same, and up ahead, James saw that even Fabian had donned their mask and gloves.

They stopped in front of the inn, but no stable boy came running up to take their horses. Marshal hopped out of the coach and waved a hand at them, saying, "Can you put your horses away yourselves? Please just let me check with my wife, I am sure you can still stay," before disappearing indoors.

James and Barty exchanged a look, shrugged, and did as he suggested, Barty collecting Fabian's horse for them while James led his horse and the baggage pony around the back to the stable. They got the beasts unloaded, unsaddled, fed and

160

watered - James imagined they must look quite amusing to any outsiders, attending these chores in full plague gear. The only other horse in the stable was a silver beauty standing quietly at the opposite end.

Barty hesitated, watching his brown mount go right to the water barrel and drink. "Do you think I should brush him down?" he asked, running a hand over the parts of the horse's chocolatey fur that were damp and disturbed with sweat and wear from the saddle.

"Let's get all our things inside first," James said, hoisting his own bags. "Then once we're sure we are actually able to stay here, you can come back out."

Barty nodded, gave his horse an apologetic pat, and squeezed out of the stall.

"Always the soft heart," Fabian observed from the end of the stable, having made no effort to tend their own horse, content to leave it in Barty's charge.

"I used to be friends with my parent's stablemaster," Barty said, stacking Fabian's saddle on top of his own in the tack room. "Learned a thing or two about caring for them. And horses are such lovely creatures, really. They can be very nice as long as they aren't mistreated."

"Did your stablemaster tell you there are no bad horses, only bad owners?" Fabian said, a sneer lurking under their words.

"Oh, no," Barty said, shaking his head. "He'd been bit too many times by Betsy. She'd never had a hand raised against her in her life, but she sure liked to take a chunk out of anyone who got near. Still, she was meaner to people who were mean back, so, it just goes to show."

Fabian sighed. "Come along, Doctor. Save your charming little tales for around the fireplace."

Barty wilted a bit, but went. James followed, casting a last look back at their horses. All the creatures were eating or drinking, aside from the silver one, who had angled its head to watch them go. The horse jerked its face back as soon as

161

it caught James looking, and nosed at its feeder, almost as if pretending to look for scraps.

Strange.

James had a prickly feeling that Fabian might be right about this place, and he didn't like it. He hurried after Barty.

They trooped into the inn, dusty, road weary and, at least in James' case, worried that they would be told to leave, that the inn was closed due to plague. They settled down in front of the fire, appreciating at least a moment of rest and warmth. Voices echoed from the back room, Marshal's familiar cheerful lilt along with a deeper, crooning rumble.

James settled back, folded his arms, and surveyed the room, searching for insight among the decor. The furniture was heavy, old, but well kept, suggesting a comfortable amount of money had been laid out both to build and maintain this establishment. The walls were of dark wood with golden settings for candles, giving the room an almost cavern-like feeling. Paintings hung here and there in heavy guilt frames, picturing men whose clothes spoke of past ages. They were all smiling, with golden rings, buttons, and in the instance of a man who wore a hat heavy with feathers and had a hook instead of a hand, a few gold teeth. Crystal ashtrays glittered on the tables, the mantle of the fireplace, and the banister leading upstairs, indicating casual luxury and commitment to quality even in minor details. All in all, the inn had a solid, safe atmosphere, promising that the troubles of the outside world would not touch one who lodged here.

Barty seemed to sense it too, for he stretched his legs out to the fire and leaned back in his seat, sighing and remarking to James in a voice muffled by his mask, "Sometimes a long journey is worth it, just for how good it feels to get to the end."

"Except this isn't the end," James said dryly. "We're supposed to go all the way to Plymouth, remember?'

"Oh." Barty considered this. "True. But, well, we'll stay here a few days, won't we, if they need our help?"

James managed a tired chuckle. "I suppose. It won't hurt

to investigate a little anyway, if this plague is once again magically based."

"If it is," Fabian interjected from a chair in the shadows, "it is far more likely there will be answers here than in Plymouth."

They turned their masked face to James, their lenses glittering orange in the firelight. "This place is much more magically charged. Any sensible mage would start here, if they sought to cause mischief."

James pushed back his increasingly-prickly feeling and clamped his jaws closed to keep a cross, 'will you shut up about the fairy tales' from bursting out. Luckily, however, he was saved the necessity of further self control when the innkeeper, followed by Marshal, swept into the circle of firelight.

"Gentlemen, welcome," she said, casting a smile on them all that shone just as much as the gold and crystal about the room. She was a tall woman, taller even than Barty, with broad shoulders and well kept, if a little old fashioned, clothing. "My dear Marshal tells me I have you to thank for his safe return. If it were not such a dangerous time here, I would embrace each of you in turn." She bowed deeply, the gold of her necklaces, earrings, and hair piece sparkling, then straightened again and slipped her pipe between her teeth. "Please accept my most sincere thanks, and accept rooms here for as long as you will stay, free of charge." Smoke wafted with each word.

James stood, and bowed in return. "It was hardly any trouble, madam," he said, impressed with her manners and presence.

Barty bowed as well, even sweeping off his hat. "We could hardly have left poor Marshal in the road!" he chimed in. "We are most grateful for your offer, madam. And I am sure we will be happy to accept...?" he trailed off, glancing over his shoulder at Fabian.

Fabian had not jumped up with Barty and Buckler. The necromancer remained seated, gloved fingertips pressed together, observing the innkeeper's every move. Once they were certain all attention was on them, however, they did stand, and bowed in a courtly, old-fashioned manner. "It has been a long time, Ida," they said, "but you have not changed, and neither has your beautiful home. How fortunate I am, to see you once again."

The innkeeper froze, dark eyes widening, then narrowing as she peered at Fabian. She stepped closer, towering over the necromancer and staring down at them, a slow smile creeping over her mouth, smoke rising between her white teeth. "Is that you, Frayn? Your voice is lighter, but the arrogance is always the same."

Fabian laughed, and pulled off their mask, red eyes glittering. "I go by Fabian, in this life."

"Ah! And your last one too, I think?" Ida chuckled, offering a hand to Fabian to shake. "I seem to remember that for a few decades everyone from up north complained about walking corpses. I wondered if you were the tyrant they spoke of."

Fabian grinned, smoothing back their hair. "Well, Ida, I don't like to boast, but-"

"You," the innkeeper said, puffing out a smoke ring in Fabian's direction, "shouldn't be here."

An awkward silence settled over all three doctors. It was hard to say who looked more surprised; Fabian, who had frozen in place, or Barty, whose beak waggled between the necromancer and the innkeeper, his eyes wide through the lenses of his mask. James almost had to bite his lip to keep from laughing

"If this is about your ring," Fabian said smoothly, "I assure you, I had nothing to do with its disappearance. I did not intend to be born into this gender, but even I have only so much control over my rebirth cycle-"

The innkeeper raised one fine eyebrow. "It might have been nice to know its continued existence was directly tied to your natural form," she said, "but no, this is not about that. I had many years in the shape I wanted."

164

James blinked at this, a sudden suspicion forming in his mind. He had heard those words before, from Fabian referring to his own condition.

The innkeeper continued, though, tapping her pipe against her teeth. "I will find another way in the future. I am not warning you as a threat, Fabian, but rather for your own sake. You know better than to show up so close to the edge of the King's lands."

Fabian snorted. "Coming here was a risk, yes, but a calculated one. You know I can manage myself, Ida."

"I know," Ida said, a rumble of warning in her voice, "that if you were in your right mind, you would not have set foot in the Wystwood, let alone in Whiston. So, either it has been so many cycles for you that you have forgotten the past, or something else is pulling you here."

"That is enough," Fabian said sharply – so sharpy that Barty cowered away from them, and James raised both his eyebrows.

The necromancer took a deep breath and let it out, clearly gathering their nerves. "I," they said with a dark smile, "remember perfectly well why it is not the safest choice to be here. I am also fully in control of my faculties. We did not choose to come here, Ida, we are only passing through on our way to Plymouth, to fight the plague there."

James had never seen Fabian's smile look so forced. He remembered all Fabian had said about the fae folk being near to this land, and wondered if that had anything to do with his theory of Fabian chasing someone.

Ida gave the necromancer a hard look, but shrugged. "Nobody," she said, "passes through Whiston by chance. But I will let you keep your pride, Fabian. I know how important it is to you."

She went to the front desk, trailing smoke. Fabian glared daggers after her, their smile almost corpse-like in its fixed nature. Ida brought out a set of room keys, one of which she gave to Fabian, one to Barty, and one to James. "You are still,"

165

she said, "welcome to stay as long as you like. If you do truly wish to help us fight this plague, I will offer you all the help I can possibly give."

"That is very kind of you, madam," Barty said earnestly. "In fact, as wonderful as it would be to rest first, I was wondering if perhaps we should go see a few of the sick before night falls completely."

Fabian snorted, tucking their key in their cloak and already moving towards the rooms. "You will be doing that on your own, Doctor," they said. "I am going to eat, and then to rest, assuming there is food to be had." They paused at the bottom of the stairs, giving Ida a pointed look.

The innkeeper's smile was as pointed as Fabian's gaze. "Insult my hospitality any further and I will throw you back into the street, necromancer," she said. "There is always food here for the hungry. And I know, I know. You are…"

Fabian grinned, a bit less malice, a bit more self deprecation, "…always hungry. Well. You know where to find me."

The necromancer ascended the stairs.

James and Barty exchanged stunned looks, and then turned their eyes back to Ida.

"Why," James asked without hesitation, "is it not wise for Fabian to be here?"

Ida smiled at him, removing her pipe from between her teeth and blowing a smoke ring over James' head. "There are people with great power," she said, "and long memories, who do not forget deeds of the past. More than that is not my place to say."

James considered this, remembering Fabian's ominous warning about not making deals with the fey folk. Perhaps Fabian had learned that from first hand experience.

"Are they in danger – are we in danger, by being here?" he asked.

The innkeeper shook her head, golden earrings flashing in the firelight. "You should be fine, as long as you are careful," she said. "As for Fabian…"

Her eyes trailed to the stairs the necromancer had taken, and she put the pipe back between her teeth in a thoughtful manner. "Well, as I said, nothing happens here by coincidence. And, considering who else was here recently…"

"Who else was here?" Barty asked, and James had to repress an eyeroll at the childish eagerness in his voice. Clearly, the young doctor was excited to be caught up in a 'fairy tale'.

Ida gave a mysterious smile, smoke whispering through her lips with each word. "Best not to speak of it at night," she said ominously. "The walls have ears." She nodded to a little mouse running down the stairs.

James frowned at the mouse, knowing exactly who it belonged to. He pushed himself up from his chair, stretching stiff shoulders, and said loudly, "Fine. On a different matter, then, I would like to speak to your local doctor, or whoever serves as such. I need all the details as to where, how and when the plague started here."

Ida tilted her head. "Maybe if you'd gotten here a month ago you could," she said, "but I'm afraid you're too late."

James sighed. "He's dead? Of plague?"

"Not of plague," Ida said, shaking her head. "Murder."

James blinked. Out of the corner of his eye, he saw Barty raise a hand to his beak, as if covering his mouth.

Director Peete had said something about Plymouth's plague doctor being murdered. Apparently they were quite close to the big city, then, if this was where he had lived.

James sat down again, gesturing for Barty to do the same, and removed his mask, setting it on the table. "I would like to hear the full story, please."

Ida nodded, and pulled up a chair for herself as well, sitting with her back straight and ankles crossed. Perfect posture, James couldn't help but notice, as elegant as her clothing and jewelry.

"It all started two years ago," she said, "or perhaps, thirty years ago. It depends on what you consider a beginning."

James gestured for her to go on with it, and she smiled, continuing. "Thirty years ago, the most powerful witch in our little town married a young doctor from a village that hated magic."

"Oh!" Barty said, removing his mask as well. "I think we met them on the way here. Do you know, their doctor just died as well?"

Ida blinked. "I did not know," she said, frowning into the fire. "If I am remembering correctly, that would have been the father of the young doctor I am speaking of."

James said, "Please continue."

She nodded grimly, and spoke on. "There is not that much to say. They married happily, and he became our doctor, living here in Whiston and traveling to Plymouth when they had extra need. He worked tirelessly and well, though his manner was cold, even disdainful at times. Many speculated his mind remained stuck in the ways of his home village and their hatred of magic, but had hidden his true nature out of love. Anyone could see he was madly in love with his wife. That never changed, in all the thirty years he was here. Until..."

Her gaze drifted back to the fire.

"Until what?" Barty whispered.

Ida turned her gaze back on the young doctor. "Until she died," Ida said, "suddenly, of plague."

She sat back in her chair, tapping her teeth with her pipe, smoke rising from her nostrils. "It broke him. Utterly broke him. He stopped leaving his house, stopped answering the door for anything but the most dire of emergencies. Passers by could hear him shouting, weeping, pleading...cursing somebody, something. But nobody dared approach him to ask."

"If nobody dared approach," Barty breathed, on the edge of his seat, "how do you know he was murdered?"

Ida gave a sad smile. "Because whoever did it left his corpse in the middle of the street," she said, "and that was the beginning of a very hard time for this town."

"Hard because you had no doctor?" James asked.

"Hard because whoever murdered him didn't stop there," Ida said, shaking her head. "Hard because whoever did it stole his plague mask and haunted the town for weeks, spilling blood in our streets and making us afraid to leave our homes at night."

"You speak in past tense," James said. "Whoever this was was caught?"

Ida's face became an impassive mask. "In a manner of speaking," she said. "We had someone pass through who specializes in that sort of thing."

"Catching people?" Barty asked.

"Hunting monsters," Ida said, pushing herself up from her chair, signaling the end of the conversation. James stood as well, but she still loomed over him by half a foot. She gave him a small smile, and said, "I imagine, since the good doctor is dead, he will not mind you using the supplies in his home. Tomorrow morning, after you've had some time to rest and recover from the road, I will give you their spare key. Perhaps you can find some answers to the questions you undoubtedly have."

James took a deep breath and let it out. He didn't need to sleep, he could have happily gone to investigate the house and stayed there all night. But...

...he glanced at his companion. Barty, now maskless, showed decided signs of wear. Red lines crossed his face from where the leather had sat, and shadows around his eyes spoke of their days on the road and the strange, additional stresses that came of traveling with a relentlessly cruel necromancer.

So, James nodded, pulling out the room key Ida had given him. "Thank you, madam," he said.

She waved away his thanks. "The least I could do, both for the sake of my town and the sake of my husband." She gave both doctors a lazy smile. "I'll be along shortly with food, but after that, try not to need anything this evening. I have not seen my Marshal in a long time, and I would like to spend the next hours in his company without interruptions."

James very carefully did not meet Barty's eye. "I quite understand," he said. "My wife was of similar mind when I returned after a long trip."

Barty choked at his side, and James had to fight to keep back a smile. "Good evening to the both of you." He turned, and went to the stairs.

"G-good evening, madam, and thank you again!" Barty said, and scurried after him.

Together they climbed the stairs, and James counted down silently in his head. Three, two, one...

At "zero" Barty burst out, "James? Do you think we've walked into some kind of trap?"

James looked past him, down the stairs to where the little mouse still sat, frozen in a shadow.

He shook his head.

"I don't know, Barty," he said honestly. "But we should be prepared for anything, just in case."

Barty didn't look terribly comforted, but he did nod, expression hardening into determination. "I don't care if we have, anyway," he said. "If we can stop the plague here, that's all that matters to me."

James smiled at him, and patted his shoulder. "That's the spirit, Dr. Barty," he said. "Goodnight. Leave all your worries alone until tomorrow."

Barty nodded, managing a grateful smile of his own. "I think I'm going to go back to the horses and see to it that they're comfortable," he said, "but I'll be in bed soon." He tipped his hat to James, as polite as ever. "Goodnight, if I don't see you."

James chuckled and tipped his hat right back. "Until tomorrow."

They parted, Barty going back down the stairs, James to his room. It was a cozy room, like the rest of the inn, all dark wood, polished accents and with a heavy, maroon bedspread promising warmth and security to any who slipped beneath the covers.

James pulled a chair away from a small side desk and sat, slowly removing his boots. A hunter of monsters, huh? He wished he were more surprised. At some point in the day, he had to admit, he'd stopped thinking about Fabian's fairy-tale warnings as pretend and began accepting them as reality. He didn't enjoy that change – not only because he was rather sure once he was out of this strange place things would go entirely back to normal, but also because, if he was being quite honest, he didn't like to think of how much danger was truly at their heels, if what Fabian and Ida had been saying was any indication.

He went to his window and pushed it open, letting in a cool night breeze and looking down over the stable.

He could see Barty below, brushing down his horse and speaking to it in soft, comforting tones.

James knew even if he suggested they leave and seek a more grounded reality, Barty would refuse. Barty would never turn his back on people in need, especially sick people, no matter the circumstance.

Barty's horse turned its head, resting its soft nose on Barty's shoulder as the boy worked.

James stayed in the window a long time, watching. The breeze blew past, ruffling his hair and scraping a few dry leaves along the street below. Barty almost seemed like a fairy creature himself, James thought with amusement, the pure-hearted hero out of an old tale, speaking to animals and curing disease wherever he went...

Movement caught James' attention, and he turned just in time to lock gazes with the other horse in the stable - the silver one.

James squinted down at the silver horse. Was it normal horse behavior for a creature like that to stare at someone on the second floor of a building? Was it normal horse behavior for it to keep eye contact for such a long time, ears pricked forward, nostrils flaring, as if it could sense something strange about James?

James shivered and pulled his head in the window, closing the shutters firmly. The last thing he wanted was some fool beast spoiling things for him and making people uneasy. Common folk were suspicious of doctors enough already, and he certainly didn't want any animal giving people cause for closer inspection.

He stood up, pushing his chair back to his desk and changing the rest of the way into his sleeping things. He hung his clothes on his chair, tucked the linen binding strips into his bag next to the bandages and gauze, and finally slipped into bed, forcing himself to relax for what felt like the first time in days.

His thoughts turned to Jessica, and he wondered what she was doing, how she was faring, with him away for the first time in a year. He hoped she didn't worry too much, and determined that when he wrote to her in the morning, he would not mention the strangeness of fairy tales and suspicious coincidences.

The blankets did not warm around him, he was dead and did not generate body heat. However, their weight was a comfort, and he closed his eyes, his wife's face and voice a soothing memory as he slipped into a darkness that was almost like normal sleep.

CHAPTER 14:
INTO THE FIRE

Barty woke to a rap on his door, a brisk, "We have work to do, Doctor," from James, and the smell of eggs and sausages seeping invitingly into his room. It was the temptation of food more than the call to work that made him leap from his warm blankets and dress as quickly as possible. After so many days of travel, a fine, sit-down breakfast was worth hurrying for.

He wasn't disappointed. Joining James at the table, he found a plate waiting for him, heaped with sausage and eggs, fried mushrooms, a toasted biscuit with butter, spiced potatoes, and even kippers. He settled into his spot with a soft groan of appreciation, taking a deep whiff of the deliriously tasty smells. "Bless Mrs. Ida," he said, picking up his fork.

James nudged a steaming tea kettle his way. "I'm not a

religious man," he said, almost smiling, "but I'll say amen to that. Did you sleep well?"

"Like a rock," Barty said around a mouthful of sausage and mushrooms. "Has Fabian been down?"

"They are eating in their room," James said. He didn't roll his eyes, but Barty got the feeling he wanted to. James had already cleared his plate, and now sat back in his chair, a cup of tea in his hands. "They also said to continue our investigations without them, they want to do things their own way."

Barty shivered. He was fairly sure that Fabian's way of investigating involved a bundle of dead rats, animated to unlife and scuttling through the whole plague-ridden town. "I hope they're alright. This whole situation seems like a bit of a shock for them."

James gave Barty a strange look, but only shook his head and sipped his tea. "Mrs. Ida," he said, "has given me the key to the deceased doctor's house, that we may assess his supplies and see if any of it will be of use to us in our efforts to help the town, once we've done a few rounds and tended to the most pressing needs of the afflicted."

"She did? That's very nice of her," Barty said, his positive feelings about their innkeeper host growing with every bite of delicious breakfast. The food really was good, even the kippers were cooked to perfection, smokey and flavorful. He was also more than a little relieved that they would be tending to the sick first. As much as he genuinely did need his breakfast to function during the day, he could not shake the internal twinge of guilt accusing him of cruelty; enjoying his delightful food while others suffered alone.

He glanced around, half hoping Ida was around so he could deliver his thanks himself and distract the accusatory part of his brain. "Did you speak with her already?"

James nodded, his expression guarded. "We shared a cup of tea a little while before you came down. We...have a few things in common."

"Really?" Barty said, looking back at James and feeling

very curious indeed. "What did you talk about?" He loaded his fork with crispy potatoes.

James was quiet for a few seconds, regarding the tea in his cup. When he spoke it was slow and thoughtful. "She told me how she met her husband, and how he loved her no matter the shape she was in. She told me of the ring Fabian had given her many years ago, that allowed her to wear the kind of body she wanted in truth, so that she was able to bear her own children."

Barty swallowed his mouthful, digesting the implications of such an enchantment. If magic allowed an anatomy rewrite for Ida, then surely there had to be a similar kind that would work for James! "Did she, um, mention if there were other rings like the one she had?"

For a moment Barty read surprise in his friend's face. James nodded, though. "More stories of fairyland," he said, and Barty thought his voice was a bit less dismissive than it had been the day before. "Rings, deals, wishes. Nothing comes without a cost of some kind, she warned me." He sipped his tea, his eyes returning to his own empty plate. "She also said that some costs are worth paying."

Barty considered this, sipping his own tea as well. "I wonder what kind price would get your proper life back."

James blinked. "You know," he said with a chuckle. "It didn't even occur to me to ask."

Barty finished his breakfast while James finished his tea, sharing a companionable, thoughtful silence. When every drop was drunk and every crumb eaten, they stood, buckled on their masks, and ventured into the streets of plague-ridden Whiston.

Barty shivered as they made for the road. Fall bled away with each passing day, and the cold of winter's approach crackled on the winds. He followed James through the town, avoiding the solemn, fearful gazes of the few people working in the streets. He hoped these people saw hope in the arrival of proper plague doctors, but it was hard to shake the loathsome curses of the previous village from his mind.

Here they would do better, he promised himself, pushing away memories of blood and screams. Here they would bring relief and healing. Especially with the supplies of a well respected doctor to aid them, and, hopefully, any records he had as well.

"Funny thing," James said, leading the way through the town to the home of their first patient. "We got the letter about the outbreak almost a week ago."

"We did," Barty agreed, making sure his mask and gloves were snug. The home before them was a fine new house, and the words, 'PLAGUE, GOD HELP YE' stood out in fresh red paint on the sturdy oak door.

"But the plague here," James said, giving the door a rat-tat-tat with his cane, "only began within the last few days, according to Ida."

Barty furrowed his brow at that. "Well, but we were summoned to Plymouth, weren't we? Maybe it was there first?"

James shook his head, putting his hand on the doorknob at the weak command of 'enter' coming from within the house. "Ida says no traveler has mentioned plague in Plymouth. They would have heard something by now, it's only a day's journey away."

"I got the impression that people don't actually come here very often," Barty said, frowning. James opened the door and led the way in, and Barty followed, barely seeing the house around him as the familiar stench of plague hit them both. Blood and sour sweat.

"People don't come here very often," James agreed, setting his walking stick aside and going to the sickbed holding a frail old gentleman. "So how would plague have come here without people carrying it?"

It was a good question, and Barty had no answer for it.

The doctors spent a busy, all too familiar morning doing what they could to treat the half dozen sickest plague victims in Whiston. The plague had either not spread very far yet or had not manifested its symptoms fully, but it seemed to be concentrated around a particular family - with an entire household ill at once, and some neighbors and cousins. James speculated that perhaps it had been spread at a family gathering. Barty wondered if it was, in fact, a similar plague to the one that had hunted Fabian, then would it be traveling down a family line, as the necromancer's had. When they questioned the ill family, however, they had no connection to any necromancers of yore. "We've been here practically since the town was founded," was the repeated story, often with pride enough to smooth their grief and fear for a moment. "You won't find any folk who've been here longer."

"If it is a curse..." Barty said, washing his hands after treating a particularly nasty, fluid-filled set of symptoms. The poor stable boy was too ill to rise from the straw. "...there certainly doesn't appear to be any motivation. I know small town families can have their drama, but I have heard no mention of old grudges here."

"We'll have to ask Ida later about the history of this family in town," James said, shaking his head and slipping his gloves back on. "But next we have the doctor's house to check. From what I heard, his wife was also of this same family line. Perhaps we'll find answers among his papers."

They arrived at a fine, old house in the center of the town. Built in a similar style to Ida's inn, it had a familiar weight and spread to its walls and windows. Barty trailed slightly behind James, looking at the yard as they passed through. The garden was overgrown now, but he could see many familiar patches of herbs and flowers, including chamomile, mint, and feverfew. A willow tree loomed over the the eastmost corner, old and gnarled with branches that trailed down to touch the grass. A wide, paved trail led around to the back of the house, likely used by a horse and carriage in past days. It was easy to see how this had been a bright place of life, comfort and security.

In the present day, however, the splendor of the home

had faded with neglect. Grass, garden and path lay silent and ignored under a dry carpet of willow leaves. The herbs in the garden were both overgrown from lack of use and wilted for want of water. The dark windows were cloudy with dust, and even the front doorstep seemed grim and uncared for, dirty with debris and some brown splotches Barty suspected were dried blood.

Both Barty and James hesitated at the entrance, trying not to stand on the blood of the house's previous occupant. Finally James cleared his throat, straightened his shoulders, and pulled the key out of his pocket. "Right," he said frankly. "In we go, then." He opened the door and walked purposefully inside.

Taking a moment to gather his courage and wishing he'd asked Fabian if ghosts were real, Barty followed, stepping over the stains and looking around.

If the outside of the house had a feel of the inn about its foundations, the inside had nothing of the sort. Brown stains caked the wood floors, leading out from one of the inner rooms. Books and papers spilled into the hallway, torn and dirty.

Even the non-brutalized aspects of the home showed signs of neglect. Unwashed plates lay in haphazard piles on desks and tables that would otherwise have been respectable, and long-dead flowers rotted in dry vases. The few paintings on the walls were dusty, their colors grayed and blurred.

Once, this had been a home to be proud of. Now, it was a shambles, a shameful story of a man whose world had ended weeks before his life had.

Barty and James looked at the mess, and then at each other. "We ought to split up," James said. "Cover more ground without getting in each other's way."

Barty squashed down an unwelcome mental translation of 'I don't want you to get in my way, Bartholomew Wayman,' and said, "Good idea, sir. I see stairs at the end of the hallway; I'll check below first, shall I? And you can cover the ground floor."

James nodded, his gaze already drawn to a half-open door revealing a room of books and papers. "Don't hesitate to shout," he said, moving to the door, "if you need any help."

"Yes, sir," Barty said, smiling despite his anxiety. It made sense that James would be drawn to a place of study. Barty walked to the stairs instead.

He lingered at the top of them, resting his hand on the mahogany banister and peering into the darkness below. Something felt almost familiar, as if he had once, perhaps in a dream, stood atop these stairs and crept down, only to find horrors, or wonders...

After a long moment, he shook his head, banishing the mental specters, and descended with a firm step and a straight back. Even if he were walking to meet some terrible fate, he would do so with pride and respectability. Doctor Bartholomew Wayman: British citizen, former sailor of the navy, and battler of plague and pestilence.

The stairs creaked under his boots. The air cooled noticeably as he descended, step by step.

His feet touched the bottom landing.

No light from the outside world illuminated the hallway before him. There were, fortunately, still a few candles, and after a few moments of fumbling with flint, steel and tinderbox, he was able to get one lit and proceed down the hallway.

A breeze ruffled the flame of his candle, making his skin prickle. How could there be a breeze here, in the basement?

He really should have asked Fabian about ghosts.

He looked into the first room and found it to be a storage area - stacked with extra chairs, a linen cupboard, and dusty crockery. The next room was similarly occupied, with barrels instead of chairs, and crates, bottles and bags. Some of the crates and bags lay open, displaying glimpses of old, wrinkled potatoes, sprouting onions and dusty squash. The bottles held more temptation for Barty than the shriveled vegetables did.

He crept closer, lifting his candle to illuminate the dark gleam of wine and the glitter of gold and silver on the labels. A well off family indeed, with such a collection of vintages.

His boot crunched on something hard. He looked down and saw an array of glittering, broken glass, covered in sticky residue. He checked the bottles again and noticed that there were blank spots on the shelves closest to the door. Clearly, he thought, shaking his head, someone had been drinking without caring what they drank, seizing only the closest bottle and knocking loose others.

Resisting the temptation to rescue a few bottles himself, he continued on to the next room. Seeing things like wine and potatoes had helped him relax a little, and he now imagined what this house must have been like when it was more of a home. Plenty of food, good wine, an atmosphere of education and respectability...all the more sorrowful that tragedy had struck, ruining the lives of such a happy couple.

He closed the door, shutting away the smells of earthy vegetables and fermented drink, and went to the next, at the left end of the hall.

Ah, now this was what he and James needed. A huge alchemist's cabinet filled an entire wall, with dozens and dozens of drawers and compartments. Barty set his candle on a writing desk and eagerly went to investigate, the smell of herbs overpowering even before he opened a drawer.

Feverfew. Catmint. Yarrow. Ginger. Willowbark. Chamomile. Dozens and dozens of herbs, dried and neatly labeled. He checked one drawer after another, delighted to find them all full and unspoiled. Some of the bigger drawers held pages of notes on the various properties of the plants, observations on what combinations produced the best results and which did poorly. There were several detailed chapters on plague and its symptoms, written in a stern, neat hand. Barty tucked these into the breast of his coat, almost shaking with eagerness, and pulled out his journal, making a list of every label he could find. He was already eager to show James his discovery. He did notice, however, that not all the labels bore the same hand as the notes now nestled in his pocket. Some were of a more flowing script, less rigid than the plague documentation. Perhaps the doctor's wife had been as much of a herbalist as her husband?

Again, a pang of loss squeezed through Barty's heart, imagining how much the doctor must have suffered, losing a woman who he had left home and family for, a woman who had shared his passions and home.

The candle danced in Barty's stinging eyes. He sniffed, wiping them dry, and frowning at the flickering flame. More breeze. Why would there be a draft in a windowless basement? He simply had to carry on. Something else was down here, something he hadn't found yet.

He shut the door and went to the next, on the opposite side of the hall.

A closet. Cloaks and coats. Scarves and blankets. A shelf with a few top hats, and some empty spaces where the dust thinned, outlining the spread of the former contents. One circular area had probably been a hat. And other, oblong, pointed space...

Barty chuckled to himself when he realized what it was, tapping his own beaked mask. Of course, the doctor had been a plague specialist. Surely he had had a plague mask of his own. Barty wondered where the mask had got to, though. If the dust was any indication, it had only been removed recently.

He made a mental note to ask Ida about that later.

Only one room left, at the back wall of the hallway. Barty closed the closet and stood before the remaining door. Here it was that his candle danced and guttered the strongest. Barty's curls brushed against his masked cheeks, and he could just hear the sighing of moving air over the pounding of his own heart. Whatever it was that was strange down here, it was on the other side of this door.

He reached for the handle.

Something clawed its way up the front of his coat.

He shrieked and flailed, trying to brush off the furry, red-eyed mass before it went for his face, dropping his candle in panic.

Only the candlestick clattered to the floor as long, sharp teeth snatched the candle out of the air, landing with a tumble and holding it high, still lit and flickering.

Barty sank to his knees before the great rat. "Fabian?" he squeaked. "Are you trying to give me a heart attack!?"

The rat twitched its whiskers at him and, proudly holding the candle in its teeth, padded over a few paces to where a heavy metal key lay on the floor.

"Oh," Barty said, rattling the locked door handle "How did you even know I'd be needing a key?"

The rat set the candle on the floor, smoothed its whiskers, and scurried back up his coat, settling primly on his shoulder.

Barty picked up both candle and key. "I'll never understand how you have the foresight to predict such things."

The rat snickered at him, and tugged on the collar of his coat. Come on, it seemed to be saying. Come on. Open the door.

Barty took a deep breath and slipped the key into the lock.

It slid in with almost no resistance, and his heart leapt.

The key turned easily under his gloved fingers. Almost before he'd willed it, the door opened before him.

He held his candle high, casting a flickering streak of light into the darkness. It fell across a stone floor, scattered papers, strange markings...

"Did you know this was here?" he whispered to the rat. "Did you know all along?"

The rat said nothing, only twitched its whiskers, leaning forward as if it could smell whatever awaited them.

Taking some courage from the rodent's eagerness, Barty pushed the door open wider and stepped into the room. It was big, easily three times the size of the other rooms in the basement. Two long worktables stretched across either side, covered in books, scrolls, bundles of herbs, sparkling crystals, and other expensive-looking implements. Many of the papers held writing in languages he didn't recognize, and runes that looked vaguely familiar.

Barty's skin tingled all over as he understood what he was looking at. "This is a laboratory," he said. "But not of chemistry or medicine. This is a place of magic."

On his shoulder, the rat gave a soft squeak of agreement.

Barty put the key into his pocket and crept inside, holding the candle higher so its light sparkled on the polished stones, silver instruments, and glass containers. "There is so much," he murmured, finding it easier to digest with someone to talk to, even if it was only a necromancer's rat-spy. "Do you think this has been here as long as the house itself? Generations and generations of mages, passing down their workspace from one to the other?"

He paused at one of the tables, hovering his candle over the papers. "This is where it would have been helpful to have a mage along," he grumbled, holding up a page for the rat to see. "Does this mean anything to you?"

The rat peered at the page, but judging by the milkiness of its red eyes, Barty doubted it could see well enough to make out anything written there. "I'll bring it back to the inn, perhaps," he said, tucking it into his coat as well. "I'll bring anything that looks recent."

He began to rummage about, making a stack of papers that were the least yellowed or faded. Once or twice he paused, reading bits of the things that were written in English. There were a great many mentions of plague, and just as many notes on how and why magic spells worked.

"I think," he said aloud, surprised, "some of these were written by the late doctor. At least, the handwriting matches the labels in the store room. But didn't he come from a family that hated magic?" He frowned, considering the pages. "Maybe he ran from his family because he was actually drawn to magic?"

He glanced over the table again, looking for more writings, and his gaze came to rest on a picture frame lying face down. He reached for it, setting it upright again, and got his first glimpse of the family in whose home he now stood.

It was a meticulous pencil sketch of three people. Dark haired and handsome faced, a lady and gentleman stood side by side, smiling. Between them a boy beamed, with black hair and fine features like his parents. "But," Barty said curiously, turning the picture over, "nobody mentioned their having a son."

Mr and Mrs. R...rs...and...1707. The words were smudged beyond legibility, the paper yellowed with age. Barty set the picture frame back on the table, frowning. "That can't be right. Maybe this is a picture of relatives."

The rat on his shoulder made no comment, only tugged on his collar, silently demanding he continue looking.

Barty went to the middle of the room and knelt in the dust, examining the runes drawn on the floor. Judging by the brownish color, he very much suspected they had been painted in blood. He ran a finger over one, and it did not smudge. "About the same age as the stains upstairs, I think," he said softly. "But what does it mean? What spell is this..?"

The rat scrambled up his hair and hat, and stood tall as it could. Barty helped, straightening up and holding the candle high to cast as much light on the blood-runes as possible.

The rat stayed a few moments, shifting slightly on his head, making his hat wobble with its weight. Then it hopped down, running around the ring and sniffing each rune in turn. Finally it scuttled back to the table, scrambled up one leg, and nudged an ink bottle.

Barty set the candle on the table and opened the ink bottle, pulling out an unmarked sheet of paper with a smile.

The rat nodded, dipped its tail in the ink, and wrote on the page, 'SUMMONING.'

"Summoning?" Barty repeated, puzzled. "But what would be summoned? Not the plague, surely?"

The rat shook its head and turned to rifle through the pages on the table.

Barty, nonplussed, shifted paper as well. He wasn't sure what he was looking for. He didn't understand much of what was written there, and half the table was a disorderly mess. Maybe if he just tidied up the chaos a bit, an answer would be revealed.

He stacked papers neatly. He set stones and crystals in a pile. He swept up spilled herbs and organized brass instruments by size.

After some moments, under a stray bundle of lavender, he found a silver ring. It was set with a great, round gem that shifted color even as he looked at it.

He held the ring up to the candle, puzzled about the nature of the stone, and admiring the way the hue changed with every flicker. He'd never seen or heard of a mineral that behaved in such a way. "Gracious," he said, "what a pretty thing. You don't suppose this could be Ida's missing ring, do you?" He paused, staring at the rainbow hues, something tickling his memory. "Only, I think I've seen a ring like this before..."

He squinted at it, trying to remember. Sometime recently, a ring just like this, with a stone that changed colors.

The rat looked at the ring a long time. Then it dipped its tail in the ink again, and wrote, "MAGMAYDON."

Oh. Of course. Barty's hand went to his arm as he remembered those cruel fingers, with their changing nail polish, and the ring of many colors. "But," he whispered. "You don't think- why would she be connected to all of this? What does it mean?"

The rat was still, very still, like the corpse it was. Barty stared at it, biting his lip, hoping for answers.

Suddenly, in a flurry of movement, the rat leapt from the table, scurrying for the door. The message was clear - time to go.

"Wait!" Barty shouted. "Wait!"

But the rat did no such thing, streaking up the stairs and disappearing.

Barty dashed up the stairs after it, ring in one hand, candle in the other. "I don't understand, come back-!" He crested the top and-

"Barty! What-OUCH!"

James had just stepped out of the office to see what the fuss was, meaning Barty ran slap-bang into him and they both crashed to the floor in a flurry of papers and candle wax.

"Sorry!" Barty gasped, scrambling to help pick up the papers. "Sorry! I just - Fabian was- there's a ring and spells and a summoning-"

"Slow down, Doctor," James said sternly. He picked up the snuffed candle first, keeping it from dripping on the papers, and only when he was sure there was no risk of damage did he get to his feet and offer Barty a hand up. "What are you on about?" He picked up the ring from Barty's mess of fallen paperwork. "Is this the ring that's got you excited?" He gazed curiously at the rainbow stone, but handed it back to Barty.

"Fabian's rat just scampered off, James. I found a lot downstairs, but I don't know what any of it means yet." Barty accepted the ring and hastily explained everything he had found, including the summoning circle, the spells, and Fabian's rat's reaction. "Maybe we should leave?"

James' expression got darker and darker with each word. "We can't leave without a full picture." He said. "I don't know what the summoning is about, but I know the doctor was dabbling in magic himself. His office was also full of spellwork. Look."

He took one of the sheets from the pile and showed it to Barty. Barty's curiosity overcame his anxiety, and he peered closely at the paper, recognizing some of the magic symbols, even if he couldn't read them. "What does it mean?"

"According to his notes," James said grimly, "he had found a spell to cure plague, and was trying to transform it into a spell to cure *magic*."

"A cure for magic?" Barty repeated, blankly. "Using magic to cure magic? How is that possible? Anyway, magic isn't a disease."

"Don't forget where he came from," James said, shaking his head. "We met the people of that village ourselves: So stubborn they'd rather die than accept help. Maybe Dr. Rivers wasn't as divorced from his heritage as he seemed."

"Oh, but..." Barty's heart sank at the possibility. How terrible a situation, to have married a famous witch from a famous magical family, and still harbor a seed of hatred the entire time. "How did you find his name?"

"All the letters in his desk are addressed to him," James said impatiently. "So the question remains, then, who was teaching Dr. Rivers how to do magic for such a strange purpose?"

Barty and James shared a heavy silence, looking at the papers, and at the color-changing ring in Barty's hand.

"He originally just wanted to cure plague," Barty said sadly, "but maybe he wasn't satisfied with just that. We ought to ask Ida."

James shook his head. "I think," he said, "we need to talk to Fabian."

Barty thought of the rat, who had showed up at just the right moment, and fled with such haste. He thought of Fabian's ominous warnings before they arrived in Whiston, and their refusal to leave their room. He thought of Fabian's sudden desire to join them on their journey, and their strange behavior before that.

He nodded. "I think you're right," he said softly. "Let's bring all this stuff back to the inn and have a chat with them."

"We ought to take down a copy of the summoning circle you saw below," James said, handing over his armload of papers. "Hold these. I'll draw it and be right back."

"Oh. but-," Barty's heart still pounded, the urgency of the rat's disappearance hovering over him. "Maybe we shouldn't linger?" Still, he accepted the stack of papers.

"If you're going to do something, Dr. Wayman, it is best to do it thoroughly, with as much investigation, observation and preparation as is necessary to get a full picture." James called back, already halfway down the stairs. "I'll be quick."

Barty said, "Yes, sir," listening to James' steps disappearing and trying not to worry. His thoughts swirled in the eddies of the Rivers' family tragedy - dead wife, murdered husband, magic and treachery, and a son whom nobody had thought to mention, who seemed to have likewise disappeared.

He looked at the ring in his palm, wondering who had given Dr. Rivers a ring identical to one worn by the head of the mage's guild of London.

The ring gleamed at him smugly, and Barty got the strong feeling that whoever had placed it was not the least bit sorry.

CHAPTER 15: UPHEAVAL

Fabian's teeth broke the skin and meat of the apple with a crunch so satisfying it should have been a crime to continue working instead of stopping to savor the moment. Unfortunately, they had to hold the apple in their jaws, appreciating the sweetness of its brittle flesh while their shaking hands worked the straps and buckles of the horse's saddle. It had been so long since they had to do such things themselves, they hoped they were remembering the correct methods for what connected where. Through this buckle, under this strap, then this little thing holds it in place...

They stepped back a moment, finally finishing their bite and taking two more, surveying their work with a critical eye. It looked about right.

The horse cared less about the saddle and more about

Fabian's apple, turning its head and flaring dark gray nostrils. "Don't even think about it," Fabian warned the horse. "I'm going to need the energy." The horse continued to think about it, trying to steal the fruit right out of Fabian's grasp.

Fabian pushed its velvety nose away with one hand and devoured the entire apple with the other, down to the core. "I," they declared around a mouthful of sweet crispness, "do not have time for this."

That being said, they checked the sky, assessing exactly how much time they did have before nightfall. The clouds were an obscene shade of pink, purpling at the edges. Nightfall would be upon them soon.

They sighed and gave the core to the horse, remembering that this beast was their fastest way out of here and should probably be bribed for good behavior.

Fabian hoisted their bag up behind the saddle. Before they strapped it in, though, they dug out a strip of jerky, putting the entire thing into their mouth, chewing vigorously. Calories, calories, they needed fuel to burn for the eternal, ravenous flame of their necromancy. They closed the bag and tied it into place.

They should never have come here.

They should never have left London.

A curse on all of it, plague and faeries and the like.

The dry jerky stuck in their throat, but they forced it down anyway, turning at last to regard the final piece of their possessions.

The great bundle filled with dead rats, now loosely closed, seemed to look back at them, large and heavy in the dust. Even as they watched, another rat returned from its scouting, wriggled into the wrapped cloth and lay neatly on top of its rotting fellows.

It was the heaviest thing Fabian had brought, with hundreds of little bodies all squeezed together. There was no question that its weight would slow the horse. Unfortunately, to be caught without the small army of vermin would be almost more dangerous than traveling slightly less-than-top speed.

No, they wanted it. The horse could cope.

They bound the bundle with rope and heaved it off the ground, but it was almost as long as they were, and their balance wavered precariously. Curse this form, they thought, panting, the bundle unwieldy in their sweaty hands. Curse the physical weakness that came with a fire of magic that burned so brightly it devoured them from the inside.

Fabian was not one who enjoyed exercise for its own sake, but when the bundle tipped over, ripping free of their hands and clumping into the dust, they swore they'd find an exercise routine to strengthen their arms and back.

No. They were strong *now*. They could do this.

Ignoring the weakness tingling through their legs, scolding themselves for lack of persistence, they knelt again, clenching their teeth and lifting with all their strength.

Up came the bundle, and they bent back, staggering to center its weight over their own hips and legs. There. They had it up.

Now they just had to get it onto the back of this accursed, massive horse. The smooth gray haunches of the beast seemed like a veritable cliff before them. Fabian's arms hurt just looking at it.

"Oh my goodness, can I help you?"

All-too-familiar boots hurried up beside Fabian, and Bartholomew Wayman's anxious face popped into view. Barty slipped his hands under the bundle, and together, they heaved it onto the horse's rump.

"You certainly have a habit of showing up when you are most needed, don't you, Doctor?" Fabian said, giving him a bitter smile and wiping sweat off their brow.

"I try my best," Barty said in earnest. Fabian took a carrot from the bin reserved for horses and munched on it, watching Barty's gaze roam from the horse's saddle to the luggage and back to Fabian again.

"Something on your mind, Doctor?" Fabian asked, offering him the already-bitten carrot.

Barty cleared his throat and shook his head, taking a step back from the dusty root and bouncing on his toes. "Well! Not exactly. But, um. It rather looks like you are leaving, Fabian?"

"Running away, more like." James Buckler strode up, his scowl clear behind the glass lenses of his mask. He held an armload of papers that Fabian very much did not want to look at.

"Oh James," Barty turned to him in protest. "Fabian wouldn't–"

"Oh, but Fabian would," Fabian said, settling the carrot between their teeth and hoisting themselves up into the saddle. "Fabian," they declared, removing the carrot and gesturing grandly with it, "has not survived this long without knowing when is exactly the best time to run away from a situation that has gotten out of hand."

They put the carrot back in their mouth and groped for the reins, which had, unfortunately, slid a bit too far down the horse's neck for them to reach.

"Fabian," Fabian growled around the vegetable, leaning forwards to stretch for the long strips of leather, "does not want to meet old enemies with long memories. Fabian was tricked into coming here, and Fabian doesn't-"

"Fabian!" Barty exclaimed, and to Fabian's surprise, he jumped for the reins, grabbing them moments before Fabian could. "You killed the mage we were supposed to bring here! You insisted on accompanying us, and you are the only person here with enough understanding of the situation to guide us! People have died - and are still dying! You can't go!"

"I can," Fabian said with dangerous calm. "Give me those reins, Doctor."

"I won't," Barty said, his brown eyes full of terror, though whether it was terror of Fabian's wrath or his own daring, Fabian couldn't say.

James stepped forward. "Nobody is going anywhere

until you tell us exactly what is going on, Fabian. We have a responsibility-"

"It's a trap," Fabian hissed, shifting in the saddle to face him fully. "Everything here - the plague, the doctor and his family, even meeting Marshal on the road. All teeth in the trap, set for me. And I..."

They looked at the sky. Almost no orange left, and the purple steadily devoured the last traces of red.

"I," they said, offering the carrot to the horse so it turned its head, pulling Barty forward - and the reins into Fabian's reach. "Do not intend to be caught again." Their fingers closed around the reins, and they jerked hard, trying to dislodge them from Barty's grip.

"Please, Fabian!" Barty begged, his gloved hands firm on the leather. "Please just wait! Please explain it to us - surely the inn is safe for one more night? Maybe we can help you!"

For a moment, Fabian hesitated, looking at the inn. Barty didn't know it, but the place was definitely the safest building in the entire town, for more than one reason. Perhaps it would be better to wait until daylight. Perhaps they still had a little time...

A wolf howled - but it wasn't in the distance. It was close, close enough to make Fabian's skin prickle, close enough to sound as if it were standing right in the street.

Fabian's innards went cold, and they smiled.

"I'm sorry, Dr. Wayman," they whispered.

Fabian dug their heels into the horse and it reared with a sudden bellow, throwing out its hooves and making both doctors jump back. Fabian caught the reins tight and yanked the horse towards the road, kicking it into a surprised gallop.

"Follow them!" they heard James shout behind them. "Grab the horses! Something's wrong here!"

Fabian didn't turn to look. They steered their horse for the village entrance - for the forest that had brought them all here. They had only traveled the road yesterday, it should still be safe.

Another howl erupted behind them. They looked over their shoulder and saw an enormous silver wolf charging down the main street, shocking in its beauty, terrifying with the redness of its sharp-tootled maw.

And behind the wolf, two more figures: Drs. Barty and Buckler, charging bareback after the wolf and necromancer, their horses unencumbered but for their bridles.

Fabian turned away. "Hurry!" They shouted to their horse, whipping the reins against its neck. "Hurry, hurry, hurry!"

The horse didn't need telling. Its ears lay flat against its head in primal terror of the pursuing beast, and it stretched its legs to a full gallop.

Fabian let the horse do what it knew best and turned back once again, laying their hands on the bundle of rats. They closed their eyes and took a deep breath, trying to blot out all fear and dread, all noise and sensation. They focused only on the small vessels within.

When they opened their eyes, red light poured from beneath the cloth, accompanied by a great clawing and squeaking. "Go!" Fabian commanded, pulling a knife from their sleeve and slicing through canvas and rope holding the rats in place. "Devour it!"

The bundle fell, and a shrieking mass erupted from it, swarming towards the silver wolf, all glowing red eyes and flashing sharp teeth.

Fabian gripped the reins once again and laughed, still watching back over their shoulder as the wolf let out a yip and began tearing off in the opposite direction. "Idiot!" they chuckled, finally turning forwards once more. "It will take more than that to-"

Another howl interrupted them, to their left in the forest.

A third joined, forwards and to the right.

And yet another, directly ahead - and Fabian's very heart froze as one, two, three silver wolves bounded out of the forest.

They all wore collars - collars that flashed with gems shining in endless, shifting colors.

"NO!" Fabian snarled, jerking their horse off the road so hard it squealed with protest.

"Fabian!"

Fabian snapped their head around. Barty and James were only a dozen strides behind, how had they managed to catch up so quickly!?

"Fabian!" Barty shouted again. "Wait! Let us help you! We need to stay together–"

But Fabian couldn't stop. It was too late - it was all too late.

They plunged through the bracken and brambles, desperately trying to think. Howls shook the air around them; over half a dozen now.

If Fabian could just find an opening in the forest - if they could just break through the trees, out onto the moor! Wolves were good hunters, but they were not as fast as a horse across open ground.

"Fabian!"

Somehow, impossibly, Barty and James were catching up. The baggage, Fabian realized, feeling almost sick, was weighing their own horse down. They should have cut the ropes.

Crashing and panting in the underbrush. Silver streaks against the dark of the forest - gaining on all three of them.

Despair threatened to seize Fabian by the throat, but - wait - was that starlight? A clearing, there, to the right!

Fabian would lose more distance by turning, but there was no other choice. They pulled their horse's reins again-

"Come on, you stupid necromancer!" James's mount put on a burst of speed and he somehow, impossibly, threw himself off his own horse and onto Fabian's, clinging to them with his undead strength and lunging for the reins. "You're going to get us all killed-!"

"You are already dead, James!" Fabian snarled, elbowing

him in the face. "Hands OFF!"

He recoiled with a shout, either because of Fabian's magically-powered command or because of their elbow.

"The wolves!" Barty shouted behind them. "So many! Who is that?"

Fabian's horse burst into the clearing, and once more they looked back over their shoulder. Barty was pointing behind the collared wolves, where the first, huge silver one had reappeared - but now it was not alone. It bore a silver-eyed rider on its back, a man clothed in a jerkin of color-changing stones.

He was not leading the charge with the other wolves. He was hanging back, directing them with motions of his hands - translated into wolf speech by his howling mount.

Understanding chilled Fabian to the bone. The rider and the wolves were not seeking to tear the trio of doctors apart.

They were guiding their course.

The wolves were herding them.

Too late, Fabian turned with horror to get a better look at the clearing ahead. Too late they saw the immense ring of mushrooms at the center of it, gleaming with an otherworldly light, as if pieces of the moon had fallen and taken root. James gasped at their shoulder, "What on earth?"

Too late. Too late.

Fabian closed their eyes. They let out a breath, relinquishing all emotion with it.

With emptiness came clarity. With clarity, insight.

It might be enough.

"Hold tight to me, James," they said.

James' arms locked around their middle with rigor mortis strength, and Fabian slipped their feet from the stirrups.

"Jump us both free of the horse!" Fabian shouted, putting all their strength of command into the words. "NOW!"

The horse broke through the mushroom ring. James jumped, pulling himself and Fabian free of the rushing beast.

Stars, wolves, and mushrooms spun in Fabian's vision.

And, just before they fell into blackness - Fabian had one last flash of sight.

Barty Wayman, still on his horse, his eyes wide with terror, falling into the ring after them.

Then the blackness closed over their heads, and silence swallowed them all.

CHAPTER 16: BAIT AND SWITCH

The pack of wolves plunged into the ring of mushrooms in a silver-furred blur, and Jeremiah rode after them, gloved hands buried deep in Shilling's mane. The wild fury and delight of the pack coursed around him - they exalted in the chase, in smelling the fear of their prey, and in the moment of freedom. A rare feeling, when one was a servant of The Faceted King.

For they were, one and all, his servants, collared by the deals of their fathers and their father's fathers. Only Jeremiah could call himself a free man, despite his debt. These creatures, for all their power and speed, remained chained beasts, at the end of the day.

The world rippled, the Faerie realm reaching through the ring and greedily pulling its creatures back into its domain.

Darkness then light. Cold. Emptiness. Furnace like heat, and finally, like waking from a dream, reality congealed back into something solid and recognizable.

Jeremiah had done it a thousand times. It was no longer an impressive experience.

Paws hit the ground, disturbing ash and dust. Confused whimpers and whines surrounded him, wet noses sniffing and searching.

"Two trails," Shilling translated for Jeremiah. "The horses went two ways!"

Jeremiah cast Shilling a critical look. The wolf bled from vicious bites on his muzzle and tattered ears, and from the red, raking scratches down his paws.

Accursed necromancer. Neither Shilling nor Jeremiah had expected the rats.

Jeremiah looked about. Beyond the gleaming pack of restless wolves lay nothing but acres of long-dead briar patches and brittle grass. He had hoped it would be daylight in this part of Faerie, but it seemed the presence of the men from the world of logic had brought their logic along with them. Night reigned here, at least for now.

'Split the pack up,' Jeremiah signaled to Shilling. *'Tell them to pursue both sets of horses. Report if you catch anything.'*

Shilling howled the message to the others, and the pack split in two, one half streaking off after the first horse trail, the other surging ahead of Jeremiah and Shilling, leading the way down the dusty hill and towards a lazy, gleaming streak of gray water.

Even in the darkness, Jeremiah was able to make out the mounted figure ahead, bent low on their horse and galloping at top speed across the ashen plane.

Jeremiah set his jaw grimly. Out in the open like this, a horse could easily outpace a pack of wolves, even the King's wolves. However, there was no nearby bridge over the river. If they could pin beast and rider against the water, their prey would have no choice but to surrender.

He tapped Shilling's shoulder thrice.

Shilling, panting, nodded, and Jeremiah held fast. The great wolf shuddered underneath him, stretching and rounding out into a magnificent silver stallion.

Horse and rider streaked out ahead of the pack of wolves. For a moment - for one wild moment, Jeremiah felt the wonder of it; of a partnership with a beast straight out of the tales. Strength, loyalty, and deadly intent were qualities he and Shilling shared, tried-and-true weapons in their arsenal. Even in the middle of a wild chase across a streak of dead land, there was wonder in such a bond, in the magic he and Shilling bore. Knowing that he, a human, and Shilling, a changeling, a creature of magic he still did not fully comprehend, were united in purpose and understanding, brought its own incomparable joy.

Shilling seemed to share Jeremiah's wonder, for he lengthened his stride, all but flying across the dead grass and ashes, shaking his mane and letting out a whinny of pure exaltation at their speed and unity.

The wolves howled encouragement behind him, answering the horse's song as if it were one of their own. The rider ahead turned to look, and even over the cacophony of canid voices, Jeremiah heard the fellow shout in terror.

Closer and closer. Jeremiah could see his brown hair and black coat.

"Not the necromancer," Shilling shouted between heavy, bellows-like breaths. "It's one of the others!"

'Keep going,' Jeremiah signed. 'We can use him, and he has nowhere to turn."

Indeed, the rider seemed to realize his fate was sealed. Ahead of him stretched the gray, nameless river, choked with ash and silt. Behind him, the wolves howled nearer, and Jeremiah drew his sword, the blade shining bright and pure, lit by Faerie's silver moon.

Jeremiah waited, holding his sword out like a beacon, expecting any second for the brown-haired man to realize he was doomed. He tapped Shilling's shoulder, and the horse called, with Jeremiah's voice, "SURRENDER!"

But the man did not surrender. He did not slow. He did not even try to turn. Instead he charged straight for the river, loosed a wild cry, and threw himself from the horse's back into the churning, murky waters.

"Oh, no!" said Shilling, skidding to a stop to avoid tumbling into the wet. "He can't do that! Where did he go? Hey-Hey!"

He whinnied at the other horse, who was splashing about very unhappily, half in a panic.

"Come over here!" Shilling said to the horse, while Jeremiah stood on his back, scanning the water furiously. "Don't stay in the water, you'll be swept away! It's stronger than it looks!"

The horse whinnied something back.

Jeremiah saw no hint of brown hair or black coat in the gray depths. He gritted his teeth, hissing out a frustrated breath.

"I know! I'm sorry! Here, I'll tell them. Hey! Back off you guys!" Shilling turned his great silver head, addressing the wolves. "You're scaring him!"

'Tell them to spread out downriver!' Jeremiah signed to Shilling. 'He will surface to breathe somewhere! We will find him!'

Shilling relayed the message, and Jeremiah slid off his back, sheathing his sword and storming along the shoreline himself.

Behind him, Shilling continued to coax the stranger's horse to safety. "Yeah, that's right! Come along back. They won't hurt you, I promise. It's safe here, see?"

The sound of hooves crunching in the dead grass. A snort from the water, and then a great splashing, as the doctor's horse scrambled out of the water and onto land.

Jeremiah glared at the dirty river. It roiled and churned, but revealed no horseless strangers. It couldn't have been more than four feet deep, judging by the way the doctor's horse -

brown - was stained gray up to the withers, but the depths was so silt-choked that the riverbed remained invisible.

"There, see," Shilling said soothingly to the horse. "You're fine now. We'll help you get somewhere you can rest and eat safely."

Jeremiah rolled his eyes, gathered up a pebble, and flicked it at Shilling to get his attention. When the silver horse looked his way, he signed, 'We aren't going anywhere until we find that man.'

"He isn't even the one we're looking for!" Shilling said, stamping his hoof.

A distant howl made both of them pause, both horses' ears pricking up.

"Anyway," Shilling continued, shaking his head, "the other horses have been caught too, says the pack. They were empty. No riders!"

'We've been tricked,' Jeremiah signed, and the words felt heavy in his hands. The King would not be pleased that so much setup, so many days of preparation, and so many servants under Jeremiahs' command had not gotten what he wanted.

"Yeah," Shilling agreed grimly. "What do we do now?"

Jeremiah stared into the muddy water, thinking. Returning to the King empty handed was not an option. Failure in the King's eyes was too costly a price to pay - better to stay away until they had at least something to show for all their toil.

'Tell the pack to return to the point of entry and resume searching - more carefully. Tell them to follow the scent of only the necromancer, not the horses or any other creature. Tell them we will be continuing our search downriver.'

Even if they could not bring the necromancer, one of the necromancer's friends would be enough of a prize - enough of a bargaining chip, that the King might forgive Jeremiah's slip.

The King would forgive Jeremiah eventually, one way or another. But the price of such forgiveness was steep. Jeremiah knew what kind of favors the King liked, in exchange for his mercy.

Jeremiah shuddered. Never again.

"What about him?" Shilling interrupted his thoughts, jerking his head at the dirty brown horse. "I know you won't leave him here by himself."

Jeremiah sighed, but Shilling was right. The Hunt was the Hunt, but Jeremiah had never been the sort of man to let duty be an excuse for neglecting responsibility.

'He can come with us,' he signed. 'We will at least lead him to greener pastures. And,' he added, a thought suddenly occurring to him, 'tell him we will get him his favorite food if he can help us find and rescue his master.'

"Huzzah!" Shilling whinnied, prancing about with eternal, boundless energy. Jeremiah shook his head. Shilling was like a child in his perpetual eagerness, but Jeremiah knew for a fact that the creature was far older than himself. Changelings were strange creatures, and Shilling was strange even by Changeling standards.

Shilling spoke to the dirty horse, translating the offer of companionship and safety into a bunch of horsey noises. The dirty horse, ears perked and seeming greatly interested, nodded, then looked surprised that it had done such a human behavior.

"It's alright!" Shilling reassured the horse. "You're just getting smarter! It happens to all animals that come here. That way it's easier to answer the King when he asks you questions."

Jeremiah turned away before the horses could see his furrowed brow, and almost tripped over a wolf standing silently next to him, watching the exchange.

"He'll be talking soon," said the wolf, his voice deep and gravely. "And not very well. Are you sure you want to take a logic-horse with us, when we have such an important task to attend to?"

He looked up at Jeremiah, his yellow eyes intent and far too knowing for a simple animal. Then he looked back at the horse, licking his chops.

Jeremiah sighed. Talking or not, a wolf was still a wolf. He tapped the beast's shaggy shoulder to regain his attention, and signed, very clearly, '*I am sure. You and your pack are not to hurt him. He will be useful to us, especially as he gets smarter.*'

"He's going to ask a lot of questions," the wolf grumbled. "They always do, at first."

'*Did you?*' Jeremiah asked, a bit surprised at this voluntary information.

The wolf nodded. "Yeah. But I soon learned I should have kept my mouth shut. What's the thing humans say?" He considered a moment, his gray ears laid back against his fuzzy head. "Ignorance," he said at last, "is bliss."

'*Perhaps,*' Jeremiah replied. '*But would you go back to being a creature of ignorance, if you could?*'

"Nah," the wolf said, giving a sharp-toothed grimace and looking back at the horses, "and he won't either, once he changes."

Jeremiah looked as well, watching Shilling lead the horse down the riverbank so they could sniff around for the rider together.

The wolf nosed his hand, making him jump with surprise. "What about you?" the wolf asked, bluntly curious as only a wolf could be. "Would you go back to how you were?"

Jeremiah glanced at Shilling. He pretended to think about the answer, even if he already knew it. Even as Shilling caught him looking, raised his head, and gave a very un-horse-like smile.

Jeremiah snorted, and shook his head.

'*No,*' he signed to the wolf. '*I made a good bargain. I am satisfied with my end of things. Now, get back to work. The sooner we catch the man in the black coat, the sooner we can all go home and have a proper dinner.*'

"Alright, alright," the wolf huffed. "You better be telling the truth about dinner."

Jeremiah more than suspected that the King kept his

wolves hungry to make them better trackers. '*I*,' he promised, '*will hunt you a meal myself, if what the King provides is not sufficient to fill your stomach.*'

The wolf's yellow eyes lit up. "Now that is motivation!" he growled with a fierce smile. "Come on, come on!" he spun on his heel, racing down the side of the river and howling to his friends. "We'll find him, wolves! Search, and sniff true! We eat our fill when the task is done!"

Howls of joy answered him, and Jeremiah let out a long sigh. He was probably going to have a lot of hunting to do, before the night was out.

"That was kind of you," Shilling said, walking up to him and resting his rubbery, whiskery chin on Jeremiah's shoulder. "You must be in a good mood."

'*It has nothing to do with my mood,*' Jeremiah argued, scratching under Shilling's jaw. '*It's about motivating the wolves to do as is required. There is a lot at stake for us here.*'

"Yeah," Shilling said, "but most people would simply threaten them." He leaned into Jeremiah's scratches, almost tipping the huntsman over with his weight. "You're being nice."

Jeremiah adjusted his footing and leaned back, bearing his teeth in a fierce grin and refusing to be tipped. '*You're forgetting something,*' he told Shilling.

"Oh?" Shilling stopped leaning and instead placed his velvety nose on Jeremiah's chest, looking into his face with brown eyes. "What's that?"

'*Our job,*' Jeremiah told him, returning Shilling's brown gaze with his own silver one. '*The hunt is not over.*'

"Well then, Huntsman! Let's keep hunting!" Shilling whinnied a chuckle, prancing before Jeremiah.

Jeremiah put an arm around his neck, swung up onto his back, and looked out over the gray landscape.

'*Soon this will be over,*' he promised himself and Shilling silently. '*Soon, we will be free.*'

CHAPTER 17: FAERIE

James Buckler opened his eyes.

The world resolved into being - sort of. Darkness stretched around him, only broken above by gaps in... whatever it was they had fallen into, letting in small slivers of moonlight.

James reached out to touch the matted ceiling. His glove snagged on something sharp.

A briar patch. They'd landed in a mass of dead, thorny vines. If not for his leather gloves and mask, as well as his long doctor's coat, James had no doubt his skin would be a mess of lacerations, judging by the length of the vine's points.

Or would it?

He frowned at the growth and pressed his hand against the ceiling of woven mesh. It did not part before his touch, only bent slightly.

How had they fallen through it and become so hidden?

Ah, *they*. That's right, he had not been alone when he fell.

He looked around and spotted a shadow amongst the shadows - a velvety void, lying flat on the ground with their hood drawn over their head.

Fabian raised their head a few inches, glancing at James. They put a thin finger to their lips, before returning to stillness.

James listened.

Growls, whinnies and howls. Snorts and scuffling. The sound of paws against dusty earth, running here and there, and then growing fainter, away from their hiding spot.

The wolves were chasing the horses. Clearly, they did not think anyone had escaped into the briar patch.

Fabian had saved them both.

James glowered over at the necromancer. They wouldn't have needed to be saved at all if Fabian had just kept their head instead of haring off in a panic.

James moved, wriggling through the dust on his belly to get closer to Fabian. Thorns snagged on his coat, but he didn't care.

"Where," he breathed, "is Barty?"

Fabian returned his look with red neutrality. "Don't you think, Doctor," they whispered back, "that you should be asking where *we* are first?"

James begrudgingly looked around. All he could see, with his eyes adjusting to the darkness, were grayish brambles, every direction he turned. The woven ceiling was no more than a foot above his head in this prone position, and the density of the stalks made it seem impossible that they would escape without significant damage.

"I care less about where we are and more about how we are going to get out," he said, low and irritable. He did wonder where they were, but not enough to give Fabian the satisfaction of being right.

Fabian seemed to read his mind, a slow, pale smile stretching across their face. "Not wise to leave too soon," they whispered. "Wouldn't want any sharp eyes to spot us standing in the middle of a sea of thorns. Follow me for a while, and perhaps we'll find somewhere safer."

"Follow you where?" James whispered back harshly, but Fabian was already moving, slipping away from him, somehow finding a way through the thorny stalks.

James cursed under his breath and wrigggled after, crawling on his knees and elbows and trying to avoid being snagged. His movements cast up little puffs of dust. Dead leaves whispered at his passing. Stars twinkled above, gleaming down through gaps in the thorny foliage cover. The moon shone just bright enough to illuminate the way, showing the sea of brambles stretching endlessly around them.

This was, most definitely, not the forest they had been charging through minutes ago.

"Alright," James growled, "where are we, Fabian? Or did I hit my head when we jumped and this is some kind of ridiculous dream?"

He rather hoped it was. It certainly felt like a dream, creeping through this weird layer of ash and dead vegetation.

"We are," Fabian said, a forced-sounding calm clear in their voice, "in the lands of Faerie."

"This is not a time for jokes." But James knew it was true, even as he denied it.

"Perhaps a demonstration would be more potent than an argument. A moment, Doctor." Fabian wormed their way forward and sat up, somehow having found a gap in the brambles big enough to accommodate them.

James followed after, pushing himself up in the small bubble of space and shaking his head. It was exactly the perfect size for the two of them to sit in, and seemed rather too convenient in shape and in timing for James' liking.

Fabian folded their legs, dusted ash from their robes, and settled thin hands on their knees. "Faerie," they began, "is not a land without rules. However, the rules here are not the same as those from the land of logic."

"What kind of rules do you mean?" James asked, bending so as not to catch his hat on the thorns. He removed it and set it in his lap, repressing a sigh, and looked at Fabian. "Do you mean rule of government?"

"I mean the rules - or rather, laws, of physics and nature," Fabian said, their tone as calm as if they were referring to a shift in the weather. "Hence why they call our world the land of law-gic."

James snorted. "Impossible."

A faint smile flickered about Fabian's mouth, but they did not laugh. "I am taking the time to explain this to you," they said, "not because it amuses me to prove you wrong..." they lingered a moment after this statement, just so it was clear to James that they did find amusement in this matter, "...but because it would be very, very dangerous for you to walk through Faerie and not understand the dangers here, both *to* you and *because* of you."

James blinked. "Because of me?"

Fabian nodded. "Faerie," they said, turning their gaze upward, to the moonlight streaming down through the brambles, "is a land ruled by desire. Where our world has a natural order of things, a 'logical' state of balance, if you will, this world is bent and shaped by the wants of those within it. Wishes, expectations, hungers, goals; all of these things change the land as we travel through it. Desire warps physicality, space, and even time."

"Impossible," James snorted again, trying to cover his deep unease. He suddenly realized how much he did, in fact, appreciate living in a world of logical consequence and universal rules. "How can a land exist simply because of wishes and desires?"

"The land does not *exist* because of desire, it *changes* because of desire. There is a difference. After all, what is magic but a manifestation of desire?" Fabian looked at him. "Every time a mage casts a spell or engraves an amulet in the world of logic, they are changing the laws of nature with their own intentions. Magic, by definition, is about breaking restraints of physics and logic for a new purpose, guided and provided by desire. This land," they gestured to the brambles stretching around them, "is shaped by the energies of people who wished for things to be other than they were. This land thrives on the power of such wishes. Every cold winter that makes men long for spring, every time of famine that brings thousands to dream of food, every person that wishes to be something that he was not born..."

Their red gaze bored into James, and he glared back.

"...all of these desires add strength to this land. Once, before the era of logic and science, it was as easy to get here as taking a walk in the forest, lost in daydream. Now, however, too many men know such things are impossible, and so the threads connecting our worlds unravel."

James shook his head. "It doesn't make sense."

"Sense is a matter of framing, perspective and experience," Fabian said wryly. "To an outsider, yes, this land does not make sense. But it is here, whether you like it or not. Just as the laws of physics exist whether you like it or not. And, just like the laws of physics, once you understand them properly, you can navigate the world around you better."

"Prove it then," James shot back. "Prove that this place is as you say."

Fabian smiled, a slow, luxurious thing that told James they had been waiting exactly for this demand.

"Much of this land," they said, "is governed by expectation. You, and the other inhabitants, expect common rules to hold true. The land itself knows it was once much more closely entwined with ours, so much is similar to what we know. Sharp things still cut, blood still flows, and death still lurks to snag those who make foolish mistakes."

They rested a hand on the ceiling of the bramble-pocket, parting some of the vines with their gloved fingers. A moonbeam, white and perfect, shone through the hole, illuminating the dust floating in the air and a neat patch of bare, dry soil in front of Fabian.

"Those who understand this place," Fabian whispered, "those who truly understand, and who are sharp of mind, firm of belief, and most of all, wield their desire like a well-honed blade..."

They reached out with their free hand, circling the moonbeam with their fingers as if intending to grasp it.

"Those people," they said, "can move through this place a little more easily."

And, right before James' eyes, Fabian snapped the moonbeam off at the hole with a sound like glass cracking, and held it out to show him. It gleamed in the darkness, illuminating the vines around them both.

James Buckler stared at the impossible strip of light in the necromancer's gloved fingers. It was about three inches across, and translucent, like clouded quartz, shining with its own light.

It couldn't be. It simply couldn't. It made his unbeating heart hurt just to look at it, in a way he couldn't even begin to understand.

Fabian chuckled at his silence, and leaned a bit closer. "Go on," they whispered. "Take it."

"It's...it's impossible," James said, reaching for the moonbeam despite himself.

"Nothing is impossible, if you believe," Fabian said, the dripping irony in their voice completely at odds with the gentleness of their fingers as they pressed the beam into James' hand. It was cold, even through his leather glove. "Believe, Doctor."

"I can't. This-" James held the moonbeam in his trembling hand. "Light does not have physical form and cannot be held or shaped by any man!"

The moonbeam flickered out, leaving his hand empty. James stared at his dark palm, both relieved and disappointed. "There," he said firmly, trying to dust away the lingering cold. "A trick."

Fabian stared intently at the emptiness where the moonbeam had been. They moved their gaze to James's face, peering through the shadows between them, right into his eyes. "You," they said, barely above a whisper, "have a very strong sense of rationality, Dr. Buckler. In this realm, that is as powerful a thing as magic is in our own land. You can bend things to how you think they should be. However..."

They leaned closer, their long hair trailing in the dust.

"Be very, very careful," they breathed to him. "Rational thought would dictate that a corpse cannot walk, talk or think."

James froze.

He hadn't even considered that his very existence depended on exactly the kind of belief and desire Fabian was talking about. If this world of Faerie was as Fabian said, and expectation created reality, would he sabotage his own existence as a living corpse if he rationalized too hard?

Fabian smiled. "I am sure," they said, reaching to snap off another moonbeam without even looking at it, "that your wife would much prefer you make it home safely to her side. I'd hate to tell her that her husband's body lies in a magical land unreachable to her. Imagine what kind of deals she would be willing to make, to get you back."

"Stop it," James croaked. "I understand."

"Do you?" Fabian held out the second moonbeam to him. It was thinner than the first - closer in size to a fencing saber instead of a machete. "Prove it."

James looked at the silvery beam of light. He told himself that it was a blade like any other - like a surgical knife, or the sword he still had back at home, locked away with his military things. It was a little easier this time, because of its shape, and because he had felt the coldness of the first beam. Cold like steel.

He took the moonbeam from Fabian's grip. This time it did not flicker, but seemed to solidify, shifting shape ever so slightly to be sharp on one end and flat on the other.

Fabian's red eyes gleamed, noticing the change. "Good," they said. "Very good. You can hand it back now."

James did so, relieved to be rid of the mental taxation that came with accepting impossibility. "Is all the land a place of madness, then?" he asked, trying to keep the strain from his voice. "Will we walk two steps and face fire, flood, abyss and eternity?"

"No," Fabian said, still smiling and snapping the moonbeam in half. The lower half they put back by its hole, where it stretched to properly beam down again. The sharp half, however, they slipped into some inner pocket of their robes, and James remembered uncomfortably that they carried a wide array of knives. "As I told you before, this land is connected to ours, even if the connections have been fraying over time. Everyone, more or less, expects it to behave something like the world of logic, and it more or less does. The people and creatures here are either denizens of the world of logic who have wandered here over the years, fae folk native to this environment, or offspring of the two."

Faint howls broke through their conversation, carrying through the night. They both fell silent, listening, but the sound did not come any closer. If anything, it lingered much further away than last time.

Fabian said, "best to keep moving," and knelt down again, crawling out of the hollow.

James followed, and only now that he knew to look for it could he see the brambles parting before Fabian, bowing before their expectation. "Offspring?" he grunted, wriggling after. "So the people here are human then?"

"Either human or human enough to believe themselves compatible with humans," Fabian said. "It is best not to dwell on it too much, especially once you see the variety of beings. Just know that the science of procreation here is, hmm, easier to negotiate with, than in the land of logic." They gave a shrug as if to say, 'It is what it is.' "There can be complications when such folk visit the land of logic. Think of all the fairy tales you have heard, of beings who turn to stone in daylight, or melt into ashes when they are slain. Many can never leave this place. Those that can are generally very, very powerful."

"Like dragons," James grunted, thinking over the classic adventures, "or ogres."

"Vampires, werewolves," Fabian agreed, smiling. "It used to be quite common for there to be a healthy amount of crossing between worlds."

"What happened, then?" James asked. The brambles were thinning, the space ahead of them growing lighter. He hoped their crawl was almost over. "There are far less rumors of such creatures now than there were in the past." Stories, yes, but no records of deaths in the mortality reports.

"Ah, and here we get to the real rot in the marrow..." Fabian squirmed past the edge of the brambles then stood up, dusting the ash from their black robes. "I would imagine it has something to do with the one in charge here."

"The one in charge?" James pulled himself free as well, and likewise stood, plucking off the twigs and thorns that clung to his clothes. They had come out at the edges of some kind of forest, the world before them a mass of either dead or dormant trunks.

"Yes. Rulers come and go in Faerie, and there are different kingdoms here just as there are in our world." Fabian dragged their fingers through their hair, freeing dead leaves.

Except, were they dead?

James stared at the discarded foliage. It was hard to be sure in the darkness, but Fabian's leaves seemed greener than the gray ash they'd settled in.

Fabian continued, "Long ago, the King and Queen of this particular realm of Faerie loved men and their ways. They kept every door flung wide open, and citizens of both worlds crossed between them freely and frequently. However, over the centuries, men grew more advanced, and more dangerous. I imagine, with the creation of things like guns, the world of logic became less safe for creatures of magic to wander into."

"As if it's so safe to wander here," James grumbled, looking back the way they came. The brambles stretched out behind them, wide and dead. "This place looks like a battlefield gone to seed, and then hit by thirty years of drought." Or, did it? Was there some green amongst all that dead vegetation?

"We will not be wandering," Fabian said, smiling. "We are going to find a way back, and then we will be leaving immediately."

"We most certainly are not," James said firmly, turning back to them, "not without Barty."

"How about a deal, Doctor," Fabian said, arching a brow at him. "We are in the land of faerie, after all. Deals are very fashionable."

James remembered Fabian specifically warning him against deals not a day before. He glared and said nothing.

Fabian laughed, and spoke on as if James had agreed. "We will both focus on what we want. I will focus on finding a gate back to the land of logic. You will focus on finding Dr. Wayman. We will see whose will is stronger, and the land will judge between us."

James didn't trust that it would be so simple. "He rode off in the opposite direction," he argued. "We need to actually search for him, not just hope for coincidences!"

"It hardly matters," Fabian said with an eloquent shrug of their thin shoulders. "If you want to find him, and he wants to find you, the energies of this place will make it so."

James wanted to argue. He wanted to say reality didn't work like that and they would never find Barty just wandering around.

But he remembered the cold of the moonbeam in his hand, and how it had flickered out when he had spoken against its existence.

He swallowed his arguments, and said, "Fine then." And then he added firmly, "We WILL find him."

Fabian smiled at him and turned away. "Unfortunately," they said, "you may have some competition, Doctor." They stepped into the trees, a black specter among the moonlit, bare trunks. "After all, we are not the only ones looking for him. Nor is he the only one looking for us."

The howl of wolves rose in the distance, and a chill went down James' spine. Somewhere out there, a pack of wolves hunted for reasons he strongly suspected had something to do with the necromancer before him.

He clenched his fists, bent his head, and squared his shoulders.

He followed Fabian into the dead forest, praying to whomever was listening that they would find Barty soon and *all* go home.

CHAPTER 18:
GUIDANCE

Barty Wayman fought for his life in the gray, silt-clogged waters of the nameless river. The current tore at him, snapping him up and down, slamming him against rocks and roots and spinning him until he couldn't tell which way was up.

His mask saved him. The break of leather held a pocket of air, protecting him from gasping water the first time he hit something hard. However, when he finally opened his eyes, he couldn't even see light to guide him to the surface.

His only chance of survival was to catch himself on something and get his bearings.

He grasped wildly at the darkness around him, but the water fought his every move. River rapids were completely different from the ocean waves of his naval training. His full length plague gear dragged him down, as if the current were a thousand hands pulling him back into murky, chill darkness.

He kept trying, however, and finally managed to grasp a great thick root of something. He wedged himself tight against the pull of the water and ripped free of his coat, letting the garment fly away with the current. His boots followed. Finally, he pointed his rapidly-filling beak towards the slight sliver of gray above and pulled himself upwards, following the root to the light.

His head broke the surface and he tore off his mask, gasping in a great lungful of air. Almost as quickly, though, he ducked back under - for not a dozen feet downriver were a pair of wolves, barking eagerly and chasing the coat he had just set free to swirl down the currents.

He covered his face with his mask once again, hoping the darkness of the leather would camouflage him against the blackened tree roots if a wolf happened to look his way, and sank into the water, head all but submerged except for the airholes on his beak. Only once the frenzied barking moved further away did he pull himself through drooping branches and waving reeds.

He knew he couldn't make land here. He would be all too easy to see, all too easy to smell. However, the river forked not far ahead. His coat had already gone down one side of the fork - if he could swim to the other and stay underwater long enough for his scent to be concealed, he might be able to depart the waters in safety.

Assuming he could control his path, in that hungry flow.

He pulled his mask off, tucked it into his vest, took one last, deep lungfull, and dove back into the murk, pushing off the root and swimming with all his might towards the left fork of the river.

It was hard going. Even though he wasn't flailing beak over bottom this time, the current pulled mightily, and his vision was limited to endless gray swirls. All he could do was keep going, and hope that if he swam hard enough, if he pushed his complaining muscles and aching lungs just a little bit further-

Ah, yes. The current shifted, pulling him to the left now instead of forward. He let it take him, swimming upwards for one more breath before sinking under entirely and gliding along with the flow, instead of fighting it.

As the waters calmed, Barty's surroundings cleared, gray silt melting away into crystalline clarity. He took another breath and sank deeper, keeping his eyes wide open. Fish appeared, drifting out of thick walls of river weed. They were colorful things he had no name for, and seemed to have no name for him, either, judging by the way they stared. His ungraceful progress felt even clumsier by comparison to their feather-light travel, for they darted around his hands and legs with effortless grace, and looked him over with eyes of gold and silver, utterly fearless.

Pretty, he couldn't help but think as he swept by. Pretty, and uncaring of the struggles of half-drowned doctors. It felt rather like a dream.

He surfaced for another breath. The world above the water seemed lighter than the darkness he'd left behind, and grew brighter every moment, as if he traveled through time of day as well as through water. But how was that possible?

At least there was no sign of wolves or sword-bearing riders. No sign of anyone, really, only a great mass of green forest that cradled this fork of the river. He floated along, trying to stay alert and wondering if there would be other dangers lurking in that forest. It was half tempting to remain among his new fishy companions, and not have to face the next stage of whatever trials this land had concocted for his personal torment.

His bare toes brushed bumpy ground, the sun-warmed current drifting to stillness, spreading out around him in a wide, clear, pond. Its bed was lined with stones so pale he almost felt he was wading in a pool of cream.

Barty lay in the shallows, gathering the bedraggled

remains of his resolve. He had to be grateful, he supposed. He had his life and his health, if not his coat, or boots, or companions.

Oh, James, Fabian... Bartys heart squeezed in his chest, the memory of howling wolves and fear for his friends dashing away his bubble of lethargy. Please be alright, he prayed, removing his mask from his vest and wiping tears from his eyes. Please, please be alright. He poured water from the dark beak, hoping the wet would not damage the leather of the single remaining token of his career.

He shook his hair out of his face, feeling very like a wet dog, and looked about, wading closer towards the pond's bank. What he saw there took his breath away.

Flowers. Flowers crowded the shoreline, taking up every inch of space, even growing half in the water so that they bobbed and bent with the ripples from Barty's approach. All colors of flowers - red, white, pink and violet, blues of countless, nameless shades and shapes. Yellow bursting through like drops of sunlight, and even some velvety black blooms he almost couldn't believe were real.

He waded closer, and knelt on the smooth stones in the sparkling shallows just to drink in the colors and fragrance, and to brush the petals with his fingertips to be sure they were real, living, growing things.

Their sweetness was fresh; so different from the sickly perfumes pressed from dead petals that Barty was used to. His spirit felt renewed, as if he, too, were a bloom flourishing in shallow waters and sunlight.

He stayed there a long moment, basking in the tapestry of color and sweetness, of breathing free, and sun warming his damp back.

Then the ripples stilled below him, and his eyes met the empty sockets of a skull, nestled among the flowers.

He jerked back with a gasp and a splash - but not before he saw that the skull wasn't alone - that what he'd taken for stones lining the bottom of the pool were, in fact, hundreds, if not thousands, of human skulls, clean and perfect, resting silently under the clear waters.

Barty scrambled for the shore, but a voice froze him in his tracks; a strange voice, accented by a soft humming that, somehow, did not interrupt the words it carried. "I was wondering when you would notice."

Barty looked up.

A figure rose from the depths of the overgrown flowers; a figure that, at first glance, seemed to be a flower too, hues shifting from the wild patterns of the blooms to shades of white, pink and gold, like dawn-touched clouds. What might have been petals, however, hung close her body like a perfectly-tailored gown, both concealing and accenting her shape.

She stepped closer, the motion as natural as a leaf swaying in the wind, her organic garments trailing in her wake. "Hello," she said, staring into Barty's face. Her eyes, while normal in proportion, were a solid, deep amber color, and glittering with segments. They were unlike anything he had ever seen before.

Barty staggered back a pace, shoving his mask back on, breathing hard. No, he HAD seen eyes like that before - compound eyes, with shifting points of black among the facets. Dragonflies had eyes like that, but Barty had never in his life met a dragonfly so big, so human shaped, or with such a voice – and such a smile. A crimson smile on still lips, painted as perfectly as any doll's. He felt like he needed the familiar protection of leather to shield himself from something so utterly alien.

"I beg your pardon," he said, and bowed, reaching to tip his hat, then remembering his hat was lost somewhere among the currents. "I - um. I did not mean to intrude in your garden-"

"Oh, there is no intrusion." She swayed closer, her smile staying the same, the points in her eyes darkening. The more Barty looked at her face, the more uncanny it seemed; the planes and shapes a perfect, artificial beauty. She wore no cosmetics, but the overall effect was similar - flat color on a smooth surface. "It's been such a long time since a human came here, I was beginning to wonder if they had forgotten me."

"Oh dear! I'm so sorry. What a terrible thing to be lonely like that." Barty edged further away from her, the water now up to his thighs. The skulls were slippery under his unshod feet, and creaked when bearing his weight. "You had many visitors in the past, I assume?" Probably the poor souls whose heads he was treading upon at this very moment.

She laughed, her garment fluttering behind her with a quickness that was most certainly not brought about by the wind. Wings, perhaps? "Polite and clever! How unusual. How delicious."

She stepped into the water, and Barty's suspicions were confirmed by a clawed, delicately pink foot disappearing under the surface, followed by another. "Not visitors, though," she hummed, stepping closer. "Suitors."

"S-suitors?" Barty squeaked, still backing away, the water back up to his ribs, his shoulders. There were so many skulls! All suitors? True, she was beautiful like no creature he had ever seen, but- "Th-that's not me I'm afraid," he said with a nervous laugh. She was close now. Reaching for him. The pond bed was steep; he couldn't step back any further without the water covering his head. "I-I'm just-"

"You're half drowned, poor thing," she purred. One pinkish-yellow, chitinous hand hooked his vest and pulled him back to shallower water. "You should let me help you out of those wet things and this...hm."

She ran a sharp finger along the length of his beaked mask, pausing at the airholes, puzzled. "Is your face supposed to do that?"

"S-supposed to do what?" Barty went cross eyed, trying to look at his own beak, and noticed a spot of green.

Something brushed against his mouth from the inside of the mask.

"AUGH!"

He leapt back, falling into the deep water and clawing the leather off his face. Flailing and choking, he paddled back to the shallows (out of reach, he hoped, of lonely or hungry insect ladies!) and upended his mask into the water, shaking out whatever had touched him.

Fresh, healthy mint leaves fell free, scattering on the liquid surface. Purple sage flowers, too, as bright and lush as if they were still growing on the plant he'd picked them from. In fact, a few more bloomed right before his eyes, floating there on the water.

"What?" Barty gasped, momentarily forgetting the danger picking its graceful way over the skulls. "But...these have been dead and dried for weeks." He scooped up the plants, setting the stalks, leaves and flowers back in his mask. They remained alive, smelling as sweet as the day he picked them, and putting out more leaves and buds even now.

"Yes," murmured the creature striding ever closer to him. "The flowers have always loved these waters. They're so... fertile."

She flashed Barty her perfect smile again. She'd moved between him and the shoreline, with the deep water once more at his back. "Come along," she said, soft and inviting. "Come sit on the grass and dry your hair. Come rest from your travels and troubles. Tell me who you are, and where you are going."

As if the skulls weren't warning enough, as if Barty couldn't see the soft, subtle flexing of her lower jaw. There was some kind of seam there, down from her bottom lip; he was fairly sure he didn't want to know what it was for.

"I d-don't wish to trouble you, madam," he tried to edge around her - but she moved to meet him, smiling. "B-but I am afraid I must be on my way. You see I came here quite by accident, I have an important mission to attend to, and-"

"There is time," she said with her painted smile. He tried to lunge past her through the water, but she sprang with shocking agility after him - her sharp hands gripping his vest and pulling him back while *another* set of arms wrapped around his middle, squeezing him close. "There is time for all manner of lovely things," she murmured in his ear, "before dinner."

For a moment Barty froze, too shocked, terrified, embarrassed and indignant to do anything, even breathe. He hated this - he felt absolutely helpless, absolutely humiliated, her hard fingers already trying to pull his shirt apart. It was just like Magmaydon all over again – just like when he was a child, with that girl who'd actually liked Chester.

But no! He struggled in her grasp, causing her to chuckle and hold him tighter. Hadn't he grown? Hadn't he learned anything since then?

What had he learned that could possibly help him now, with the flash of a red mouth and pale, pale teeth out of the corner of his eye, poised to-

"MADAM!" he shouted suddenly, firmly. "This is VERY UNSAFE BEHAVIOR, and AS A DOCTOR I simply cannot allow it!"

She paused. "You cannot allow it?" He got the distinct impression she had never been spoken to in such a tone of voice in her life. For one surprised moment, her iron grip loosened.

He tore free of her grip and turned to face her, clutching his now-ragged shirt closed and drawing himself up to his full height. "Do you have ANY IDEA," he demanded, pitching his voice to be as much like his dear friend Doctor James Buckler's as possible, "how many DISEASES can be transmitted through just the kind of tomfoolery you are insinuating?"

She stared at him. It took every scrap of will power for him to stand his ground and not flinch away, for the seam in her lower jaw had opened, revealing rows and rows of needle-sharp pseudo-teeth. Then she closed her mouth, looking genuinely puzzled even with her neat smile back in place. "Diseases..?"

"Syphilis!" Barty proclaimed, pointing an accusatory finger in her direction. "Why, you might not even know you

have it at first! A single mysterious sore on your lips or other delicate areas, turning into a rash, and then fever, headache, muscle ache, and more and more sores!"

She backed away from him, looking decidedly uncomfortable. "I do not have any sores-"

"That you know of," Barty said darkly, advancing on her. "Some of them lurk inside, where they cannot be seen. And that is only one of many afflictions common as a result of such behavior! There's chlamydia, which induces painful urination, discharge and bleeding - or even gonorrhea, which brings both itching and a pus-like discharge from-"

"Stop! Enough!" She retreated right out of the water, a few yards away from him. Her alluring human form became instead a more natural, if still beautiful, insectoid one, with clear wings on her back and a segmented body. Her painted lips warped into an equally-painted looking frown. "Cease your words, mage of logic, I feel your spell reaching for me." She pulled at her wings, and shivered.

"Oh, oh, I beg your pardon." Barty scrambled out of the water, as far away from her as he could manage, but not so far that he couldn't keep an eye on what she was doing. "I'm not a mage, though, I am afraid I must correct you. Mages use magic. I am only a doctor." He brandished his beaked mask, wondering if such a creature would have heard of plague.

She crossed two of her arms over her abdomen, folded a third across her chest, tapped her chin with the claw of a forth. "A doctor," she repeated. "What does a doctor do then, without magic? Seems a significant disadvantage."

"Oh, well! Doctors study very hard to cure disease and injury through natural means, using plants and other remedies." He gestured to the flowers.

She stared at him with her faceted, unblinking eyes. "Is that what you were just describing?" she asked. "Diseases? Not a curse?"

Barty nodded, his expression solemn. "The diseases I spoke of are very common in...um." He glanced around. "In my world. I assume this isn't Devonshire."

She grinned at him. It was still frightening, the contrast between her painted lips and sharp teeth, but it seemed a far more natural expression than her decoy smile from before. "Devonshire is on the other side," she said, as if it were obvious. "You are in the realm of Faerie now." She spread her wings, fluttering them so they caught the light and sparkled, a rainbow of color as bright as the flowers below their feet. It made a jaw-droppingly beautiful display, however inhuman. "Or, to be exact," she folded her wings again. "You are in the kingdom of the Changelings."

"Is that what you are?" Barty said, curious despite himself. After all, she'd changed before his eyes, shifting color and shape. "A changeling?"

She nodded. "I," she said, standing tall and proud (at least two feet taller than Barty), "am the Guardian of the Living Waters by the Springtide Gate. Once, men of logic fought for the right to be sent to me, for what better way to die, than to be consumed by one so eternal and beautiful?" She gestured over the skull-ridden pond. "What better reward, than to be permitted to pass a single flask of Living Waters back to family in the realm of logic, to heal any injury, restore any weakness? Countless were the suitors who perished by my-"

"Did you say gate?" Barty interrupted.

She gave him a sideways, disapproving look, and he quickly covered his mouth in what he hoped was an apologetic manner. After a moment's stare, she nodded. "Yes," she said. "The gate is not far from here. Men used to pass through it with regularity."

"I would very much," Barty said, "like to see this gate."

She considered him in silence for a time. Then her painted smile stretched wide, (it was fascinating to see the color move on her face of its own accord, as if an invisible artist had decided to paint her lips wider) and said, "Perhaps we should make a deal?"

Barty hesitated. "Um," he said, vividly remembering

Fabian's warnings from the day before. "I was told I am not to make any deals with Faerie folk."

"Oh?" The Guardian of the Living Waters tilted her head. "Who told you this?"

"Um." Barty was very sure Fabian would not want to be mentioned to such a person. "Someone who knows about such things."

"But Doctor," the Guardian leaned closer to him, close enough that he could see the pale facets in her segmented eyes, "you don't even know what I would ask of you."

Barty gripped the straps of his mask, ready to use it to beat her back if he had to. He did not want those hands on him again. "I believe I could guess-"

"Could you?" she stepped closer, towering over him. "Then how, Doctor, could you blame me, after all you have described?"

"Huh?" That didn't line up with what he'd been thinking at all. He immediately felt guilty for his assumptions, and curious about her true proposal. "Maybe you had better explain."

"Teach me," she said, "how to be a doctor."

He gaped at her.

She stood tall, proud, and inhumanly gorgeous, her petal-garments rippling in the breeze. "These things you described," she said, finally settling down on the flowering grasses so she was eye-to-eye with Barty, her amber gaze both alien and sincere, "these diseases. I have seen them before. I lost many daughters to them, long ago. Always, we had thought them a kind of strange, cruel curse - something the humans had sent as vengeance for us feeding upon them. But if I am understanding the meaning behind your words correctly, it seems it is an affliction from which humans also suffer?" She tilted her head, the facets of her eyes glittering.

Barty swallowed hard, and nodded. "It is very common, in our lands."

"And," she continued, "You are a doctor who knows how

to stop such suffering?"

Again Barty nodded. "My most recent studies covered exactly that-"

"Perfect!" She rose again to her feet in a swell of eagerness, wings fluttering behind her and making the flowers wave their heads, swept up with the wind of her passion. "I must learn this skill. I will see the end of these diseases, for all my family."

"That's very noble of you," Barty said, touched by her sincerity, dizzied by the implications of teaching such a creature standard human medical practice, and worried about the lack of comparability between human and insect anatomy. "But I am only a beginning student of the medical arts myself-"

"Do not fret," she looked him up and down now, her eyes lingering on his form in a way that made him decidedly uncomfortable. "I know such lessons take time. I will accompany you on your journey, and you can use that time to teach me. Behold, my level of sincerity-!"

She ran her hands along her figure, and her petal-clothing shifted, losing its organic shape and shortening into a neat white vest over a delicate, frill-edged pink shirt, with golden buttons and red trousers. Somehow she even made her extra arms disappear. Like Barty, she was barefoot, her clawed toes pale against the grass and flowers.

She spread her two remaining arms, and turned in a slow circle. "How is this?"

"Fantastic," Barty said faintly, impressed despite himself. He would have been far more flustered to have someone so shapely change clothes in front of him if she were not still so very insectoid. As it was, he could not help but add, with a sort of helpless, horrified fascination,"Doctors often wear wide hats as well, and, um, at least right now, we wear long coats and masks, to protect from the plague."

He held up his beaked mask, careful to not let the plants spill out, but showing her the shape.

"Hmm," she peered at it closely. "Put it on again, and let

me see how it sits."

He obliged, shifting the leaves so they brushed up against his cheek instead of his mouth and slipping the leather straps over his damp curls .

She looked a moment longer, then put her hands on the sides over her face and smoothed them forward. Her face morphed under her touch, until she looked much more like a bird than an insect.

There was still a mouth-line of red, though, making the pale beaked face appear as if it had been drinking blood. "How is this?"

"V-very impressive," Barty said with an approving nod. "You are quite talented with your, um, changing."

"It has been some time since I had a guest to show off to." She glanced down her back with a coy smile, shook her shoulders, and created a translucent, gossamer cloak, clearly still wanting to have wings even in this shape. "So, you agree to our deal, then?" She looked at him, still coy, but there was an intensity behind her smile that made Barty uncomfortable. "I will show you the gate, and you will teach me how to be a doctor?"

Barty hesitated. Unfortunately, he didn't see any other way he could get out of here. Surely Fabian would understand that he didn't have a choice, but...maybe there was a way to make this a bit safer?

"How about this," he offered, making his voice as kind and reasonable as he could manage. "You show me the gate, and I will give you three lessons in exchange - one lesson for showing me the way, one lesson for arriving there, and one extra as thanks." He didn't think he would leave just yet - he didn't know where James and Fabian were and he had no intention of abandoning them - but it would be useful to know the way out, when he did find them. Also, limiting the exchange to three lessons seemed a lot more manageable task than promising a title which may or may not be tied to the educational system of England.

She considered his proposal, her eyes impassive and richly amber in the unchanging sunlight beating down on them both. Steam rose from Barty's wet clothes.

Finally she nodded, offering her hand and a smile that parted the bird-like beak, revealing more sharp teeth. "Very well," she said. "It is a deal, Dr...?"

"Barty," said Barty, smiling, shaking her smooth, chitinous hand and trying not to feel like he was making some terrible mistake in dealing with the very first fae he met. He even took off his mask, tucking it into his vest so he could smile at her properly. "Very nice to meet you, miss. What would you like to be called in return?"

She showed more teeth. "You could call me 'sweetheart' or 'darling.'"

Barty went pink and let go of her hand, already regretting revealing his face. "Ahem. Perhaps something less implicative."

She chuckled, letting her features smooth back into their original shape. "Iris will do, then."

"Iris," Barty repeated. "Well met, Iris. If I had my hat still I would take it off for you, but I am afraid it was lost in the current, along with my coat and boots."

A shame, really. If the clippings in his beak had sprouted so gloriously after contact with these strange waters, imagine what the herbs in his bag would have done!

On a whim, he pulled his flask out of his vest pocket, drained the whisky in a hearty swig, and filled it from the magical waters. You never knew, after all.

She watched his movements with curiosity, but did not stop him. "If you lost them in Faerie, it is unlikely you will get them back." She turned, striding away from the waters and towards the forests. Her steps were light and swaying, even with only two legs.

"Oh?" He put the stopper in and tucked the flask back into his inner vest pocket, hurrying to catch up with her. "Why is that?"

"Human items are extremely fashionable in higher circles," she explained, picking her way delicately over the flowers. "The smallest fae will wear thimbles and handkerchiefs as marks of rank. The larger and wealthier will have true garments stolen from human towns, or fashioned after what they think is human, and the nobility, while sneering at the antics of the others, will imitate all the latest human trends, adding their own embellishments and pretending they were the ones who thought of it first." She smiled and shook her head. "Many a deal I have made with the nobles, trading away the clothes of my suitors for seeds or services. Many a time I have attended parties, only to see the same garments I traded away, renewed and made grander and more splendid, but still clearly human, even as they scoff at humans for being lesser beings."

"Lesser beings?" Barty repeated, frowning. "We aren't-"

"Most of you don't have any magic to speak of at all," she said.

"But apparently you don't even have doctors here," Barty argued back. "What kind of society doesn't have healers?"

"We do have healers," she said, tossing her head. The petal-shaped tresses covering her head grew a few inches longer, falling about her shoulders like hair. "It is only silly human diseases that they cannot work with. The Living Waters I guard would heal any injury of flesh, any wound of the spirit or heart. But, diseases?" She shook her head. "They flourish when in contact with the healing power of the waters, like weeds in a flower bed. Any of my daughters who catch human disease must stay far away, for fear of dying by its cruel workings."

"Oh! That is just like mage healing." Barty remembered how Cassie and Liz had described the limits of magical remedies over a year ago. Healing applied to all living beings - including the living disease causing the host's discomfort. "I am surprised you continued to, um, spend time with human men, if this is such a common and dangerous occurrence for you and your daughters."

She grinned at him. "A wolf must hunt when hungry, even if the deer are ill."

Barty looked away. "S-so, ah. I believe I promised you three lessons, didn't I? Let us start with identifying features of each disease I mentioned before, and then we can move on to common treatments..."

They walked together, and he spoke as best he could on what he had been studying with James only a day earlier. Signs and symptoms, treatments and remedies. Iris listened attentively, asking questions here and there for the sake of clarification, but not once needing him to repeat himself. In fact, the nature of her questions made Barty realize very quickly that she was fiercely, almost frighteningly, intelligent. He couldn't help but think that she would, in fact, make an excellent doctor, with proper time and training.

The landscape changed as they walked, the verdant greens and colorful flowers fading away, leaving ashy ground and brown, withered stalks in its place. Standing, dried-out trees appeared here and there, like lone soldiers among the ashes. The light, too, faded, dulling to red and then purple as they left the sunshine behind. Barty trailed off in the middle of describing the proper application of motherwort to glance back the way they had come.

Far behind, he could see the splotch of green, bright and welcoming in contrast to the dominating, ashen landscape of old death.

He gestured to the dead trees, looking back to Iris. "What happened here? Why is it like this?"

She paused, following the gesture with her gaze. For a long moment she was silent and unmoving, a slight breeze stirring the petals that made up her hair and clothing. When she spoke, her voice was much, much softer. "We have a King in Faerie, but no queen."

"Oh?" Barty furrowed his brow. "What does that mean?"

She shook her head at him, turning once more and

continuing to walk. "If you had not proven so eager in answering every question I ask, I would make you pay for this answer. But as you have shown me sincerity and generosity, I will answer in kind. You remember how I spoke of the faerie love for human things?"

Barty nodded.

"The Faceted King loves human things most of all. All human things - jewelry, clothing, carriages, creatures. Everything he can get his hands on, he must have."

"But why? This is a land of magic, and he is the king – surely he can get anything he wants from his own land?"

She nodded. "You have spoken the very problem."

Barty frowned, repeating his words in his head. 'He can get anything he wants from his own land...'

Iris smiled at him, waiting patiently.

Barty thought about what rich people sought back in England, and his mind drifted to the near eternal history of war that the Monarchy boasted so highly of, conquering lands and bringing back treasures. So, perhaps following that line of reasoning... "Do you mean it is because he can have anything he wants here, he only wants things that are not from Faerie?"

She nodded. "And because he is the King," she said, "he can trade away pieces of this land to get what he wants. If he wishes to lay claim to a painting made by human hands more unique than anything he could ever make himself, he can offer precious stones so beautiful they will drive anyone who looks upon them mad - never mind that his own people died shaping those stones. If he wants a farmer's albino sheep born into a black flock, he can trade the fertility of a hundred acres of his own forests. If he wishes to have a human servant in his palace, to demonstrate to his peers his own might and superiority, well..." she shrugged. "I am sure you have heard the old tales of such things. Trade a man's desire in exchange for his firstborn child."

She rested a hand on a dead tree, its bark dry, lifeless, colorless next to the delicate yellow-pink of her carapaced hand. "He is never satisfied. He does not die. And so he slowly trades away all we have, in exchange for filling his own palace with human wonders and human servants. But..."

She closed her eyes, and the tree blossomed to life, covered in pink flowers and smooth leaves, shimmering and ghostly against the dark sky.

She opened her eyes and looked at the flowers, her expression wistful. Then she removed her hand, and the illusion immediately faded back to skeletal, bare branches. "...they remember what they have lost."

"Why does nobody stop him?" Barty asked, stunned both by the horror of the situation and the beauty of Iris's display.

"He is the King," Iris replied, and continued walking.

"But surely there are more of you than there are of him!" Barty insisted, hurrying to keep pace with her. "Why not band together and-"

Iris smiled. "Fae folk do not form armies like humans," she said. "The complexity and delicacy of that degree of bargaining would prove impossible. How would one place value on a life risked for a common cause - how would one pay appropriately for the labor, the risk to limbs and sanity? How would you even begin to assess the degree of effort required of each fighter to earn their payment so as to properly satisfy the deals made?" She shook her head. "No. At least in this country, changelings stick to family groups, or boroughs, at most. Who would risk the lives of their families fighting for the good of neighbors they do not even speak to?"

Barty couldn't even begin to answer this question. He looked down, troubled, and something gleamed at him as he passed. He stopped walking, crouching by a dead bush and staring between the twigs.

Was it his imagination, or did he see a little dry figure there? Half buried in ash, one frail wing so transparent it was barely visible...

He shivered and stood, hurrying on after Iris. The

enormity of the death around him seemed like something worth fighting to prevent, but he did not know how to explain that to someone who came from a culture where war was not, in fact, a historical solution.

Then again, he supposed he couldn't see his own neighbors banding together to fight the Queen of England, no matter how much they complained about taxes.

"We're nearly there," Iris said, snapping him out of his thoughts.

Barty looked around. Not much had changed, except the dead trees were denser now, crowding out most of the view of the horizon. The sky had darkened as well, returning to the night-time hue it had been before he'd stepped into Iris's territory. Weariness tugged at his bones, his body reminding him he'd worked all day treating plague before riding and swimming for his life.

"Well, I've kept my half of the bargain so far, right?" he said, looking at Iris. "Are you pleased with the lessons I have given you?"

She gazed at him, her expression even more difficult to read in the darkness. "I am, and you have, though you owe me one more still. I would like to be able to identify these plants that you have been describing."

"I can get some from the other side of the portal and bring them to you," Barty said eagerly. "Then it would be a proper lesson indeed."

Iris nodded, unsmiling. For some reason, her serious expression filled him with far more dread than her sharp-toothed grin. "It would, indeed, be a proper lesson," she said.

Barty's eagerness faded. He glanced around, searching for any cause of her shift in personality. He saw nothing - only the forest of skeletal trees.

"So, where is the gate?" he asked, looking back at Iris.

She gave him an unreadable amber stare, then sauntered over a dozen paces to two identical trees standing side by side. "It is here."

Barty followed, noting how the branches of the trees reached across to each other, entwining at top and bottom, forming a natural circle. "Gracious," he said, "are all ways between Faerie and my world circular?"

"Yes," she said. "Doors are easier to open that way."

Barty examined the branches. They were dead, hard, and brittle, and didn't seem terribly magical.

He picked up a handful of ashes and tossed it through the circle.

Nothing happened.

He, very tentatively, reached a hand through the space as well.

Nothing continued to happen.

He looked back at Iris. "The gate does not appear to be open."

She tilted her head to one side, considering the gate for a few moments. "No," she said, "it appears it is not."

Barty let out a great breath of exasperation. "But we had a deal-!"

She stepped closer to him - suddenly tall, very tall, as she had been when they first spoke. "Our deal was that I would show you the gate," she said.

"But- but obviously I wanted to go through the gate!" Barty protested.

"Then you should have specified so," Iris, Guardian of the Living Waters, said. "You did not specify. You said only that I needed to show you the gate."

She gestured to the empty circle of branches.

"I have shown you the gate. You have given me only two of the three promised lessons. I require the third, unless..."

She leaned close to him, her chin-seam parting to show all those teeth, an image of absolute hunger and intimidation.

"Unless you would break our deal, Dr. Barty. You are free to do so, I do not mind taking payment by force."

Barty shrank back, terrified, hurt, feeling like ten kinds of fool. This was exactly the sort of thing Fabian had warned him about. "No," he said, fighting back panic from his voice. "No, I do not mean to break the deal. I-"

He took a shaking breath, retreated a few paces, straightened his back once more. *Chin up, Dr. Wayman*, he told himself firmly. *You made a stupid mistake, and now you must pay the price, or, better yet, salvage the situation.*

He let his breath out slowly, and looked Iris square in her faceted eyes. He needed an open gate, and he needed an excuse to make her bring him to one. "I cannot finish the last part of the lessons," he said, "unless I can access my world. I normally carry the correct plants with me, but they were lost during my time in the water. Clearly, then, in order for me to complete your last lesson, I need an open gate to get the plants. That is logical, is it not?"

She glared at him, segmented eyes gleaming in the darkness. No, it was more than that. Her gaze was a force - he could feel her will trying to bend him, to seek out the weakness in his argument and use that to break him and make him keep his word some other way. It hurt, it made his breath come short, made his hands shake and cold sweat trickle down his brow. He was an insect to her - a small, stupid creature, toying with forces far beyond his comprehension.

But he knew he was right. It didn't matter what she wanted - there was only one, logical answer. He bent his mind to this concept; the idea that he needed the actual plants to show her. There was no choice she could force him to make that would change the reality of the situation. That thought, that he was physically incapable of changing the truth of things, was all that kept him upright. If not for this truth, he would have instead fallen to his knees in tears, begging for her forgiveness for daring to thwart her will.

It was terrifying. All the more terrifying because he had underestimated her. He knew, with absolute certainty, that if he had tried to lie or fool his way out of this, he would have ended up worse than dead.

"Spoken like a true creature of logic," she said at last. "I cannot deny the truth of what you say."

He sagged with the release of pressure, swaying but forcing himself to stand straight. Some of his courage returned, and he was able to force out more words, "Then it is for your benefit as well as mine that we find a different gate that is open, or open this one, somehow. If you wish to be a true doctor, we must do things the correct, practical way."

She parted her jaws in a soft hiss. "The only one who can open or close the gates is the King himself."

Barty perked up. He had definitely noticed how much Iris disliked the King. Perhaps this represented a way out of his predicament. "Well then," he said, his tone businesslike, "I suppose we will have to go to the King and ask him to open the gate, won't we?"

"Yes, I suppose we shall," Iris said, her words dripping sarcasm like a flower dripping nectar. Her temper seemed to be manifesting in her shape - the neat crispness of her vest and trousers becoming marred by jagged edges, and pale red veins blossomed across all the garments. She gave Barty a steely look, then tossed her head, flicking her petal-hair over her shoulder and regarding the world around them. "It is near impossible to find the King," she said, "unless one has a very pressing need, has been summoned by him, or knows someone who is in his service."

She strode past Barty, making for a small clearing in the trees. He followed after her, keeping his back straight and his steps steady, hiding his nerves as best he could. Part of his mind whirled with questions. Was there some way they could entice the King into summoning them? Did Iris perhaps know anyone in the King's service? "Well, we do have a need-"

She shook her head before he could finish. "The King would not consider enforcing someone else's deal a relevant need."

Barty frowned, worry pricking at his insides. "Then what is your suggestion?"

"Neither of us have been summoned by him," she said,

gesturing from Barty to herself with a clawed hand. "But I believe we know someone who is in his service."

"We do?" Barty said, stumbling over a tree root. It was getting harder to see; the clearing ahead of them was flooded with moonlight, but past that, the trees thickened into a wall-like blur of black. "Who?"

Iris gave Barty another unreadable look, then turned her gaze to the dark forest. "Huntsman," she called. "You have been following us for some time now. Did you hear what we have been discussing?"

A shadow moved among the shadows. A man stepped forward into the moonlight, dark skinned, silver eyed, silver haired, silver sword gleaming in his hand.

Before Barty's heart could stop with terror, however, the man sheathed the sword, and spread his empty hands. He then moved them in a peculiar manner, looking at Barty.

Iris also looked at Barty. "Do you understand finger-speech?"

"Oh!" The man was a mute. Barty shook his head, embarrassed. "I am terribly sorry, I am afraid I have never had the chance to learn it."

"He said that he has been watching us for some time and he understands our situation," Iris translated. "He says he might be able to help."

The man held up his hand in a 'wait' gesture. He put his fingers to his lips and whistled, looking off into the woods.

Barty struggled to adjust to this sudden turn of events. "I beg your pardon," he said to the man, "but are you not the same fellow who was chasing me, with that same sword, not too long ago?"

The Huntsman turned his strange silver eyes on Barty and raised an eyebrow.

"He clearly put his sword away, " Iris answered with a painted smile. "Do you want help or don't you, Doctor?"

A clip clop of hooves sounded from further back in the trees.

Barty, feeling very odd indeed to be having this conversation in front of a man who had been trying to murder him not long ago, explained to Iris, "In the world of logic, it would be considered extremely foolish to go off alone with someone who had just tried to kill you. I assume you were trying to kill me, sir?" He turned back to the Huntsman. "Or else you wouldn't have drawn your sword!"

The Huntsman shrugged, and signed something in response, his expression both grave and amused.

"He says he only intended for the blade to intimidate, not harm," Iris translated, smirking. "He had hoped you would surrender when you saw you had nowhere to run." She watched his hands with interest, raising a painted eyebrow. "He says the King is, in fact, quite interested to meet you, and it is his duty to escort you to the palace."

Barty blinked. That seemed far too convenient to be trusted. "Does the King want to help me?" He asked cautiously.

The hoof beats were getting closer. Barty glanced over just in time to see a magnificent silver horse trot out of the trees. "Sorry for the delay!" the horse said in a rich, excited baritone. Barty's mouth dropped open. "I was trying to convince him to stay behind, but he wanted to come too."

"So it's settled then," Iris said, speaking over the horse as if he didn't exist. "We will go with the Huntsman and ask the King to open the gate. Then you will get your plants, and come back and give me my third lesson."

The Huntsman's eyes narrowed, and he signed something to Iris. She glared back at him, and said, "Don't you try to pull any of that on me. I found this boy first, you cannot just-"

"Oh, but the KING can," the silver horse said.

"But do you take me for a fool!" Barty cried out. The others turned to stare at him, but he spoke on. "The both of you have already tried to harm me at least once! Why should I trust what either of you have to say at all?"

"Barty? Barty!"

240

Barty was almost bowled over when a second horse plowed into the clearing, rubbing its brown face up and down Barty's tattered shirt. "Barty! Barty! Barty safe!"

"What - what!" He spluttered, clinging to the beast's mane to keep himself from being knocked over.

"He was very worried about you," the silver horse said accusingly. "He's only just learning to talk, and he keeps asking where you are!"

"Barty!" the horse said, now sticking its velvety nose in Barty's face and breathing deeply. "Barty safe! Good boy. Good Barty!"

It was all too much. Barty was exhausted, scared, desperate, overwhelmed, and now his horse was talking to him in the sweetest, most innocent way possible.

He hugged the horse's long face, and burst into tears.

Everyone else fell silent, watching him weep. His horse tried to nuzzle the tears away with its warm, soft nose.

The Huntsman tapped Barty on the shoulder.

Barty looked up, choking back his sobs.

Slowly and clearly, so all could see, the Huntsman signed, *"I swear on my title as Huntsman: no harm will come to you, Doctor, as long as you are under my protection,"* his silver horse translated.

Iris folded her arms and sighed.

Barty, touched despite his tears, wiped his face on his sleeve. "Mr. Huntsman-" he began.

"You can call him Jeremiah, if you want!" the silver horse interrupted. "And I'm Shilling! Hey- what!?"

The Huntsman had cuffed the horse on the side of the head. Not hard, but enough to express the irritation evident in his face.

Shilling stamped his hoof. "Everyone knows Barty's name! It isn't fair that he doesn't know ours! It's only your common-use name anyway, master!"

The Huntsman sighed, but nodded. He looked to Barty, waiting patiently for him to continue.

Barty swallowed hard. "I, um, I appreciate your offer, Mr. Jeremiah, sir, and Mr. Shilling…"

He stopped.

What could he possibly say? He'd made nothing but mistakes since he'd come to this horrible place, but whether it was the Huntsman's sincerity, Iris's irritation at the offer of protection, or his own horse's concerned, kind snufflings, his heart spoke to him loud and clear about what he had to do.

He took a deep breath. "I appreciate your offer, and I am pleased to accept it. Thank you sirs, for your assistance in my time of need." He swallowed hard, steeling his nerve and standing tall.

There was only one way out of his situation, and all he needed was the courage to seize it.

"Take me to the King."

CHAPTER 19: COMPLICATIONS

Fabian's ears were ringing.

The necromancer stared at the man that should have been dead, the man they had killed with their own hands twenty two years ago.

The Huntsman Jeremiah - hunter of monsters, slayer of the evil tyrant Lord Fabian, stood there alive and well, chatting with Barty, with the changeling, and with the silver horse. His hair had gone gray with age, true, and he spoke with his hands instead of his mouth, true, but Fabian would know those eyes, that face, anywhere.

"Fabian?"

James' hand closed on their wrist, halting the fingers that had begun to creep towards one of their many hidden knives.

"What are you doing? We can't just rush in."

Cold stone tiles. Hot blood, gushing free. Racking pain in their chest.

"Fabian!" The hand on their wrist tightened.

The world was graying at the edges. They forced themselves to breathe, forced themselves to relax enough to jerk their arm out of James' grasp.

"I'm fine," they rasped, pulling their cloak close about their shoulders. They tore their gaze away from the little group - the Huntsman was helping Barty up onto his saddleless horse - and looked at James, forcing a smile that hurt. "You're right, Doctor," they said, drawing up their hood. "We can't just rush in. Not unprepared as we are. It would be suicide."

Fabian and James stood a ways away from the group, well hidden behind a dense cluster of dead trees. It seemed, Fabian observed with wry humor, that their own will and James' will had been equally strong, for they had found both Barty and the gate. If what Fabian's rat was overhearing from its hollow among the roots was correct, however, this gate would not serve their purpose.

"You cannot leave me behind!" A ringing, angry voice interrupted Fabian's thoughts, drawing their attention back to the little group in the clearing. "I saw him first! He is still bound by my deal!" The faerie changeling was indignant, her pinkish-white petals shifting to a redder shade of mauve at the edges, visible even in the moonlight.

The Huntsman shook his head, signing something back that neither Fabian nor their rat could see.

"I'll remember this," Iris said, her words as cold as a spring frost.

"I'm so sorry, madam," Barty interjected, playing the peacemaker as ever. "I will uphold my end of the bargain. I already promised you. But you know this is necessary - all it will take on your end is a little patience."

"While you tell me to be patient, I worry for the safety of my daughters!" she retorted bitterly, voice loud enough to be heard even without a rat spy. "How can a cure be within my grasp, and I must patiently watch it ride away to *his* castle?"

"A cure?" James whispered at Fabian's side.

"I believe Barty promised to teach her a little something of doctoring," Fabian said. "Apparently the indignant madam's daughters suffer from a variety of diseases common among humans who enjoy procreational pastimes."

James' head turned sharply back to the Guardian. She remained standing in place, watching the two humans ride away with unconcealed resentment flowing from every inch of her stiff form.

"Come on," James pushed past Fabian, walking towards the clearing without bothering to hide himself.

Fabian had to hurry a few paces to catch up with him. "Now who's rushing in without being careful?"

James only snorted. "What on earth do I need to be careful of? I'm already dead, remember? Anyway, she'll be able to tell us where they are going." He pulled out his mask and strapped it on, clearly wanting to convey his status without having to explain himself.

"You didn't give me time to tell you what kind of creature she is," Fabian said, lowering their voice as they got nearer. "You are going to find yourself in a very uncomfortable situation, dead or not."

James paid them no mind, pulling his coat straight and making sure his hat was sitting evenly. "I," he said, "am a doctor, before I am a corpse. And that, *Lord* Fabian," he put more scorn into the title than Fabian felt was strictly necessary, "comes with responsibilities."

"Such as getting yourself eaten?" Fabian murmured, but James ignored them, and walked into the moonlit clearing.

The changeling was more than a little surprised, even stepping back a pace at his sudden approach, despite the fact that she loomed a good foot and a half over him. "Another human? Is there a gate open here after all?"

"Madam," James said earnestly, "is it true that you have

245

family members in need of medical attention?" His voice rang clear, despite the mask. Fabian supposed that after a year of practice the doctor knew how to project properly.

She stared at him with her strange, glittering eyes. "I had no idea eavesdropping was such a widely accepted human custom," she said. She ran her hands over her face and form, smoothing away the plague-doctor-style outfit becoming something much more feminine and shapely. "You'll have to tell me more about what the humans are enjoying these days, sir."

She smiled at him with her painted mouth, and slid closer.

James stepped back automatically, and Fabian repressed a snigger at how quickly the tables had turned. Dr. Buckler really should have listened to his elders.

Still, the undead medic soldered on. "Dying is common," he said, lifting his chin in defiance. Fabian had to admire his iron resolve, even though they still thought it foolish in this particular instance. "Diseases left and right, death by childbirth, starvation, neglect-"

The faerie sighed and delicately pushed his beak back with a pale finger. "Are all human men so boring," she said, "or only the doctors? You ARE a doctor, aren't you?" she ran her hand along the full length of the mask. "I have just spent half an hour learning all about these attractive pieces of apparel."

Fabian choked back a laugh, and quietly slipped their mask on too.

James jerked his head out of her touch. "Madam," he said sternly, "I am a married man. I am only here to talk about the condition of your-"

"That doesn't bother me," she purred, following after him and snagging lapels of his coat.

Fabian cleared their throat, stepping around the trees and into the clear moonlight. "I beg your pardon," they said silkily, "but the gentleman you are harassing, is, indeed, a doctor, and renowned both for his skill and his intelligence.

However, if you persist in your carnivorous intentions, you will make him into a foe, instead of a friend."

Slowly the insectoid changeling turned and faced Fabian.

Fabian folded their gloved hands across their stomach. "Think of it," they said, "as friendly, well-intended advice."

Then there was a tearing noise – James Buckler wrenched himself free from her grasp with such force that his coat split around her sharp fingers.

Fabian sighed. "Was that really necessary, Doctor?"

"Entirely," he said, coldly. He stepped away from Iris, smoothing his coat and fixing his hat. Trying, Fabian could see, to re-don the professional bedside manner that he prided himself on. Fabian wondered how long it would last.

"Temper, Doctor," Fabian said, letting a smile creep into their voice. "You haven't made a very good first impression on, ah..." they turned to the Guardian, who had watched Fabian with unblinking intensity since they stepped into the clearing. "Iris, was it?"

She didn't reply. She stared at Fabian, and then shifted her head slightly, looking back at the trees Fabian and James had come from.

Fabian glanced too, a hand slipping to their knife. Did she see others behind them?

Nobody was there, however. Only the trees, dead but for a few small shoots of green waving in the dry wind.

The Guardian looked back at Fabian, and seemed to shrink down into herself a little. "Who are you?" she said. "I know you...but I do not know you."

"You do not know me," Fabian agreed pleasantly. "As for who I am, it is irrelevant at this time. What *is* relevant is that he," they pointed at James, "is a specialist in all diseases that afflict the female form, and you," they pointed at the Guardian, "have a pressing need for his services, do you not?"

"How do you know that?" Iris's face faded several shades paler, ending up white as a Rose of York.

"Does it matter?" Fabian shrugged. "It is the truth, as much as his healing talent is the truth. Now, if you will both kindly set your egos aside, we can proceed in a much swifter manner. We do not have time to spare."

"Is that so?" Iris turned to face Fabian. "Are you in some manner of hurry, Doctor?"

Fabian did not correct her, content to let the medical title obscure their true nature. "As you may have deduced," they said, smoothing their hands over the leather feathers of their mask, "that was our companion you just gave to the emissary of the King."

Iris picked some strands of Dr. Buckler's coat off her sharp claws. "He did mention that he was looking for his mentor."

"That would be Dr. Buckler there," Fabian said, gesturing to James. "And you will not find a man with greater skill or knowledge on the subjects of healing the female body. I suggest that we all take a breath, find some civility in our hearts," Fabian pressed the tips of their gloved fingers together, striking a pose of mocking patience and calm, "and discuss how we can best proceed, and be of use to each other, in a fair, civilized way."

James glared at Fabian, and Fabian could almost hear his mental accusations of hypocrisy. Fabian stared back, silently daring him to speak them aloud.

Finally, James shook his head and turned back to Iris. "Come on then," he said, with a gentler tone. "Tell me what your daughters are suffering from, and I will do my best to help them."

Iris stared at him. "Are you trying to give me a gift, Doctor?" she asked, her voice dangerously calm.

"Nonsense," James said. "I'm a doctor. Helping sick people is my job – my responsibility."

Iris tilted her head, considering him. "Healing people," she observed, "is…your nature."

James, after a moment's hesitation, nodded.

Iris relaxed a fraction, her colors returning to a delicate, floral balance of pinks, whites and yellows. "Very well," she said, turning and walking through the trees. "Follow me back to my territory. I do not like being so exposed out here in the dead lands."

"I doubt anyone likes it out here in the dead lands," James said wryly, following her.

Iris sighed, leading them back into the shadows of the trees. "It was not always this way."

"That much is clear," James said, looking at the dead forest. He tugged at a vine in passing, and it crumbled to dust. "I imagine this whole place used to be alive."

"Correct," Iris said. "But that changed when we lost the Queen."

"I don't see what a member of political royalty has to do with the health of the native landscape-"

"Just as the King has the power to take or trade away the life force of this land," Iris said, "so too the Queen had the ability to return it. To help it grow anew. As long as there was a Queen of Faerie, the land could recover from any injury. But without one..." she gestured at the dead trees. "What is dead, stays dead. What is lost stays lost."

"One would think," Fabian interjected with grim amusement, "that the King would learn, and stop trading away the bounty of his own lands."

Iris only shook her head. "He does not change," she said. "He does not learn. He only seeks to enrich and entertain himself. After all..." her doll-like lips shifted into a hard, bitter smile, "he is the King. He does as he pleases."

"I am starting to understand why you saw overthrowing a monarchy as a viable solution," James grumbled to Fabian.

Fabian grinned under their mask. "I always knew you'd see things my way eventually, Doctor."

Iris looked at Fabian again, her curiosity a palpable, sharp-edged thing. "Did you overthrow a monarchy?"

Fabian waved away the question. "That is a story for

another time," they said. "Doctor, why don't you tell the lady something of your credentials and experience."

James Buckler was all too happy to share details of his education and work in the field. Iris attended his words with intensity, occasionally asking questions on such topics as "Why do human females die when giving birth?" and "How exactly does cutting someone open to take out their child help them survive better?"

Fabian only half listened to James's answers, though. Their attention was on their surroundings – especially on the dead trees slowly giving way to live ones, and the ashy ground changing into grass, and then flowers. Just as Fabian had hoped, they were returning to the Living Waters Iris guarded.

Even James slowed his lecturing when he noticed the change in scenery. His masked face swiveled left and right, taking in the flourishing trees and overabundance of blossoms. "Is this," he said, sounding awed, "how Faerie is supposed to look?"

Iris nodded. "The flowers were born from gifts from my previous suitors, but all of Faerie used to be this green and thriving." She peered at the multitude of colors. "These," she trailed a finger along a vine of blue-violet buds, "grew everywhere, once upon a time. And these," she nudged a sprig of white blossoms, pale and unexpressive next to their more colorful fellows, "especially liked damp areas."

"Why, but that is Elderflower!" James exclaimed. "They have healing properties - antiseptic, and anti-inflammatory as well. In fact," he looked around at the flowers, reaching over to pluck a bright burst of yellow growing near the great pond. "These marigolds are excellent for coping with insect bites-"

"Doctor," Fabian cut in, sharply, "stay away from the water."

James looked surprised even with his mask on, but stepped away, still holding the flower. "Why?"

"The Living Waters have magical properties to them. I do not know how they would react to your...ah...condition, and I would rather not find out unless I am quite sure nothing terrible will occur." Fabian said. It was mostly true. There was another possibility, though, that Fabian did not really want to deal with right now; not in such a dangerous, unpredictable place.

James looked more closely at the pool, saw the masses of skulls, and took another step back. "Right."

"The only insect who bites around here is me," Iris said, pulling the marigold from James' hand. "But I am curious, Doctor. Tell me about this condition you have." Her eyes glittered with mischief, and she reached teasingly to try and steal James' hat as well. "Is it like the ones you are teaching me? Did your wife give it to you?"

James caught her wrist, gripping hard, so hard Iris let out a hiss of pain. "Do not," James growled, very softly, "suggest such things about my wife. This is your only warning."

Iris tugged at her arm, but James's undead strength was enough to keep her held. She glared at him, and then the glare melted into a wicked-looking smile, especially wicked because she parted her jaws enough for all her teeth to show. "I can see why your wife enjoys you," she said, the words throaty, almost a purr. "There are not many men with strength like yours."

She bent over the hand still holding her fast, toothy jaws spreading wider. "Surely she won't mind if I just take a little taste-"

James slapped her.

The blow snapped her jaws shut. She staggered back, reeling, only his grip on her wrist keeping her from falling.

Fabian sighed. "James-"

But James wasn't listening. He pulled Iris back towards him, his voice still dangerously calm. "This is your last warning. I am happy to help you, but disrespect my wife or my body one more time, and this entire interaction is over."

Iris rubbed at her jaw, a bright, crimson growth veining out across the petals of her figure. "How... *dare you...*"

"James," Fabian said more loudly, once more letting their hand slip to their knife handle. "Apologize, quickly."

"I warned her very clearly," James said, still gripping the faerie's wrist with merciless strength. "If this is a lesson I must also teach, so be it-"

"I brought you to my beautiful home," Iris hissed, growing a foot in height and spreading crimson, translucent wings. James staggered back, releasing her arm. "I trusted you as men of honor and truth, and this is how you repay my graciousness-!"

"It is her nature, James," Fabian said, drawing their knife and backing away. "She did not intend to assault your dignity!"

"She did intend it!" James snarled, but he was also edging nervously away. "She was about to bite me, Fabian! I will not tolerate-"

"You are the one who cannot be tolerated!" Iris screeched. Her distorted, open face no longer resembled anything human. Six insectoid legs poked out from under her petal-like garments. "If you think you are immune to my wrath simply because you have something I want-"

She pounced on James, lifting him up by the coat like a scruffed cat, despite his struggling. "Then THINK AGAIN!"

And despite Fabian's shout of "NO!" she hurled James Buckler into the waters.

He fell with a shout and a splash.

No, no, no! Fabian dashed to the water's edge, staring at the spot where James had fallen.

James broke the surface, gasping and drenched. "It's alright!" he called back hoarsely, having to pause and cough a moment. "It's not that deep." He waded back towards the shore, coughing and fumbling with the buckles of his mask.

Fabian sighed. They looked at Iris, who was shrinking down again to a pretty, person sized, delicate thing with a rather smug expression.

"If you've just done what I think you've done," Fabian said, fighting back the desire to cut that smug expression off her face with their knife, "you have cost me a great deal of preparation and security."

She recoiled from Fabian's tone, despite still being significantly taller than the necromancer. "I'm sure I don't know what you mean," she said, but she didn't sound so sure.

Fabian stared at the doctor - at his sodden brown coat, at the mask leaking with the Living Waters, at the way he awkwardly splashed up the banks, slipping on smooth skulls.

They could already tell. They could feel it, down in their core, like a flexed muscle suddenly gone slack.

This was not good.

Fabian forced themselves to take a deep, deep breath.

Dr. Buckler stepped out of the water, his sodden boots crushing the lakeside flowers. He was still coughing, almost doubled over with the strength of his gasps. "Absolutely preposter-" he choked around the liquid. "An overreaction -" he stopped, heaving further. "Never been so..." more coughing. "in all my life - BLAST THIS MASK."

James tore off his leather beak, chucking it among the flowers. Fabian shook their head, trying to ignore the dread settling neatly between their ribs. "I think you had better sit down, Doctor."

James had doubled over, hands on his knees, face red from hacking. "What on earth is wrong with me?" he gasped.

"Most men choke when water goes into their lungs," Iris snipped, peering curiously at his face, at his mask, back at his face again. "I believe it is a hazard of having lungs, isn't it, Doctor? Or are you supposed to be an exception?"

"I am not most men!" James snapped, his voice grating like a rasp. "The only reason I must breathe is to speak! I am of the walking dead!"

A tense silence fell. Fabian looked down, carefully examining their leather gloves, noting a slightly skinned knuckle that needed mending. They kept their breathing calm and steady. Everything was under control-

"Who told you you are dead?" Iris asked. "You look fairly

alive to me, even if you're as wet as a drowned rat."

"Of course I'm dead!" James snapped. "I've been dead for over three years now! I-"

But he stopped, coughing again furiously. He had to take a few moments to just breathe and get himself under control..

Fabian closed their eyes, but it hardly made a difference. In their mind's eye, they could see it happening: Dr. James Buckler realizing something was different, realizing that he'd never coughed so terribly in those three years, that the heat from his red face, the cold of the water against his skin, the sudden heaviness of his heart in his chest meant...

Fabian could see him pulling off his wet glove, taking his own pulse...finally understanding...

"My God," James croaked. "My God, I'm...I'm alive."

Fabian kept their eyes closed. They didn't want to see the tears in the grumpy doctor's eyes, even though they could hear them in his voice.

"My God..."

James fell to his knees among the flowers with an audible thump.

Then a silence, broken only by the soft lapping of the Living Waters at the edges of the lake, and James' labored breathing as he fought back sobs. Fabian looked at him then - at his bent, shaking form, and wondered if there was joy in his now-beating heart. Perhaps he was thinking of his wife or his future. Perhaps he was shaken by the return of his mortality.

Finally Iris moved, stepping through the wet grass towards the doctor. Fabian watched her closely, not trusting her to leave James unbitten, but she only sank down in the damp at his side, and put a hand on his shoulder.

"It is alright," she said, and there was gentleness in her voice, even though she most likely did not understand his turmoil. "You're safe here. Nobody else will see you."

James Buckler sank his head into his hands, hiding the first tears he had shed in the three years Fabian had known him.

Fabian's jaw tightened.

"Safe you say." They smoothed both hands over the feathers of their mask, fighting down cold, empty fury. "Far from it, Guardian. Do you realize what you have done to him?"

Iris raised her head, staring unblinkingly at Fabian. "The waters returned him to his natural state," she said. "So he was telling the truth? He was dead before?"

"He was safe before," Fabian hissed.

They didn't want this. They didn't want to have to explain themselves. They didn't want this conversation to happen in front of James.

James, who now lifted his head a fraction, staring at Fabian with wide, overflowing eyes.

Fabian ignored him, raising their voice to Iris as if their words were a shield to be braced in time to parry a blow. "He could not be touched, not by disease or weapon, not by time, or-"

"Or my wife." James interrupted, disbelief warring with horror on his features. He pushed himself up, his clothes still dripping, and wiped the tears from his face. "Safe? You think I was safe, trapped in a corpse's shell?"

"You survived the plague, didn't you?" Fabian shot back at him. "You survived being stabbed, and captured and who knows what else, because I-" They caught themselves, swallowed down the words. No – it was a mistake to explain this now-

James's jaw dropped, and Fabian could all but see the pieces click together in his mind. "You," he breathed, his expression darkening, his eyes still red with tears. "You did this to me... on purpose?"

There was an almost pleading quality to the accusation, as if James wanted Fabian to deny it.

But Fabian did not deny it.

Fabian remained very still, letting their hands slide into their cloak. They looked James in the eye, glad that their mask still concealed their face. "I saved you, Doctor. You had been thrown into the river and drowned. I found you and-"

James pointed a finger at Fabian as if he were brandishing a spear, impaling their words. "When you brought Ruphys back," he said, his voice rising, "he returned as a living man! Flesh and blood! A beating heart! I helped you birth his child!"

This was true, but Fabian made no move to admit it.

James continued, his hand now gripping his own chest, "But me – when you brought me back, it was as this..." he struggled for words, "...monster!"

"I had limited options." Fabian had never seen James this angry: the lifeblood pounded through him, visible in a vein that throbbed in his forehead, in the sweat of anger beading on his brow, in the dilation of his gray eyes. He was gloriously, terribly alive in all his fury.

Fabian closed a hand around one of their knives, though they did not step back. The last thing they wanted was to kill the very doctor they had fought to save, but if he lunged for their neck now, they would not hesitate. "I needed you alive, James. Not susceptible to plague, and-"

"Why not return me properly!" James roared into Fabian's masked face. They automatically braced an arm against his chest, keeping him from moving any closer. "Why not give me true life and bring me back later if you have to! Why condemn me to this miserable-"

"Because I COULD NOT bring back any of the plague victims!" Fabian snarled, shoving him back a pace. Their self control was slipping, but they suddenly didn't care one drop. Old pain bubbled up before they could stop it, infecting their voice. They stalked forward, grabbing James by the wet collar of his white shirt, jerking him close again. "You think I didn't try? My OWN CHILDREN, JAMES, WERE THE FIRST VICTIMS!"

That shut the doctor up. He gaped at Fabian, his gray eyes wide in horror and understanding.

Fabian forced their fingers to uncurl and stepped away from him, breathing heavily. They tried to steady their hands, tried to ward away the adrenaline racing through them, making them shake. "My children," they rasped, "were the first to die. And then my grandchildren - my siblings, and cousins. My daughter - my mother, in this life, was gone in three days. She suffered greatly. And I, I with all my knowledge, all my power, all my magic..."

They hated this. They hated remembering, they hated feeling, they hated every accursed part of the conversation that was happening right now, from the sudden sympathy that had replaced James' anger, to the tears sliding down their own face, hidden by their white, beaked mask.

"I could do nothing. I was...powerless."

Silence from James and Iris.

Fabian turned away, ignoring them both. They forced themselves to take a deep breath. Another. They smoothed their gloved hands down their robes, as if they could soothe away all emotion.

Control. Everything was about control.

This was neither the time nor the place to slip.

"That plague," they said, calmer now, "was designed to destroy me. Anyone who died of it, I could not bring back with any semblance of mind or soul. I invested in young Dr. Barty because he had demonstrated immunity far beyond any he was near – probably due to the complete disconnect between his heritage and mine. But you, James..."

They forced themselves to stand straight, forced themselves to turn and face the doctor. "You, I couldn't be sure of. I did not know if our lines were joined somewhere, back along the twisted trails of time. So yes, Dr. Buckler, I let you die, even if I did not kill you by my own hand. It was the only way to save you."

They stared at each other across the flowers. James still glared, but gone were the hatred and accusations of before.

Finally he turned to Iris and asked in clinical tones, "How long will this last?"

She considered his question. "I am not sure," she

admitted. "These," she gestured at the skulls, "did not come back when they were wetted, so something about you is different from them, even if you are dead. Your healing may be permanent, like a battle wound healed. Or, perhaps, it may last only as long as you have some of the water in your system. I think, ah…"

She peeked at Fabian, who made no acknowledgement of her attention.

"It was your friend here who helped you walk as a dead man, yes?"

James nodded. "Not sure I'd call them a friend," he said gruffly, "not anymore."

Fabian sneered, even though neither could see it. "Blame me all you like," they said, "but you know my actions were correct. It is only logical, Doctor."

He shook his head. "I trusted you," he said bitterly. "Lord knows why I did, but I trusted you."

"That was your first mistake, wasn't it?" Fabian said sarcastically. "Or did you forget who I am?"

James scowled at them and turned away, stripping off his sodden coat. "There will be consequences from this."

"Oh, yes," Fabaian said, nodding. "For now you can die, Doctor, like any man. You can be pierced by arrows or split by a sword. You can hang, choke, or even drown." They looked at Iris. "Thanks to her."

Iris tilted her head, a pinky-white picture of innocence. "You didn't tell me he is dead," she said. "I only thought if he had a disease the waters would punish him for striking me."

"Ugh!" James suddenly burst out. Fabian and Iris both looked at him - but he had turned his coat upside down, shaking out what looked like piles of damp leaves. "All my herb are growing! They've come back too! And my bag-, blast it-"

He ripped open his doctor's bag and dumped its contents clear of the leather. Out fell more green things, taking root even as they hit the already-densely-populated ground. Up sprouted his precious supply of sage and mint, rose and camomile, and countless other things. He stepped back, awestruck.

Iris moved closer, however, examining the new plants curiously. "Ah," she said. "These must be the very same plants Dr. Barty had told me he needed to get back to the world of logic to retrieve."

"Of course they are," James said stiffly, already pulling a knife from his things to take new clippings from the still-growing foliage. "Who do you think trained him in what he was supposed to be carrying? I did."

Fabian bit back the correction that they, too, had contributed to Barty's plant lore. James probably didn't need to know they'd taught the boy a few poisons as well as antidotes.

Iris gave James a coy look, "Then," she said, "you have fulfilled his part of the bargain for him, for the last thing he had promised me were the right kind of plants for treating my daughters."

"Well," James grumbled, waving at the plants, "you certainly have them now, and I'll wager you can spread them as far as you like for a never ending supply."

"That is a great gift indeed," Iris said, slipping closer to him.

James pointedly sheared the head off a rose and stripped away the petals, keeping only the hips to put back in his bag. He said nothing, keeping his thunderous glare on Iris, letting the crushed petals fall.

She only smiled at him. "A gift must be returned," she said gallantly, plucking a rose as well and pulling away the petals with smooth motions of her hard, pale fingers. "And as you have given me *such* a grand gift, then I believe I know just how to reward you in return."

"Do tell," James said in a tone of voice that, to Fabian's ears, was actually saying 'shut up.'

Iris seemed not to hear the undertext, however, and brought the handful of loose petals to her mouth, breathing deeply before she answered. "I have decided," she said at last, "that I will help you find your friend. Only then will our status be even, Doctor."

"I already told you I am not interested in deals." He tore free a sprig of sage with such violence that it came up by the roots.

Iris pulled the roots away from him and planted them back in the ground, giving him a handful of leaves instead. "I will behave myself," she promised, "and if you think my gift puts you back in my debt, well...I suppose you will simply have to teach me more of your healing arts on the way."

Ah, there it was. Fabian rolled their eyes, but said graciously, "We would be most grateful for your assistance in finding our young friend, madam, despite what my damp companion is trying to argue."

Iris hesitated, but nodded to Fabian. "I am glad at least one of you has proper manners," she said, though she again seemed less at ease with Fabian's attention on her.

Fabian bowed low. "Well, you have done me a great favor, madam. It is the least I can do to be gracious in return."

"A favor?" she looked confused, and even more wary. "I do not know what you mean. I thought I had ruined your protection over the doctor."

James snorted, but Fabian ignored him. "You did," they said calmly, folding their hands and striding towards the water. "And if we are being honest, that alone, I believe, would put you seriously in my debt."

Iris' mask-like face went a shade paler. "It had nothing to do with you-"

"However," Fabian spoke over her, "you have the means to repay me immediately available, with no harm coming to you whatsoever."

She gave Fabian a puzzled look, glancing at James in hope of an explanation. "Have I?"

James frowned, but as Fabian drew nearer to the edge of the water, his eyes widened in comprehension. "Good lord," he said. "You don't mean-"

"I do," Fabian said soothingly, spreading their hands over the water. "I do."

And it was so easy, here in Faerie; so easy to feel their power flowing through them, to channel it, to reach with threads of will and command to every neatly-stacked pile of bones in the lake, and summon them - demanding their obedience, their service, and their loyalty.

The Living Waters rippled. They churned. Iris and James both stared, their faces horror struck as, one by one by one, the bones of the dead rose out of the waters of life. The pond erupted with skeletons, all perfectly white and preserved, shining with the gleam of sunlight catching the liquid pouring down their bones.

One by one they trooped out of their damp prison, lining up neatly behind Fabian in rows. Slowly the water level fell, and the banks glittered with exposed, red agates set in dark, clay-like soil. The flowers were swift to converge on this soil, sprouting with voracious speed that was almost dizzying to look at.

Fabian's hands shook, but they kept them raised - kept the power flowing as more and more skeletons rose, until finally the clear waters were empty of white, showing only the dark gray lake bottom, with the occasional flash of crimson, like drops of blood on a velvet shirt.

Fabian sank to their knees at the water's former edge, breathing hard. A glance over their shoulder showed hundreds of skeletons standing in perfect rows, drying under the eternal sunlight in slow, lazy curls of steam.

They'd never raised so many dead in this lifetime. Convincing old bones to move was far harder than fresh corpses, but they'd done it. They'd done it.

Their neck ached under their cowl, the metal of their necklace of power hot, searing against their skin.

"James," they croaked.

The doctor hurried over. "Are you alright?" he asked gruffly. So much for holding a grudge.

261

Fabian made a weak gesture at the water - now several feet further away. "Just thirsty."

James nodded, and trooped down over the new flowers, paying no heed to the ones he crushed. He rescued a jar that had once contained leeches from among the growth, made sure it was empty, then went and filled it from the water. This he brought back to Fabian. "Never knew using necromancy broke your legs."

Fabian managed a chuckle, shifted their mask up, and took the jar in both hands. "I'll be fine in a moment."

They drank deeply, feeling their strength return - more than return, the power of the waters flowed through them, refreshing every fiber of their being. Before they knew it, they'd downed the whole jar, feeling more awake and well rested than they had since the nightmares began.

Good. They wouldn't have to sleep for a while. No risk of further dreams.

They handed the jar back to James, wiped their mouth on their sleeve, and pushed their mask down. Wordlessly, James collected his own mask from the flowers, then offered Fabian a hand, which they accepted, rising to their feet.

Fabian surveyed their skeleton army. Rows and rows of pristine bones, standing in attentive silence, flowers of many colors poking up around their fleshless toes.

A shame they wore no armor, but one couldn't have everything.

"Now," Fabian said with a smile, "If you will be so good as to lead us, madam, we can begin our march. Barty and the Huntsman may have horses, but even horses need to sleep, and if my guess is correct, we do not."

Iris did not answer.

Fabian looked at her - as did James. She had gone a greenish shade of white, a hand over her gaping, toothy jaws, staring at the skeletons.

And then she bowed low to Fabian, her petals all a-tremble with emotion.

"I hear and obey," she whispered.
Fabian smiled.
"Lead on."

CHAPTER 20: DETOUR

Jeremiah was beginning to wish he'd never agreed to this job.

He hadn't intended, originally, to take the young doctor under his protection. He'd expected a long chase with eventual victory; accepting the fellow's blubbering surrender, then escorting a captive who was meekly terrified, confused, and silent. Or perhaps he'd expected something more straightforward - knocking the fellow out and tying him up, carrying him to the King like a gift with a bow. Jeremiah was not a cruel man, but he was used to hunting monsters, and monsters...

"Is this right?" the doctor asked anxiously, showing Jeremiah his hands.

B-a-r-t-y the gloved fingers signed, using the letters

Jeremiah had just taught him.

...Monsters weren't like this. Jeremiah repressed a sigh, and nodded.

Barty's face broke into a beaming smile. "Wonderful! This is so interesting to learn. I truly do appreciate you taking the time to teach me a little bit about this hand-speak."

Jeremiah hesitated, then signed back at Barty - Shilling translating aloud, *'People do not often ask to learn it.'*

"I suppose it isn't often that people expect to spend a few hours in your company, is it?" Barty asked with a sheepish smile. "I mean, it seems like we're going to be riding a while, and we don't have much else to do." He patted his brown horse, who had also been attending the conversation with pricked ears. "Thank you again for the ride, sir."

"You, good Barty!" The horse said happily.

Shilling snickered, and Barty blushed. "Perhaps I should be teaching him more words as well."

"I've been teaching him so far," Shilling said proudly. "We were just doing names when we found you."

"Shilling!" Barty's horse agreed.

"Really?" Barty looked impressed. "Did he tell you what his name is?" And then, to the horse, "Do you have a name, sir?"

"Barty!" said the horse eagerly.

Barty laughed, and even Jeremiah wiped a hand over his mouth to repress a smile.

"That's my name!" Barty said, still grinning. "You need your own name." He looked around, then asked Jeremiah, "How did you name Shilling?" He spelled out S-h-i-l-l-i-n-g alongside his spoken question. Well, actually he spelled 's-g-i-l-l-i-n-h,' but he was still very clearly doing his best.

Jeremiah shook his head, both at the error and the question. He signed 'h' back to Barty, then showed him the sign for a shilling, instead of spelling it out. By the deep woods, he didn't want to be drawn into this silly conversation, but the young doctor had something about him that made it easy to let his guard down. Jeremiah answered the question, once more with Shilling himself translating for Barty's benefit. *'Shilling has his own name aside from the one I gave him, but true names are not shared in this land. I gave him something easy to remember, because of his silver color,'* he hesitated, then added, *'also, it is a pun on the term 'shill'.* "What is a Shill?"

That last was Shilling's question, not Jeremiah's. The silver horse looked to Barty for the answer, apparently having decided that he liked the young doctor.

Barty said, "A shill is a person in a crowd who acts as a sort of...hm. Pretend customer, I suppose? Or a decoy? Usually it's to help sell something, or to encourage people to take a risk in gambling. Sometimes people feel safer putting their money at risk when someone else does it first." He considered the concept a moment. "I guess that makes sense for you, because you can pretend to be other creatures, right? You were the wolf before, and now you are a horse."

Shilling nodded, pleased at being remembered. "That's right! I can do more, too, look!"

He suddenly became a silver giraffe. Jeremiah hissed, clinging to his neck to keep from falling off. Shilling stopped, bending slightly to keep him seated.

Barty gasped and applauded at the transformation. "Amazing!" he said. Then he laughed, running a hand through his curly brown hair. "I saw it with my own eyes and yet I still cannot believe I am seeing it!" He shook his head. "I feel I am supposed to be far more afraid than I am, but I have witnessed so many wonderful things since I got here. I cannot help but appreciate that I get this chance."

His horse, apparently not as impressed with the transformation, turned his head to nudge Barty's boot. "Name!" he insisted. "Name horse. Thank you."

Jeremiah tapped Shilling impatiently, but Shilling pretended not to notice, walking with slow grace in his newly-acquired shape, despite his rider slipping a few dangerous inches. Jeremiah cast Barty a glare, knowing full well who Shilling was showing off for.

Barty was not paying attention to Jeremiah, though, instead considering his own horse's request. "Well, let me see. I could choose something for your color," he stroked the horse's shoulder, "which is brown. Or, I could name you for something special that you do, which is talk, I suppose, or run..."

Jeremiah could tell that Barty was speaking these ideas aloud not for his own sake, but for the sake of the horse, using words for simple things that the beast would understand easily.

The horse certainly listened, his ears turned back towards Barty, even as he continued walking forwards. "Run... brown..." he repeated, chewing over the words as if they were new flavors.

Suddenly, Barty smiled. "I know what's brown and runs. The river Thames! It talks too - it babbles and whispers. What do you think, horse?" He patted the horse's neck. "Would you like to be called Thames?"

"Yes!" The horse nodded, his mane flopping about with his eagerness. "Tems!! Good. Good Barty."

"I see he's coming along well."

Jeremiah turned his head downwards. The talking wolf - mentally, Jeremiah had named him 'Gravel,' for the sound of his voice - had reappeared, trotting alongside Shilling. The wolf's yellow eyes roamed up and down Shilling's long legs and neck, and he shook his head. "Not good to attract so much attention around here."

Jeremiah prodded Shilling's shoulder. The great giraffe sighed and shifted down again, once more a silver horse.

"Good lord! A talking wolf! Is he another friend?" Barty asked, trying to peer around Jeremiah at the wolf.

Jeremiah ignored him. *Make your report,* he told Gravel.

Jeremiah could tell the wolf was uneasy. His ears lay flat, and the hackles on his shoulders bristled. "The road has changed," he growled.

Jeremiah sat back, surprised. Then he leaned forward again, signing as quickly as he could, *What do you mean? How* could the road have changed? The King himself is waiting for us.'

The wolf licked his chops anxiously. "The only thing I can think of," he said, "is that someone on our path has a need greater than that of the King."

Jeremiah stared at the wolf, his shock bleeding slightly into wonder, even curiosity. 'That is an uncommon occurrence,' he said. 'Where are we being taken?'

The wolf pointed with his muzzle. "If my nose is correct," he said, "we are going to one of the boroughs. But the scent is off. Strong, and foul. Something is wrong there."

Jeremiah's heart sank. He didn't have time for sidetracking. The King waited for him, and would not be pleased with any delays, roads or no roads.

Before he could ask further questions, however, Barty butted in, touching his forehead as if tipping a hat. "I beg your pardon for overhearing," he said, "but I have to ask - what does it smell like?" His brow was furrowed in worry, as if he already suspected an answer.

The wolf faced him. "Like blood," he said. "Like excrement, and rot. Like sickness."

"Plague," Barty breathed. "Even here. Well, sir," he glanced at Jeremiah, "there's your answer."

'My answer?'

The young doctor nodded, tapping the beaked mask hanging from his belt. "I am a plague doctor," he said firmly. "It is I that is needed."

He spoke with such resigned confidence, Jeremiah felt no need to argue. He simply sighed. 'Run ahead and tell them we are coming,' he told Gravel, hoping to get the distraction over as quickly as possible. 'And send one of your pack to tell the King what has happened.'

Gravel gave a snort. "I don't envy the one delivering that message," he said, "but it will be done."

'Thank you,' Jeremiah signed.

The wolf gave a last nod and bounded off, a howl rising as he went.

Shilling snorted and shook his head. "I don't like going to the boroughs," he said, prancing a little in his steps.

Jeremiah gave his neck a few strokes of reassurance. '*I know. We won't be there long - and they will have other things on their minds than giving you a hard time.*'

"Excuse me-"

Jeremiah looked over at Barty again, raising both his eyebrows. The doctor blushed, aware he was interrupting the silent conversation. "Sorry to keep bothering you. But you see," he gestured down at his disheveled, damp form, "I lost all my supplies in the river. Will there be anywhere I can pick herbs on the way? Or will it all be..." he waved a hand at the dead trees and ashy ground, "...like this?"

Jeremiah frowned, thinking. He didn't spend much time in the boroughs - they weren't fond of his profession, and some found Shilling's presence insulting. '*I cannot answer that in any sureness,*' he said at last, shrugging. '*Keep an eye out. Perhaps we will find something.*'

Barty nodded. "You hear that, Thames?" he said to his horse. "Keep an eye out for plants, alright?"

"Plants!" Thames agreed. "Alright, Barty!"

Shilling sighed heavily, his great ribs shifting Jeremiah's legs. He turned his head with a mournful expression. "We can't let anything bad happen to them, master," he said, his voice unusually low and serious - as if Jeremiah himself were speaking the words of his heart aloud.

Jeremiah nodded, but said nothing. He didn't know what would be demanded of him or of Barty - and he didn't know how far the King would push his authority. Jeremiah would do what he could to protect the young doctor, but that was not entirely a comfort, because when faced with the Faceted King, there was not much one could do.

'*Let's hurry,*' he told Shilling, nudging the horse into a trot.

***

Dawn broke as they neared the borough, the strengthening sun casting streaks of gold among the deep, purple shadows. Jeremiah was glad of it - both for his own sake, as he preferred to face social situations in full light, and for the sake of Dr. Barty, who had been nodding off on his horse, almost falling more than once.

"Sorry," the young doctor apologized with a yawn. "I worked a full day treating plague before we even got here."

'You are missing your chances to identify herbs,' Jeremiah told him. *'Look, there is more life here.'*

For indeed there was. This close to the borough, the King had left the lands alone, and trees grew with proper leaves, vines displayed their verdant splendor, and shrubbery and bracken overtook the twigs and dust, carpeting the earth with thriving plant life. Jeremiah felt far more at ease, reminded of the forests where he'd honed his trade.

Barty nodded, glancing about at the green and signing *'thank you.'* He was picking up on the signing language quickly.

Jeremiah couldn't remember the last time someone had wanted to speak to him in his own way - a fact didn't want to think about now. It was just going to make all this harder.

"So," Barty said, leaning over the side of Thames' back to try and get a better look at the shadowy underbrush. "What kind of people live in this borough?"

Jeremiah replied and Shilling translated, allowing the doctor to keep looking and hear the answer. *'It depends which borough we're being taken to. They are all similar in that they descend from old, old faerie families. They band together to have authority and representation under the King's rulership. The families themselves, however, are drastically different. Shilling comes from the borough of Shifters - you've seen his shape changing ability.'* "I'm very good, aren't I?"

Jeremiah gave Shilling a gentle tug on the mane, silently scolding him for interjecting his own commentary into the conversation.

"That's amazing!" Barty said, glancing up from his search to look at the horse in admiration. "What other boroughs are there?"

'There's lycans - similar to shifters, but with their transformations limited to a single beast, and often directed by seasonal or lunar periods. There's the mageborn, who are completely obsessed with pushing the limits of magic - if you can think of an enchantment, they've probably tried it. There's the Yoldenfolk, who are... I'm still not sure what they are. I think they lived here long before humans arrived-'

"What do the Yoldenfolk look like?" Barty asked eagerly, his search forgotten.

Jeremiah shrugged. *'Like things of the land - like stones or water, trees or earth. It's debatable whether they live in a borough at all, or are just everywhere, and maintain a borough only for the sake of communication with outsiders. And then there's - oh. Well, here we are, anyway.'*

Jeremiah pointed ahead. Through the trees, though still deeply immersed in the forest, pale blue lights huddled together; windows, he could see as they neared, lit from within in a shade completely different from firelight. Beside him, Barty leaned forward in his shadow, peering eagerly at the periwinkle shine.

'They call themselves 'Decided,' Jeremiah explained, Shilling's voice of translation clearly unhappy with where they ended up. *'According to legend, they were once changelings closer to the nature of Shifters; but instead of honing the ability to shift, they settled on forms they liked and kept them. Strange shapes – forms between forms - nothing truly reflected in nature.'* "They think they're better than everyone." Shilling added his opinion once more. "They think they've achieved perfection in form and that anyone who still shifts is unstable and uncivilized. But they don't know how fun it is! And just because they make up their own shapes doesn't make them better than Shifters, either!" Shilling shook his head, fluffing his silver mane. "We appreciate the beauty and variety of the natural world!"

Jeremiah gave a little huff, irritated at his tale being spoken over again. *'They can be reasonable folk,'* he told Barty, *'but Shilling is right - many of them, especially the older generations, tend to look down on anyone who appears too...'* He hesitated, searching for the right word. *"raw."*

"So what should I do?" Barty asked, clearly worried about his own role in the ever-approaching meeting. "I'm just a human - will they still listen to me? Will they accept medical help from someone who is, uh, raw?"

'Believe it or not,' Jeremiah leaned across and poked the doctor's beaked mask where it hung from his belt, *'this might help your case. Even if you can't change, you have the decency to hide your nakedness.'*

Barty looked thoughtful, but pulled the mask from his belt and buckled it on. "I wish I had my hat," he said mournfully. "And my coat. I wager they would help too."

'You can borrow my spare cloak if you like,' Jeremiah offered. *'It has a hood.'*

Barty accepted with obvious relief. So it was that, as they rode up to the heavy gates that barred entrance to the walled city of the Decided, Jeremiah felt like he was at the side of a particularly large bird, for the hood of his spare cloak was a good one, deep and long, and between the black leather of the doctor's beaked mask and the gray, color of the cloth, Barty looked very much like a hooded crow.

Jeremiah rode with his own hood down, face unhidden keeping his silver eyes, gray hair, and dark skin plain for all to see.

Clear, too, was the scar across his throat. Even here, in the borough of the Decided, they would know who he was.

Hunter of monsters.

They approached the dark gates, the heavy, cloying scent of death wafting between the metal-wrought shapes of flowers and fantastical beings. Barty gave Jeremiah an expectant look, but Jeremiah only shook his head and gestured to the gate. If the doctor was the reason they'd come here, the doctor could be the one to deal with the Decided and their problems.

Barty laid hold of a great brass knocker in the shape of an owl-cat and knocked, the sound ringing out clearly, resonating off the walls of the homes beyond the gate. Jeremiah wondered how the buildings looked to Barty. He still remembered how he'd felt, the first time he'd seen them; sophisticated structures painted so heavily in dark colors, one could not tell the material they were made of. Each building was adored with intricate, endlessly complex designs of silver, copper and gold worked into the wood and paint, proudly showing the history of the occupants. Judging by Barty's staring, it was a lot to take in.

The heavy gate remained closed, however. No heads poked out of windows, no curious children or animals ran along the cobblestone road up to see who had knocked.

"Don't they know we're coming?" Barty asked anxiously. "We sent the wolf ahead-"

A noise interrupted his worry. The clopping of hooves, slow and deliberate - strangely patterned after a day spent riding horses. Horses, after all, had four feet alternatively clipping the ground.

These hoofbeats were paced like a man's steps instead.

A single figure emerged from a smaller building to the left of the gate. He wore a long tailcoat, black as midnight, with patterns of leaves in gray, and buttons of silver. The rest of him, however, was covered in dense, dark fur, from the bases of his four arched, ribbed horns, all the way to the joints where his legs ended in hooves. His face was goatlike, or at least, Jeremiah thought wryly, as if someone had started with a goat, and then decided to remove as much flesh as possible. Gaunt was the ideal word, with deep shadows, bony angles and yellow eyes that glittered at the travelers out of dark sockets.

He surveyed the travelers in silence, his horizontal-pupiled eyes flicking from Barty to Jeremiah, lingering on the scar across Jeremiah's neck, and finally taking in the horses.

At last he gave a small nod, and spoke in a deep,

rich voice that contrasted chillingly with his menacing appearance, "We have been awaiting you."

He lifted the bar holding the gate closed. His hands, Jeremiah noticed, were something between hooves and proper fingers, finely boned but with black, claw-like tips taking up the entire last joint.

"W-we came as fast as we could!" Barty said. "Though I am afraid I may not be as much use as I wish to be, as I have lost most of my supplies on the way here."

The gatekeeper eyed Barty impassively. Jeremiah wondered if he was actually being impassive, or if his skin-and-bone face was simply not capable of showing emotion. "Nevertheless," the fellow said, "you must do the best you can."

Jeremiah snorted to himself. Yes, that was just how the Decided asked for help. *You must.*

Still, the horned gentleman opened the gate for them, and closed it again once they had ridden through. From behind they could see a black mane that fell down past his shoulders, and a long, thin tail with a brush on the end, like that of a lion.

The gatekeeper put the key back in his pocket. "Please leave your raw beasts in the stables," he said, looking directly at Shilling.

"Hey!" Shilling burst out, "I'm more than just a beast!"

The gatekeeper shook his head, his expression unchanged. "You certainly have not Decided," he said, "and you are not here to help. Therefore, you will be cared for, but you must remain where your presence will not distress those who are ill."

"Decided?" Thames repeated, surprising Jeremiah and Barty, who seemed to have forgotten for a moment that his horse could talk.

The gatekeeper treated the question seriously, however, turning to the horse and nodding his four-horned head. "You," he said, "are still Deciding what you want to be. This one," he pointed at Shilling with a dark nail, "refuses to Decide."

Shilling grumbled. The gatekeeper looked to Jeremiah.

"Explain it to him, in a way he will understand."

Jeremiah sighed, but dismounted, stroking Shilling's long face with one hand, signing with the other. *'They asked the same of you last time we were here, my friend. Think about it like humans and clothes.'*

"What do you mean?" Shilling asked sulkily.

'In human society, very small children can get away with not wearing clothes because they do not know better. But if an adult man were to walk around without clothes, it would be embarrassing for him, and perhaps arouse great feelings of dislike in other humans.'

"But that Decided ISN'T wearing proper clothes! If a man walked around in only a coat and his bottom sticking out-"

Barty, overhearing, choked in the middle of requesting supplies from the gatekeeper. He hurriedly went off to deliver Thames to the stable, a hand over his mouth.

Jeremiah had to repress a smile, but nodded. *'You are correct. If he were a human in human society, his manner of dress would not be acceptable. He, too, would have to wait out of the way while the rest of his companions attended to business.'*

Shilling signed, but nodded. "Fine," he grumbled, "but I won't wait in the stable."

He shifted, turning into a very small serpent. He slithered up Jeremiah's leg, over his shoulder, and finally onto his head, curling himself around Jeremiah's brow like a silver circlet.

"There," he said, in a very small hiss. "Now I can still help translate for Barty, and I just look like one of their silly decorations they have everywhere."

Jeremiah smiled. *'That is a clever solution.'* He looked to the gatekeeper. *'Is this acceptable?'*

The gatekeeper, who had apparently been ignoring them and examining the clasp that held his coat together (silver, in the shape of twisting vines) nodded. Jeremiah wasn't sure if he was imagining it, but he thought he detected amusement in those strange yellow eyes. "It is well," said the gatekeeper. He glanced back to where Barty had gone, and, once the masked doctor hurried to rejoin them, said, "follow me."

Jeremiah and Barty followed. The rising sun now penetrated the leaf cover above, dappling the houses of the borough with light and warmth. Jeremiah, who had been here only once in the distant past, found himself admiring the metalwork on the homes. Here was one with a bear and sheep motif, and large, hulking shapes moving within, silhouetted against their windows. There was a small home worked all over with copper mice and butterflies, with a figure in a pale dress and silvery wings ushering two squabbling youngsters indoors, holding them each by their large ears as they fluttered and squalled in indignant protest. Yet another home bore so many different creatures on the outside in so many shades of metal it was near impossible to guess what sort of folk slept within, but as the house was one of the largest and grandest they had passed yet, Jeremiah wagered that it was someone well respected among the community.

"What can you tell me of the sickness?" Barty asked the gatekeeper, "and how would you like to be called, sir?"

"I am called Grimley," the gatekeeper gave a small bow, "and the situation is thus: not two days ago, one of our number returned from a journey to the King." He walked with his hands behind his back, steps slow and deliberate, and his manner of speaking reminded Jeremiah of how men of the church spoke - with a steady, almost rehearsed tone.

Grimley continued, "She was in poor condition - thin and dirty, red of eye and with blood on her breath. She collapsed as soon as she was through the gate, but managed to tell us what happened: she had been imprisoned by the King for many days, and had only escaped by..." Grimley paused with a shiver that ruffled his mane, "...changing her form - becoming small enough to slip through the bars and escape the castle."

Barty, looking puzzled, asked, "What reason did she give for her imprisonment? And has anyone else fallen ill since she returned? Is she still alive?"

Grimley hesitated, and Jeremiah sensed embarrassment behind his dignified pause.

"Berthelia is...full of grand notions for the world. She speaks constantly of improvement and growth, despite there being so few who agree with her desires. It is not the first time she has petitioned the King for the establishment of safe trade routes, or inter-barrow schools. However..." his voice took on a mournful edge that sounded at least a little genuine, "...I fear it may be the last. I can only assume she went too far in her suggestions, and the King took insult. As for your next question..."

Grimley sighed.

"Everyone who cared for her has fallen ill as well. It starts with a fever, and a cough. Then sore spots under the fur, and reddening eyes. As soon as we realized what was happening, we quarantined all the afflicted, but that did not stop it from spreading to at least a dozen. There may be more by the end of the day."

He cleared his throat delicately.

Barty cast Jeremiah a grim look. "I was right," he muttered. "Plague. Probably the same one we saw in Whiston. But why is it here? Surely it is not easy to pass disease from the human land to Faerie?"

'It is not,' Jeremiah agreed. 'Almost all the ways between are closed.'

Grimley flicked his tail in an impatient manner, as if annoyed that they bothered consulting each other when he was right there. "Berthelia was held in the prison," he said again. "She mentioned other prisoners who were ill. I would assume that one of the prisoners is a human who failed in his deal, and is being punished for his crimes."

Barty frowned. The tone of Grimley's voice made it clear that this was to be expected of humans - there was no shred of sympathy for a sick prisoner.

"As for your last question," Grimley continued, "she yet

lives, but we do not know for how long."

"Take me to her," Barty said. "And I'll need hot water, and - this is going to be so hard without my herbs, but if you'll give me pen and paper I will write a list of what I need."

Jeremiah touched the doctor's shoulder to get his attention, then signed to him, with Shilling translating, *'They won't have much in terms of of healing herbs. Disease is rare in this land - you had best make your list of things equally used for cooking or dyes.'*

Barty looked stricken at this, raising his gaze to Grimley. "Is this true?"

Grimley nodded. "We Decided do not succumb to ills as humans do. It is a mark of weaker existence to be prey to such things."

Barty stared at him, eyes wide behind his mask. "Weaker existence!" he repeated at last, and Jeremiah was amused to hear, for the first time, anger in the young doctor's voice. "You mean sheltered existence, I suppose! Otherwise this is terribly embarrassing for you, isn't it, to ask a weaker being like a human for help in fighting off an illness that you are supposed to be above?"

Grimley shook his head - much like a horse would shake its mane to be rid of flies. "It is," he agreed solemnly, "deeply embarrassing. And yet," he looked at Barty with both his strange yellow eyes, "we love our families more than we dislike strangers. And so we will stoop to this depth of humiliation, if it will save those who are suffering. Do you understand, human?"

Jeremiah could see Barty's jaw clench as his pride and compassion warred within. He wondered if the indignity of being referred to as a lesser being made the doctor reassess whether he wanted to help after all. On the other hand, Barty's heart was that of a caregiver - even Jeremiah could see that.

In the end it seemed the latter of the two impulses won out; for Barty said stiffly, "It is for her sake that I help, and not for the sake of a people who are so...so..."

"Aloof," Grimley said, not at all insulted. "We know what we are."

"Well maybe you ought to be trying for more than that," Barty snipped back at him, pulling the hood of his cloak more firmly in place.

Grimley swished his tail, giving Barty an unreadable look. "And who are you," he said, "to be telling us what we should and should not do?"

"I'm the fellow you are asking for help!" Barty said. "And I'll give it to you whether you like it or not, so lead on!"

Jeremiah had to repress a chuckle. It was gratifying to see the doctor flash some backbone for the first time since they'd met.

Grimley shook his head, but did lead on. They walked past the homes, gardens and streets, orchards and wells, and even a water-powered mill, churning away in the dawn light. Finally, after having traveled through what felt like the entire borough, Grimley stopped in front of a small, unguilded building. He gestured at it with one hoof-nailed hand. "This," he said, "is where she lies, along with those who had been her caretakers and have since fallen ill."

Jeremiah hesitated, but Barty didn't - marching straight up to the doorway. He glanced over his shoulder at Jeremiah. "You should not come in," he said. "You don't have a mask, and I would not want you to risk plague."

Jeremiah couldn't stand idly by while the doctor endangered himself. He pulled his scarf out from under his gear, wrapped it around his face, and asked Barty, *'Will this suffice? I imagine a second pair of hands would be useful to you.'*

Barty, after a moment's hesitation, nodded. "Do please be careful," he said. "Don't touch anything if you can help it. And watch out for fleas."

Fleas? Jeremiah didn't understand, but he nodded. Shilling slithered down to his shoulder and promptly turned into a small silver frog - to catch any threatening fleas, Jeremiah assumed.

Together, he and Barty entered the sickroom, leaving Grimley waiting on the street.

The air reeked of sweat, blood, and other fluids Jeremiah didn't really want to think about. Once this had been a modest sitting room, cozy with furniture and a simple table arranged around a fireplace. Now, however, it was a place of despair, with six figures bundled on the floor and one on the couch.

Barty was already examining the bodies on the floor, his touch gentle but unhesitating. "Why," he observed softly, "they're all wolves! Like the ones you travel with Jeremiah, only...different."

Jeremiah leaned over one of the bundled forms. Sure enough, a wolfish figure lay there, though his paws were more hand-like, with long, claw-tipped fingers that still retained canid-esque pads. It was clear by how he lay, flat on his back rather than on his side like a true wolf, that he was a creature of upright posture.

"Wolves often try to join the Decided," Shilling explained in his little froggy voice. "They are pack animals. It is easy for them to want to belong to something."

Barty gaped at Jeremiah and Shilling. "Are you saying... are you saying the people in this town were animals first? Animals who grew into human shapes?"

Jeremiah shrugged, and signed, '*That is often the case, but not always.*'

"Wow," Barty breathed. "So that is why Grimley called Thames 'undecided.' He could turn into one of them too, if he wished? This place is so wondrous."

"Isn't it, though?" said a weak voice from the couch.

Barty and Jeremiah both moved to look.

There lay the most unusual creature of all. The immediate comparison was a lion, but no lion had vivid green scales arranged like jewelry along its snout and cheeks, nor catfish-like whiskers protruding from a golden furred muzzle. Twin pale, forked horns arched back over the being's coppery mane, and purple-red skin showed through at the lip and eye where no fur grew.

Jeremiah let out a surprised breath of recognition. He gave Shilling the frog a little prod to get his attention, then told Barty, '*She is of the Primus family - they were the first ones in this borough. You saw their house, it was the one with the greatest variety of animals decorating the sides.*'

"Oh, I see! So, ah..." Barty cleared his throat. "You are Berthelia Primus, madam?"

Barthelia nodded, just barely cracking open eyes that were as green as her scales. She managed a weak smile, rasping, "I am, though I don't know for how much longer."

When she caught sight of Barty and opened her eyes a little wider. " Oh! You are..."

A cough interrupted her - a terrible, wet cough that made it sound as if air couldn't possibly get past all the fluid within. She fell back, exhausted and wheezing. "I am sorry," she whispered, flecks of red covering her sharp, leonine teeth. "I didn't realize I had brought disease back to my home. I am afraid..." her eyes filled with tears. "I am afraid I have murdered all the hopefuls with my carelessness."

Barty stroked one of her gold-furred hand-paws. To Jeremiah's eye he looked like a man who knew the worst was coming, but did his best to hide it, his shoulders slumped as if a great weight had settled on his back. "Don't worry about them," the doctor said soothingly. "Save your strength for yourself, Berthelia-"

"Please," she said with a grimace, "call me Theli." Her voice caught on her name, and she had to stop, breathing deeply and slowly, her catfish-like whiskers drooping.

Barty nodded. " Theli. Ah... I have asked for some hot water, um. I don't... I don't actually know how much I'll be able to help you, for if your illness is the same I came into this land seeking the cure of, it is magical in origin-"

She opened her eyes again, staring at Barty with pupils that dilated from slits to round orbs. "Magical...?" She spoke the word in tones of wonder, rather than fear.

281

Barty faltered a moment, but continued on, "B-but maybe I can make something that will at least soothe your pain a little." He shook his head. "Gracious, if what Grimley told me is true, and you caught this in the King's own dungeon, I wonder if there will be anyone left alive when we get there."

Theli's heavy paw closed on the front of Barty's cloak, and she pulled him closer, interest kindling in her eyes, visibly lending her strength. "Tell me," she said, her curiosity outshining even the heat of her fever. "Tell me more about these things. About...the magic behind this illness, and how it is cured, and why you are going to see the King. I want..." she let him go, covering her mouth to cough more and falling back once again on the pillows. "I want...to know all. I have...a notebook under my pillow. Give it to me and I will write down all you say."

Barty gave Jeremiah a puzzled look. Jeremiah shrugged, and signed, '*I will go find the hot water.*'

He left Barty explaining everything to Theli. The doctor had, he observed, taken out the book, but was writing in it himself, intuiting that his patient didn't have the strength to keep up with his words.

Jeremiah returned to the street. Grimley was still there, waiting.

'*Hot water?*' Jeremiah asked. And also, because he couldn't help his curiosity, '*Is she always so fixated on new information?*'

"She questioned the human the moment she saw him, didn't she?" Grimley asked, amusement creeping into his voice even though his face remained stoic. "Yes, curiosity has ever been her strongest trait. It runs in her family. It skipped a generation with her father, but her grandparents and great grandparents were always exploring other realms and seeking out exciting discoveries. In fact, the rumor is that the reason the Primus members are so extravagant in their appearance is because Berthelia's great, great, great grandmother explored all the way into the human lands. She was so impressed with everything she saw, she simply could not Decide on one or two, and chose pieces of five beings to be her Decision."

'*I am surprised you know so much of their history,*' Jeremiah said, raising an eyebrow at the stuffy, arrogant gatekeeper.

"Ah, well. I did some traveling myself, in my younger days." Grimley said in a tone that was both proud and did not invite further questions. "And, if I am not mistaken, here comes your hot water."

A large creature puffed its way up to them, a heavy kettle held in two paws. It was one of the bear-shaped folk, Jeremiah observed, but with curling ram's horns and wooly, carefully styled fur.

"Hot water," growled the newcomer, offering the pot to Jeremiah while avoiding looking at his face. "And we do not have most of the other things you ask for - willows do not grow in this place, nor do many of the plants on your list. There is only garlic," he handed over a small bundle.

Jeremiah repressed a sigh. Why had they even been summoned here, if the things needed to cure people were not available? He accepted the hot water and bundle of garlic anyway, and bowed low to the wooly bearer.

The fellow turned without another word and ambled away, clearly quite annoyed at having to come such a long distance for a mission so beneath him.

Jeremiah shook his head. '*I doubt the doctor will be able to accomplish much, with only hot water and garlic, but I imagine he will do his best with what he has.*'

Grimley nodded. "That is all we can ask for." He hesitated, then added, "Berthelia... reminds me of an age when things were different. I do hope you can help her pull through."

Jeremiah nodded, finding his dislike of the goat-man lessoning some. '*We'll do what we can,*' he signed, and went back to the sickroom.

He found Barty pacing up and down, Theli having fallen asleep again. As soon as Jeremiah entered, the young doctor spun to face him.

"I can't do this!" he whispered, his voice cracking. "She's dying even now! All of them have plague tokens under their fur - all of them have bleeding gums, red eyes, fever - and I! What do I have? Nothing! Not even the amulets I bled for, all my supplies were lost in the river! Did they at least send us something to help?"

Jeremiah sheepishly showed him the garlic.

Barty let out a manic laugh, pulling at his curls with both fists. "What am I even doing here, sir?!"

Jeremiah set the steaming kettle on the table, and gripped Barty's shoulders with both his hands, steadying him. He didn't need to sign - for Shilling knew his heart well enough to say the words they both meant. *"All you can do, Doctor, is do what you can."*

"But what can I do?" Barty whispered, and Jeremiah could hear his tears, even as the lenses of his mask fogged from heat and moisture. "I have nothing! No herbs, no amulets, no knowledge of where this curse lies-"

"You do have something!" Shilling said suddenly, "I smelled it on you before! What is in your mask, if not herbs? What is that sweet smell?"

Barty froze, his hand going to the leather beak. "I...It is only mint and sage, but...but I suppose a soothing tea is better than nothing." He paused a moment, then added, his voice a bit more hopeful. "M-mint and sage that...that were revitalized in the Living Waters."

That made Jeremiah raise his eyebrows. *'I think,'* he signed, *'you had better set about making that tea, Doctor Barty.'* He handed the pot over.

Barty accepted it with trembling hands. "S-see if they have any cups, will you sir, please?" He removed his mask, and, pulling out the leaves from within the beak, began shredding them into the pot.

Jeremiah obliged, searching the cabinets of the little house. He found a half-eaten, very stale loaf of bread, and some dried out old apples. A crumbly old cheese and a handful of dried beans joined his collection, and a half-empty sack of rubbery turnips. Finally, in the same cabinet as a stack of chipped plates and a collection of old, tarnished silverware, he found half a dozen tin cups, which he lifted out in a stack.

He brought the cups back to Barty. *'Judging by the state of their cupboards,'* he signed, *'they haven't had much to eat lately.'*

A flash of anger crossed Barty's face. "For all the Decided's 'superior nature,'" he muttered, the words as low as they were sharp, "they have a very subpar way of taking care of the needy in their community."

'Are humans any better?' Jeremiah asked wryly.

Barty hesitated. "Some are," he said at last, and began to pour tea into the cups. "I don't suppose there was any honey in the cupboards? A little sugar might do well for their strength."

Jeremiah shook his head. *'Only turnips.'*

"Bring them along, if you would be so good," Barty said, already picking up cups. "We can light a fire in the hearth and make a turnip soup with the rest of the hot water. They might not even be able to get it down, but it's worth a try." He pulled his mask back over his face, and returned to tending his patients, bearing cups of the mint-and-sage tea.

Jeremiah nodded and went, first to light the fire, then back to the cupboards. He retrieved the turnips, as well as the beans, and set them on the table. After a moment spent watching Barty coax Theli into drinking a bit of tea, he drew his sword and, using the part of the blade nearest the handle, began to chop the roots as best he could.

One by one, Barty took cups of herbal tea to all his patients. One by one Jeremiah diced the turnips, throwing them into a pot he found, along with the garlic, the beans, some of his own supply of salt and dried pork, and the rest of the hot water from the kettle.

By the time Jeremiah had finished with the last root, Barty returned to the table, his expression grim. "I was able to wake them to make them drink - I believe Theli has the worst of it, the others fell ill more recently, and all at the same time. From what I understand, they thought being the ones to care for her would gain them favor with the Decided." He shook his head. "Honestly, making those they view as 'lesser' expose themselves to disease so they don't have to help themselves? This whole place is ill, not just Theli."

'That's often the way of things, unfortunately,' Jeremiah told him, heaving the pot off the table and over to the fire. He hung it there, then stepped back, wiping his hands on his tunic. 'Now what?'

"Now we wait," Barty said, shrugging weary shoulders. "You don't have to stay here if you don't want to. I imagine they have better lodgings somewhere, for a servant of the King."

'I am not his servant,' Jeremiah signed sharply. 'I am a Huntsman, and I have been hired to do a task. It is not the same thing.'

Barty looked surprised, but accepted the correction. "I do beg your pardon," he said, tugging on his hood again. "I was not aware."

'It's alright.' Jeremiah walked towards the fire and sat down beside it, with his back against the hearth, folding his arms. He closed his eyes, making it clear he didn't want to speak about the subject further.

"We'll stay," Shilling told Barty, seeming pleased about it.

"I'm glad," was Barty's soft reply.

Jeremiah heard the shift of cloth and leather as Barty settled down on the other side of the fireplace. Soon the doctor's soft, steady breathing joined the ambiance of the fire and boiling stew pot.

Jeremiah remembered Barty had already worked a full day of trying to cure plague even before he'd arrived in Faerie.

He wondered what it was like, living a life keeping people alive, instead of ending creatures too terrible to tolerate.

He pulled out his sword, and looked at it.

It was a bit sticky from chopping turnips.

He took the edge of his cloak and cleaned the blade, wondering if he had saved as many people as the young doctor had, by killing, instead of healing. He laid the weapon across his knees, watching the firelight dance along the steel.

He didn't realize he'd nodded off until words shook him out of his dozing state. At first he thought he'd dreamed them, only, they came a second time.

"I said, is anybody there? What is that good smell? I'm starving!"

Both Jeremiah and Barty sat up, Jeremiah's sword clattering to the floor. As one they turned to the couch.

Theli was sitting upright in her blankets. Her mane was mussed, her fur rumpled from where the plague pockmarks had been, but her green eyes were bright and clear. Even her catfish-like whiskers had some perk to them.

Barty jumped up immediately. "Turnip stew!" he gasped. "I'm afraid it isn't much, madam, but it's hot and healthful!"

"I would very much like some, please," she said, her ears perking in eagerness. "And also, can you tell me who you are, and where you come from? And what did you put in that tea?"

A sound of snuffling and stirring accompanied her words - the wolves, too, were lifting themselves up, wet noses twitching in hopeful appreciation.

Jeremiah retrieved his sword and slid it back into its sheath, then reached out to pat the back of Dr. Barty, whose eyes visibly overflowed with tears. The doctor's gaze drank in the room of formerly-dying patients, now stirring with miraculous life.

"Of course," Barty said at last, casting Jeremiah a grateful look but moving towards the fire. "Of course! I'll bring food to everyone."

Jeremiah tapped Barty's shoulder and signed '*I'll fetch bowls*,' unable to repress a smile.

Barty hugged him, quite to Jeremiah's shock. "Thank you," he said, his voice muffled against Jeremiah's shoulder. "And I don't just mean... well. Thank you, sir."

Jeremiah didn't particularly like hugs - he avoided physical contact with people as much as possible. However, he could feel Barty trembling, and managed to gingerly pat the doctor's back a second time.

"You're welcome!" Shilling sang in a froggy cheep, sounding justifiably proud that his suggestion had worked.

The doctor laughed and let go of Jeremiah, reaching to give Shilling a little pat as well with one gloved finger. "Y-yes, thank you too, Shilling. That was a brilliant, brilliant idea. Thank you both."

'Let's serve the soup,' Jeremiah signed, hurrying to fetch the bowls before Barty tried to hug him again. Even as he went to the other room, he could hear Theli starting up with her questions again. "That mask, what does it mean? Were you seeking to join the Decided as well? A beak is a very difficult transition from a mouth, I will warn you."

"I am afraid not! This mask is for protection from plague."

Jeremiah gathered up the bowls and returned to the fireplace. 'At this rate,' he signed to Shilling, 'The good doctor is going to start a new trend among the fae, with that mask.'

"That would be an improvement!" Shilling said, stealing a sliver of turnip with his long tongue. He promptly yelped and dropped it. "Ow! Remember when they heard humans were wearing wigs?"

'Every changeling through the realm had straw, fur, or hair dripping all over them.' Jeremiah chuckled, picked the sliver of turnip off the floor, and handed it back to Shilling. The little changeling gnawed on it happily with his toothless gums. Jeremiah took soup to each recovering patient while Barty explained plague and plague masks to Theli. At least Theli was letting him speak, so fascinated she didn't eat the soup Jeremiah pressed into her claws until Barty asked her to. Even then she sipped automatically, her gaze not leaving the doctor's face.

Jeremiah handed a bowl to each wolf. They were sitting

up now, looking puzzled but alert. One of them grabbed his sleeve and asked in a surprisingly clear voice, "Is this real? Are we cured?"

Jeremiah pressed the bowl of soup into the wolf's hand-shaped paws, but looked to Barty for the answer.

Barty hesitated. "I don't know," he said finally. "I don't know if this is a permanent cure, or a temporary reprieve. My advice is to gain what strength you can, and pray that we find, and stop, whatever is causing this illness."

The wolf nodded. "Even if it is only a few days," he said, "I bless you for it. I want to help, if there is anything I can do."

'Focus on resting for now.' Jeremiah told him.

The wolf nodded and began lapping up the stew.

Jeremiah stepped away.

He could not remember the last time his heart had felt this heavy.

What was he doing? Helping sick creatures, while also bringing their doctor to the King, who had nothing but ill intentions? Was it really worth gaining his own freedom at the price of such a kind soul being made captive?

Should Jeremiah risk the wrath of the most powerful being in all of Faerie - a being that knew his full and true name - by advising Barty to run, instead of continuing on his quest?

And yet, he knew even if he warned Barty of the danger, the doctor would press on. The King was a selfish, conniving creature of closed heart and open cruelty, but it was still true that the key to the cure for the plague lay in the King's hands.

From what Jeremiah had seen of the boy, he was not one to be easily dissuaded from his goal.

Jeremiah had no choice but to continue. No choice, but to look at his own part in this charade, and wonder.

Was there another way?

CHAPTER 21: READJUSTING

James Buckler thanked his benevolent stars he had a student to teach.

Iris's presence meant he could pour his focus and energy into something controllable - something he was master of. When listing to her the bones of the human body, one by one, he did not have have to pay heed to the way breathing was shockingly important again, or how his heart beat so strongly against his sternum he could practically hear it, or how both his chest and his lungs ached because when he'd put his bindings on that morning, it had been on the body of a dead man who didn't need to breathe, and now the regular movement of his diaphragm and ribs kept him in a state of constant discomfort.

The dust didn't help - every cough was a further

vexation.

He didn't know when he'd have a moment of privacy to adjust the tightness. He'd just have to endure, and focus on his talented, if slightly irritating, student.

"I still think," Iris said, looking at her own chitinous hand, then back at the clinking, clattering mass of skeletons following behind them through the trees, "that it is silly for me to have to learn the names of human bones when I, myself, do not have bones." She flexed her fingers, making them grow uncannily long, sharp and dark, proving just how illogical the idea of bones was to her species.

James sighed. "Then you can spend some time developing names of the different plates that form your exoskeleton," he said, "but, logically, it would be wise to follow an anatomy vocabulary that is already well documented and understood. Hence, I am teaching you the names of human bones. Now, tell me."

"Distal phalange, middle phalange..." she recited the full list back to him, tapping each joint of her fingers as she did. It was impressive - he'd only told her the names once. James shook his head. If she really persisted in her goal to become a doctor, she would be an excellent one.

Assuming she could resist taking bites out of her patients.

He reminded himself that her patients would most likely be fae folk of her own species, and pushed back his doubts. She was lucky she didn't have to face any of the challenges he himself had gone through, when he first entered medical school.

He tugged at his collar, the tightness of his breath all too familiar from those days.

Iris stopped her recitation, giving him a curious look. "Are you alright, Doctor?"

"Fine," he said shortly. "Just not used to having to breathe so much." They'd been on the move for a few hours now, trekking their way across the dry, dusty dead lands with their bony army in tow. James had no doubt that the dust rising behind them could be seen for miles. At least the trees were a little greener; a smattering of leaf cover kept some of the sun off their heads. James knew Barty was still far ahead because he and the Huntsman had horses, but surely Fabian was less used to walking long distances than James was...

Actually, James had no idea if that assumption was accurate. He did not know how Fabian spent most of their time, though he assumed much of it was in some kind of private research laboratory.

"Are we going to be traveling much longer?" James asked, looking at his student.

"I am not sure," Iris said, looking at the now-leafy trees. "Usually it stays bare all the way to the King's castle, but it seems Dr. Barty took a detour of some kind. We are headed into a great family's territory."

"Do you know which family?" Fabian asked from behind.

Iris flicked her wings, startled, taking a moment to compose herself before giving the necromancer an acknowledging, polite nod. "If the roads have not changed terribly since I last wandered the lands, we are following Dr. Barty to the Borough of the Decided."

"Aah," Fabian nodded, and smoothed back their leather feathers. "Good. I can work with the Decided. If we were going to the Lycans, I would be fearing for his safety."

James had no idea what the Decided were, and was only half paying attention. He glanced over his shoulder at Fabian, and Fabian's cadaverous army. There were consistent oddities about the necromancer's presence in this world; like how Iris seemed afraid to displease them, and how Fabian moved through the land so easily, and how they seemed to know as much about the places they went as Iris herself.

James looked behind the necromancer, and, similar to what he had observed in the briar patch, some of the trees they had passed were now putting out small green leaves. Was that a side effect of necromancy, or something else?

There was clearly more to Fabian's history here than ancient travels. Unfortunately, James doubted the necromancer would offer an explanation unless faced with dire consequences.

"Do we have any kind of plan?" he asked, pushing back his suspicions but determined to keep an eye out for further evidence. "We want Barty back, but even if we get him, the door will still be closed."

Fabian turned their masked face to James. Somehow, the angle made it look like the seams of the pale beak were smiling. "I am going to ask the King nicely," they said.

James looked again at the rows of undead skeletons marching behind them. He had to admit, asking nicely while at the head of an undead army was a valid strategy. "And you?" he changed his line of questioning. "How are you holding up, marching this far with so many puppets to attend to?"

Fabian hesitated. "When we get to the Decided, I would very much like to politely ask them for some supplies. Particularly, food."

James had suspected as much. The necromancer put on a brave front, but they were doubtless spending copious amounts of energy to keep the parade going. They were probably exhausted and ravenous.

James gritted his teeth and turned away, forcing down a twinge of compassion. He should be feeling no sympathy for the one who'd sentenced him to a life imprisoned in a corpse. However, as much as he wanted to hate Fabian for all they'd done, his impulse to look out for his patient's health remained a strong force within his very soul. If he added how recently the necromancer had borne a child to the list of things that would make this journey difficult for them...

He shook his head irritably. "How much longer?" he asked Iris.

"We're almost there," she said, also looking curiously at Fabian, and then back to James. She'd settled into a form more on the inhuman side now, he noticed, with four arms, clearly visible wings, and her pink-white-yellow coloration considerably brighter. "My advice to you is to put on your masks, if you want any shred of respect."

James gave Fabian a glance, hoping for an explanation, but the necromancer said nothing, seeming content to leave James in the dark.

"Fine," James said flatly, buckling his beak onto his face. "I suppose I'll see for myself."

When they arrived at the ornately-wrought gate, James had to admit to himself that no amount of explanation would have properly prepared him for the creature guarding it. It looked straight out of a mythical nightmare, all boney angles and jutting horns. The being put a hand on the gate as if to steady it, and though it was certainly difficult to read any expression on a face that seemed a twisted mockery of a living animal, James thought he saw surprise in those inhuman yellow eyes. The skeletal, dark-furred head turned slowly, taking in each weary traveler, and last of all their undead escorts.

Finally he took his hands from the gate, and stepped back. "I don't know what you want," he said gravely, "but I cannot let you bring such a threatening invasion into our borough. You would do well to turn around and leave."

"Really, Grimley?" Fabian said, folding their arms. "After all these years and all these miles, this is the welcome you give me?"

The creature - Grimley - snapped his head around. Even with his face so skull-like, it was easy to read the shock in his features.

He looked from Fabian to the now-still rows of skeletons and back again. Slowly he slid the bolt open and stepped through the gate.

"Fiia?" he said, his deep voice much softer. "Is it...is it really you?

He was interrupted by a sudden, explosive commotion on the other side of the gate. Shouts and growls echoed through the streets, then a figure came dashing into view, running full tilt on two legs, though the being was so far from human James had to shake his head to be sure he wasn't hallucinating.

"It's NOT right!" She - at least, James assumed it was a she, by the inflection and pitch of her voice - shouted. She skidded around the corner, all flying copper mane, lashing golden tail, and bared, white fangs, snarling over her shoulder at a gaggle of creatures hot on her heels. "More falling sick! And you're not going to do anything to help him! Well if you won't do something about it, I will!"

"BERTHELIA!" roared another creature - taller, grayer, but with similar mane and body structure to the first. He ran full tilt as well, but kept tripping on the hem of his long, robe-like night-blue garment. "You are ill and need to stay in bed! You cannot go galavanting across the countryside after some human!"

"You could have sent someone else to help him, but you didn't!" she shouted back, now bolting towards the gate. "I won't sit around while - hey! Let GO OF ME!" These last words turned into a completely inhuman roar as another creature - something between a scaly turtle and an explosively feathered peacock - grabbed her about the middle. She pulled the creature's head-feathers until it released her with a shriek, then sprang free, sprinting with all her strength for the gate. "Open wide, Grimley!"

Grimley, indeed, opened the gate wider, if only to keep Berthelia from running smack into it.

She dove through and slammed it shut behind her, panting, then wrapped both clawed hands around the bars, as if holding them closed. "N'ol!"

The bars glowed briefly, then went dark again.

"How dare you!" the greyer, dignified version of her, presumably her father, shouted at her, more snarl than speech. "Using human magic on our own territory!" He'd stopped in his tracks, though, not even trying to open the gate, instead drawing himself up to his full, behorned height. He was impressively large - James was quite glad there was a locked structure between his own newly-vulnerable form and this creature of frosted fur, blue scales and antler-like horns.

Berthelia stepped back from the bars, grinning and dusting off her paw-hands. "Maybe if you spent less time shut away from the world, you'd know the counterspell!"

"We do not sully our claws with human magic in this land," her father growled back. "You are a disgrace to our family!"

The other creatures, looking embarrassed at such a public row, began to slink away, scales and feathers and fur disappearing into various doors along the road.

"You're a disgrace to all living creatures!" she shouted back. "Even humans care for each other! They have doctors who travel, risking their own lives to heal others! But you won't risk your pride to help your own people!"

"You are a spoiled, ungrateful child!"

She laughed and turned away, though James could see the sparkle of tears in her green eyes. "I stopped being a child long ago," she said to the world at large. "It is only- oh."

She blinked, seeing, apparently for the first time, the crowd of plague doctors and skeletons that were her audience.

She assessed the gathered travelers, her catfish-like whiskers twitching, nostrils flared. Now they were closer, James could see a glitter of jewelry about her - two rings in each ear, and a necklace with a stone as green as her scales around her neck.

Finally her gaze settled on Grimley. "Friends of yours, gatekeeper?"

Grimley hesitated. "Er, well-" He glanced back through the gates, but Berthelia's family were walking away, apparently done with the entire affair.

"I am Fabian," Fabian said, stepping forward and bowing smoothly. "And my traveling companions are Dr. Buckler, and Iris," they pointed to each in turn. "We are just passing through. Though, in truth we had hoped for some food and shelter on our way, as it has been quite a long, tiresome journey."

"We are also looking for our friend," James said, irritated that Fabian did not ask about Barty first. "Has a young doctor passed through here? He would be wearing a mask like ours." He tapped his beak pointedly. "He was in the company of-"

"Of the Huntsman, Jeremiah!" Berthelia finished for him. "Yes! It is he I was hoping to follow. He left a few hours ago while I was still asleep. Really, can you imagine! Sneaking off like that and leaving only a note behind! He knew I wanted to come with him, and yet-"

"And yet, if what you said was true," James said sternly, "You have been ill, madam? Surely bed rest and plenty of food and drink are more appropriate for you than traipsing around the country."

"Do not speak to me as if you are my father," she growled, baring long, sharp teeth.

James stepped back a pace. It was shocking how much more vulnerable he felt now that he knew things like 'bleeding to death' were possible for him once more.

"Peace, peace," the gatekeeper spoke, sliding between them. "It seems everyone here is tired and desperate to find the young doctor. Why don't we all step along to my cottage and have some tea and victuals? I am sure tempers will settle much more easily with food."

"I will state," Fabian said icily, "that it would not be wise for anyone to share space with this creature if she is, indeed, infected with plague."

"Oh, don't worry," Berthelia said, brightening up despite the necromancer's rudeness. "I'm better now. But, if it's any comfort, I came prepared, hold on a moment. And don't call me a creature, it's very rude! My name is Theli."

She swung a large pack off her back. Digging around in it with her paws, she pulled out a clearly homemade, but well crafted, plague mask, complete with beak and herbs.

She buckled it over her face, her curved horns sticking out between the straps. It was a beautiful mask: the stitching clean and neat, with small, silvery designs worked into the leather. Far fancier than any plague mask James had seen, to be sure.

"What do you think?" she said, her voice muffled but sounding pleased with herself. "Not bad for a first time, eh?"

Stony silence met her from the assembled group. James folded his arms.

She hesitated, then said sadly, "There are a few people in the borough who are falling ill, alright? Anyone who came to check on me has a fever now. They didn't want to tell the human doctor - it's a very shameful thing to be sick, amongst our people; but I overheard them talking. If it spreads so easily, the whole borough will be sick before long, won't they?" She shook her head, and pulled off the mask, tucking it back into her pack. "Someone has to do something. I know Dr. Barty went to see the King already, and he's planning to offer to help with the sickness in exchange for opening a gate, but I think the King is more likely to listen if more people ask him."

"The same King that threw you in the dungeon with a sick human to begin with?" Grimley asked.

Theli hesitated. "Well...Barty will still probably need help. Perhaps breaking out of the same dungeon? At least I know where it is."

James looked to Iris, who shrugged. "I have not spent enough time in the King's company to know the ways of his castle. There is no harm in having another to lend intent and purpose to our journey."

James looked to Fabian.

The necromancer considered Theli thoughtfully. "I noticed," they said at last, "that you used a spell to seal the gate."

Theli perked up. "Yes I did! I learned it from the Mageborn in exchange for some, ah... s-spell components." James wondered what sort of spell components caused her to hesitate. She clearly came from a place of highly magical creatures - perhaps clippings from a fish-lion's claws or fur from a bear-sheep's coat could power a spell?

"Do you think," Fabian asked, "that you would be able to perform written magic as well as spoken magic?"

"Oh yes, we use written magic all the time," she said, nodding eagerly. "Every house in the borough has wards of warmth and strength worked into the wood - though it is forbidden to learn any new spells, only a few old ones."

"I think," Fabian said, looking at James, "that we have our mage we needed for the amulets."

"Great," James said, refusing to be impressed. "Now we just need Barty back and we can begin plastering on bandages as gangrene consumes the population."

"Gangrene?" Theli repeated, puzzled.

Fabian sighed. "Dr. Buckler is pointing out that it would be futile to attempt any preventative measures against the disease while the root of the problem is still flourishing. Before we make any kind of amulet or treatment, we must break the curse powering the plague."

"But there is a cure already," Theli said, tilting her head. "Barty treated us - he had some kind of tea. He said it was mint, I think, and sage, from somewhere called the "Living Waters?""

James and Fabian looked at Iris.

She smiled, ran her hands over her face to return it back to beak form to match the rest of the group, and shook her petals out into a long coat. "Look at that," she purred. "I'm already going to be terribly helpful, aren't I?"
**

At Fabian's insistence of needing food and rest, they all went along to Grimley's home. It lay solidly in the middle of the iron fence, half in and half out. The boney-faced Decided assured the group that no member of Theli's family would pester them here, as 'he himself was not a very reputable person, and the Decided tended to look down on disreputable people.' When James asked him what he'd done to damage his reputation, he only smiled, far more widely than a goat-shaped face was meant to accommodate, and said, "Oh, I liked to travel in my youth."

He guided them all to a somewhat cozy living room full of mismatched chairs and a well-worn couch, all of which were covered in books. James helped him clear sitting space, and caught glimpses of titles such as "A Midsommar Night's Dream" and "Comedia de Calisto y Melibea." In fact, no two books seemed to be in the same language.

"Can you read all of these?" James asked, putting the books onto the shelves in alphabetical order.

"Yes," Grimley said, pushing the chairs into a circle around a low central table. "I used to collect them in my travels."

"Books or languages?" James said, watching Fabian claim the couch while everyone else chose a chair. James sat as well, perching reluctantly on the couch next to Fabian. Lord, he was tired. The soft cushion made him want to just sit back and close his eyes.

"Both," Grimley said. "The patterns of language are satisfying, and the more one can communicate, the better one can travel to points of cultural interest."

"Grimley's the one who got me wanting to travel to begin with," Theli said, pulling her chair closer to the table and once more searching through her bag. She retrieved a slim leather-bound volume and opened it to a blank page, produced a pen, and began scribbling notes. "He told me all sorts of amazing tales, when I was a little girl." James could just make out the words '*successfully escaped the village, preparing to visit the King*' in neat, quick handwriting.

"That is why I was assigned the task of Gatekeeper," Grimley said. He brought in an armload of foodstuffs from the kitchen and began to lay things out on the table: a large cheese, several loaves of bread, a dozen apples, a jar of something that could have been olives, six smoked fish, a flagon of wine and a flagon of water. "The counsel determined that someone who had already had dealings with the beyond world would not be as 'disturbed' by outsiders as a local who had never passed the borough walls."

James looked numbly at the food, only now realizing that he could eat any of it, even the apples. Even the bread. He reached for one of the fruits, then hesitated, Fabian's earlier warning coming back into his head. "We are not supposed to accept gifts?" he said softly, looking to the necromancer for confirmation.

"Oh, we aren't accepting gifts," Fabian said. They pulled off their mask, grabbed an apple, and chomped into it as if they hadn't eaten in three days. "This is bribery."

"Bribery?" James repeated, removing his mask and taking an apple as well.

"Grimley is offering me a bribe of food so that I do not break down the gates with my undead army and take all the rations I want," Fabian replied, their red eyes glittering. They reached for the wedge of cheese next. "Isn't that right, old friend?"

"Exactly correct," Grimley said with a prim nod. He made a neat little sandwich with layers of bread, fish, and olives. "Any rational person would do the same."

"Would you really?" Theli asked, freezing in the middle of tearing a fish in two. Iris patiently awaited the other half beside her. "Would you break down the gates, um, Fabian?"

Fabian gave Theli a slow, sharp smile. "Pray you don't have to find out."

Theli blinked, as if it had only just occurred to her that there was a possibility that the humans she'd teamed up with were not purely altruistic. Iris, too, looked unsettled, her now-humanoid face shifting a shade paler. She daintily nibbled at her fish, though, her unease not great enough to disrupt her hunger.

James tore his gaze away from her jaw-mandibles, contemplating the apple in his hand instead. It was a rich, deep red, almost black, and smelled wonderful.

"Once we've rested," Fabian said, now stuffing a fish between two chunks of bread, "I would like to see your boneyards."

"Boneyards? You will not touch our dead." Grimley flicked an ear.

"Not the ones of your citizens. The ones of your animals - or do your sheep and cattle have no bones?"

James bit into his apple. His mouth immediately filled with juicy sweetness, flowing over his tongue and throat as he chewed, cool, refreshing, unbelievably delicious. He closed his eyes, swallowed the first bite, and took another, letting Fabian and Grimley's discussion wash past him, and hoping nobody noticed the tears he fought to hold back.

It had been over three years since he had been able to eat anything but meat.

He wished he could share this moment with Jessica.

Or even Barty.

But both of them were far away. He was surrounded by strangers, and Fabian, who had sentenced him to a lifetime of living death. He had no choice but to push it all back; no choice but to fight down the feelings of gratitude, awe and disbelief that warred within his chest, around his beating heart. He took another bite of apple, allowing himself this small moment of blissful appreciation, outwardly pretending it was not a miracle that he could do it. Pretending it was not the best thing he'd had in what felt like an eternity.

He sank back into the cushions of Grimley's couch, deciding to let Fabian handle things without interruption, though the necromancer's hunger seemed unquenchable as well. Every word they spoke was now muffled by mouthfuls of bread, cheese, fish and fruit.

James drank water, but no wine. That, at least, he could save for when he reunited with his wife. What would she say, he wondered. How would it feel, to finally be able to kiss her properly, for his own heartbeat to reply to hers when they were close...

It was with these warm thoughts that he drifted off, succumbing to the deep, rolling power of true exhaustion.

Fabian could handle things.

For the first time in three years, in the home of a stranger and surrounded by wondrous fae creatures, James Buckler slept.

CHAPTER 22: THE FACETED KING

Bartholomew Wayman stood before the King of Changelings and prayed. He prayed for steady hands, for an unwavering voice, and for the wisdom of how to speak to one so powerful.

The King sat upon a white throne - marble, straight edged, with no cushions between him and the pristine stone. On either side stood guards. One was white furred, and Barty knew enough now to recognize him as one of the Decided, with great, deer-like antlers and long rabbit ears that fell around his shoulders. The other guard was either a living tree or doing very well at disguising herself to be so, her papery skin lightly patterned like birch bark, her head a crown of leafless branches. Both of them bore spears and wore identical pale tunics. Swords rested in white leather sheaths at their waists.

Their paleness seemed specifically chosen to contrast the man sitting between them. The Faceted King wore long, gauzy robes which shifted in hue even as he held still as the stone he sat on. They rippled lazily from fiery red to sapphire blue, from deep forest green to twilight purple. Upon his head sat a crown of white gold, filled with stones that shifted in color like light in a dewdrop. About his neck, wrists and fingers lay countless pieces of jewelry of every material - gold, silver, copper, brass - each more heavily ladened with stones than the last. Barty had no idea how the man could stay upright with such a weight upon him, but upright the King remained, one elbow resting on the arm of his featureless throne, the other raised so he could watch the sparkle of his rings with every twist of his fingers. The effect of his splendor, combined with the colorlessness of his servant and the room at large, seemed to state that all the color in the world belonged to him alone. Even his skin shifted to match the hues of this clothing, dark, and light, and dark again.

It was terribly distracting. Even more disheartening, the grand fellow did not even look Barty's way, his gaze fixed on his own jewelry.

Barty took a breath, straightened his spine, and spoke his piece anyway.

"First, um, Your Majesty, I thank you for granting me an audience with such speed."

Indeed, once they'd gotten within the castle grounds, the King's servants had all but flown Barty through the palace, ushering him to the King with a swiftness that had left his head whirling. Jeremiah had remained at his side, warning Barty several times, spelling out the warning because Shilling had refused to enter the castle, *'Be polite. Be careful. Do not fight, or you will die.'*

Between the warnings and the speed of movement, Barty hadn't had a moment to take in his surroundings, though the blur of color and light in his memory would surely resolve into something beautiful and impressive with time.

He cleared his throat and continued. "S-second of all..."

He glanced aside at Jeremiah, who kept his silver gaze on the floor. Hearing Barty pause he looked up, met Barty's eye, nodded briefly, then looked down again.

Barty took courage from it.

"Second of all," he began again, "I am here to offer you a service, Majesty." He bowed deeply, wishing once more for his hat if only so he could remove it in proper respect.

The King leaned forward, his hair changing color and length until it landed at long, golden tresses, trailing past his ankles. His eyes, momentarily blue, fixed on Barty, and an indulgent smile played about his temporarily-slender mouth. "A service? How very generous of you, Doctor. I am most curious to know what it is." He sat back again, his hair once more shortening, this time to a blood-red spray of tight curls. His clothing shifted to match, becoming shades of yellow and orange, until the man looked like a stationary flame, or pile of fall leaves. His skin was brown as bare twigs.

Barty swallowed hard, throat dry. "Y-yes sir," he said, bobbing his head. His mask was off, he held it in his hands, but he knew that the lines from wearing it all day would still be quite visible upon his pale face. "Y-you see, sir, you might not be aware, but-"

The shades of red and orange darkened, even though the King did not move.

Barty pressed on as bravely as he could manage, "T-there is sickness in your land, sir. Your own subjects are falling ill with disease; a lethal form of black plague. I may only be a human from the kingdom of England, but I have some knowledge of curing illness, sir, and if you would allow me-"

"Let me see if I understand," The King held up a hand, silencing Barty and smiling icily. His clothing shifted once more to match his mood, becoming shades of winter blue and stark white, even as his hair grayed and straightened and his skin went so colorless it was almost albino. Impossibly pale eyes regarded Barty, lips with almost no definition speaking words of mocking sincerity under a freshly-sprouted, close-cut white beard, "You come into my land, trespass through the homes of my subjects, disturb the workings of the plague I myself created, and you expect me to give you permission, nay, assistance, in your unwelcome interfering?"

Barty's jaw dropped. For a moment he couldn't say a thing, and then when he spoke, it was with a disbelief that only the barest fingernail-hold of politeness kept from becoming outrage. "*Your* plague?"

"Of course it's my plague," the King said, smiling. He rested an elbow on the pale arm of his throne again, and shook his head so that all traces of frost left him, golden, wavy locks dangling at his shoulders, golden silk trailing down his body, golden eyes staring at Barty through heavy, golden eyelashes. "Do you really think any illness could survive in this land without my permission? Do you think I have so little control over my kingdom that I could not choose if, where, and how disease is able to spread?" He tisked softly.

Barty cast an agonized look at Jeremiah. The Huntsman had closed his eyes, his still jaw clenched. Barty couldn't tell if he had known the answer all along or only suspected it, but there was no surprise on his face at the King's outrageous revelation.

"But," Barty said, wishing his voice wasn't quite so high, trying not to be sick at the memories of the bodies of villagers contorted by decay, or the Decided shivering in the grip of merciless illness, "but why? Why would you afflict humans, and your own people-"

"Think about it," the King said pleasantly, folding his hands across his chest. He remained in his golden form, sparkling slightly as if he sat in a sunbeam. "What have I achieved, by spreading this plague? You're a clever boy, aren't you, Doctor? I'm sure you can come up with an idea."

Barty tried to think, but it was hard to focus over the ringing in his ears. What had been achieved by the plague coming back?

People in the human world had died. What help was that? And...

"We're here," he said finally. "Myself, and...and the others." James. Fabian.

Fabian, who had warned of old grudges and long memories.

Barty's lungs felt like they were full of ice. Fabian had been right, all along. "This was all a trap."

The King smiled.

"But how could that be worth it?" Barty burst out. "All this death and suffering! What is it about F-" Barty caught himself in time, deciding not to even use their common name, "m-my companions that you would do so much just to get them here?"

"Your companions?" the King laughed. "All in good time, Doctor."

He stood up, and suddenly all his garments were black, his hair went black, and his eyes deepened to bloody red.

Just like Fabian's.

"What I want to talk about is *you*," he said softly, stepping down from this throne.

Barty gaped at him. Even the voice sounded close to Fabian's, the inflections all too familiar, though with an accent he couldn't quite place. "Me?"

"Yes, Doctor, you," the King purred. He trailed down the steps. "You burn with passion, Doctor. Passion to heal, to help. So much so that you were able to make an antidote potion out of nothing but leaves and hot water."

"Those leaves came from the Living Waters," Barty argued. "I didn't do anything!"

"Didn't you?" asked the King, drawing closer. "Didn't you believe they would work? Didn't you wish it, with every fiber of your soul? And are you not, yourself, a fount of healing who has literally shed his own lifeblood for the sake of others?"

Barty gaped at the King. Everything he said was correct. Barty had never thought of his own work in the anti-plague amulets as a magically significant factor, but a thousand spells of healing were tied to his very blood. "But," he said, "what do you want from me, s-sire?"

"I want," the King said, his smile like a knife, "your name."

The command slammed into Barty. He all but shouted "BARTY!" before he clapped both hands over his mouth and shut his eyes, struggling against the sudden, fierce compulsion that tore through his mind under the King's gaze.

"Barty?" The King repeated, and Barty could hear his amusement, even as he fought against the impulse to keep speaking, so powerful his knees buckled. "Short for Bartholomew, I assume? And your last name?"

Barty shook his head, both hands still over his mouth, eyes screwed shut.

The King sighed, and Barty heard him turn away. "Make him speak," he told someone.

A pause of silence, interrupted by the creak of leather and rustle of cloth. Barty realized in horror that the King had been addressing Jeremiah. What he heard was the Huntsman's hands moving, signing his reply.

However, whatever the Huntsman said had not pleased the King, for the bejeweled man sighed sharply and shifted his orders elsewhere. "Do it."

Barty snapped his gaze open in time to see the two guards in white descending the stairs. On impulse he backed away, but the King grabbed his arm, smiling and keeping him in place. "Do you really think," he asked softly, his colors rippling to a white-flecked blue-green that made Barty think of the endless, uncaring expanse of the ocean, "that you can defy me? Even a simple human King would not allow such a thing, and I-"

He slipped back just in time for his guards to step forward, each towering creature seizing one of Barty's arms.

"...I am no human King. Now, boy. Tell me your NAME."

The guards pulled Barty's hands away from his face.

"Bartholomew Wayman!" the words tore out of Barty in a sob, and he collapsed in their grip, trembling.

"Bartholomew Wayman," the King repeated, smirking like a cat with a faceful of cream. Barty shivered, feeling the King's intent tighten on him. "Tell me, Bartholomew Wayman, the true names of both your companions."

Barty could feel the words building in his chest. He could feel the names bursting within him, fighting to be set loose.

But the faces attached to the names swam before his vision. Although he trembled, although the command pulled at him like strings attached to his flesh, the pain of resisting the King's will was less than the pain of betraying those he cared about.

"No," he said, sweat dripping down his brow.

The room went still. Even the guards holding his arms looked stunned.

"No?" the King repeated. A wisp of smoke escaped his lips with the word, but he closed his eyes, frowned, and opened them again, focusing on Barty with a gaze that shifted colors like light on a soap bubble. "You cannot tell me no. I have your name, Bartholomew Wayman."

Barty shivered, but knowing he had been able to deny the King once gave him courage. "No," he said more firmly. "I won't tell you."

The King breathed out a single, trembling breath. Then he said, "You will," and with a sudden flurry of movement that sent silky cloth flying all around him, he pulled a sword free from one of his guard's sheaths, and raised it high into the air. "You will!"

Barty flinched back, closing his eyes as the blade swung towards him, expecting hot pain, bracing for a scream of defiance and terror.

Something shoved in front of Barty. He staggered back. A shattering clang echoed through the room.

Barty opened his eyes.

Jeremiah stood before him, his hunter's blade drawn, the

length of scratched metal shining in the pale light. Pieces of the King's sword clattered onto the floor.

Faerie metal was no match for iron-based steel.

The King stared at Jeremiah, speechless. "How dare you," he breathed, color swirling in his clothing, his hair, his face.

'This is the land of Faerie,' Jeremiah signed back. Barty couldn't see his expression, but he could almost feel the tension in those broad shoulders. 'I am following the law of the land. To bring Barty here, we made a deal – I swore no harm would come to the boy as long as he is under my protection.'

"Who gave you permission to swear such a deal?" The King asked. A ripple of green veined his cheeks, and more smoke trailed up from between his teeth.

'I do not need permission to conduct my duties with honor,' Jeremiah responded. He kept his blade up, a single line of steel protection between himself, Barty, and the King.

The King's kaleidoscope eyes narrowed. "Very well," he said.

He turned away, making once more for the stairs to his throne.

"You have fulfilled your commission to my satisfaction," he called as he ascended, one step at a time, his voice almost bored. "I am satisfied with your services and relieve you of any further responsibility. Your debt is paid in full. I am taking this boy into my own care and protection."

He waved a hand, and his guards immediately pounced, gabbing Barty by the arms and dragging him toward a door behind the throne's pedestal.

Jeremiah remained in place, shocked, lowering his sword.

The Faceted King settled on his throne, crossing one leg over the other, his garments all a uniform, scale-patterned shade of green. His eyes, yellow now, focused intently on Jeremiah. "You are a free man, Huntsman." his words echoed around the room, though he barely spoke above a whisper. "Be gone from my halls."

"W-wait!" Barty called, shaking free of his shock and fighting against the clawed hands holding him. "Wait!"

But it was too late. The King pulled a cord, a bell rang somewhere, and a dozen more guards in white marched into the room, surrounding Jeremiah with spears and prodding him towards the entrance.

Jeremiah looked at Barty, and Barty could see his own dread reflected in his friend's face.

"Put the doctor in the dungeon with the other," the King called. "And see that the Huntsman finds his way out promptly."

"You can't do this!" Barty tried to struggle, pulling against the heavy hands that held his elbows like iron bands. He couldn't break free, but he did manage to hook his bare foot against the doorframe, bringing them all to a halt. "Stop! Please!"

The King laughed. "If he is too bothersome," he said to the guards, "make things easier in whatever manner is convenient! For his own good, of course, we wouldn't want him to hurt himself on the journey."

The guards nodded, and the behorned rabbit swung the butt of his spear into the air.

Barty tried to shout "No, no wait-!" but the spear struck him square on the head, and his vision exploded into stars, his limbs falling limp.

The world faded in and out of focus. Blackness swirled over him in waves, as if his consciousness were suspended in a rolling sea.

The guards dragged him down a carpeted hallway to a flight of stairs.

He sank under the waves.

Arguing voices penetrated the blackness.

"You open it."

"No, I threw in the last one. I'm not risking breathing that air again."

"Give me his mask then."

Someone pulled the mask free from his grip - how he still had it, he didn't know. The sound of a door opening followed.

Once more the dark washed through him.

When next it drained away, he lay on cold stone, and something smelled terrible. Terrible, yet familiar. The darkness was just within reach, but he could not shelter in its painless embrace. There was something he was supposed to do, something he had to be doing. It was urgent.

His head throbbed.

Barty pushed himself up before he could even open his eyes, and stayed there a moment on hands and knees, trying not to be sick, trying to keep his balance despite the world spinning around him and his own trembling. He didn't know if the nausea was from the smell or the bump on the head. Pain warbled through his skull.

Through the pounding and the dizziness, however, he heard something. A ragged, raspy breathing. A rumbling, regular drone. A wet drip, drip, drip.

He opened his eyes, and saw the stripes of pale and dark before him.

Bars, he realized dully, looking up and squinting against the light. He was in a prison. In a cell.

And he wasn't alone.

He reached forward, gripping the iron bars and using them to pull himself up. They were cold, and dirty, leaving flakes of rust on his bare hands.

On the other side of the bars was a bench, where some kind of masked guard sat, bulky arms folded and head bowed. The flickering lantern at his side illuminated a cloth mask hanging down over his face, long and rust colored like some kind of executioner, but with no eye holes. His tunic was a dirtier, bloodied variant of the guards in white, and even bloodier gloves of the same material covered his heavy hands. At his side hung a great sword, brown and caked with...was that also rust? Or just more blood?

The droning noise was this creature's snores, the cloth over his long face moving with every breath.

The dripping noises, however, were from within Barty's own cell.

Slowly he turned away from the bars, keeping tight hold in case the movement made his head spin more.

Striped bars of light fell across many forms. Many still forms.

The so-called jail was closer to a mortuary.

Corpses lay wedged into every corner and edge of the stone chamber - creatures of all shapes and sizes but too contorted and filthy in death to identify. Barty looked at the one closest to him - a fellow almost humanoid, but with something wolfish about the angle of his sideburns and gray-black coloration of his hair. Blood had left dark trails from his eyes and mouth, and numerous plague-tokens, now brownish, spotted his skin.

Barty had no doubt that if he checked the other bodies, he would find more of the same. Theli had said there was plague in the King's dungeon, and here Barty was - a plague doctor in the dungeon, but too late, far too late, to help anyone.

He was so used to feeling helpless, it shouldn't have bothered him much.

The tears trickled down his face anyway.

He closed the man's yellow eyes.

Drip, drip, drip.

Barty looked up. The noise was coming from the back wall.

He saw now why all the corpses were at the edges of the room. They'd tried to stay as far away as possible from the figure chained to the stone, a figure in dark clothing, with skin pale as death where it wasn't plague-blackened.

The man, for it seemed to be only a man, had been bound most cruelly. His back lay against the stone, his hands suspended together above his head. Barty stepped closer and saw the dripping was from those hands. They had been impaled with an iron spike, blood trailing down the spike's length and onto the unconscious face. An iron lock kept the spike sealed in place, preventing the man's escape.

Another step closer. Dry blood had sealed the man's eyes closed. Barty could see his black hair falling down his shoulders, and his shirt had been torn open, revealing a chest defaced with lacerations.

Despite all the abuse, however, he yet breathed, in shuddering, slow rasps.

This tortured soul, in the midst of all the death and decay, was still alive.

As if in a daze, Barty pushed himself away from the bars. He stepped over the rotting bodies, around the piles of filth scattered on the stones, and knelt at the man's side.

To Barty's practiced eye, every sign pointed to a human body in its last gasps of life. The plague tokens mottling the man's skin were an outraged shade of red, and very numerous. The blackening necrosis that came when the disease caused so much swelling it suffocated the very flesh it inhabited had even reached the man's face. The mangled hands were alternately pale and dark, bloodless from their elevated position. The blood caked over his eyes was so thick there was no way he could force them open even if he wanted to.

It looked like he had been here for weeks, but what man could survive in this condition that long?

Was there anything Barty could do, with no herbs, no supplies?

Was it even possible to heal someone so far gone?

Even as Barty's mind asked the question, his heart answered it. He had to try, no matter what the reality was. He had to try.

Barty reached to touch the man's throat and feel his pulse

The man jerked with such violence it made Barty jump. "Who-!" snarled the man, but the rest of the words were lost to a sudden, violent fit of coughing.

"I'm sorry!" Barty gasped. "I'm sorry - I didn't realize you were awake! I'm a doctor, I want to help you."

The man, shaking and wheezing, did not reply. He only slouched back against the wall, the drip-drip-drip of his spike faster now he'd moved.

He was probably too exhausted to say more. Barty wondered if he'd even understood the answer he'd received.

"It's alright," Barty said soothingly. "I'm not going to hurt you." He reached again for the man's pulse. "It's alright. You're safe."

The man let out a sharp breath that might have been a snort, but didn't pull away from Barty's touch, this time. "Safe," he said in almost a whisper. "Right."

"Well, I mean-" Barty faltered, knowing how silly it sounded when the man was dying of plague and also imprisoned in a faerie dungeon. "Safe from me, anyway. I won't harm you. I've treated many patients with plague." The stranger's pulse was shockingly strong, under Barty's fingers. So strong that Barty wondered if he'd made a mistake, and had to bend down to put an ear to the fellow's torn chest to hear for sure.

"Plague..." The man repeated, the word breaking in his raw voice, rumbling through his chest under Barty's ear. He stopped though, seeming to understand what Barty was doing, and letting him get a clear listen.

No, Barty had not made a mistake before. The heart beating under all those cuts was steady and strong, even if his breath rattled wetly.

The man said something else, again muffled because of how Barty was sitting, but he just caught, "-oft."

"I beg your pardon?" Barty said, sitting up so he could hear properly.

The man paused, licked his pale, thin lips. "Water..?"

Barty's heart sank. "I don't have-"

But then he remembered.

He DID have water. He'd refilled his flask from the Living

Waters after draining all the cider from it.

"Oh," he said. "Oh. Yes! Water! Just hold on a moment sir, I'll help you."

Heart pounding with excitement, he checked his pocket. Miraculously, the flask was still there, heavy with its liquid contents.

"I'm going to let you drink some," Barty said, "but don't go too fast, understand? And I'll use some to clean you up a little - at least to get all that stuff out of your eyes. Is that alright?"

The man nodded. Barty opened the flask and held it to the fellow's lips. He drank in long, grateful sips, his adam's apple bobbing with each swallow.

Barty gave him a good while and then gently pulled the flask away. "I'm so sorry," he said, "but too much at once can make you ill even with normal water. I don't know about this stuff."

He set the flask aside, then tore the sleeve off his shirt. Folding it into a sort of pad, he tipped the flask onto the cloth, and began to sponge the dried blood away from the man's eyes.

"What is your name, sir?" he asked, his old habit of chatting with his patients to take their minds off their troubles present even now.

The man hesitated. When he next spoke, his voice was much less raspy, clear and soft, with a strangely elegant accent. "I don't know."

"Well, that's alright, sir." Barty didn't want to upset the fellow if he could help it. "You've clearly been through a lot, and it is to be expected that your memory might be a little hazy. I'm going to touch your face now, don't be surprised." He dabbed at the caked-on blood. Immediately upon coming in contact with the water, the hard brown crust became quite easy to wipe away, bright, red and liquid, as if...

As if it were fresh.

Barty shivered. The Living Waters seemed to be re-animating the blood itself. Still, he persisted in his task.

The man held quite still, allowing his face to be cleaned. "You," he said at last. "Who are you?"

"Dr. Barty, at your service," said Barty. "Although I suppose I'm not much of a doctor right now without my supplies. Still, one must make do with what one has, in a pinch. And this," he cast his eyes around the corpse-ridden room, "is certainly a pinch."

"Heh." The man had laughed that time, Barty was sure of it. There was definitely a small smile on that pale face. "That's putting it lightly."

The man opened his eyes.

For a moment there was a flash of green - bright green, as if a light were shining through glass, but then it was gone, and the fellow had normal, if certainly still quite vivid, verdant eyes.

Barty managed a weak smile, trying not to stare. "Some things are easier to bear when you put them lightly, sir."

"Perhaps," the man said, his voice still soft, but definitely stronger than it had been before. His gaze traveled down Barty's figure, lingering on his torn sleeve and bare feet, then returned to his face. "It seems I owe you my thanks, Dr. Barty." He glanced around the cell next, flicking to the bodies, then the Jailer, then back to Barty. "You are," he said, "the first to try and help me."

"What?" Barty said, startled. "Really? But you are bleeding!" He rang out the bloody water from the rag, poured more from the flask, and started to dab at the fellow's chest next.

"They were all afraid," the man said, a touch of sneering derision in his voice. "Afraid of the plague, and afraid of what they thought I would do to them if they got close. This..." he moved his wrists, the chain rattling and more blood splattering down onto his face, "...is a punishment reserved only for very strong and wicked wizards, so they whispered to each other."

"Are you a mage, then?" Barty asked gently, wiping the

fresh drips off his forehead. "That's wonderful. We need a mage to help make our anti-plague talismans." He paused, frowning at the cuts on the man's chest. Now that he was thinking about magic, and now that he was looking more closely at these marks, he recognized some of the shapes. There were familiar runes there, carved in a layered circle.

"Did…you didn't do this to yourself, did you?" he asked, staring at the mage's face. "This looks like a spell."

"No," the man said firmly, trying to bend and look at the marks. The movement put pressure on his hands and their spike, and he flinched, letting out a soft noise of pain. He eased back against the wall, breathing heavily. "They did that to me," he said, and this time Barty knew he didn't imagine the green gleam of light in those eyes, nor the anger in that voice. "When they brought me here, they carved that into my flesh, and threw me here to rot."

Barty dabbed further at the bloody runes. They were cleaner, but not closing even with the help of the Living Waters. Whatever magic was in them seemed to be holding them open. "I am so sorry," Barty said. "These don't seem to want to heal. I don't know why you're here, but nobody deserves to be treated this way."

The man was silent, watching Barty under half-closed lids, that dangerous green gleam still present. "Do you truly want to help me?" he asked at last, as if Barty tending his hurts weren't evidence enough.

Barty gave a sad chuckle and wrung out the cloth once more. "Of course I do," he said. "I'm a doctor."

"A doctor," the man murmured, his gaze going momentarily distant. "I think…I was also…" He shook his head, as if the thought were a fly he didn't have the strength to chase. "If you want to help me, Dr. Barty," he said, his words firmer now, "you must free my hands of the spike. I may be able to recall a spell of healing, but not when I'm touching iron."

"Oh, right! Of course. Um…" Barty examined the spike. It was, indeed, impaled right between the bones of the man's palms. It was a miracle that the thing hadn't pierced an artery, Barty thought grimly, but perhaps whatever spell was on this fellow only worked as long as he was alive. The lock was the main obstacle, but thanks to Fabian, Barty thought he could pick it open. A truly nasty piece of work. Removing it was not going to be fun for this poor fellow.

"What should I call you, sir?" Barty said, pulling two slender pieces of metal from his shirt pocket and setting to work.

The man made a small noise of pain at Barty's actions, but after a moment to catch his breath, he managed an answer. "I have…heard others referring to me as 'The Raven.'"

"Doctor Raven, then?" Barty smiled at his feeble attempt at humor. "You must have been a plague doctor, like me. Did you train in London? Oh blast-" The lock came open, but Barty's tool snapped in half when it did. Some kind of magic, probably. Barty sighed, but supported the fellow's hands while letting the metal fall free, clattering against the wall.

Again, the man hesitated. Barty wasn't sure if it was because he was searching for a lie to tell, or if it was because he was simply seeking for the answer in a mind that had been so tormented over the last few days, or weeks, it was refusing to function. "I don't know," he said at last, with a small shiver. "So much is…is gone. Ah-"

He groaned when Barty shifted his grip on his hands, and laid his head back against the wall. His face had gone a nasty shade of green.

"I'm terribly sorry," Barty said, meaning it. " I know this hurts, but the pain will pass. Perhaps when you are well again, memories will begin to come back." He took a deep breath. "I will be able to pull this spike out," he said, shifting his support to the Raven's wrists, "But you are going to be bleeding very freely. It will also hurt a good deal, I'm afraid."

The Raven met Barty's gaze, and swallowed hard. "Do it quickly."

Barty nodded. "Relax as much as you can," he said. "I'll

count down for you, try not to tense up." He was reminded very vividly of a similar moment a year ago, in the depths of a well. He wondered where James was, and prayed that he was alright.

"Three," he counted "two-"

He pulled the spike free. The Raven cried out in agony, collapsing against Barty.

Barty dropped the spike to catch the man. He was surprisingly heavy, heavier than Barty would have expected from so long in such a tortured state. "You did it!" he said soothingly, just holding on to the fellow, hoping his presence was reassuring. "It's out! You're free!"

"My arms," groaned the man, "are burning-" he stopped, coughing violently. Barty only now remembered that his patient was suffering from plague as well as injury and horrific muscle cramps.

"Circulation coming back, I imagine," Barty said, rubbing the man's back. "Combined with the level of blackening in your hands, I shouldn't wonder if you'll be immobile for-"

But the Raven was already moving, pushing away from Barty with bleeding hands and staggering to his feet.

Barty jumped up too. "S-sir I think you should sit down-"

The Raven paid Barty no heed. He seized the spike from the floor and, before Barty could stop him, drew a fierce slash down his own chest.

Right through the center of the circle of runes.

Then he collapsed again, gasping in pain. Barty barely managed to catch him, lowering him gently to the stone floor.

A deep growl behind them both made Barty freeze. He turned, looking over his shoulder.

At the bars of their cell stood the Jailer. He'd been roused from his slumber by the commotion. Now he towered over them, seven feet tall, rusty sword in one hand, the other gripping the bars of the prison as he stared at them both through the veil of his executioner's hood.

The last thing Barty needed was a fight, or someone telling the King he was helping his prisoner break a spell. His mind raced, and for the second time since his journey into Faerie, his solution was to draw upon the technique of his dearest friend, James Buckler. "Why are you just standing there?" Barty snapped, putting James' force of authority and knowledge behind the words.

The Jailer stopped growling, clearly confused.

"I need soap and hot water to wash these wounds!" Barty ordered, fighting down the desire to break into a mad laugh. "You're the only one who can get those things! Well? Hurry! We don't have much time!"

The Jailer hesitated, then gave a nod and another rumble. The motion made Barty shiver - whatever face was under there, it wasn't human, judging by how it distorted the cloth. Barty couldn't help but stare as the huge fellow turned and walked away, dragging his sword. Despite the tunic, trousers and boots hiding his feet, it was easy to see the creature's legs bent back at the knee.

A minotaur, perhaps?

"I can't believe that actually worked."

Barty turned back to find the Raven staring at him, astonishment written all over his face.

Barty gave him a lopsided smile. "I have an excellent mentor." He proceeded to tear the sleeve off his other arm and rend it into strips. "Do you know any spells that can unlock the door?"

The Raven thought for a moment, but shook his head. He was still covered in old and fresh blood, but he'd regained a little color in his face. "I might have once, but..."

Barty repressed a sigh - a mage, but with no magic, for the moment. Wasn't that just like his usual luck? "Nevermind," he said kindly. "Let's get your hands and chest taken care of, and maybe we can think of a plan for when he gets back." Barty had some vague idea of trying to subdue the Jailer when he unlocked the door, but the creature was so very, very big.

322

Anyway, if he really had gone to get supplies to help them, Barty didn't want to hurt him.

"Or I can let you out!" said a tiny voice, once again from behind them.

Barty turned, a smile already breaking out over his face. "Shilling? Is that you?"

"It's me!" Shilling raised himself up off the floor - a small, silver snake, with a loop of keys caught in his coils. "I am being so brave right now!"

"You are, you are!" Trying to keep his hands steady, Barty quickly turned back to the Raven, washed his bloody palms with the rest of the water from the flask, and bound them up as best he could with the strips of his shirt. "Dr. Raven, meet Shilling, a friend of mine. Shilling, this is-"

Shilling's little snake mouth had fallen open upon seeing the patient, but he closed it with a hiss of horror. "Barty!" he said, recoiling from the bars. "Don't you know who that is? That's the Raven!"

"Yes, he told me already." Barty turned back to Shilling, puzzled by his shock. "He needed medical attention, and I gave it to him. No person should be kept like this, no matter who they are."

Shilling looked doubtful, but eventually he nodded. "I guess...he does seem to be behaving himself at the moment. But be very careful, Barty!"

A hand touched Barty's arm, and the Raven was suddenly right there, his gaze on the snake. He looked to barty next, his stare seeming to bore right into Barty's soul. "I will behave."

Barty looked boldly into those eyes, and asked, "Does my companion speak the truth? Should I be worried about your history, sir?"

The Raven's gaze flickered briefly back to the snake, but he soon met Barty's eyes once more. "You have nothing to fear from me, Doctor," he said, his voice soft. "I will cause you no harm. You have my word. And I do thank you for your help." He gave a subtle bow. "Truly."

Barty blushed, but even though he wondered why Shilling was so concerned, he felt he could trust the prisoner's word. "It's what I do."

"I think it's who you are," the Raven said with a strange, small smile, "as much as what you do."

"Aha, maybe." Barty's face felt even warmer. He stood up and cleared his throat, walking over to the bars to retrieve the keys from Shilling's coils. "W-well! Let's hurry along then."

He picked up Shilling, draped him gently about his own shoulders, and unlocked the door. "Ready to go?" He looked back at his patient.

The Raven nodded. He plucked the iron spike from the floor, tucked into his belt, then wiped his bandaged hands on his pant legs, already heading for the door. "Let's," he agreed. Then he made a face, looking at the filth his trousers had left on his hands. "Perhaps, at some point, we can stop somewhere for a change of clothing."

Barty looked down at his own garments as he stepped through the bars. Both sleeves gone, boots lost to the river, trousers tattered, dirty and blood stained. "I think that is an excellent idea," he said, shutting the door behind them and locking it again. "Do you know where we can find something to wear, Shilling?"

Shilling slithered down Barty's side, and onto the floor, where he changed into a handsome silver fox. "I do!" he yipped. "Follow me!"

He took off down the hall.

Barty and the Raven followed after him as quickly as they could.

Barty could only pray that the Jailer would take a long, long time returning. Maybe if they got enough of a head start, they could get away without anyone knowing they were gone.

CHAPTER 23: WINDING

The child followed the smell of food.

Her stomach rumbled with an all too familiar demand, but she ignored it, trending carefully through the undergrowth with bare, calloused feet, resting her small hand on tree after tree to keep her balance and not risk breaking so much as a single twig in her approach.

The smell was so good it was almost unreal. Despite seeing nothing but trees, she could identify the things waiting ahead - broiled meats, roast vegetables, sliced fruits, aged cheeses, fresh bread... everything she had been dreaming of. Every memory of goodness that she'd dwelled in during the hungry months waited for her, just ahead.

Part of her thought this was a dream, but when she'd looked down at herself, she still had the same matted, filthy hair, and the same fingernails caked with grime, where they had not been torn away completely from digging for roots or climbing for birds eggs.

In her dreams she was never helpless like this. In her dreams, she was revered, respected, worshiped, even. A thousand voices whispering her name, a thousand eyes shining with hopes that she, only she, would notice them.

Now, however, she was dirty and small, clad in nothing but a tattered tunic taken from a dead soldier, his knife secured to her belt. Now she was hungry, in the months after her village had been decimated, and scared, knowing winter was coming. She knew it was unlikely she would survive on her own. Already the air had begun to bite her small hands. Already she shivered, deep in the night, buried under the pine needles and leaf litter that were the best the forest could provide.

And it would only get colder.

Where there was food like what she was smelling, though, there would be more. Fine clothes, probably. Maybe even blankets. Money would be useless to her - anyone of her size caught with money would only be robbed - but the other things she would be able to use.

Closer and closer she crept, the red-tinged light of afternoon bathing the bark of the trees in harmless shades of flame, the breeze wafting just enough to know she was going in the tantalizingly correct direction.

She closed her hand around her dagger. If there was a man there, she would kill him. She had done so before. If not, she would take what she could, and run before he got back.

She took three more steps, turned a corner around a massive old yew, and paused, her eyes widening.

In a perfectly circular clearing before her, illuminated by light streaming through the trees, lay a massive feast. Every dish she could imagine had been arranged on an enormous blanket rich with gold and silver embroidery. The dishes, too, were gold and silver, filled to the brim. There were steaming cuts of every kind of meat imaginable, from venison to pheasant, and entire loaves of crusty, perfectly-baked breads. Fruits she had never seen in her life lay in heaps, some cut open to display tantalizing, sparkly flesh colored like a shower of gemstones. A wheel of cheese made from dozens of wedges of different varieties lay in the center of the spread, and sweets glittered brightly, scattered about the dishes as if whoever had arranged the meal couldn't decide where they would fit.

The girl wiped a trail of drool from her chin and looked around. Nobody was there. The only sign of how the feast had arrived was a splendid carriage parked across the glen, with one white horse still hitched and an empty space where another had been. The remaining horse pricked its ears curiously at her, and shook its head with a sound of bells, but made no other noise to give her away.

Carefully. She had to do this carefully. If she was clever, and she knew she was clever, she could make off with a lot more than a single meal.

She went for the bread and cheese first, knowing they would keep the longest. She gathered up as much of an armload as she could manage before scampering off. She knew these woods, and ran first to an old oak with a hollow center. She shoved bread and cheese into the crevice and ran back. This time she hesitated, and, reasoning she would need strength to continue her raid, crammed a slice from one of the meat platters into her mouth.

It was unlike anything she had ever tasted; full of salt and fat, bursting with the flavor of herbs she could not name. For a moment she forgot her task and simply stood there, chewing, not even seeing the rest of the feast as she savored the magical slice.

Once she swallowed it, she had to have more. Breathing hard, she immediately crammed two more pieces into her mouth.

Good. So good. Tears blurred her vision while she chewed, but that only made her angry. She snapped out of her fervor – this was no time to get emotional! – and once more ladened her arms with bread and cheese. Once more she ran off, hiding the goods closer this time so she could get back to the feast more quickly. Once more she returned and, rewarding herself for her hard work, took some kind of pastry. She bit into it and found it was filled with...

meat? Mushrooms? She couldn't tell. It was rich with gravy and onions, and before she knew it she was on her knees, devouring it and two more before she could stop herself.

No, she silently screamed, no! This was her chance! If she did not focus she would die!

Tears of frustration ran down her face. Still chewing the pastry and with another in her hand, she looked around for anything that might serve as a blanket or coat.

There was nothing. Only the stretch of food resting on the spread cloth - far too much for her to pull along into the forest. Really, she could have begun throwing the dishes off and clearing the blanket to be taken, but despite her internal shrieking to hurry, she could not bring herself to damage food when she spent almost all her waking hours consumed by hunger.

Just looking at it was making her lose self control. An entire smoked trout was in her hands that she didn't remember taking, grapes dangling from between her fingers, and she alternated between gnawing at the fish and crunching the grapes, forcing herself over to the coach, pulling open the door with one hand, the other supported the mass of food that normally would have sustained her for a week.

Ah, here was a coat - a very fine one at that. It didn't have the fur she would have hoped for for warmth, but it certainly seemed made of something that would keep her protected, and many layers of stuff too, the outside some kind of wool that seemed to gently shift colors in the sunlight, like the colors on a bubble of soap, and the inside a creamy, silky texture that would feel good on her skin when the cold grew so intense it made her elbows crack.

She managed to pull the coat out, but the fish was down to bones in her hand, the grapes gone between her chomping teeth.

She stood there a moment, and felt true fear. She was afraid to turn around and see the feast again. She knew she would be drawn back. She understood that there was, perhaps, something wrong, that no one would leave so much food out without thinking to guard it. The only people who did such foolish things were lords, and all the lords she knew of would not hesitate to kill a filthy little *child who spoiled their picnic.*

She looked at the fish bones in her hands, blurry through her tears. Slowly, she closed her fingers around the bones. What was better? Dying, starving and cold in the winter? Or dying with a dagger in her hand, stolen food in her stomach, and a fancy coat on her back, plunder from her own daring?

She put the fish bones between her teeth, slid the coat over her shoulders, (it was too large for her, but she didn't care) and drew her dagger.

She was never one to accept dying at all, in fact. Not even when her village was being burned and raided by soldiers. Not even when everyone she knew had perished defending it.

She kept her eyes down and walked to the very edge of the blanket. The smell of the food brought saliva pooling around the fish bones, but she clutched them tight in her teeth, a ward against opening her mouth to anything new.

She chose a corner of the blanket where the most meat and bread lay, and began to cut, slicing through the rich cloth and making a smaller blanket that she could both manage to wrap around the food and use to cover herself later.

It was surprisingly difficult, though; the cloth of the blanket was very fine, and very thick, and her knife was dull after long months of use on less forgiving materials. Still she hacked and sawed, sweat dripping down her brow and drool trickling down her chin at the smell, the smells...she'd eaten loads, and yet she was still famished.

No, no, she had to focus. Focus. The presence of the single horse with his bells behind her was a warning. Someone had brought all this here. Someone would be returning.

She sawed and cut. She focused so hard and so efficiently that she didn't realize until too late that the jingling of the bells was accompanied by another nose: a steady clop-clop-clopping of hooves, getting closer...

A hand closed over her shoulder, and a smooth, beautiful voice said in her ear, "Well well. I thought to catch a little sunlight, and instead I found myself a shadow."

She snarled and leapt away - or tried to. Somehow the coat she'd stolen tangled her feet and she went sprawling in the dishes, slopping food everywhere with a great clatter of silver and gold.

The man - at least, she thought it was a man, though she'd never seen any man or woman so beautiful - only chuckled, running a pale hand through silvery-gold hair. In fact, all his clothes were silver and gold, as if he had dressed just to match his picnic.

The girl struggled to her feet, knife out and pointing at the man. She'd dropped the fishbones in her fall, but she knew her face was still smeared with all the crumbs and grease of the food she'd stolen. "You don't scare me!" she snarled at him.

He only smiled at her, the expression as beautiful as the rest of him, as beautiful as the feast, full of warmth and light and pleasure. "Then you are either," he said, "very brave, or very foolish, little one."

"I'll not take any of your names," she said coldly. Unfortunately for her, even though she was in danger, the food did not cease to smell amazing. Her eyes were drawn back to it against her will, watching the steam rise and the juice sparkle.

She jerked her gaze back to the man and his smile. "That's too much for one person," she said. "Who else were you waiting for?"

"Why," he laughed, "whoever would join me. Today, that seems to be you, child who speaks like an adult."

He ran a hand over the blanket and it mended itself where she had been cutting. She stared, open mouthed, as with another gesture of his hand he righted all the spilled food as well.

Magic.

She tore her gaze away from the cloth and glared at the stranger. "I remember before I was a child. In my old life."

He stared at her for a long time. When he spoke next, it was almost a whisper. "I would hear more. Please sit with me."

Her instincts screamed at her to run.

She looked again at the mended blanket, the righted tureens of food.

Instincts had their place, but the lure of what this man represented was stronger. After all, was it worth running, just to die in the winter cold a few months from now?

No. It was not.

She sat on the blanket, still holding the dagger, and did not reach for the food. A new hunger had awoken in her, one so real and from so deep within it made even the gleam of the enchanted feast seem false and foolish.

This man had power.

She wanted such power.

With power like that, she could survive the winter.

With enough power, she would never have to be afraid or hungry or cold ever again.

"Who are you?" she said, managing to make the words wary instead of hostile.

"I am but a traveler in this part of the world," smiled the man. "I am searching for someone. Someone wonderful, and worthy. Do you know anyone wonderful?"

The girl snorted. "All the wonderful people have died," she said. "They were killed, and them that did the killing went away."

The beautiful man met and held her gaze. When she stared back without flinching, his brow furrowed, and he was first to break the stare, glancing around at the feast. "You must have been alone and hungry for a long time," he said. "Won't you eat a bit more? With my permission, this time."

The girl's stomach growled in agreement with this offer, but she folded her hands in her lap, around the dagger, and continued to stare at the beautiful man. "No."

His eyes widened, and for a moment he didn't look human at all, but like a thing trying to pretend it was human and forgetting out of surprise, his features too extreme, too falsely perfect, as if they didn't actually belong together. He caught himself, though, and relaxed back into his smile, balance returning to his face. "No? You only want your food if it is stolen, wild one?"

"I do not want your food," she said, clenching her jaw so that no other sounds of hunger could escape.

He seemed to hear the unspoken words anyway, chuckling softly. "Is there," he said, sitting across from her so that their knees touched, "something else you want more?"

Her heart fluttered in her chest. He was so close, and so much...so much everything that anyone ever wanted to be. Rich, beautiful, powerful. She could feel all those things pulling at her, trying to impress her, but she was too hungry and tired, and too aware of her death before her, and the deaths of everyone she knew behind her, to forget the truth she had learned in those weeks of frigid starvation: no man of power ever truly cared for smaller men, let alone children.

"I want," she said flatly, "protection. From the cold, from hunger, and from men who would hurt me, or those that are mine. I want revenge on those who took everything from me. I want to be the hand of the dead, reaching from beyond the grave, to teach the living that they have done wrong, and that they should fear to do more wrong."

The beautiful man was silent for a moment, listening to her more intensely than anyone had ever listened to her in her life.

Then he leaned closer, the red sunlight gleaming in his silver-gold hair and his silver-gold eyes. "I hear your three wishes, little shadow," he said softly, and reached to capture her hand.

She let him, some part of her knowing already that as soon as she'd spoken the words aloud, it was too late to take them back.

He smiled at her, running his fair thumbs over her rough knuckles. "And if I can give you these three things," he said. "If I can give you food and shelter," he made her hand into a fist, and uncurled one finger, the first wish, "revenge on all who harmed you," a second finger, her dirty nails a stark contrast to his pearly skin, "and the power of the fear of the dead, will you give me three things in return?"

"What three things?" she asked warily. She wanted to pull away from his soft touch, but at the same time... she wanted him to stay, to continue holding her aching hand in his soft one, as her mother had done, any time she was upset.

The man hummed out a smile. "I want very simple things,"

he said coyly. "I would ask you for now only to go with me. To come live in my castle, and learn my ways, and be someone whose company I can enjoy."

"Those things are far from simple," the girl said dryly. She did pull her hand away then.

He caught it, however, and pulled it back with a laugh. "Fine, fine, clever shadow. For food and shelter, then, you will live with me, and be my company as I desire." His eyes gleamed, then, with a strange, inner light. "Is this a satisfactory agreement?"

"I will agree," she said with a wary nod, "but I won't pretend to be satisfied." She didn't really understand why a man who was so rich and splendid would want things like company from a dirty child like herself, but she had heard tales of such things happening before - village girls who went to live with young noblemen. She supposed she would learn soon enough, one way or another.

"Heh, we will see about that." The more she denied him, the hungrier his expression became. She knew hunger - she felt it herself constantly. His, as he revealed it, was almost a match for hers. "The next thing I will ask of you will come when you are a bit older...but I will pay for it in advance, with the last thing you asked - the power over the dead will be yours, though it is one of the most valuable gifts I have ever traded for. Do you agree?"

"It is foolish to agree when I do not yet know what you are asking," she said, putting some of winter's ice into her words. "Your power had better be worth it. Yes, I will agree - ah!"

As soon as she said it, something swirled through his hand into hers - something colder than winter and hungrier than a pack of rabid wolves. Something that settled into her core and burned and churned like a snake in throes of death.

He made his last demand then, as she was gasping and shivering with the new power settling into her bones. "My last thing I demand of you is that you come back to me always. In each life that you awaken in, I would see you again, child who does not forget her past...."

There was a snap, and her neck was suddenly encased in something cold and heavy.

He smirked at her then, and for the first time, his face was not beautiful. "The second gift I gave you," he said, "will take care of your last request. Once you have mastered your power, you will be able to seek your revenge."

"That means you only gave me two things," she growled, feeling the thing around her neck. It was a collar! But it reflected light back onto her hand in shades of yellow - a golden collar?

He shrugged. "The two gifts will take care of your three wishes."

She gaped at him. Everything that had happened had been so magical, and so...true! But somehow he had lied, even within the middle of it?

Her gape turned into a glare. She tugged at her collar, tears burning in her eyes. "Take this off me," she demanded. "I don't like it."

"Once I am sure you won't try to break our deal," the man said, smiling his eternal, false smile, "I will remove it. But until then, you will remember..."

She bent almost in half, gasping, trying to pull the collar free. No matter how she tugged, however, she could not budge it. No matter how she felt along its edges, she could find no seam.

"You will remember," he whispered, "that no matter if or where you try to escape..."

"No!" she shrieked.

"I will always, always-"

"Fabian!" Ruphys' arms around her as she cried aloud in her sleep. "It's alright, Fabian, you're safe-"

"Fabian?"

Fabian snapped their head up.

It took them a moment to re-orient themselves - to recognize that this green, early-fall forest was not the pre-winter one of their dream. The man speaking their name was neither Ruphys nor Faerie foe, but James Buckler, looking at them with a frown. They were seated not upon a picnic blanket but upon the hard back of an undead cow skeleton, the ridges of bone cushioned with their own folded cloak, plodding steadily forward. James, too, rode a skeletal creature, as did Theli and Iris behind him. The ladies were having some kind of argument, and following them marched the undead hundreds.

"Fabian," James said again, and Fabian once again forced their attention his way. "Are you alright?"

"Yes, yes, fine, Doctor." Fabian waved a hand. "Simply dozing from the monotony of the road." Half true. The other half of the truth was that maintaining all these undead soldiers, even with the assistance of their magic-enhancing necklace, was exhausting. They had not been practicing necromancy on this scale since the purging of the plague rats from London over a year ago. So too, they were hungry again, and tired from the rigors of the journey itself. So too, they had not recovered from the days of travel before getting to Faerie, nor from the trials of bearing a child before that.

Really, they were lucky James had said something. It would have been humiliating indeed if they'd fallen off their steed all together.

Grimley, who rode on Fabian's other side, pulled out an apple and offered it, the red bright against his hoof-like fingers. "I seem to remember you burn through your meals more quickly than most."

Fabian gave the dark-furred fae a wry look. He had, upon requesting to accompany them on this journey, produced his own half-style plague mask, neatly concealing the top half of his face and muzzle. His horns poked through the silver-trimmed black leather, and his yellow eyes somehow looked perfectly correct amongst the delicate ornamentation. The mask did not encircle his whole jaw, leaving him free to speak clearly, unlike Fabian and James' masks, which had a tendency to muffle.

"You don't have to be wearing that," Fabian said, accepting the apple regardless. Their own mask hung from their belt. They sank their teeth into the very real, slightly sour fruit. Dream food it was not, and they were quite happy for it. Grimley had remembered correctly. Why couldn't Fabian have dreamed about past adventures with Grimley, instead of one child's mistake that had cost multiple lifetimes of freedom?

"It is amusing to dress the part, and fit in with the rest of the group," Grimley gestured at James's mask, hanging from one of his mount's vertebrae, and Theli's, swinging from one horn of her undead cow as she bickered with Iris. "Anyway, I want to practice wearing it before we reach the castle. It is better to get used to things ahead of time, not while plunging into imminent danger."

Fabian rolled their eyes, but couldn't quite repress a smile. Grimely, for all his stiff posturing, did like a bit of fun now and then. "What are they arguing about back there?" Fabian asked, not wanting to think about the castle just yet. The voices of Iris and Theli rose with passion, and the necromancer had half a mind to turn and silence them both.

James snorted. "Iris thinks we should simply kill the King when we meet him."

"Which is completely unreasonable!" Theli shouted. Her voice was rougher in anger, her claws out, gripping the bone of her mount. "Assassination is not how you generate understanding and peaceful relations between districts-"

"But you already aren't getting those things," Iris said calmly. "The boroughs do not talk or trade amongst themselves. You cannot even find each other without magical assistance."

"Nonsense!" Theli tossed her head, her glorious copper mane shimmering in the bright sunlight. "I've been able to find my way between boroughs for years, and I learned magic from the Mageborn and lunar cycles from the Lycans and-"

"That was before the King knew what you were doing," Iris spoke over Theli, arranging her pale head-petals neatly as if to contrast the wildness of Theli's mane. "Have you been able to go to and fro once you told him of your antics?"

Theli's ears drooped. "No."

"The King is the one standing in the way of the peace you seek," Iris said, the gleam of victory - or perhaps hunger - in her segmented eyes. "Killing him would be the quickest way to bring cooperation between the peoples."

"Killing the King," Fabian said, not turning around but speaking loud enough for both of them to hear, "would be the beginning of an era of upheaval, war and chaos like neither of you have ever witnessed."

Both ladies fell silent at the words. Finally Theli spoke, "What do you mean?"

Fabian beckoned, and Theli's and Iris' skeletal mounts quickened their pace so they could be side by side with Fabian, saving the need to shout. "The Land of the Changelings," Fabian said, gesturing to the spread of leafless trees around them, "must have a King. All the citizens expect a King. The land itself has learned to expect a King, hence why the roads obey his will. Do you know of any time when there was no King in Faerie?"

Theli shook her head, but Iris said, "I do know that the Kingship belonged to a family of dragons, many generations ago."

"Ah, yes," Fabian gave a bitter smile. "The son and heir of the dragon line fell in love with a human and abandoned crown and castle to chase 'true love,' leaving the land to rot in the hands of whoever wished to replace him. A fairytale indeed. You see what happens when a king, even a dragon king, leaves the throne free for the taking?"

Iris and Theli exchanged unsure glances.

Fabian leaned towards them. "Another king steps forward to take it. Who wants such a crown the most? A person who desires power, luxury and splendor. A person with no real understanding of rulership and all the work it entails - for anyone who craves trappings of material wealth and social power cares little for the labor that comes with being responsible for the lives of many. You understand where I am going with this."

Theli nodded. "The Facited King rose to power because there was no system in place to choose someone better," she said, "and he hasn't exactly put any structure in place for a successor. Another King who took his place could be just as bad..."

"Or worse." Fabian said, smirking. "Imagine one who demanded all first-born children be sacrificed to her endless appetite." They gave Iris a pointed look, but the floral changeling only smiled, showing all her sharp teeth.

"But what if we made one of our own people King?" Theli asked, eyes shining with eagerness. "Someone who would want to use power for the good of all-"

"Envisioning how a crown would fit over your horns?" Fabian asked, amused. "Well, I cannot blame you for your ambition. How much have you studied governmental policy, Theli?"

"Governmental...you can study that?" Theli looked surprised.

"Of course you can. You can study the policies of past rulers, to see where they failed and where they succeeded. You can study the history of your country, to know what problems and patterns tend to arise. You should also have a strong understanding of economics – you know about economics, I assume? Supply and demand - market values and trade regulations?"

Theli's shoulders slumped.

"No?" Fabian chuckled. "I am afraid even the best intentions will descend into chaos if one does not have the knowledge and experience to support their implementation."

"Is that what you did then?" James asked sharply, glowering at Fabian over his shoulder. Privately, Fabian wondered if the tension in his voice was from more than the conversation topic. How many hours has it been since his dunk in the Living Waters? Fabian wondered if his new-found liveliness would wear off, once the magical liquid left his system.

James continued, "You studied economics, and government policy, and history, before claiming the throne at the tender young age of twenty three?"

"I did," Fabian said, turning to face James. "And I also recruited the best courtiers I could find over several lifetimes. You remember my servant Wilfred?"

James nodded stiffly.

"He has a gift for economic comprehension and manipulation that I have never witnessed in another soul, living or dead."

A memory flashed in Fabian's mind - Wilfred holding little Willamina on his lap, looking anxious and awestruck at the tiny form, with Ruphys reassuring the undead genius that it was alright to relax, he wasn't going to drop her...

Fabian shook the memory away. "He kept the kingdom running smoothly for 40 years. I had, and still have, many such servants; men and women gifted in their understanding and specialties. That is, you see, the true key to being a good king." Well, that and the courage and heartlessness it took to decimate your political opponents, but Fabian didn't expect this group of dew-eyed idealists to understand that part.

"Yeah, that worked out real well for you," James said, words so heavy with irony it was a marvel they didn't break his jaw. "Don't you love how people assassinate the Kings they think are doing a brilliant job?"

Fabian shrugged. "Just because I'm a genius doesn't mean the common fool can recognize it. Anyway..." they hooked a lock of hair behind one ear. "There's a good reason I didn't 're-apply' for the position. I was replaced by a puppet - a descendant of the old monarchy, with strings pulled by courtiers who had hungered for the power and influence lost in the old days. The citizenry celebrate the return of the 'true Queen.' If the common ignoramus would rather be run by greedy fools than a brilliant and charming strategist, then they are earning their own ill fortune. I intend to stay well out of it."

A pensive silence stretched over the group. Fabian

counted the seconds, and at exactly twelve, as they expected, James said, "I have serious trouble believing you would just drop your ambition for-"

"It wasn't ambition," Fabian spoke over him, their impatience rising. "Honestly, Doctor, is it so difficult to imagine that I sought to rule England out of a desire to make it a better place to live?"

"*Impossible* to imagine!"

"Why so impossible?" Fabian spread their arms, as if they weren't aware of the army of skeletons encompassed by the gesture. "Why would I want to *ruin* the world, Dr. Buckler? After all, *I am the one who will still has to live in it*, lifetime after lifetime!"

That shut him up. That shut them all up. Iris and Theli's argument lay forgotten in the dust of their passing army.

With every step, the trees thinned around them, and the pale shape of the Faceless King's castle grew steadily clearer.

"Then," Grimley broke the silence, politely inquiring, "what is it you propose we do, once we get to the castle, if not kill the King?"

Fabian jerked a thumb over their shoulder at their army. "I'm going to tear his castle down stone by stone until he opens a gate to let us out." Spoken as if they were sure it would work. Knowing it wouldn't be so simple.

Grimley eyed them as if he had heard Fabian's unspoken worry. "I suppose there is little room for error."

"What error could there possibly be?" Fabian asked, tilting their head. "He has no army. He doesn't believe in having many armed, trained beings around that might take issue with his rule. He keeps no pet mages to fortify his castle. He doesn't trust any with power that he himself does not possess. I imagine he has to make a deal, too, any time he needs a bit of complicated spellwork done."

Like the plague curse, they thought wryly.

"The most he has is a light guard assembled of brainwashed faecaught who have been promised to him since

340

birth, and even those have little more than basic combat trailing. They will be no match for an army of undead guided by an experienced strategist."

"These things you say are true," Grimley gave a nod.

"So you see," Fabian said, allowing themselves a bit of smugness, if only to soothe their nerves, "there really is no weapon he can wield against me. Er. Us."

The castle drew nearer, as if the road itself were being pulled along into the entrance like a worm into a hungry bird's beak.

Fabian tried to pretend every step didn't fill them with dread. They wrapped their fingers around a vertebra of their mount, and glowered at the approaching castle.

'You are not finding me this time,' they told him, 'I am finding you.'

"It is hard to imagine a King that cares about the needs of his people," Iris mused. "If such a king did rule in Faerie, I expect all the land would come to petition him with requests. I myself would, on this very journey."

Theli pricked her ears forward at that. "Oh? What would you ask for?"

"I would request for the gate to be opened again near my home," Iris said. "I wish to travel more to the lands of logic, and properly learn doctoring. Also," she grinned hungrily, "I miss the visitors that would find their ways to me. Nothing yet matches the enjoyment they bring me with their tributes."

Fabian rolled their eyes, but paid close attention to this exchange. After all, learning what motivated people was a key step to controlling, er...inspiring them to cooperation.

"And you, Grimley?" Theli asked. "What would you ask for, if we had a king who granted favors?"

"Hmmm..." Grimley swished his tail. "I, too, would like to travel in the human lands. It has been many years since I added to my collection of books. I would enjoy some new reading material."

"And you, Dr. Buckler?" Theli turned to James.

Fabian all but felt the castle increase its approach with James' desire not to have this conversation. The doctor didn't answer right away. Fabian wondered whether it was because he did not want to share his personal feelings, or because he still hadn't decided which of his needs was most pressing. They wondered, yet again, just how alive he was under all those layers.

"I don't know," the doctor said at last, his short tone making it clear he did not wish to be pressed on the matter. "Getting our hopes up at this stage is foolish anyway. It is better to focus on the task at hand."

"Indeed it is."

Fabian drew the party to a stop at the edge of the forest. The oaks, beeches, and birches ended in a neat line, right before the castle walls.

"Remember," they cautioned the party, "we are not here to bargain. We are here to demand. We will not fall prey to any deals, gifts, or offers, as anything that tempts you will doubtless have a hook meant to pierce right through your gills. The King likes to bribe and to trap."

They resisted a shiver, remembering their own cage of so many years.

A golden collar around their neck.

Cold stones on their back.

They firmed their voice, speaking with sharp, unmistakable callousness, "If you make a foolish choice because you believe lies and whispers, I will not save you. I will leave you to rot in your own freshly-dug grave. Is that understood?"

Even as Fabian spoke, their skeleton army marched around the living party members, lining themselves up along the stone walls, bleached bones an almost perfect match to the pale bricks forming the castle defenses.

The assembled group of the living nodded, their shared anxiety nearly palpable in the still air.

"Very good," Fabian said. "Now, brace yourselves - we

will knock until a messenger is sent out to ask our demands."

They smiled, a sharp, tight thing.

"I predict it will not take three knocks before those doors open."

"Get on with it," James said irritably.

"Please, Doctor. Allow an old necromancer their theatrics," Fabian said with half a bow his way.

They turned their mount back towards the castle, and lifted their hands, closed their eyes, focusing on the strings of power connecting them with their cadaverous army.

Four hundred skeletal fists raised into the air and fell against the stone as one enormous cracking noise, making the whole wall release a puff of dust.

"One," Fabian said lazily.

Again the fists raised and fell with a cacophonous crunch. A few pale stones loosed, crumbling down with an audible clatter.

"Two..."

A rattle of metal and a creek of hinges interrupted the knocking pattern.

Fabian opened their eyes, grinning. "Voilà..."

A figure in a white robe stepped out of the gate and bowed to the company. Its yellow, slit-pupil eyes were set deep in a white crocodilian face, and it carried a spear in one clawed hand. The other hand bore a scroll, from which it began to read, "By order of the King-"

"We accept your surrender," Fabian said, waving a hand. "Open a gate so we can get out of-"

"- you are all cordially invited to a feast celebrating your arrival and the future alliance between families and peoples."

Fabian froze.

"The King promises his full hospitality to all guests as long as they abide by the rules of decency while within his walls, and thanks every member of the party for taking the time to journey across the lands in order to-"

"NO." Fabian shouted.

Everyone turned to look at them. Fabian's vision tilted - they couldn't read the expressions on their companion's faces, but they didn't need to. It was all they could do to keep their clenched fists from trembling.

"We do not accept hospitality," they said with forced calm. "We make a demand-"

"Maybe we should hear him out?" Theli said breathlessly. "I mean, I know what we agreed, but this is exactly what I hoped for-"

"Don't be a fool!" Fabian snapped. "It's a trap! Of course it's a trap!"

"The King has promised hospitality," Iris pointed out. Her colors had faded slightly, as if she were trying to match the outfit of the guard out of politeness. "The binding power of that promise is older than he is. Old as the land itself. Surely you know this."

"It doesn't matter! He is bound by no law but his own!" Breathing heavily, Fabian was fumbling for their daggers before they realized it. They wanted to fight - they wanted to run. They could do neither, and the war that waged between the two desires was pulling them apart at the seams. "Better to kill this messenger and send the King his head than to-"

"Fabian." James' hand closed on their arm. Not tightly, he wasn't threatening them, only offering them a point of contact. A grounding. "Nobody is agreeing to any deals. Surely there is no harm in gathering more information before we proceed?"

Fabian wanted to shout at him. They wanted to shake him till his hat fell off and snarl into his face that there was *all* the harm. They leaned close to James, one hand gripping his lapel, the other still holding their dagger. "Every moment," they breathed, "in his presence is a chance for him to win. Agreeing to the rules of hospitality means *I* cannot strike out at him first without sacrificing the protection of those very same rules. This is *exactly* how we lose the advantage here!"

James met their fury calmly. "You yourself said we are

not here to kill him. Unless you can open a gate yourself, Fabian, we need him willing to bargain."

As angry as they were, as terrified as they were, Fabian was not a fool. They could see Iris and Theli meeting each other's eyes, silently agreeing with James. They could see Grimley's awkward averting of his gaze, for he knew as much as Fabian did that one simply could not turn down hospitality offered so openly and honestly, or all of Faerie would turn against you.

Fabian knew, too, that somewhere in those stone halls was Bartholomew Wayman, and if Fabian didn't agree to the invitation, Dr. Wayman might not survive his visit.

"Fools," they whispered, hating the tears that burned in their eyes. "All of you, damned fools, damning me along with you."

They straightened their spine.

"Fine."

They tucked all anger, terror and frustration away in neat little boxes, placed the boxes in a chest, and closed it with locks of steel.

If this was how the tide of the war would turn, they would simply pull out more suitable weapons.

Blood would spill before the night was out.

"Fine," they said again, louder. "We accept the King's hospitality, as long as he does, truly, abide by the rules of decency."

The pale crocodile bowed low enough for them all to see the neat braid falling down his back scales. "Please follow me, and, er..."

The messenger, for the first time, showed some signs of nervousness. "Please leave your mounts and escorts outside, as the feast hall does not have room to accommodate them as well as all the other guests."

"Other guests?" Fabian repeated, heart sinking further.

Theli and Iris were already scrambling down from their steeds. Fabian pressed their lips together and had the other mounts kneel, allowing all members of the party to dismount.

"Yes, other guests!" The crocodile's slit pupils dilated in wonder, staring at the skeletal creatures. "It is an occasion of great joy and celebration."

"And what is the occasion?" James demanded, stepping over to offer Fabian his arm. Fabian accepted in silent gratitude, hating his thoughtfulness, even though they knew their shaking legs might give out if they didn't have it. They were so tired.

"A most wondrous announcement, known only to the King! But, um…"

The crocodile hesitated, looking at each member of the party. Then he leaned closer, saying in a low, trembling voice, "You haven't got any more of those masks, have you?"

"Why?" James asked sharply. Fabian turned their head back to the creature as well, suddenly much more interested in what he had to say.

"N-no reason," if crocodiles could sweat, this one would be. "Um, if anyone asks, the rumors aren't true."

"What rumors?" Fabian said, a flutter of hope making its way through their locks and chests and boxes protecting their heart.

The crocodile swallowed hard, throat-scales visibly quavering. "Th-the rumors of the plagued prisoners escaping. Everything is under control. We have nothing to fear." He said it too loudly, as if someone had made him rehearse it several times.

Fabian and James exchanged a look, and for the first time in what felt like an eternity, Fabian laughed.

"Please," they said, bowing to the crocodile and then resting their arm once more on James', "lead the way."

He nodded, rolling up the scroll and turned back. The doors opened wide enough to accommodate the entire party at once. The revealed castle grounds were full of pale birches, white flagstone, and a black-leafed morning glory trailing its way around a fountain that sparkled and danced, glittering in the midday sunlight.

The crocodile tucked the scroll into his tunic, bowing low to them all and gesturing down the central path of the courtyard to a pair of huge silver doors emblazoned with golden dragons. "This way."

Dozens of memories flashed through Fabian's mind upon seeing those doors. Long-buried emotions tried to claw their way through Fabian's defenses.

Fabian took a deep breath, gripped James' arm a little more tightly, and smiled into the torrent of light and memory and feeling.

They had come here of their own free will. They would leave of it too.

Just as they had before.

"Tell the King," they said, at last letting go of James and smoothing their dirty, travel-worn robes, "that he had better lay a more impressive table than last time I was here."

They made a show of yawning and stretching, for any watching eyes to see they were completely at ease.

"I'd hate to come all this way and find the fair the same as it's been for the past five hundred years."

The crocodile looked like he'd rather bite off his own tongue than convey such a rude message to his master, but he bowed again, scampering ahead a few paces. "I-I'm sure you will find all our accommodations completely satisfactory."

"I doubt that," Fabian chuckled. And, strangely enough, the chuckle combined with their facade of carelessness eased some of their internal tension. "Your King knows very little about accommodating people of taste. And I..."

They slipped their hands into the sleeves of their robe, feeling the comforting, reassuring weight of their loyal daggers.

They could do this.

They had to do this.

"I am never satisfied."

CHAPTER 24: REUNION

Jeremiah ran down the pristine white halls and hated every second of it.

He'd never so badly wished for his voice. He wanted to snarl, to scream, to hiss Shilling's name so the stupid changeling would come back. Probably for the best that he couldn't, though, as technically he wasn't supposed to still be in the castle. Technically he was free, all his favors paid for, and he and Shilling should have been miles away by now, maybe even back in the world of logic.

Instead here he was, sprinting over pale stone and pausing at each doorway to peek inside and whistle softly.

Shilling? Shilling?

Nothing greeted him but silence. Nothing showed its face but memories - cursed memories, memories of pain and humiliation and discomfort, the King's words and the King's smile and the King's hands... ugh. Shilling knew how much he hated it here. Shilling hated it too, for he felt Jeremiah's emotions as if they were his own. It was why Shilling stayed in the stable, rather than face the King at Jeremiah's side.

Jeremiah should never have told him what had happened in the throne room.

"You just let them take Barty?" Shilling had demanded, outraged. "Why didn't you fight them?"

I tried to! Jeremiah signed back angrily. *I faced the King himself! I was outnumbered!*

Shilling stomped his silver hoof. "We aren't leaving him there!"

Yes we are, we are getting out of here right now–

Jeremiah had reached for Shilling's bridle, but too late. The horse shifted into a tiny silver grass snake and zipped away, through the stable door, through the morning glory and birches and finally slithering his way into the servant's entrance, squeezing under the crack of the door and disappearing from sight.

Jeremiah had had no choice but to follow him, cursing in words he couldn't speak aloud.

Luckily the castle staff were used to seeing him around and hadn't questioned his sudden appearance.

Luckily the King had been occupied with something else going on; the walls had shaken only moments ago, and panicked servants ran hither and thither, setting the long table in the grand hall and preparing guest rooms. Jeremiah overheard them whispering among each other, 'undead army' and 'Berthelia of the Decided' and also 'Guardian of the Living Waters' passed from mouth to mouth faster than a spreading plague.

Jeremiah understood, all too clearly. An undead army meant only one thing.

The necromancer was coming, with allies.

More than enough reason for Jeremiah and Shilling to

get out and away, as quickly as possible. If Fabian were anything at all like the King, there would be no forgetting and no forgiving.

So where the hell was Shilling?

Something strange was happening to the hallways - he'd just come this way, but the length had shifted even as he passed through.

The King was changing the castle.

Jeremiah needed to find Shilling and get out of here.

He whistled again, daring to be a little louder.

He got a growling bellow in return.

Just in time he ducked into a room, fighting every instinct of haste and closing the door in painfully slow silence. The heavy clomping of boots and scrape of sword on stone passed by on the other side, and he shivered, knowing very well that there was only one creature that size the King kept on his staff. So, even the Jailer was out on the prowl. Maybe that meant Shilling had accomplished what he wanted and gotten Barty out. At least Jeremiah didn't have to search the dungeon. But then where on earth-

Something clattered to the ground behind Jeremiah.

He had only a moment of warning - a chill down his spine that made him spin, drawing his sword, just in time to block an iron spike swinging at his face. The resulting crash between his blade and the spike drove him back into the door which flew open, spilling both himself and his attacker into the hallway.

Eyes glowing green. Black hair. Filthy skin. The Raven, bleeding and feral, wrestled Jeremiah to the floor, kneeling on his middle and using both hands, one bloody, one bandaged to try and drive the spike into Jeremiah's face. He looked an absolute madman, his features twisted in a snarl of unending fury. Even with both of Jeremiah's hands locked on the handle of his blade, the spike inched closer and closer to Jeremiah's face-

"SIR!" A horrified shout came from back in the room.

Dr. Barty sprinted out, dirty, barefoot and with his shirt half undone. He grabbed the Raven's wrists and pulled his hands away from Jeremiah's face. "Stop that at once!"

Shilling came speeding out as well, in silver fox form, and flung himself over Jeremiah's chest and face, worming his way between Jeremiah and the threatening human. "No, no, no!" he whined. "Don't hurt him! My Master!"

"He's the one who captured me and brought me here!" the Raven spat. He was in utter disarray; shirtless and gore-covered, green eyes blazing with the same unnatural light they had the night Jeremiah had caught him. However, despite his fury and the strength Jeremiah knew could easily overcome any normal man, Barty was able to pull him off, the doctor's hands both firmly clenching the Raven's spike-wielding ones.

"I am sure there is an explanation!" Barty gasped. He put himself between the Raven and Jeremiah - Jeremiah could not see his face, but he could hear his sincerity "I believe you, sir, that you have suffered terribly here. But this man - Jeremiah the Huntsman, he has already risked his life to save me once! Please do not harm him!"

The Raven's eyes were riveted to Barty's face. "He is part of this," he growled, soft but accusing. "The plot to spread this plague. He is complicit!"

Jeremiah stayed down, but he silently stroked Shilling, then put up his hands to sign so the changeling could translate for him. "*I did not know,*" he signed. "*I did not know that you were anything but a murderer. I did not know that you were part of a larger plan. I am the Huntsman - I hunt monsters. I do not get involved.*" He hesitated a moment, his gaze caught on the slow-healing magical runes carved into the Raven's chest. "*The King used you to work a spell?*"

"Of course he did, you-!" The Raven tried to step past Barty, but Barty once again planted himself firmly in his path. The Raven glared at Barty, then looked down, closed his eyes, and spoke tight words through gritted teeth. "The spell they carved into me was one that was meant to keep the plague going. I..." for a moment he looked sick, dizzy. "I...I don't know how I know. But the knowledge is there. Where did it come from?" He looked to Barty, almost frightened, as if asking him for help. His blood dripped down his unbandaged hand onto the white marble, pooling beside his bare feet. Clearly Barty had been in the middle of changing his bandages when Jeremiah had burst in.

Jeremiah pushed himself up enough to sit, but left his sword on the floor, showing he would not attack. *"You do not remember?"* he signed, surprised. *"How can you not know? Don't you know who your mother was?"*

"My...mother?" The Raven stared at Jeremiah, and suddenly there were tears in his eyes - tears that dripped red and black down his face. "Mother..." he said again, his voice breaking. "I...I don't remember..."

Barty took the man's hand in both of his own. He held it with unhesitating gentleness, stroking his thumbs over the bandages. "It's alright," the doctor said softly. "It's alright."

The Raven closed his eyes, swallowed hard and did not move, clearly suffering, clearly calmed by the doctor's touch and presence.

Jeremiah wondered just how many times Barty had spoken those same words to his ill patients in the past. And, although he sighed to admit it, unless this was a very, very good act, Jeremiah did not think the Raven was lying about his loss of memory.

"His name," Shilling said suddenly.

'*What?*' Jeremiah looked at the fox, puzzled.

"Whatever deal he made with the King," Shilling said, looking back gravely at Jeremiah, "he traded away his name to get what he wanted. Everything he was that made him *himself*, his family, his history...the King has it all now. The Raven would keep his basic knowledge, but everything that is *him* has been taken, except for whatever motivation he had to make the trade to begin with."

'*The King can take someone's name away entirely?*'

Jeremiah asked, puzzled. The King knew his own name, but he'd only ever used it to control Jeremiah, not to modify his memory. He turned his gaze back to the Raven - the bloody fellow gripped Barty's hands tightly with both his own, as if the young man were his only anchor in a stormy sea. Tears still trickled silently down his face, but he was listening to every word.

"He can, if you agree to give it to him," Shilling explained, his voice unusual somber. "And he can replace it with whatever he wants. Any command. Any idea. Half the Kingsworn have no names anymore." He turned his foxy face back to the Raven and Barty. "You're lucky you escaped before the King ordered you to act. And you better understand right now: if the King sees you and gives you a command, you won't be able to disobey him." He shook his head, and shivered. "You should never have given away your name."

"B-but the King knows my name," Barty said, turning to cast a fearful look at Shilling. "Am I doomed too?"

Shilling looked troubled, but Jeremiah shook his head. *'He wasn't able to command you the first time without a lot of effort,'* he signed. *'He must be missing something. I've never seen someone resist the way you did. Do you have a different name you didn't tell him?'*

Barty nodded. "I do. My birth name, in Hebrew."

'Good,' Jeremiah signed heavily. *'Don't share it.'* He looked to the Raven, who seemed to have recovered somewhat, wiping the bloody tears off his face and cradling his still-bloody palm. *'Can I stand up now? I won't attack you.'*

"Stay on the floor," the Raven said, a dark, unspoken promise in his voice.

"Oh, sir-" Barty began, exasperated.

But Jeremiah held up a hand, bidding them both to stop. A noise over their chatter...yes, there it was, coming down the hall towards them. Heavy steps. The sound of dragging metal.

Whoever Jeremiah had passed before - the Jailer, most likely - was coming back, doubtless attracted by all the shouting voices. '*Hide!*' he signed to the others.

Barty and the Raven didn't need telling twice. They hurried out of the hallway, back into the room.

Jeremiah followed as well, one hand clutching Shilling to his chest, the other snagging his sword. He stayed crouched low in case whoever it was suddenly turned the corner. Sometimes breaking the pillar of the human silhouette was enough for a foe to miss you.

The steps were slow, however, slow enough so that Jeremiah had time to get to the room and shut the door behind him. Then, under the watchful eye of the Raven, he lowered himself back down again, propping his shoulders more comfortably against the wood. He looked at the Raven and raised an eyebrow. '*Acceptable?*'

The Raven's mouth twitched. "Acceptable." He, too, went back and sat in a chair. Barty followed, picking up the bandages once more.

Now that Jeremiah was in the room he could see what the men had been doing. There were a few stacks of clean clothes on the table, as well as an assortment of boots, belts, and gloves. In fact, the entire room was lined with shelves and chests, with multiple closet doors half open, showing splendid arrays of garments inside.

Jeremiah frowned around at it all. '*What is this place?*'

"I think it's some kind of store room? Or spoils room?" Now that Barty had re-bandaged the Raven's hand, he was trying, with gentle futility, to tend to the wounds on his chest. The wounds seemed to be reluctantly closing, but they still oozed, the floor around his chair peppered with red drops. "There are so many different kinds of clothing here," Barty explained, "and in all sizes - I think this is where the King must store the things he's traded for, or taken...none of it seems faerie make to me. I mean-"

He held up a shirt - well, once it had been a shirt, now it was half a shirt as it had been stripped to make rags. "This is just simple cotton. Good quality, but I'm fairly sure I have one just like it at home."

He tore another strip off, and went back to dabbing. "I wish I had my needle and thread," he said miserably. "Or at least hot water - or even some water left in my flask. You really can't remember the healing spell, sir?"

"It dances just beyond my recall," The Raven sighed. "I can almost see it, but not quite." The Raven didn't seem terribly disturbed by the young doctor fussing over him. His green eyes were on Barty's face, and only seemed to remember Jeremiah was there when the hunter cleared his throat. He cast Jeremiah an annoyed look, but Jeremiah didn't let it stop him.

'*I think,*' Jeremiah signed, and Shilling spoke, more to Barty than the Raven, '*we have all been used.*'

'What do you mean?" Barty repeated, frowning. Even with his attention on Jeremiah, he continued applying pressure to the wounds.

'*The Raven was tricked into giving his name - making him into a monster. I assume you sold yourself for vengeance?*'

The Raven paused - a moment that stretched into something unnatural, his eyes going completely unfocused, his breath slowing, and his silence filling the room with near-smothering weight.

Then, at last, he said, "my father," and once again, that strange green light flashed in his eyes. He made a noise of discomfort, and covered his face with a hand, breathing hard.

Jeremiah frowned at him. He carefully let one hand settle on the handle of his sword, signing with the other for Shilling to translate. '*Your father was Dr. Rivers, correct?*'

Another silence, but this one was less like a gap in presence and more like a gathering of deadly intent.

"Stop talking," the Raven said.

Jeremiah knew that story - everyone in Whiston knew the story - that Dr. Rivers had come from a village that hated magic, and married the most powerful witch of the generation. '*I think Dr. Rivers was used as well,*' Jeremiah said, though he could feel Shilling tensing on his chest, clearly not liking how upset the words made the Raven. '*I think someone gave him an incomplete curse and told him that if it were completed, it would cure plague from his village, and then magic from his family. I think someone needed that brilliant mind of his-*'

"Shut up-"

'*To finish a curse that would go along a family line. Maybe the doctor even had his intelligent and magically gifted wife help him with the puzzle. Maybe she unwittingly crafted the very nature of her own death. And then, when the doctor had done the dirty work and, in the process, accidentally killed his wife, the King offered a deal to his son, who was all but mad with grief-*'

"I told you to shut your mouth!" The Raven's chair clattered across the room. He lunged for Jeremiah. Jeremiah threw himself to the side, fumbling for a weapon. Before either of them could connect, however, the door was pulled open with such great force that it tore clean off its hinges.

The Raven skidded to a stop, slipped on his own blood and fell flat on the floor. Jeremiah rolled to his feet, sword in both his hands, Shilling scrambling to get back on his paws.

An enormous figure loomed in the doorway - bloody robes, hooded head, sword dragging at his side. The Jailer looked from one combatant to the other. Steam rose around his hidden face from the kettle he clenched in one dirty, gloved hand. A deep, grinding growl echoed through the room, making the steam swirl away from him.

Jeremiah lunged, sword flashing. The Jailer swung his own blade with impossible speed, blocking just in time. Sparks and chips of rust flew, and Jeremiah dodged back, narrowly avoiding a blow so powerful it would have taken his head clean off.

"Stop, stop!" Barty leapt forward, right between the two combatants. He put his back to Jeremiah and held up both hands towards the Jailer. "Sir!" he exclaimed. "You brought the hot water?"

Jeremiah's mouth fell open.

The Jailer turned his attention to Barty, and his growl

stopped, replaced by a softer rumble as he nodded. He gave Barty the steaming kettle, then dug around in his robe and produced a few almost-clean rolls of bandages and a bar of soap, which he also handed over.

"Thank you so, so much," Barty said, absolutely beaming at the creature. "You have done really well!"

The Jailer stood a bit straighter, clearly pleased by the praise.

Jeremiah could not believe his eyes. This had to be magic.

"There is just one more thing," Barty said, carefully staying between the Raven and the Jailer, blocking the creature's view of his former prisoner. "I really, really need a needle and thread to do some sewing work. Do you know if anyone in this palace has a needle and thread? One of those curved needles would be best."

The Jailer tilted his head - the motion making it even clearer that his executioner's hood hung over long horns. Finally he nodded and turned away, dragging his sword back out the door and down the hall, apparently on his way to find what Barty wanted.

The Raven finally pushed himself up off the floor, staring at Barty. "Are you," he croaked, "a wizard? Did you bespell him?"

"What? No, of course not! I'm a doctor, not a magic-user." Barty carefully set the hot water and bandages on the table, and ushered the Raven back into his chair.

'Then how on earth did you do that?' Jeremiah demanded, equally puzzled.

"I - well! I just gave him a chance, you see." Barty seemed embarrassed. He settled some of the rags in the hot water, and worked the soap into a lather. "S-sometimes people aren't so bad, if you just give them a chance to do the right thing. Right, sirs?" He looked meaningfully between the Raven and Jeremiah.

Jeremiah sighed, and sheathed his sword.

The Raven gave a soft laugh, shaking his head and settling back in his chair. "You really do believe that, don't you."

"With all my heart," Barty said, giving him a pat before going back to his bloody task of cleaning wounds.

"Believing has a lot of power, in magic and in Faerie," Shilling piped up. "You probably did bespell him, in your own way."

"And have I bespelled all of you, too?" Barty asked, his tone suggesting only amusement at a foolish idea.

There was a silence as Shilling, Jeremiah and the Raven exchanged glances.

Barty sensed their silent agreement, blushed and cleared his throat. "Erm. Anyway, what I want to know is - why would the King want to curse a family line, anyway? I mean, it sounds like this is the development of the curse that was sent to take down Fabian. That's the only other spell I know of doing such a thing."

'You tell me," Jeremiah said. *'Look at the aftereffects of the entire chain of events. Does it shed new light on why you and your companions are here, now that you know the King brought the plague on purpose?'* He stepped out into the hall, re-claiming the door and tilting it against the doorway. There was no saving the hinges, but it would still be shelter from prying eyes. *'And can you go a little faster? Anyone could walk in here, not just the Jailer.'*

Barty shook his head. "I'm trying... and I can't really see what he has gained," he said, switching to a fresh rag and going back to his bloody cleaning with more urgency. The Raven's jaw tensed, but he remained silent. "I mean, we all got stuck in Faerie, but I think Dr. Buckler and I were just caught up by mistake. Probably who he really wanted is Fabian, right? Since they were his original target-"

'Are there other doctors besides you and your mentor and Fabian who know how to stop this plague?' Jeremiah asked. He stayed near the door, listening for footsteps.

Barty hesitated. "Not really."

Jeremiah grimaced. '*How, exactly, do you stop it?*'

"Well, we had to physically break the spell. It was carved into the coffin of one of Fabian's old bodies. Destroying it caused the plague to go from being a magical, always-lethal disease to a natural infection. After that, then we made amulets to protect people from normal infection-"

"How is this amulet made?" the Raven asked. Sweat dripped down his brow - the soap and hot water must have stung quite a bit. "Is this the same one you wanted my help with?"

Barty paled a few shades. "It's...it's made with magic, and...and some of my blood, since I have some kind of natural immunity to plague and no blood ties to Fabian..."

Jeremiah sighed.

"However!" Barty burst out, clearly wanting to downplay his own, dangerous importance in the present situation, "Since we got here I think we have another cure! You see I made tea with mint leaves that had grown after being in the Living Waters and-"

Jeremiah held up a hand to make Barty stop. '*You are telling me,*' he said, '*that not only are you and your friends the only people alive who know how to stop the King's plague, but you also came to Faerie with blood ties to however many dozens of people you gave these amulets to? Specifically for keeping them safe from this same disease?*'

Barty looked absolutely miserable. "Hundreds by now, actually," he said, in a very small voice. "If not thousands. We were trying to protect as many people as possible."

Another silence. "Not ideal," the Raven said. "If the King has you, he has a blood link to each and every one of those people."

'*He must have known that if the plague showed up again, the people who broke it the first time would come running,*' Jeremiah said, shaking his head. '*Just as he knew Fabian would want revenge on whomever had given the plague spell to the mages in the first place-'*

"Is THAT why Fabian wanted to come so badly!" Barty gasped.

Well, One reason. Jeremiah ran a thumb over the scar on his throat, knowing very well who *else* Fabian would like revenge on and deciding not to bring it up. *'I don't care about the necromancer,'* he said. *'The King can have him. But you, Barty, don't deserve to be mixed up in all this. I'd rather see you and your friends out safely.'*

Barty hesitated in his work, setting down the cloth he'd been using to dry his patient's wounds and tore more strips from the shirt. "Fabian IS my friend," he said, though the words were a little too firm. "I won't be leaving without them."

'You don't sound so sure.' Jeremiah raised an eyebrow. *'Hasn't traveling with him showed you his true colors by now?'*

Barty turned away, winding the strips around the Raven's chest, closing the worst of the gashes. "Everyone has a dark side to them, when pressed," he said softly. "I'm sure they were only doing the best they can, as anyone does." He cut the bandage free, tied it off, then wrapped the remainder into a small bundle, which he pocketed.

'That kind of naivety can get you killed,' Jeremiah signed bluntly.

"That kind of belief can save a man's life," the Raven answered sharply. Then, in a softer voice to Barty, "Come on, the hunter is right. We must hurry." He pulled a black shirt from the pile and slipped into it, digging out a vest and coat as well.

Barty glanced over at Jeremiah, clearly unhappy, but firming his resolve. "What does the King want with Fabian anyway?" he demanded.

The Raven, gently, shoved a clean shirt and coat into Barty's hands, in a silent bid for him to hurry. Barty immediately swapped it for his shredded one.

Jeremiah rubbed at his face, feeling deep in his soul that he was the wrong person to be conveying this information.

'Fabian is-'

To his immense relief, however, his words were interrupted by a noise outside. Footsteps - many footsteps, this time, marching down the halls and opening doors. '*We don't have time for this*' Jeremiah signed, clenching his jaw. '*The King wants you both. You understand by now what he has to gain by spreading a plague that only he holds the cure to?*'

"Yes," Barty said grimly, struggling into a tight-fit vest and coat. "And I can only imagine how much worse that will be if he uses me to get a hand in the mortal world. Can you get us out of here, Jeremiah?"

'*I can try, but it would be easier if we had someone more in tune with the castle. It's already been shifting, even as I searched through it. Also, ideally you two should hide your faces.*' He peered out the cracks of the broken door to judge how much time they had to hide, then frowned. '*They're all bunched at the end of the hallway...Why is everyone out there wearing plague masks?*'

Barty and the Raven blinked, and as one, smiled at each other.

'*What?*' Jeremiah asked, irritated. '*Why are you smiling?*'

"Well, er. Since the one who is supposedly spreading all the plague has escaped," Barty pointed to the Raven, who was already walking back into one of the closets, "I assume everyone is afraid of catching the disease."

"Which means," the Raven came back out, holding a handful of masks. One was Barty's mask, one was the very same mask the Raven had worn when Jeremiah had first caught him, and one glittered, shining and gold against the Raven's black gloves,"we shouldn't stand out too much from the crowd, in these." He tossed the golden mask to Jeremiah. "We'll hide in the closet until they pass, then go the other way."

Jeremiah caught the mask, turning it over in his hands. The gold coloration made it look more like a costume prop than something actually meant to protect against illness, but it still had the glass lenses and long beak of a plague doctor.

The footsteps and opening doors drew closer.

"Should we choose a costume for you that better suits the mask?" Barty asked, doubtfully looking Jeremiah's rough huntsman's clothing up and down even as he moved towards the hiding place. "The gold doesn't really match the rest of you, it'll be easy to see you're not supposed to be here."

"I'll choose something for him," the Raven said with an ominous smile, stepping back amongst the clothes.

'*This is ridiculous*,' Jeremiah signed impatiently, edging away from the door. '*We are going to get out of the castle as fast as possible, there's no need-*'

Gasps and shouts outside. A now-familiar growl, and the scraping of a heavy sword on stone. Feet running away at top speed.

The Raven came back out of the closet with a ridiculously shining coat of gold and silver. "Put that on," he said, tossing it at Jeremiah.

'*Wait-*' Jeremiah tried to tell him, but it was too late. For the second time in twenty minutes, the door was jerked free with a crash, and the Jailer stuck his hooded head through the doorway, rumbling at Barty and offering something in his cupped, dirty-gloved hands.

A curved needle, and a spool of thread.

Barty accepted the proffered items, but then cupped the fellow's massive, hands in his own. "You, sir, are a wonder and a gift. Thank you so much. I appreciate all you have done for us more than I can even say."

The Jailer hummed, sounding delighted even to Jeremiah's ears and not drawing his hands out of Barty's grip.

"Do you feel up to one last thing?" Barty asked him. Behind the young doctor, an impatient Raven gestured 'hurry up' at Jeremiah.

Mentally cursing, Jeremiah struggled into the gold-and-silver coat, slipping the accompanying mask over his face. The Raven plopped a broad, golden hat on Jeremiah's head, a half-sized topper on Barty's, and settled a familiar, full size one on his own.

"I know we have already asked so much of you, sir. But your kindness is clearly as great as your strength. May I beg one more piece of assistance from you?" Barty looked up at the Jailer, still holding his hands, his brown eyes wide and sincere. "Could you assist us one last time, and lead us out of this place?"

The Jailer looked into Barty's face for a long moment. Then he nodded with another rumble, reached out, gave the doctor's tophat a clumsy pat, and clomped back into the hallway.

One by one, masked, coated, and hatted, Barty, the Raven, and Jeremiah followed, Barty slipping the needle and thread into his pockets.

Shilling, now a silver lizard ran after, clawing his way up Jeremiah's arm and settling on his shoulder. "Look," he said, "they left behind a lot of bath linens!"

Jeremiah peered down the hall. Sure enough, there were piles of towels and sheets on the floor where the frightened staff had dropped them. *You think they weren't looking for us?*

"I don't think they'd have run from the Jailer if they were!" Shilling said. "I think they were just setting up rooms. A lot of rooms, if those stacks mean anything."

But why? What guests would they be expecting? The King almost never hosted parties or galas, as far as Jeremiah knew.

"I don't know." Shilling gripped Jeremiah's shoulder tightly in his reptilian claws. "I think there's something more going on here, Master."

Jeremiah's gut twisted. Yet another thread in his path, each one connected to a trap meant for himself or his friends. *One thing at a time, Shilling,* he signed. *One thing at a time.*

He followed the others down the hall, a hand on his sword, senses strained for any approaching threats.

It was all he could do.

He prayed it would be enough.

CHAPTER 25: REGRETS

James Buckler stood in the hallway, peering into his assigned quarters with no small amount of distrust.

He could hear Theli next door in her own room, for she kept exclaiming aloud in wonder, "This is a vast improvement over the dungeon! Oooh, where are these curtains imported from?" Meanwhile, the sound of splashing water emitted from Iris' chambers on the other side, copious amounts of steam billowing out from under her door. Neither of the Faerie natives showed any hesitation, or even fear, about making use of their guest rooms, despite knowing all they did about the King, and the things he had done.

Either their faith in the rules of hospitality were utterly

unshakable, or they were simply so used to the ruination of their world that the danger around them didn't even register.

James, however, was not comfortable.

He stepped into his own room and closed the door. Around him stretched walls of wood paneling, alternating layers of pale and dark browns that invoked an idea of sunlight shining through shadows. An oaken desk with an oil lamp sat close to the door. A soft, upholstered chair with a matching footstool and side table stood across from a currently-unlit fireplace. The combined effect gave a feeling of subtle wealth without extravagance. Open drapes and mid-sized windows offered a clear, bright view over the stone walls and across the land. It was all too easy, with this view, to see where the healthy forest ended and the dead lands began. The living foliage formed a green ring around the castle, perhaps a mile thick, as if someone had drawn a circle with a compass.

What disturbed him most, however, was not what lay beyond the window, but what lay on his bed.

Someone had set out a very fine set of clothing - out of date for the current fashions, perhaps, but acceptable - a rich brown coat of almost military cut trimmed with gold, a creamy silken shirt, polished boots, pressed trousers, and even a wide-brimmed doctor's hat with a fantastical plume of speckled feathers. Nestled on the bed alongside the clothing was a heavy leather belt, with a gold-handled sword resting in a gilded sheath, rather like the ceremonial swords given to ranked military officials. James didn't need to draw the sword to know it would be razor sharp.

On top of the outfit, however, rested a neat little roll of bandages.

James stared at the bundle, his face heating. They were clearly meant to replace the ones currently binding his chest. How did the King know? Nobody was supposed to know.

He grabbed the bandages off his bed and stuffed them in his pocket, pulling the door open so hard it bounced off the wall and storming across the hall to Fabian's room.

Who had told? Had it been tortured out of Barty? Had Fabian let it slip? Surely this was the beginning of blackmail-

He raised his fist to pound on the door, but angry voices drifted out, and he found himself hesitating, listening.

"-you, of all people, dare tell me to calm down." Fabian's voice, the cold anger sending prickles over James' skin. "You know how hard it was for me to get out of here the first time. And now these idiots just waltz us back in, complacent as sheep! They'll all be butchered, and I will be thrown back to the wolf-"

"Temper does not become you," replied an amused voice. Grimley, James realized. "Though it certainly keeps your life interesting."

"Shut up," Fabian actually snarled the words. "I know why you're here, you voyeuristic sadist-"

"You alway were able to turn a phrase like a dagger in flesh," Grimley's sounded not at all chagrined. "I am no different from any man who enjoys reading a good book."

"Of course," Fabian said, mocking, "and just like any man, you choose to help your so-called friends make their 'books' the most *interesting*, instead of sparing them pain or suffering-."

"Well, do you read books that are boring?"

James couldn't blame Fabian for getting annoyed - Grimley sounded more punchable by the second.

Fabian sighed. "I can't believe I'd forgotten how insufferable you are. You're lucky my knives are all locked in the guard tower-"

"Think of me as a historian. I simply-"

"Like to see history happening yourself, yes, you've only told me about a thousand times."

"Not in this lifetime I haven't."

A pause. When Fabian next spoke, it was in a much softer voice. "How long has it been, Grimley? Seven?"

"Seven," he agreed. "I'm impressed it's taken him this long to find you, though what on earth made you come here willingly I can't imagine."

A moment of silence. James held his breath, having very much suspected an answer of his own for quite a while now.

"The dreams started again," Fabian said at last, so quietly James almost couldn't hear them, "and with them, the obsession."

"Vengeance," Grimley spoke the word with near-imperceptible relish.

"I was assassinated in my last life," Fabian's words were both bitter and self-deprecating. "Then they sent a plague after me in this one. I thought outside of Faerie I would be free of this, or at least have more control, but-"

"But the gifts of the fae cannot be escaped," James very much didn't like the thinly veiled delight that accompanied the sympathy in Grimley's voice. "So you returned? For revenge?"

"I returned to put an end to it!" Fabian snapped. James had never heard them lose their temper so easily in conversation. Either they were very high strung indeed, or this Grimley was a close enough friend that they were comfortable bickering with him. "If the dreams were coming back like that, it could only mean one thing: he was looking for me, tugging at the strings of our deal." More pacing, James could imagine Fabian running their hands through their long hair. "When he starts playing his games, people around me die. The more distance I put between myself and my family – " They stopped. James didn't need to hear Grimley's noise of understanding to know that this was more than Fabian had meant to say.

"You're running to protect them," Grimley said. He sounded genuinely moved, but by now James knew he was as touched by the novelty of the 'story' as he was by the actual sentiment. "After all these years, is there a patch of softness in that cold heart, necromancer?"

"Keep talking about my heart and I'll cut yours out of your chest, goat-breath," Fabian said, and James could hear the forced, sharp smile behind the words. "What does it matter?

Here I am, and I will permanently deal with the problem, whatever it takes. I will not go back to what I was."

James knocked on the door.

Silence fell behind it, and after a few moments Fabian said, "Who is it?"

"I need a word, Fabian," James said, keeping his tone short and stiff.

The necromancer sighed, though whether from annoyance or relief, James wasn't sure. "Come in then. Grimley was just leaving."

James pushed open the door in time to see an unmasked Fabian and Grimley exchanging glares. Fabian's grin was all steel, and Grimley's was his usual skeletal smirk, though the set of his furred ears somehow managed to convey that he was enjoying himself. The goat-man bowed low, first to Fabian, then to James, his movements graceful despite the weight of his crown of horns. "I believe we will be called to dine any minute now," he said. "While I have the utmost respect for whatever your conversation will be, may I advise you to keep it brief?"

"All the more reason for you to shove off, dear Grimley," Fabian said, their polite tone at complete odds with the rudeness of their words.

Grimley nodded sagely at the wisdom of Fabian's suggestion, and, with James stepping out of the way, went out the door.

Fabian slid across the room, closed the door after him and locked it with a pointed snap.

"Now then," they said, turning to face James and composing themselves into their more familiar personification of control and calm. "What can I do for you, Doctor?"

James pulled the bandages out of his pocket and showed them to Fabian. "These," he said calmly, "were on my bed, alongside a suit of clothing that I assume I am supposed to change into."

Fabian took the bandages, turning them over in one slender hand, before raising their red eyes to meet James'. "Unfortunate."

No guilt in that crimson stare. James swallowed hard. "How much does...does *he* know about my...condition?"

Fabian once more dropped their gaze to the bandages, frowning. "I have no way of knowing," they said at last. "He always has more information than anyone can explain. Think about how he was able to manipulate us into coming here." They sighed. "This is exactly why I tried to stop us from falling into this accrued bear trap."

They looked back into James' face. "Assume the worst," they said. "Assume he knows everything; your family, your history, your hopes and dreams. Assume he knows everything you do not want him to know, and he will use it all against you. Think deeply, Doctor, on what you will do if he makes threats or bribes to make you stick your head through his noose."

James stared at the necromancer, disbelief and helplessness warring in his chest. "But how is it possible? How could he know any of it?"

"Everyone has their price, Doctor," Fabian shook their head. "Unless you alone know your secret, there are a thousand ways he could find out. Spies on the wind, hearing your every whisper. Spirits in the water, watching your every move. Bribes, or blackmail, to anyone you have spoken to." They held his gaze. "You don't think our fair innkeeper back in Whiston would have told him what he wanted, in exchange for her ring back?"

James felt the blood drain from his face. He and Ida had had a lot in common, and it had been a relief to speak outright on their mutual condition. "She of all people would know not to betray that kind of trust."

"And what if it wasn't presented as a betrayal?" Fabian tapped the bandages in their hand. "What if it was phrased as, 'by the way, I would like to give a gift to the intelligent human doctor who is paying my castle a visit - can you make any suggestions?'"

James closed his eyes. It made all too much sense. Ida would have been more than eager to help him achieve the same dream she had enjoyed for so long, especially if she would get a new ring out of it as well.

Fabian tucked the bandages into his vest. "You should have let me knock the walls down, Doctor."

"Perhaps." He sighed, opened his eyes, and said, "Any sign of Barty?"

Fabian ran their fingers along their jaw, thoughtful. "No," they said, "and that is a good thing."

"How can that be a good thing?" James asked, annoyed.

"Because the first place I checked was the dungeon."

James could easily imagine a little undead creature scurrying through the halls as Fabian's eyes; perhaps one of Fabian's old rats, stowed away in their pocket until now, or a new one they had acquired since entering Faerie. "Then where is he?"

Fabian gave a dry smile. "Judging by the whispers of the servants, he is still in the castle, along with another escaped prisoner."

"Is that also a good thing?" The only other prisoner James knew about was-

"If it's is the plague-infected rascal that we've been hearing about ever since we entered Faerie," Fabian said, cracking the knuckles of their left hand. "No. No, it is not a 'good thing.' Especially since we have with us the *one person* who guards the very waters that grew the plants Barty used to cure said plague, and also *another person* who likes to travel between boroughs, regardless of her own safety."

James's insides went cold. Iris and Theli.

"I should have let you knock the walls down," he said, feeling sick.

"You should have," Fabian agreed, seeming far more bitter about being right than James had ever seen them. "But, well, my army remains outside. It isn't too late." They turned away from him. "If I were you," they said, "I would not wear whatever the King has provided, unless you want to signal that you are amiable to his terms."

The necromancer picked something up off the bed - a white garment, soft and shimmering, long and delicate. They turned their lip in a sneer, and tore it in half, dropping the pieces on the ground. "On the other hand," they said, stepping on the cloth and continuing across to the window. "You might wear it if you fancy a little subterfuge. Pretend you seek the King's good graces and wait for a moment to stick a knife somewhere soft."

"I don't intend to stick a knife anywhere." James followed them, looking out the window as well. Fabian's view showed not the forest, but the courtyard, the orange light of sunset casting a warm glow on the white stone.

Fabian chuckled. "I doubt you could if you tried. He wears many wards against such things; protection from magic and curses, from iron and steel." Fabian drew the curtains across the window, leaving the room dark but for a thin ray of sunlight slipping through the heavy velvet. "Every necklace hanging around his neck is another ward. Every ring, another illusion, or another shape stolen from someone else. He could transform into a bird and fly away, or a tiger and maul you to shreds."

James digested these words, looking at the ribbon of sunlight. He remembered the cool weight of the moonbeam he'd held earlier - was it that same day? It felt like a week ago.

As if reading his thoughts, Fabian pinched the fabric closed on two sides of the curtain, making the beam of light even more slender.

"Why did they bother taking your knives away, then?" James asked, reaching out almost despite himself. "If he is protected from attack anyway..."

"I believe," Fabian said, watching James' hand intently, "he just likes to make me feel helpless."

James closed his hand around the sunbeam. It felt warm

on his palm, and brittle, like glass.

He took a deep breath, closed his eyes, and imagined it really was truly a sun-warmed piece of glass. With a single motion of the wrist he snapped it off, and only then did he open his eyes again.

"Is he protected from this?" he asked, gesturing with the blade of sun.

Fabian's red eyes gleamed. "I do not think any wards have been invented to protect flesh against sunlight," they said. "One would risk freezing to death. Was there a sword included in the outfit the King gave you?"

James nodded reluctantly. "I suppose you think I should replace it with this."

Fabian smiled at him. "Clever lad."

"You don't think someone will notice I've got a gleaming blade made of sunlight hanging from my belt?" James already regretted being clever about this. It felt too much like Fabian was setting him up for an assassination.

The necromancer shrugged. "Wrap the end in something that will hide the glow. Hmm, if only you had something good for wrapping...like bandages..."

James rolled his eyes. "Why are you having me do this?" he said. "Surely you could make a sun-sword yourself. Or is your cloak full of sunlight daggers already?"

Fabian drew their cloak open to show the lack of glowing weaponry. "I would be suspected immediately," they said. "And I trust you of course, Doctor, to only act when it is the right thing to do."

James squinted at the cloak. He could have been imagining things, but he thought he saw a glimmer of something pale and silvery...

"Would a dagger made of moonlight be invisible during the daytime hours?" he asked.

Fabian let their cloak fall closed again. "Interesting theory," they said. "We should investigate it when we are not being politely held as prisoners in the home of a hostile entity."

James shook his head. "You still haven't answered my question," he said. "Why *me*?"

"Because, Doctor," Fabian threw open the curtains again, letting the reddening light of the sunset flood the room. "Of all of us, you have the most founded, logical and steadfast mind. In this world of magic and belief, logic such as yours is more powerful than you realize. You are, at your very core, a mage of logic, with powers most devastating in this land of Faerie."

James couldn't see how logic would help him get anywhere with a blade of sunlight. Still, despite his better judgment, he found himself rather pleased by Fabian's assessment. The idea of his inherent rational qualities and years of study granting him logic as a tool to be wielded in the same manner as magic was immensely gratifying. "It is a shame that my so-called magic powers can't do something similar to Ida's ring."

Fabian gave him a secretive smile, and a wink. "Who knows?" they said. "Maybe with enough practice, they could."

A bell rang out in the castle, echoing through the halls. Fabian sighed, the smile vanishing from their pale face. "Well, Doctor," they said, "brace yourself. We are called for supper."

A bustling in the hallway told James that others had understood this summons as well. "Doctor? Fabian?" Theli spoke from behind the door, eager and excited. "Are you ready to go? I'm starving!"

James repressed a sigh and opened the door, "Yes, we were just discussing-"

He cut off at the sight of Theli. The leonine changeling had swapped out her traveling coat for a sleeveless dress of green silk. It cascaded down to her ankles, and her clawed hind paws were now encased in golden sandals. Likewise, golden bracelets adorned her wrists, golden earrings hung from her furry ears, and golden rings fit snugly at the base of her curved horns. She even had golden beads wrapped into her mane.

"Isn't it amazing?" she said, seeing his stunned look and twirling in place. Her baubles tinkled and glittered. "I can't believe they have so many things that actually fit me! Usually I have to bring all my own clothes whenever I travel - do you think he really means it, Doctor? Do you think he has decided to open the ways and let us all work together now?"

James almost didn't have the heart to dash her hopes against the rocks of reality. Still, he knew that in this situation at least, it was better to be grimly prepared than naively optimistic. "I don't think so," he said, managing to make the words sympathetic instead of sharp. He hesitated, then added emphatically, "But you know, Theli, I do think you are pursuing a good cause. The goal you chase is noble and worthy, regardless of what the King or anyone else says."

The expression of disappointment that had momentarily darkened her features vanished, replaced instead with surprise, and then a broad smile. "R-really? My whole family thinks it's a foolish dream-"

She took the hand not holding the sun-blade in her own, which was a very strange feeling of fur and paw-pads against James' gloveless fingers. He found himself flustered, and also very forcibly reminded of Barty. "They are the fools," he growled, gently pulling free and striding quickly back to his room. "Improvement only comes to those who work for it."

"Doctor, where are you going?" she called after him. "We're called for dinner-"

"I need to change," he called back. "If you're eager to go, go ahead and save me a seat."

"What a good idea! Are you ready to go, Iris, do you want to come along with me?"

Iris opened her door just as James closed his. He caught a glimpse of her finery - shades of deep purple and gold, but left Theli to exclaim over her colors and perfume, (which, indeed, James could smell even though the closed door - he was already not looking forward to sharing a table with her during dinner). The two fae women moved away, the sound of their steps fading down the hall.

James, after a moment's hesitation regarding the new

suit of clothes with mistrust, decided Fabian's idea of subterfuge held enough merit to warrant the switch. He did the best speed change he could manage, shedding his old things and slipping into the new ones, and fixing his own bandages so he could breathe a little more easily, preferring to keep the extra set as emergency medical supplies. He was glad he could make his adjustments by feel and had no need for the mirror - the last thing he wanted was anxiety about his anatomy layered on top of all the other stressors.

Last of all, he removed the sword from the sheath and slipped the sun-blade in its place. As Fabian had suggested, he bound the 'handle' of the blade with cloth, imitating as best he could the wrapping style the real sword bore.

Only after he'd fit the belt around his hips and fastened it did he take a deep breath, run his fingers through his hair, and step in front of the mirror.

His own reflection looked back at him; sharp, neat, respectable, with the same no-nonsense expression that was as much a tool as anything else in his arsenal.

Still him, despite everything.

A knock sounded on his door. Fabian's voice, "Coming, Doctor?"

"Coming."

He opened the door and stepped out to meet Fabian. The necromancer cast an approving eye up and down James' form. "My, my. Smart as paint, Doctor."

"Let's just get this over with," James said, offering Fabian his arm despite the crossness of his words.

Fabian chuckled and slid their arm through his. "Of course," they said. "Onward, to dinner, destiny and destruction, hopefully in that order."

"I'd prefer discretion and discovery," James said, beginning to walk. "Especially if it leads us to Barty. Perhaps some disappearance, for dessert."

The white crocodile servant approached them as they left the guest suite. He now bore a white plague mask that had a scale pattern similar to his own skin - it was unusually long, to accommodate his snout. "Allow me to show you the way to the dining hall-"

"Please," Fabian sneered, "in the King's palace, is it even possible for us to end up anywhere else, if it is not his will for us to do so?"

The crocodile looked awfully sheepish for a reptile. "No. But, ummm... Are you sure you don't want to wear masks?"

"Why?" James asked, eyeing the white-scaled construction on the creature's face.

"They, um," the crocodile lowered his voice, looking about fearfully, "they still haven't caught the escaped prisoners."

"Have you been warning all the guests of this situation?" James demanded, his ire rising. "If there is a significant risk of plague, it is extremely inadvisable to be hosting a large social event!"

The crocodile's yellow eyes darted back and forth. "I am not disagreeing with you," he said, "but the King's will is law here, and-"

"Good lord." James pulled his arm free of Fabian's and turned to go back to his room and get his mask.

"Be a dear and get mine as well, won't you, Doctor?" Fabian called after him, not taking their eyes off the nervous crocodile. "Theli and Iris will need theirs as well..."

"Yeah, yeah," James grumbled, throwing his door open again and storming back to collect his mask.

Guests coming. Plague loose in the halls. Barty missing. It was, entirely, a recipe for disaster.

He had a sinking feeling that that was exactly what the King wanted.

CHAPTER 26: MAJESTY

"This is the third time we've ended up here," Barty whispered, hovering at the entrance to the King's dining hall.

The Jailer had done his best: leading them through the pale corridors, hiding them in a room whenever someone passed, and trying different hallways when it was clear from the noise that the King's party lay just ahead of them. No matter which way they went, unfortunately, they always ended up at this same arched entrance, with eager chatter, soft music, and rich food smells drifting towards them, tugging with the gentleness of a beckoning finger.

"Maybe the way out is through the dining room somehow," the Raven whispered back, peering through the archway over Barty's shoulder.

'More likely the King ordered every hallway to only lead

to one place,' Jeremiah signed, Shilling, now a small silver bird, translating for him in Barty's ear. Barty had no doubt that the changeling had chosen that form specifically so his beak matched the group's chosen attire. *'If anything was confirmation that he wants to spread plague to his guests, this is it.'*

Barty's heart sank. He was fairly sure the magical-curse aspect of the plague had been removed when the Raven destroyed the spell on his chest, but he could not be certain.

The Jailer rumbled something softly, clearly doing his best to make it a whisper too.

"He says," Shilling translated, "that the only way out is with the King's permission, and the King is in that room."

Barty had been afraid of that. He sighed and peeked into the dining hall.

It was a massive room - almost cathedral-like in its size. A single long table of pale wood stretched across the entire center, covered with a lacy white cloth. A veritable feast steamed all along its length, roast meats and fowl, seared fish, fresh breads, fruits and vegetables... Even though their group was thirty feet away, huddled in the doorway, Barty's stomach growled at the glimpses he got between the many guests. And such guests there were! Horned guests and guests with feathers or fur. Guests made of wood or stone or ice, chatting amiably and passing dishes from hand to hand. All manner of colorful garments were present, and some guests appeared to be wearing nothing at all (Barty quickly averted his eyes from the more human-shaped anatomy on display).

Strangest of all, however, was not what made them different, but what unified them.

Every guest had a mask. True, some were only half-masks, allowing the guests to eat and chat without hindrance, but it seemed everyone was making an attempt to either keep themselves safe or blend in with those who were trying. The effect was rather like looking at a giant room of tropical birds, with no two sets of feathers alike.

Barty pulled back around the corner, dizzied by the splendor. "I've never seen anything like this in my life," Barty whispered to the group. "The variety and the craftsmanship and diversity of beings.... It almost makes it worth all we've been through, to witness such a sight."

"Worth risking plague and execution you mean?" the Raven said, amused. "I suppose there is value to stopping and smelling the roses even when trapped in the bleakest of life's pits..."

"There are always pits," Barty said seriously. "If I waited for fair weather to appreciate the roses, I'd be holding my breath for an eternity."

"I'd like to appreciate some of that dinner," Shilling complained, hopping along the rim of Jeremiah's hat and down the length of his mask to get a bit closer to the food. He made a show of taking a deep breath, trying to inhale as many of the scents as possible. "They have STEAK there! Can't we sneak in and steal some steak?"

Jeremiah signed something at him, and he managed a scowl despite being a bird. "If a hawk can eat meat I can too-"

"There's Dr. Buckler!" Barty gasped, pointing. He'd almost missed James in the crowd. His friend wore a splendid uniform which fit right in with all the magnificent outfits, but Barty would have recognized the stiffness of his posture anywhere. Like many of the feasting guests, James' mask rested at his elbow while he ate. "And that's Theli sitting at his side! And, oh dear, Iris is next to her, and that..." Barty's breath caught a moment, a pang going through his chest. "Fabian..."

Fabian, sitting with their mask on and an empty plate. They toyed with their silver dinner knife and surveyed the merry-makers, to all appearances perfectly relaxed, but Barty knew they were anything but, if they weren't eating the feast before them. The necromancer never turned down free food.

Barty wondered if they were angry; after all, they had tried to warn him and James, over and over, of the dangers of this land. Barty wondered what Fabian would say, when they found out he'd rescued the very person who had been enchanted for the sake of spreading plague.

He pushed down his anxiety. Fabian and James were alive, and that was a good thing. Barty had found them, and that was also a good thing. He would deal with the conflicts of the future as soon as he managed to live that long.

"What we need," he said softly, "is a way to either get in there and talk to Dr. Buckler, or cause some kind of disturbance that will bring him out here."

"I thought we were going after the King?" the Raven's whisper sent a shiver down his spine. Something about that smooth voice, and not being sure if he was plotting aid or assassination…

"Absolutely right sir, but the safety of my friends is my first priority," Barty said.

'*We may not have a choice,*' grim words signed by Jeremiah.

Barty drew himself up and turned around. "Let me be perfectly clear," he said. He did not raise his voice, nor did he speak with any emotion but calm, frank sincerity. "I understand that we need the portal to escape. However, I am not leaving this land without my companions. If things are dire, and we have only one shot, you may go ahead without me, but I'll not abandon them for anything, not even my own freedom."

The Raven and the Huntsman stared at him, and he felt his cheeks heat under their stunned gazes. "Apologies for being forceful," he murmured, turning back around to look at the room. "I just needed to make my position clear."

"Don't apologize," The Raven shook his head, a smile in his voice. "I quite enjoyed it. I'll stay by your side, Dr. Barty. We'll see your friends to safety."

Barty gave his friend a grateful smile. The Raven's vote of confidence and promise of help were a comfort.

"We all will," Shilling said, happily hopping from the Jeremiah's beak to Barty's, so he could peer into one of Barty's lenses. "And with all of us working together, why, what could possibly go wrong?"

"Your attention, please."

Every face in the room, including Barty's and his companions, turned towards the head of the table in a swarm of beaked alignment.

The King held up a bejeweled hand, smiling at the sudden focus of attention. Barty wasn't sure how he'd failed to notice him before; he sat on a polished stone platform raised above the gathered crowd, with no table and no food before him. His previous finery had been replaced with garb of silvery-golden material, and gold and silver leaves woven through his white hair like a growing crown. An echoing pattern of embroidered foliage trickled over his collar, sleeves and hem of his robe.

It was not he who had stilled the crowd, however, but one of his servants - the nervous crocodile, in fact, standing before his throne and addressing the assembly, reading from a scroll clutched in pale, trembling claws.

"His Majesty the Faceted King of Changelings offers his gracious appreciation to all the assembled representatives of the peoples of the land, and expresses his hopes for many future gatherings of a similar nature..."

"What should we do?" whispered Barty to the others. "Everyone is fully distracted now, but if we try to slip in, the King will certainly notice."

The crocodile spoke on. "His Majesty wishes all to observe that today is a day of great note, for not only have we not had a gathering of this grandeur in the last four hundred years..."

"Maybe I can get James's attention, hold on." Barty dug in his pockets and came up with the roll of bandages. It wasn't much - just the leftovers from what the Jailer had brought him - but it was something. "I hope I don't miss."

'Don't,' signed Jeremiah. "It's too far."

The crocodile droned on, "As you all may have observed

upon your arrival, the land is beginning to heal. The years of decline and loss are coming to an end, the trees are beginning to sprout anew..."

Barty took a few steadying breaths. He focused on James Buckler's stiff back. He aimed carefully with the roll of cloth.

"There can be only one reason for our beloved land coming back to life!" The crocodile bowed and stepped behind the King's throne.

Barty tossed the bandages. They hit James on the shoulder and bounced onto the table. James jumped, looked down at them, confused, twisted in his seat, and saw Barty. Even at this distance, Barty saw his eyes go wide.

The King appeared not to notice. He rose from his throne and glided forward a pace, smiling around at his assembled subjects. His prismatic eyes swept the room, shifting purple, green, red, yellow, like a collection of gemstones set in the silver-gold band of the rest of his outfit. "I am pleased to announce..."

James looked up at the King, his face going a shade paler. He looked back at Barty, dropped a hand below table level, and made a shooing gesture. "Go," he mouthed. "Go!"

Barty couldn't go - not without his friend. He pulled off his mask so James could see his face. Shilling gave a cheep of protest and fluttered back to Jeremiah's shoulder. "Come with us," Barty tried to mouth at James, beckoning.

James finally noticed there were others with Barty. His eyes went wider as he took in the crowd - The Raven, Jeremiah, the Jailer.

All of them also began to beckon, trying to get James to sneak away from the table.

James hesitated, then reached over, about to tap Fabian on the shoulder.

"...that for the first time in four hundred years, I am going to marry. At long last, my beloved bride has returned to our land, and to me. Fiia," the King cast his smile down the table like a spotlight, and every beaked face in the room turned...

...looking right at Fabian.

"Join me now for a dance, to celebrate our reunion after so many years apart."

Barty's gasp was buried in the sudden muttering that broke out in the hall. Guests craned their necks, a few even standing to try and see who the King was talking about. Apparently Fabian's leather-feathered mask was causing some confusion.

James, Barty was stunned to see, didn't look at all surprised. If anything he had a greenish tinge, as if he were about to be sick.

Which was odd, because as a dead man, he shouldn't be changing colors like that.

Fabian, at his side, hadn't moved. Head resting on their hand, they continued toying with their knife, as if the King hadn't been speaking to them.

This caused more confusion among the guests, whispers of 'Where is she?' getting louder. Even Barty began to wonder if perhaps there had been some mistake, and the King hadn't meant Fabian at all-

The King's pristine smile didn't shift an inch, but his gaze hardened, his silvery-gold clothes frosting a shade colder, now bringing to mind brass and steel instead of gold and silver. His voice, however, was unphased. "Fiia, my sweet, I am sure you do not want to be embarrassed by an escort of armed guards. Please, do as I say, and *come here.*"

His will rippled across the room; a palpable thing that made Barty catch his breath. It was a powerful summoning, pulling not only at Fabian to obey but also at the rest of the crowd, summoning their wills to compel the necromancer into obedience. Barty was glad it was not directed against him, he would have buckled on the spot.

Fabian, however, didn't turn a feather. They twisted the silver knife in their hand, to all appearances admiring the shine on the blade. James nudged them with his elbow, and

only then did they look up, as if waking from a daze. "Oh, hm? Was someone speaking to me?"

They made a show of looking about the room, taking in the gazes from the assembly. Eyes of every color and shape, framed by hollow-socketed masks, stared back at them. Every whisper died, every ear hungry for what they would say next. Barty had to choke down a highly inappropriate stab of laughter. He had the sudden feeling that Fabian was exactly where they wanted to be - in command of all attention.

The King frowned, and glanced at his guards. One stepped forward, awaiting his command.

"There must be some mistake," the necromancer said, their voice clear and carrying despite their mask. "His Majesty was not speaking to me, dear guests. My name," they put a hand to their chest, inclining their head as if introducing themselves to the room, "is Fabian."

James snorted. Iris, on his other side, chuckled. An amused titter ran through the room, and immediately the King's spell of command was broken, dissipated amongst the laughter of the guests as they turned in their chairs, still looking about for the real 'Fiia.'

For a moment, rage flashed across the King's face, his eyes blazing orange and his face darkening to an almost greenish hue. But a blink later his icy smile returned, his robes back to their warm, rich splendor of gold and silver. "Who am I to deny my bride her fancies," he chuckled, and his servants obediently chuckled with him. "Very well, Fabian. Wear whatever name you like," his eyes glittered, red, green, blue, "but I will always, always find you."

Barty wasn't sure, but he could have sworn he saw Fabian shiver.

The King held his hand out in Fabian's direction, his many rings glittering in a rainbow display of light and wealth. "Now, my dear..." and behind him, more pale servants produced instruments, a trickle of music floating its way into the wide hall, "come and share this dance with me."

Fabian stood, stretched, and sighed. "As a personal favor to Your Majesty," they said, sounding bored, "I will share one dance. But I promise no more than that."

The King smiled his beautiful smile, and Barty could have sworn he saw eagerness in those color-swirling eyes. "We," he said, "shall see."

Fabian stepped away from their chair, patting James on the shoulder, bending only a moment to whisper something in his ear. Barty caught a glimpse of his face, and the worry he read there sent a chill through his heart. James nodded, whispered something back, and Fabian looked over at Barty for the briefest moment.

Barty swallowed hard, but before he could react, Fabian had already turned away.

The necromancer walked down the dining hall, every face watching their booted steps and the swirl of their fur-trimmed cloak. The King stood waiting, smiling, hand outstretched, as if he were summoning Fabian with a spell, or even a line of thread. To Barty's eye, it seemed that, somehow, the closer Fabian got, the more the King came alive, a living, breathing person instead of a royal figurehead. By the time Fabian was near enough to accept his outstretched hand in their own leather-gloved one, the King's chest was visibly rising and falling with eagerness. He stood in silence, his eyes swirling with so many colors they were impossible to identify, locked on Fabian's mask.

The nervous crocodile stepped forward, beckoning frantically to the musicians and stammering to the audience, "All guests, please feel invited to join in at your leisure!"

The music clattered to life like a sudden fall of rain.

And Fabian and the King began to dance.

Fabian was dwarfed by the King - his splendid crown of white gold with color-changing gems only added to his appearance of towering over the necromancer. However, despite his grandeur and his height advantage, despite his being the one to lead the waltz, and the hunger in his smile, it was Fabian who Barty couldn't tear his eyes away from. The necromancer drew the eye, with their dark robes and pale mask and red lenses and their ability to somehow, even now, make it clear that they were only humoring the King's request. They knew every step of the dance perfectly, so much so that they could swirl their robes in time with each lilt of the music. Their dance was rather like watching a pampered dog badgering an alley cat, the dog's crude posturing and growls only accentuating the cat's graceful disinterest and confidence.

Someone nudged Barty's ribs, snapping him out of his entrancement. "Now's our chance," the Raven whispered. "Give me your hand. Do you know how to waltz?"

"I, what?" Barty turned to face him, blushing despite himself. "I, er, I learned long ago - sir I don't understand what-"

"We can move through the crowd without attracting any attention this way," the Raven nodded towards the center of the room. "Look, the guests are joining in."

Barty looked. Indeed, pairs were breaking away from the tables, moving out to the open floor to dance.

"Follow my lead, whispered the Raven, offering his hand. "I'll get you to your friend."

Barty furrowed his brow, peering into the Raven's eyes. The idea was a good one, and the Raven's tone was genuine, but Barty knew the man well enough to recognize that the green gleam behind those lenses meant trouble. "Please be careful," Barty said, taking the Raven's hand in his own.

"No promises," the Raven said. His face might have been masked, but Barty could hear the charming smile in his voice. He rested a hand on Barty's hip and pulled him closer. "Now, follow."

Barty had to bite his lip to not make an embarrassed squeak. His emotions were telling him a lot of things he most certainly didn't have time to process at the moment. He drew a breath, pushed every tingly feeling away, and focused on nothing but determination to do the thing right. "Lead away, sir."

They slipped into the hall, moving in time to the music. It took Barty a few moments to get the hang of the pacing and steps - it truly had been quite a long time since he'd practiced, but the Raven was patient and gentle with him, his steps light and flowing, his hands a steady guide for Barty's movements.

For a moment, Barty forgot he was supposed to be doing something other than dancing. For a moment, cradled by the music, held by the Raven, floating together with grace and melody, he simply danced. The dance felt like a thing that happened to other people, not him. His world was not one of grace and beauty, but of filth and illness. And yet, here with the Raven, he almost felt he belonged.

"Nearly there," the Raven's calm voice cut through Barty's daze. Right, focus. It must be the music, enchanting and distracting him. He could see the Raven's purpose now, for there were James and Theli, dancing carefully only a few steps away, James keeping a sharp eye on Fabian. Barty glanced back at the door they'd entered through. Only the Jailer remained, swaying his veiled horns to the music. The Huntsman had vanished.

"I'll leave you with your doctor friend," The Raven said, but his glowing gaze was trained on Fabian and the King. Barty had a sinking feeling it wasn't Fabian that drew the Raven's attention. Too late, Barty remembered that the Raven's bargain had been one of vengeance. "Ready now," The Raven's whisper was barely audible over the music. "Switching partners in three, two…"

And then Barty was somehow in James' arms instead of the Raven's, that familiar mask filling his vision, that firm grip keeping him on track and in time with the music.

"James," Barty choked out, tears filling his eyes. "I'm so glad-"

"Hush, Doctor," James' voice was gentle, despite his command. "And don't forget yourself - we are using titles here."

"R-right, right, my apologies, Doctor," Barty sniffed, blinking rapidly to clear his eyes. "I'm so glad you are alright." Somehow, despite his tears, he didn't lose the timing of the music. He and James stepped perfectly, hand in hand, turning and swirling with everyone else.

"Are you alright?" James' words, urgent and relieved. "Have you been safe?"

Barty nodded. "Safe enough, but it was a near thing sometimes. We have to get out of here Doctor. He's plotting to use us to spread-"

"I know," James cut him off, turning him with care. "We figured it out. You're right, we must go. Have you found a way home?"

Barty shook his head, the weight of reality making his steps heavier once more. "All signs point to the King as the only way out."

James sighed. "This will make things difficult. Tell me of your allies, and what you know of the castle."

Barty did his best, there in the middle of the dance floor. He had to press a little closer to James to be heard while also keeping his voice down, but the doctor tolerated it with good grace, keeping Barty firmly near, leading the waltz while Barty quickly recounted how he had met each of his companions, emphasizing how Jeremiah had helped him both with treating patients and saved him from the King, how the Raven had been cruelly held and orphaned, and even how the Jailer (who really seemed not to be all that bad a fellow) had come to their aid with both supplies and guidance.

"The Raven says I bespell people," he told James, a wry smile in his voice. "But I don't believe it for a moment."

James' expression was unreadable behind his mask, but he squeezed Barty's arm affectionately. "I am very glad," he said, "that you found good friends to help keep you safe. Your kindness has served you well, even in this world." He shook his head. "I would explain our new companions to you, but I believe you have already met both of them."

"Theli and Iris, yes," Barty said, worry infecting his voice. "They are in just as much danger as we are, Dr. Buckler. Iris guards the waters with the cure and-"

"And Theli goes between every borough, as a perfect vector of plague," James shook his head. "I can only hope what you say is true about your Raven being cured, but if the King can just re-apply that same curse to anyone, we need a more permanent solution."

"What solution could there be?" Barty said, an all too familiar feeling of helplessness coiling around his spirit. The music seemed to agree with him, winding down to a mournful stop. "There is no higher authority to report him to."

Someone tapped him on the shoulder. "May I," a deep voice said behind him, "have this next dance?"

Barty turned and found himself in the shadow of a towering figure, all curling horns and black fur. It took him a moment to get over the shock, but eventually he managed, "G-Grimley?"

Grimley bowed, swishing his tail. "I believe," he said, "I am to help you along to your next partner."

"My next - oh!" Barty glanced at Fabian, who, though they had not yet managed to escape the King's clutches, was looking right at him over his Majesty's shoulder. "Er, yes, of course. Thank you, sir!" Barty accepted Grimley's hoof-nailed hands, casting a last, apologetic look at James. "I'll come find you again, Doctor," he said.

James nodded, his gloved hands already gripped by Iris's greedy claws. He didn't look happy about it. "Don't dawdle, Doctor."

Barty nodded, and cast a nervous look up at Grimley. The music started up once more, a livelier tune this time. He hoped very much he wouldn't step on the dignified Decided's hooves.

"I am glad to see you again sir," he said, and, thinking a bit of flattery never hurt anyone, added, "your mask looks truly splendid."

Grimley's velvety ears perked a fraction, the compliment

clearly pleasing him. "Thank you," he said, "I made it myself."

"Really!" Barty found himself leading this time, and only then realized that the tune was a popular one in the human world. Of course, he had forgotten Fabian's words: the fae enjoyed human trends. "You have quite a talent. Perhaps I should commission my next mask from you."

"I doubt you could afford it," Grimley said with no hesitation. Still, Barty could hear his smile. "I was hoping to speak to you, Doctor, before passing you along."

"Oh? Well, here I am, sir, at your service." Barty lifted his arm long enough from Grimley's to tip his hat.

Grimley's yellow eyes glittered with amusement, behind the mask. "I wanted to be sure," he said, "that you understand the significance of Fabian's presence in this world."

"I beg your pardon?" Barty didn't think now was the time for gossip.

"You have not been traveling with them," Grimley whirled Barty a little faster than Barty felt was strictly necessary, he had to clutch the fellow's coat to keep his grip. "You have not seen," Grimley continued, "how the land heals with their passing."

"What?" Barty could not comprehend where this was going. "Why would Fabian's presence be healing the land?"

"Fabian," Grimley said, "was, is, and possibly always will be, the rightful Queen of Faerie."

Barty stumbled, Grimley's strong arm the only thing keeping him from falling flat out. "What?" he gasped. "What are you saying?"

"Fabian's powers of necromancy are drawn from this land," Grimley said, his normally stoic voice taking on an edge of glee at getting to reveal this information. "It is a power that was only ever meant to belong to royalty - for it is tied to the eternal regeneration of the life-force of the land of the Changelings. Perhaps you have seen a token they wear, a necklace of red stones? Those stones are a direct channel to Faerie. The land that normally heals itself with the presence of the Queen is healing now - not because of any action that Fabian is taking, but simply because they are here. Every day that Fabian is gone, the land dies further, for once upon a time-"

"No, no they only have power over corpses-" Fabian's magic had nothing to do with land, this wasn't making sense.

"- long, long ago," Grimley continued, as if Barty hadn't interrupted, "Fabian made a deal with the King of Faerie-"

"They wouldn't!" Barty spluttered, but every word of warning Fabian had delivered suddenly made too much sense. They knew the ways of the fae folk from experience. They had been here before, had been trapped by deals before. They had been afraid to return, afraid of anyone else making a deal...

...just as they had made a deal, one they had been trying to escape for who knows how long.

"- and the King never forgets his deals," Grimley continued. There was no mercy in the yellow eyes watching Barty through that beautifully crafted mask. "Don't you see, Doctor? Fabian, although they fight it, belongs here as much as I do."

Barty had no words. Too much understanding flooded him - Fabian's ruby eyes. Fabian's power that had no equal or likeness in human magic. Fabian's cycle of rebirth, and the obsession with revenge that had pulled them away from their lover and newborn child. "All this time," he whispered, "all this time they had a kingdom waiting for them..."

"And yet it was not enough," Grimley said, with mock sadness. "Why be satisfied with a kingdom you are freely given, when one can be taken through your own power and superiority?"

The words sank like stones into Barty's heart. The world around him seemed to blur as if his own understanding were changing reality. He remembered stories of The Necromancer Tyrant of England, who had slaughtered, without hesitation, any who dared oppose his rule. "Why are you telling me this?" he said, almost pleading.

"Because," Grimley said, still supporting Barty with as much gentleness and strength as he had since their dance began, "I want you to truly understand who you are dealing with. And because I think this story will be infinitely more interesting, if you know the truth."

"Interesting," Barty repeated hoarsely. "Right."

"Ah, speak of the devil," Grimley slowed, and the rest of the dancers had to part around them, like a stream around a stone. "I have your little Doctor, your Majesty."

"I'm sure you have, Grimley," Fabian's familiar, sarcastic tone cut through the music. Leather-gloved hands pulled Barty from Grimley's grip. Red lenses flashed dangerously in the fading sunlight. "Why don't you go play with the King, Billygoat? He's so lonely over there by himself. It would be most helpful to me if someone were to occupy his time and allow me a few moments of privacy..."

Barty slipped trembling fingers under his mask, wiping the moisture from his eyes. As he did, he caught a glimpse of the King. The crowned liege paced alone, before his throne, staring at Fabian. Then his gaze snapped up, and he saw Barty.

His perfect mouth split in a wide grin that filled Barty with dread. Barty quickly looked down, watching his feet and Fabian's, allowing the necromancer to dictate their movements.

Fabian, however, continued to guide Barty through the dance - steadying his steps even though they themselves were acting as the follow - making it look like Barty was leading with grace and confidence. "Pick your beak up, Doctor," the necromancer said lightly, giving his arm a squeeze. "Your hat is slipping."

"Fabian-" Barty's voice cracked on the word. He stopped, cleared his throat, took a breath, tried again. "Congratulations."

For a beat Fabian hesitated, confused. Nobody watching them would have caught it, and while they didn't lose a breath of timing with the instrumental flow, their grip on Barty's arm tightened. "I don't understand you, Doctor."

"Congratulations on your upcoming wedding," Barty said, more firmly. Something flickered in his chest. Not anger - not yet - but a seeping, simmering feeling of betrayal so strong, he could not find words to express it.

Fabian had had a kingdom waiting for them for centuries, and yet they'd conquered England when she was on her knees from plague, back in 1666, maintaining a bloody reign of terror that lasted 40 years.

Fabian had a beautiful home and family, all the while leaving the land that needed them to slowly wither away and die.

Barty remembered the miles of dead trees. The small, gleaming wing buried in ashes.

Fabian chuckled, but there was a new tension in their movements, a stiffness in the arms keeping Barty close. "Please," they said. "As I told you before we were dragged into this misadventure, Doctor. I have no desire to rule in this lifetime."

"But you did before," Barty said, staring at them, his voice rising despite himself. "You killed how many for a crown, Fabian?

Fabian's grip tightened further, and Barty winced. "Do not mock me," they hissed, and Barty caught a glimpse of their wide, wild eyes behind their red lenses. "You know why I made those choices, Doctor. You know that life was better for all under my rule. No more wars for glory, killing half the young men in England in selfish pursuit of spoils. No more corrupt Church, destroying and shaming all who were different, or poor, or alone." They leaned closer, their whisper velvety and dangerous. "It was I who avenged your parents, boy. It was I who dragged the men who had flung torches onto a synagogue, screaming, into their graves."

Barty choked at that. His steps faltered, bringing Fabian to a standstill. "If you're so much better than any other King," he managed, voice shaking, "then why not stay here and help these people? The land is dying, Fabian. The people suffer under an unjust ruler at every turn. This kingdom needs you, and-"

"This kingdom," Fabian's words sounded as if they were being squeezed out through gritted teeth, "comes with a King. And I-"

Barty almost laughed. "Is that the issue? Don't tell me it's something you couldn't handle! Whatever happened to Ruphys being 'well used to sharing your time?'"

He hadn't meant to bring that up. He'd hoped to never think of that moment again. Unfortunately, to his shame, his hurt at being toyed with (not even a week ago, though it felt like a lifetime) still hadn't completely healed.

The words stopped Fabian cold. They stood very still for a long moment, the dancers around them casting curious glances but politely flowing around the duo. Barty all but trembled in Fabian's grip, the lenses of his mask fogged over from the heat of his internal, churning aches.

Fabian stared at him, took a deep breath, and shook their head.

Then, to Barty's utter shock, the necromancer stepped closer, slid their arms around him, and held him close in an unmistakable hug.

"I realize," they said, so softly in his ear there wasn't even room for their usual cutting irony, "that I am not the person you want me to be, Barty."

He was so much taller than they were, they practically had to rest their beak on his shoulder.

"I am not kind. I am not selfless. I have seen too much darkness in the hearts of men to love them unconditionally, as you do. I am not a hero in disguise. And you have suffered because of the distance between what you wished me to be and what I am."

Tears welled over in Barty's eyes. He listened, entranced, to the words he had needed to hear for a long time.

"However," Fabian said, continuing to hold Barty close,

running their fingers through his curls, "I am, right now, the very best Fabian I can possibly be. Because of Ruphys and Mina. Because of James. And yes, Doctor, because of you. Think, Barty; the hours we spent together, working on a cure and the risks we both took, to free England from plague. We are not so unlike, you and I. We both seek to change the world, in our own ways. To better it for all who need it most."

Barty closed his eyes. He could not deny their statements. Now that he was calmer, he of course knew more than anyone, had known for a long time, that Fabian genuinely sought to improve the lives of man, even if their own methods were a bit twisted. No other ruler had lifted up as many groups as Fabian had, during their rule. Mages, immigrants, religions of all sorts: all had been granted shelter, during Fabian's time as King. Those who used violence and acted out of hate had been punished severely, which consisted of much of the death toll during Fabian's reign. Fabian cared, and here was confirmation, in their own words.

He put his arms around them, holding them close, accepting their truth, who they were, and who they were not.

They leaned their head against his shoulder, and he felt their relief even through their layers of velvety cloak and embroidered robes.

"However," they continued, "if I were to stay here, with that...person..."

A shudder went through them, even wrapped in his arms.

"I would become," they whispered, "something much, much worse."

And Barty understood.

He had seen the King with his own eyes - witnessed his true nature. His cruelty and selfishness might be similar to Fabian's, but where Fabian's reign, though a bloodbath in its own right, had improved the lives of many, the King only sought to improve his own lot. Where Fabian had lived countless lives among men, seeing and experiencing their suffering and hardship, it seemed the King had never spent a day outside of his castle, and cared nothing for the safety of even his closest servants.

It was clear to Barty that, for someone like Fabian, marrying the King would be absolutely repulsive.

Neither would a marriage solve the underlying problem. Even if Fabian's presence in the land brought the dead areas back to life, The King would still rule - he would just have more to trade away to further engorge his riches and power.

"How," Barty whispered, "do we get out of here?"

Fabian let out a long breath, giving him a last, tight squeeze. Clearly, they understood the significance of his choice of words. "*We*," they said, pulling back at last to look into his face, "will have to either find a way to convince the King to unlock a door, or-"

"Your attention please!"

Once more the nervous crocodile's voice rang out across the room. Once more everyone stopped where they were, turning to look, the music swirling to a graceful halt as if this interruption had been planned.

"His Majesty the King would now like to present gifts, as thanks for his bride's safe delivery!"

Barty winced, turning back to look at the King.

The man was staring at Barty, and if looks could kill, Barty doubted Fabian's necromancy would have been able to bring him back. The King's gaze communicated that Barty's insides would look much better on the outside, and the edges of his gold-and-silver layers had tarnished to a sickly greenish-black color. He quickly smoothed his glare and his tarnish away, though, as the eyes of the room rested upon him, smiling out at the crowded hall.

"Would Fabian's escort kindly come to the front of the room, that the King himself might bestow his blessings upon them?"

Fabian gave a soft chuckle. "It begins," they whispered to Barty. They slid their hand down his back, wrapping their arm around his middle. "Come along, Doctor, and prepare yourself for the worst."

Together, Barty and Fabian walked to the front of the room. Barty could hear James and Theli, Iris and Grimley, detaching from the dancers and following behind. He wondered once again where Jeremiah had got to. At least, when he reached the front of the room, mounted the dias, and turned to face the crowd, Barty could see the Jailer. The big creature feasted back at the long table, helping himself to a few of the steaks abandoned during the dancing. Barty had clearly been mistaken about the Jailer's species - no cow had had *ever* had that many sharp teeth-

"It shall never be said," the King began, smiling around at all the assembled folks, "that I do not show appreciation to those who aid my kingdom."

He waved a hand, and his pale guard approached, half a dozen soldiers in white. Barty could not tell if their spears were ceremonial or functional, but the pale leaf-bladed tips gleamed like steel. Not all the guards were armed, however. Several bore silver trays instead of spears. "Please, my worthy guests, remove your masks, and let the kingdom see to whom they owe their gratitude."

"I don't suppose I'll get a gift too," a voice whispered in Barty's ear. Barty had to repress a gasp - the Raven had somehow come up onto the stage! He was at Barty's elbow, stooped low so as to be hidden behind him! Barty reached up, fiddling with his mask and shielding his mouth with his hand. "Sir," he whispered, "it's too dangerous! What if they catch you?"

"Let them try," the Raven said, and Barty heard a bloody edge in that polite tone. The Raven had not removed his mask.

"For Berthelia of the Decided," the King continued, and one of the guards stepped forward. As he did, a fair amount of cheering erupted from the crowd - Barty looked over and saw, with some surprise, that Berthelia's father was there along with other Decided from the borough. Apparently their quarrel was forgotten now that Theli was being royally honored, "I grant an official title."

The lid of the tray was whisked away. There, resting on a velvet cushion, lay a shining golden badge shaped like a shield. Barty could just make out the words "Royal Embasarry" in iridescent lettering emblazoned across the center.

"You," the King said, smiling at her as if he'd never in his life dreamed of imprisoning her in a dungeon filled with plague-ridden corpses, "will become an essential part of our new future, ensuring cooperation and communication between all the peoples of my kingdom."

Theli gasped and beamed at him, tears sparkling in her eyes. "It's all I ever wanted!"

The King smiled serenely, and turned to Iris. "For Iris, Guardian of the Living waters," he said, "I have heard it said that you miss having company, and came here seeking my blessing to open a door."

"I don't understand," Barty whispered to Fabian. "Why is he giving everyone what they want?"

"It is conditional," Fabian whispered back. They had removed their mask, their red eyes not leaving the King for a moment. "This is what you get if you follow along with what he says, and agree that you were only my escort." They gave a bitter laugh. "A bride-price."

"I will reopen the very door you once had," the King continued, still addressing Iris. Another lid lifted, revealing a key made of gold-veined wood. "You will be free to invite as many visitors as you like, or even to visit the other side yourself, and find whatever it is you desire. The guard of Kingsworn will protect the gate, to ensure it remains safe for you and your daughters to use."

Iris said nothing, but her amber gaze rested on the key, looking wistful. The audience again applauded, especially the members who looked to be made of stone, wood and crystal.

"Your accepting these gifts would be the equivalent of handing me over," Fabian murmured to Barty, speaking through a sharp, bitter smile. "You must reject them all and make it clear why you are doing so. He is trying to buy you."

The King awarded Grimley next, with a certificate granting unlimited access to the royal records room. Grimley's tail swished, but he, too, said nothing. Barty had the distinct feeling that his side-set goat eyes were watching the King and Fabian at the same time.

"We need some kind of counter-offer then?" Barty whispered to Fabian. "Some way to persuade him to just let us go home without all this stuff?"

"A counteroffer, or a threat. If we can think of something convincing in front of this audience," Fabian said, nodding ever so slightly to the staring crowd, "If we can refuse him on some grounds that make us look noble or self sacrificing, it might work. He won't want to appear a bad King in front of the people for whom he is claiming he will build a new future, and every audience loves a hero of the people."

"For Dr. Buckler..."

James stepped forward unsurely, and the tray for him bore yet another velvet cushion, this time with a ring of braided gold and silver.

"An enchanted ring," the King said, his eyes swirling with colors, his smile oozing benevolent understanding, "which will allow the wearer to be, truly, in the flesh, the kind of man they wish to be."

Barty closed his eyes.

How cruel. In front of all these people, dangling a gift that was both a dream come true and an unmistakable taunt. The King was offering James something that would be impossible in their own world, while also showing the depth of the King's own dangerous understanding.

Barty wished there were some way they could say yes, for James' sake.

He opened his eyes, and saw James standing, rigid, unyielding, not even looking at the ring but instead glaring at the King's face. Clearly James, too, understood what these offerings truly meant. James would not falter, even for his own dream. Barty had no right to either.

Barty firmed his resolve, just as the King turned to face him. "For Dr. Barty."

Yet another silver tray. This one contained an envelope of pristine white paper.

"A cure for plague."

Time slowed to a stop.

Barty stood, unmoving, staring at the envelope. How many hours had he wished and prayed for this? How many people would live, if he accepted? Did he even have the right to say no, as a doctor? Did he have the right to palace the happiness of a single person above the health, the very lives of thousands?

Except...he'd already found a cure.

He'd cured plague, here in the land of changelings. He'd found a wizard, too - at least, the Raven said he knew enough of magic to be able to help with the talismans.

Not only that, but modern medicine improved daily. Maybe someday soon they wouldn't even need magic for a cure.

Barty drew a deep breath, stepped forward and picked up the envelope.

He held it high in the air for everyone to see, ignoring the King's smile of glee.

"We do not accept these gifts," he said loudly.

The room tittered. The King's smile turned into a thing of brittle ice, his eyes rippling to orange. "What?"

Barty bowed deeply. "His majesty is unendingly generous and hospitable," he said, as sincerely polite as he had ever been in his life, "and we are, all of us, grateful for these offerings. But we cannot accept, for I am afraid the King has made an incorrect assumption."

The room fell silent. The King turned to face Barty fully, his face blanching two shades sallower. "You dare," he said softly, "tell me I have made a mistake? You dare refuse my gifts, human?"

"I will not allow even an accidental lie to linger before your majesty," Barty said solemnly. "I am a man of truth and integrity, as every doctor must be, as every humble servant of the people must be."

He bowed to the audience. The murmurings seemed to approve.

"We did not come here to deliver Fabian to you," he said. "Fabian is not ours to give. We only seek the way home, back to our own world. For while your kingdom is full of wonders beyond our experience, we have responsibility to our own people, and must return with full swiftness, to tend the sick, and the dying."

The King's smile twitched at the edges. "You do not think that my gifts would aid you in your duties?" he said, projecting the words to the audience even as he glared daggers at Barty. "Are you not required, as a "servant of your people," to take this unfathomably perfect opportunity?"

"My responsibility extends only to my own capabilities and resources," Barty said, and for the first time, he found himself believing the words, accepting his limitations and the responsibility that went along with them. "The moment I justify causing someone else intentional harm, even if for a greater good, I have failed as both a doctor and a man. I am willing to do the work it takes to cure plague in the ways I know are effective. I will not betray the trust of a friend for a quick solution, especially not for one I have no proof works."

A smattering of applause broke out in the room. The King looked furious. Theli, crestfallen, James, proud.

"That," the King said coldly, "is a pathetic and cowardly excuse. How will you justify the deaths of every plague victim you could have saved simply to shield your friend?"

The crowd fell silent.

Fabian laughed. Every eye, including the King's, snapped to them in shock.

"How can you expect him to understand, Barty?" they

said, sweeping up to stand at his side. "This so-called King has no comprehension of anything you just said. Concepts of loyalty, responsibility and justice mean nothing to him. Even his gifts confess his true selfishness."

They waved a dismissive hand at the row of gleaming silver trays.

"A badge binding a true agent of the people into his own personal service. A key that comes with armed soldiers who will guard the healing waters against any but those whom the King would allow to pass. Thinly masked bribery and threats." Fabian's sneer twisted every word. "I wouldn't be surprised if-"

"But my dear Fabian," the King spoke over Fabian's words, still smiling. "You have not seen the gift I have brought for *you*. I think you will find it quite irresistible."

He snapped his fingers. Another pair of guards dragged something forward: a man, bound hand and foot, which they dumped at Fabian's feet. A man in a green-gray cloak, with armored gauntlets, silvery hair, and a gem-studded tunic. A silver serpent lay knotted around one of his arms.

The Huntsman Jeremiah, and Shilling.

"No!" Barty shouted, leaping for his friend.

The Raven restrained him, grabbing his arms and pulling him back. "Don't!" he hissed in Barty's ear. "There are too many guards!" And indeed, six guards stepped between Barty and Jeremiah, spears held ready.

"But!" Barty desperately looked to Fabian. He expected the necromancer to sneer and fold their arms. He expected them to shake their head and tell the King he was a fool.

But Fabian stood frozen in place, staring down at the captive man before them. Barty could hear their breathing - hard and tight. A bead of sweat trickled down their pale face.

Barty didn't understand why they hesitated.

"You see?" The King said, stepping closer to Fabian, circling the necromancer and the man on the floor like a hunting dog who had cornered a fox. "I do understand, child. I know how you crave vengeance upon the scoundrel who ripped you from your previous life. I remember my promise of that day, long, long ago. This..."

He held up a bare knife - Barty recognized it as one of Fabian's.

"...is who you truly are."

Jeremiah looked up at the necromancer. His hands had been bound, and the King of course hadn't bothered with a gag. Understanding and fear were all too clear in his silver eyes.

Fabian, hand shaking, accepted the knife from the King.

"NO!" Barty shouted. "Please, Fabian!"

Fabian knelt across from Jeremiah. They gripped his hair and pulled his head back.

The Huntsman, breathing deeply, swallowing hard did not struggle. The great, jagged scar across his throat was visible to all.

Fabian stared at it for a long, long moment - traced the full length of it with the tip of their blade.

"Can you speak?" they said at last, their voice tight as a coiled spring.

Jeremiah shook his head as best he could with his hair still in their grip.

Fabian took their knife, and with a single slice, cut the bonds at his hands.

"Who," they asked him, with such ringing clarity the words echoed across the stone hall, their hand still gripping his hair tightly, "hired you to assassinate me?"

They returned the blade to his throat, but did not damage the skin.

Jeremiah hesitated. Shilling, his translator, was unconscious.

"Answer them," Barty urged. He pulled free of the Raven, hurried around the stunned guards, and knelt at Fabian's side. "I'll translate."

Jeremiah nodded, and slowly began to spell, Barty reading out each word one by one. 'The Church, the mage's guild, and the royal heir to the throne of England-"

"So you want more vengeance upon them?" scoffed the King, "I'll grant that to you as well. The streets will run with blood-"

"...made a deal with the King, and he sent me to do their bidding."

The silence that fell seemed too great for the hall to contain. Every eye focused on the King, who had gone as white as the walls, except for his ever-shifting eyes.

Grimley was the first to break the silence. "Tisk, tisk. You sent an assassin against your own intended bride, your Majesty?"

The King forced a smile back onto his face. "She was not my bride at the time."

"Wait," James spoke over him, stunned and angry. "The plague that we stopped, the one that targeted Fabian - that came from you as well, didn't it? I saw your ring among the papers developing it-"

Jeremiah nudged Barty. *'Help him.'*

Barty immediately started untying Shilling. At least the snake was breathing.

"You don't understand," the King said, still smiling. "They claimed I had not kept my word. Even I must keep my word, when a deal is made-"

"And what of the deal you made with me?" Fabian demanded, standing, "all those years ago, when you promised me my vengeance." Their words were loud enough for the whole room to hear, but their crimson eyes remained fixed on the King, their smile a terrible, terrible mirror to his, full of a hunger Barty could barely stand to look at. "You, in the same breath, promised me protection. Is this how you protect someone? By arranging their assassination, and the deaths of their children?" They laughed, and angry mutterings broke out in the audience. "It seems I am indeed still owed vengeance, Majesty."

They twirled their knife, the blade as sharp as their smile.

"Vengeance against you!"

The King's robes blazed with blinding light. Multiple people shouted in pain, and Barty threw up his hands, trying to shield his eyes.

Someone grabbed him, dragged him backwards. Someone pressed a blade to his throat. "How about a different deal, then, if you don't like my initial offer," the King hissed, digging the steel in deeper until Barty gasped and stood on tiptoe to avoid it. Blood trickled down his neck.

"First," the King said, loudly, "drop the knife."

Barty's eyes were still dazzled from the light, but he heard Fabian's weapon clatter to the ground.

"Now," the King said, a smile returning to his voice, "if you don't want me to split your friend at the seams, you will all leave. You may even take the key and use my personal door. I am sure Lucius can show you the way."

Barty's vision was clearing. He could see James, pale and panicked. "Let him go!" he demanded, voice hoarse.

"Ah, ah, ah," the King dug the knife in deeper, and Barty whimpered. "I give the orders here, Doctor."

"How can you do this!" Theli demanded. Her mane was bristling, teeth bared. "You promised us the protection of hospitality! Faerie itself will not forgive you!"

"I would have kept my word," the King said smoothly. "But now you'll leave with none of it. I will give you a count of ten to go. Lucius! Guards! Take our guests away."

The white crocodile and the guards hesitated, looking at the audience. Barty could understand why; the rising tide of angry voices was beginning to echo off the stone walls. "The King himself broke a deal? No one can break a deal in Faerie. No king has ever broken a deal. And the rules of hospitality have been sullied-" Accusations passed from mouth to mouth, growing louder.

Iris folded her arms, looking cooly offended. Fabian bowed their head, breathing hard. And Grimley...

Grimley, at the back, Grimley, boney faced, impassive,

eternally smiling...

Grimley turned his head, every so slightly, as if watching something.

"I am the King!" the King shouted at the audience, his robes blazing brightly again until the assembled cried out in pain. "Faerie belongs to me! I make the rules, and if I choose to break them then-hrk!"

He suddenly let go of Barty. Barty gasped and leapt blindly, and James caught him. Barty turned just in time to see the Raven - the Raven, still masked, his eyes hidden behind tinted lenses - had grabbed all the King's necklaces from behind and pulled them tight, cutting off his words and air.

Even as he did, though, the King gave a choked laugh, and began to pull away with inhuman strength. "You cannot kill me," he said, his strained voice rising to a roar, necklaces of silver and gold snapping, scattering stones across the platform. "Do you know how many lives I have stored in these rings? Do you know how much power I have gathered-"

Fabian was on him in a moment. They plunged a blade into his chest, right over his heart, and even though Barty looked away, feeling sick, he'd still seen it was a blade like no other, made of near-invisible pale light.

The King bellowed.

"I am interested to know," Fabian purred, snapping the blade off at its entry point, "just how many lives you do, in fact, have saved up." They dropped what seemed to be a handle onto the floor. It bounced once with a noise like glass, then vanished in a flash of soft light.

"Moonlight," James breathed.

The King shrieked, blood pouring down his white robes. "What have you done!?"

He fell to the floor.

Fabian knelt before the King, smiling as blood spread on the pale marble. "I have pierced you with a blade of moonlight, Majesty," they said. They reached out, removing his crown, tossing it away from him onto the stones. "And indeed, your lives have healed you. You healed right over the hole where it penetrated, sealing it inside your body."

The King retched, coughing. More blood splattered down onto the stones.

"Did I pierce a lung?" Fabian wondered aloud. "Did I impale your heart? Who can say? But it is only a crescent moon now, Majesty. Imagine the pain once the moon is full. Or, hmm, should I even call you 'majesty' any more? I don't believe you are fit to rule."

"He most certainly is not!" Theli's father answered from the crowd, full of outraged indignation. "Sending assassins and plagues against the Queen! Failing to keep his deals! Breaking the rules of hospitality right in front of us all by threatening his own guests! That is no King of Faerie!"

Grimley, behind them all, started clapping.

Iris, a hungry smile on her face, joined in.

The Jailer at the back of the room joined as well, and soon his gloved hands were muffled by the applause from the whole room, everyone jeering and booing as the King coughed more.

"You cannot, you caNNOT," the King screeched. His entire form flickered - faces, skin colors, hair length, showing briefly before disappearing like a snuffled candle flame. "You cannot do this to me! I am the King! I am-" his words distorted into a deep roar. "I AM THE KING OF FAERIE!"

The rest of his necklaces shattered. His skin lost all semblance of humanity, bursting out in green scales. His robes ripped as wings sprouted from his back, and his hands grew great, black claws. "I AM THE KING," he bellowed again, through an enormous red mouth, jagged with sharp teeth. "I WILL KILL YOU ALL-AUGH!"

He had turned into a dragon. Or at least - he had tried to. Something was wrong with his hands.

"His rings," Barty breathed. "They're cutting into him-."

And indeed, though the King tried to limp forward on all fours, he collapsed immediately, more blood dirtying the stones.

"YOU..." he howled, twisting his long neck around to glare at Barty with swirling eyes full of hatred. Even scaled like this, he still flickered, as if this, too, were not his proper form. "THIS IS YOUR FAULT! YOU CHANGED HER! I'LL KILL YOU-" He lunged for Barty, propelling himself with his coils like a giant, deformed snake.

James Buckler shoved Barty to the side, drawing a sword that blazed like sunlight. With a single, clean slash, he sliced through the charging beast's face.

"AUGH!" The beast's howl shook the entire dining hall. Blood splattered. Claws screamed against stone. The dragon tried to recoil but could not stop his momentum. He bowled into James and Barty both. Barty was thrown to the side, but James had been directly in front of the beast-

"James!" Barty screamed as his friend disappear under the massive bulk of scaled flesh, sun-blade swinging.

Barty skidded. He scrabbled against the blood-slick platform. He fell to the cold stone floor, cracking his head.

All went black.

CHAPTER 27: CONSEQUENCE

He couldn't move. Blackness encompassed him. A massive weight smothered him, his face pressed between stone and scales.

Someone far away cried, "Can anyone see him?"

He tried to call out, but could not. There was simply no air in his lungs.

"The sword! It's there, glowing!"

"Quick, shift the coils! You there - you're strong. Come help!"

Darkness and pressure turned to light and freedom. James Buckler opened his eyes.

A huge creature with a hooded face towered over him, hoisting the dragon's bulk away from his body. The hooded one peered down at James, made a rumbling noise, and dumped the scaly coils off to the side.

"Thank you. Good job." Fabian gave the creature's muscular arm a pat and knelt next to James, their red eyes scanning him up and down. "Still alive then, Doctor? No need for my services?"

James carefully wiggled his fingers, his toes. No pain, no tingling. He took a breath, braced himself, and turned his head back upright.

Crunch. Ow. In his medical opinion, neck bones weren't supposed to do that.

He grimaced at the necromancer. "No need for your services," he said, pushing himself up. No shakiness, no pain. He felt for his own pulse. No heartbeat, either. "But, I think... not so alive."

"Hm. Fascinating." Fabian watched him, relief quickly hidden behind professional interest. "Do you think that is because my original spellwork still has a hold on you, or did the effects of the Living Waters simply wear off by the time you were crushed?"

"I would wager the latter," James said. He tried his arms and legs, found nothing broken. "I was already feeling a bit strange at dinner, and I'm not sure I breathed at all during the battle." He snapped his head up, suddenly remembering. "Barty!"

"He yet breathes," Fabian reassured him, a smile tugging at the corner of their mouth. "Bumped his head, but I'm sure he'll be awake within a few minutes. Before you run to his side, however, don't forget your badge of honor..."

"My what?" James said, already half crouched to slide off the dias.

Someone tapped him on the shoulder. He stood, looking up at...whatever the great creature was who had lifted the beast off him. The creature rumbled, and offered him something long and shining.

The sword of sunlight, now stained with dragon's blood.

James hesitated, said, "Ah, thank you," and took the

sword back. He wiped it on his borrowed trousers, and slid it back into the sheath. He wasn't sure if it was his imagination, but the light that composed the blade seemed a good deal redder than it had been when he'd first gotten it.

He glanced at the dragon. "Dead?"

Fabian squinted at it too. "No. In shock, perhaps." They grinned at James, and a steak knife appeared in their hand as if by magic. "Shall we fix that?"

"Absolutely not," James said sharply. "You can't just kill an unconscious man."

"He's not a man at the moment," Fabian said, twisting the dagger longingly in their slender fingers.

The dragon coughed, groaned, and shifted back down to person size with a wet smearing noise. His humanoid form lay still at the center of a massive dragon-sized pool of blood. He did not wake, but continued to breathe with an unfortunate gurgling sound, his face flickering to a different shape and color every few moments, his clothes stuck on crimson-stained white.

Fabian stared at the fallen king with immense dislike. "He won't last long anyway," they said.

James frowned. "We should bind him, and also find some way to dig the shard out."

"Dig it out?" Fabian repeated, as if the words were disgusting in their mouth. "Do you know how difficult it was to make any kind of lasting injury upon this oil-slicked weasel of a king?"

James shook his head. "It doesn't matter. Now he is helpless, and hurt. He needs healing and a fair trial." Even though Barty was still unconscious somewhere, James could hear echoes of the young man's voice in his demand for justice.

Fabian shook their head. "This is Faerie," they said. "There is no court system. There are no trials. What then, Dr. Buckler? Would you drag him to the human world and try him as a mage?" They gave James a brittle smile. "I'm sure he'd love that. So many new minds to bribe with promises of their wildest dreams coming true."

James gave a heavy sigh. "Let's just tie him up for now," he said, glancing around, wondering if there was any rope in the decor they could use to bind the unconscious ruler. "I need to see to Barty."

"Good idea." Fabian knelt by the ex-King and used their knife to slash off the long sleeves of his robe, then cut these into ribbons and bound the King's wrists, knees and ankles.

James left them to it and went to the edge of the platform, carefully avoiding the puddles of blood and hopping down to the floor.

A silver fox ran up to him immediately, weaving its way through the legs of the crowd. It all but danced on the spot with anxiety. "You are the other doctor, right? Barty's mentor?"

James, touched, said, "I am. Can you take me to him?"

"Please come," the fox whined. "He is asleep and will not wake up. We did not know how to help him."

Cold fear settled in James' chest. "Lead the way," he said, and followed the fox through the crowd.

The crowd itself was trying to process what had happened. The hall flowed with voices of speculation and ripples of astonishment, shock, and anger. James heard the word 'dealbreaker' more than once.

"Was anyone else hurt?" James asked the fox, squeezing past two rocky creatures deep in grinding conversation.

"My back aches something terrible!" The fox said, pausing to look up at James with sad silver eyes. "And the Raven hasn't said a word, he just sits by Barty's side. We don't know if he's injured."

"I'll look you both over after I tend to Barty," James told the fox. He could see them now, a neatly-dressed young man hunched over a dark, motionless figure on the ground. The Raven - James supposed he must have pulled Barty's unconscious form out of the way of the milling crowd. Now the young doctor lay still, his caretaker brushing the curls back from his face.

James, moving closer, studied the face of the other man with professional interest. He noted eyes ringed with dark exhaustion and lined with suffering. He saw pale skin patched with black, though it seemed faded, as if it had been healing for some time. He saw worry embedded deep in those green eyes, and one pale hand on Barty's forehead.

James looked back to the fox. "Is there anyone I can send to my room to get my medical supplies?"

"I can go!" The fox shifted into a silver hound. "I will follow your scent to your room."

"Thank you," James said.

He knelt at Barty's side, peeling back one eyelid, then taking his pulse. He did not look at the Raven when he said, "You are the son of the doctor from Whiston?"

The Raven stirred, surprised. "I - yes. How did you know?"

James glanced up at him, then down again. "You have your mother's eyes, your father's jawline. Also, your mask." He indicated the beaked leather mask in The Raven's other hand. "Dr. Rivers was a specialist in plague, and yet there was no mask in his house, only an empty space on his shelves."

The Raven fell quiet.

James pressed an ear to Barty's chest. The boy breathed well, at least, and his pulse beneath James' fingers was steady.

The Raven broke his silence. "You were in my home?"

"We took some of your father's supplies to treat the people of the town," James said, unapologetic. "They were dying, and they had no doctor to help them." He checked Barty's head next, threading his fingers through the brown curls and gently pressing along the skull for any signs of fracture. "There was a drawing of you as a child with your family. It was not difficult to make the connection." He found a sizable lump on the back of Barty's head, and though it was a little bloody, there seemed to be no damage to the bone.

The Raven looked away. "I am sorry," he said, soft and hesitant. "If I... If I had been in my right mind-"

"Too late now," James said bluntly. "We did what we could for them, before we got sucked into this whirlwind of an ordeal. If the curse really is broken, as Barty suggested," James pointed to the Raven's chest, "the citizens of Whiston stand a chance of survival."

The Raven bowed his head. "I am glad to hear it. And... Barty...?"

James managed a fractionally-less-grim smile. "I don't find anything serious here, at least in terms of the condition of his skull. He definitely has a concussion, however, and will need several days of close observation, as well as plenty of rest."

The Raven's eyes snapped back to Barty's face. "Blessed luck," he whispered. "I feared-" he shook his head, closed his eyes, opened them again, looking to James this time. "I know the signs. I will be on the lookout." He hesitated, then asked politely, "Is it safe to wake him?" deferring to James' authority.

James patted Barty's chest. "I think a nice pitcher of water would accomplish that just fine, if you want to do the honors. If that doesn't work, my bag has smelling salts. "

The Raven's green eyes shone. "I," he said, "humbly volunteer."

James met those shining eyes. "I hope you understand," he said, very seriously, "that this young man is very precious to quite a few people."

The Raven smiled, not shying away from James's gaze in the slightest. "If I may be so bold," he said, "I have known Barty only a few hours, but I would, without question, consider myself to be among those people."

He stood and went to the tables for a pitcher of water. James remained sitting at Barty's side, looking out at the crowd. The guards were attempting to usher the guests back to their rooms, but many attendants refused to leave.

Probably wanting a say in who would take charge since the King was out of commission, James thought sourly. At least some folks had things other than ambition on their minds.

Theli's parents were all but drowning her in a massive hug, and the strange hooded creature that had freed James was back at the tables, helping himself to more steak. Poor fellow, James thought. It probably took a lot of food to keep that massive bulk going.

The Raven made his way back to James and Barty, neatly weaving around the chattering groups, pitcher in hand. A silver hound trotted behind him, James' doctor bag held carefully between its sharp teeth.

James accepted the bag with thanks, and nodded to the Raven, giving him permission to pour the water.

The Raven, pressing his lips together in focus, held the pitcher close to Barty's face and allowed a tiny trickle of water to run out onto the young doctor's forehead.

James sighed, reached over, and tipped the pitcher in the Raven's hands so that half its contents gushed onto Barty's face.

Barty immediately opened his eyes, gasping and coughing. "W-what! What!" He sat up, the Raven jerking the pitcher away just in time to avoid a collision. "What happened? Ouch-"

Barty winced, swaying and putting a hand to the back of his head. "Is J- oh you're here, James! Er, I mean, Doctor." Barty flushed, looking around to see if anyone had heard his slip. "I'm glad you're alright, sir. And you, sir!" He beamed at the Raven. "You both were amazing! I'd have been dead twice over if not for you!"

The Raven's pale cheeks flushed a shade pinker, and he set the pitcher aside, wordlessly offering Barty a handkerchief.

James, however, rolled his eyes. "Probably not for long," he told Barty dryly, pulling out bandages and gauze from his bag. "We do know a necromancer after all."

"Oh!" Barty looked startled, then thoughtful, accepting the handkerchief and mopping his wet face. "That's true."

"What about me!" Shilling demanded. "I was very helpful just now!"

"Yes, you were!" Barty agreed, reaching out to rub behind the hound's ears. "And where is your master? Is Jeremiah alright?"

The dog rumbled, leaning happily into the rubs. "Yes, he is fine! He only sent me to check on you. Oh! I had better go back and tell him you are alive!" He bounded off immediately, causing gasps and scoldings from more than one of the guests when he darted between their legs.

James shook his head at the excitable animal. "How are you feeling, Barty?"

Barty grimaced. "My head definitely aches like I cracked it on stone."

"Which you did," James said, gesturing with a finger for him to turn around.

Still seated on the floor, Barty obliged, scooting so his back was to James and he was facing the Raven. "But other than that, I'd say I'm fine." He held still while James spread a poultice on the bump, layered gauze over it, then wrapped bandages around his head to keep it in place. James watched Barty's eyes - how they traveled from the guests, to the Jailer, to the platform where the fight had taken place. He could practically see the questions forming in the young doctor's chest - but he also observed that Barty's gaze was clear and steady.

"What happens next?" Barty burst out. "Is everyone else alright? Will we be able to go home soon?"

The Raven, too, seemed interested in answers, his eyes flicking from Barty to James and back again. James wondered just what had happened between the fellow and Barty to inspire such loyalty, though knowing Barty, it wasn't hard to guess.

"I don't know what happens next," he said frankly, tying off the bandage with care. "I hope we'll be able to go soon, if what the King said was true and there is a door within the castle that can be opened. As for being hurt, everyone seems to have escaped unscathed, except for the King, and I doubt he'll be going anywhere anytime soon."

As if on cue, a yelp echoed through the hall. There was a great clatter, a noise of a scuffle, someone shouted, "grab him, don't let him get away!" and then a pure white rabbit with color-changing eyes went streaking down the hall and out the door, leaving a trail of crimson on the pale stone as it ran.

James and the Raven both jumped to their feet, but the beast was gone almost within a blink.

James was sure that if his heart were properly beating, it would have given a sinking sensation now. How much harm would the ex-king cause, bloody, afraid and humiliated?

He settled back to the ground, and growled, "I hate this place."

A silver hound tore after the rabbit, baying at the top of its lungs. Jeremiah the Huntsman was not far behind, drawing his sword.

The Raven hesitated for a moment, a green light flickering into his eyes. He looked at James. "I know I just said I would stay with Barty, but I wonder if perhaps it would be more helpful to ensure-"

"Just go," James said with a sigh, "and good luck to you."

The Raven gave a nod, and then he was up and running, following after rabbit, hound and Huntsman with surprising speed.

Barty watched them go, brow furrowed in worry. "I hope they'll all be alright."

"I've no doubt they will," James said. He gave Barty a serious look. "But I don't want you chasing after them, Doctor. You've had more than enough excitement, and most likely have sustained enough head trauma to cause notable illness."

"I'm already feeling better, sir," Barty said, though meekly.

"I'll believe it if you go a week without vomiting or headaches," James said, making it clear that a week's work of observation was not optional.

Barty sighed, but nodded. "May I at least go thank

Fabian?" he asked. "They saved us all, you know."

James sighed. "I know."

He pushed himself off the floor and offered a hand to help Barty as well. Barty took it gratefully, and once James had pulled him up and was satisfied he was not going to fall right back down again, he led the young man back to the platform.

Fabian was there, along with Grimley, Iris, and a dozen guards. At present it seemed the necromancer had been attempting to determine who was next in the chain of command, but judging by Fabian's irritated gesticulations, nobody knew much of anything.

"Absolute nonsense," Fabian said, tossing their hair and sweeping over to James and Barty. "This is why a government should never be ruled by a single person. Always have multiple levels of authority, boys, if ever you attain a position of leadership. If all the threads are held in one hand and it disappears, everything simply falls apart. Apparently, he didn't even have a real captain of the guard." Fabian snorted.

"Does that mean the monarchy is going to fall?" Barty asked, clearly worried that they had overthrown the entire government by accident.

"It means there will probably be a civil war, or something else horrible, while everyone tries to be next to claim the throne." Fabian shook their head. "Look."

There were already several eyes on the crown lying on the dias not ten feet from their little group. Some humans in fancy robes were inching closer and trying to pretend they weren't. Theli's father, in particular, seemed to be urging his daughter to go pick it up. Theli shook her head repeatedly, but her eyes lingered on the pale circlet.

"Oh, for the love of-" James handed Barty to Fabian, then hurried over and picked up the crown, glaring at all the hungry eyes.

He returned to his companions, still glowering, feeling the pressure of a dozen gazes sharpening on his back. Barty stared at him with wide eyes. "Are YOU going to become king of the Changelings, James?"

James snorted. "Absolutely not. I already have a profession, thank you very much." He thrust the crown at Fabian. "Here."

Barty gasped. Fabian stared at the crown, then looked back at James, at Barty, then at the crown again. They drew themselves up and turned away, running their hands through their hair as if they were smoothing down the feathers of their mask. "I already decided," they said, a strange tension in their voice, "that I don't want to rule. I explicitly told both of you, multiple times, I am not interested in a throne."

"You yourself said the person who does this job should have knowledge of policy, history and so on," James said, unwavering. "You said someone should be able to delegate, which you know how to do. You know this land, Fabian. You have your pet specialists in economics and so on-"

Fabian closed their eyes with a pained grimace, as if every word James spoke was another nail in their coffin.

"Plus, I don't think the King was lying when he said your power was tied to this world. I've seen the trees budding as we passed, Fabian. You don't owe the King anything, but your presence in Faerie means all the harm wrought by him will begin to heal. Don't you think you owe these people at least an attempt? At least a little time, for recovery and stability?"

"And what of me?" Fabian asked in a whisper, eyes still closed. "Am I not owed a chance to live my life as I like, James Buckler? After all I have lost - I simply want to live in peace with the man I lo...with the man I choose, and-"

"So bring him here!" James gestured to the great hall, with its massive table, extravagant decorations and gaggle of servants now cleaning up the mess. "You'll have everything you could want or need! Your children will be protected by castle walls, and if you tire of rule, you can simply train one of them to take your place. If they have half your ambition, Fabian, I'm sure they'd spring at the chance."

Fabian opened their eyes, staring at him, a smile

twisting across their thin lips. "You truly are," they said, "a heartless bully, Doctor."

James pushed the crown into their hands. "And don't ever forget it."

This time Fabian accepted the circlet. They turned it in their leather-gloved fingers, admiring the shine of the metal and stones. Then, with care, they set the ring of metal upon their silky black hair.

The effect was immediate. The stone of the castle faded from white to gray in a ripple spreading out from Fabian's feet. The trees, visible through the great glass windows, swayed as if in a great wind, creaking and groaning. The servants in white gasped and stumbled, their uniforms becoming garments of black and silver, colors of all sorts bleeding into their skin, scales and bark. Even the sky itself changed, the twilight deepening into blackest midnight in less time than it took to draw a breath.

Fabian looked around at the stunned crowd, a sardonic smile on their pale face. "So begins the reign of the Necromancer King of Faerie." They chuckled, pulled their robes straight, spread their arms, addressing their audience. "Well, my Changeling subjects...it has been a long time." They stood tall, the red stones in their now-spiked, ominously black and silver crown glittering to match their eyes. "I trust you will all be patient, and accommodating, as we work together to better our futures."

For a moment, only silence greeted their words.

Then Grimley chuckled. He began a slow clap, nodding his horned head with approval, and called, "Long live the King!"

Barty, absolutely speechless, started to applaud too.

"Long live the King!" The nervous crocodile, now a creature of dark scales and red accents, joined in much more eagerly. "Long live King Fabian!"

It was like watching a magic spell unfold. First one, then two, then a dozen members of the assembled faerie races started applauding as well. "Long live the King!" they called. "Long live King Fabian!"

Theli and her family joined in. Even the eager humans who had been eyeing the crown moments before, and the creatures of stone and water, and the rest of the guards. Even the Jailer, so full of steak he'd sat right down on the floor, resting his horns on the table to recover, added his voice, bellowing wordless approval so loudly his cloth mask fluttered.

Fabian faced them all, spread their arms, and bowed, basking in the cheering as if it were sunlight.

Barty, still clapping, leaned over to whisper in James' ear. "I can't believe we put the most hated tyrant England has ever known back on a throne."

"At least it's not England's throne," James whispered back, applauding with the rest.

***

They eventually dispersed the crowd from the dining hall, with implied-promises from Fabian about 'meeting to discuss the future' in the upcoming days. Most guests declined to stay in the castle at all, preferring to leave immediately and tell their communities about the regime change.

Fabian was all for it, using whatever mysterious powers the King's crown gave them to set each guest off on the shortest path to their destination. James preferred to monitor his patient rather than participate in farewells, so he stayed out of the way, keeping an eye on Barty and watching Fabian's back in case any of the guests decided that the sequence of Kingship shouldn't have ended where it did.

Nobody seemed to feel that way, though. James supposed that the land coming back to life made Fabian's claim over the position fairly obvious.

Barty, under James' observation, sat quietly, letting others handle the excitement and allowing James to check his condition every hour or so. He seemed subdued, though James couldn't quite tell if it was from his injuries or simply exhaustion.

James assumed he himself would have felt exhausted too, if he weren't so solidly returned to being dead. There were perks to the condition, he supposed. He kept Barty's water glass full and insisted he eat a bit of the remains of the feast. Barty meekly did as he was told, slowly but surely making his way through a plate of bread, fruit and steak. James was pleased to see that Barty's appetite, at least, had not been damaged by his fall.

They ate in shared silence, watching the crowds slowly filter away. It was remarkable to see Fabian step into their new role, their confidence shining brighter than any stone in their crown with every order given, every pledge received, every ally soothed with promises of tomorrow.

The necromancer was probably going to be absolutely insufferable after this. James almost didn't mind.

It was well past midnight by the time everyone had gone. Grimley decided to stay in the castle, but immediately disappeared into the records room with instructions not to be disturbed. James wrote up a new list of anatomical terms for Iris to study, which she was doing with great focus back in her own room. Theli's family insisted on taking her home, and she'd agreed only on condition of returning to the castle first thing the next day to help form the government.

Once every guest had departed, Fabian invited James and Barty to join them in one of the bigger guest suites.

"Why a guest suite?" James asked, helping Barty stand. The boy was steady enough on his feet that James dared hope that there would be no lingering effects from his injury. "Aren't the royal chambers yours, now?"

Fabian gave a thin smile of dislike, said "I refuse to sleep anywhere near the King's bedroom," and promptly assigned it to the Jailer, telling him he could sleep on the biggest bed in the castle for as long as he liked. The Jailer, all too happy to oblige, immediately set off down the halls.

***

Barty, James and Fabian sat near the fireplace in the guest suite. The Jailer's cacophonic snores were but a distant rumble, an almost-cozy backdrop to the crackle of the flames. James and Barty had settled on a couch, and Fabian had claimed a huge, plush chair in front of the fire. The necromancer held a steaming cup of drinking chocolate in their hands, and had ordered beef broth for James, and tea for Barty. They all sat in silence for a time, holding their warm drinks, simply processing the events of the day. James still believed he'd made the right call handing that crown to Fabian, but part of him worried.

"What will you do?" Barty said at last, looking much better than he had all evening. The healing powers of chamomile tea, James thought with wry amusement. The young doctor sat in his shirtsleeves, his curls wild around the bandages, looking at Fabian intently. "Will you live in faerie, Fabian?"

His words were only encouraging, but James could see the sadness in those brown eyes. Apparently Barty's soft spot for the necromancer persisted, even now.

"Well..." Fabian sipped their chocolate, gazing into the flames. James was reminded very strongly of when he'd first met them, almost two years ago now. "I don't hold by 'forevers,' but I certainly will be spending a lot of time here getting everything sorted out." They cast Barty a sideways look. "I hope you'll be comfortable spending a good amount of time here as well, Dr. Wayman."

Barty blinked. "What - me? Why?"

"I need people I can trust," Fabian sipped their drink again, watching Barty carefully. "In addition, there is no public healthcare system at all, in the land of Changelings, and no medical school, either." They turned their crimson gaze on James. "I think you both could be quite useful, if you can bear to leave England for a time."

Barty looked delighted, but James did not answer right away. "I do have," he said slowly, "steady work, and patients who depend on me, in London still." He shook his head. "Either way, I would have to discuss it with Jessica first. I can make no promises."

"Ah," Fabian's eyes glittered, reflecting the firelight. "Speaking of things to discuss with your wife..." They dug in a pocket of their new royal tunic, and pulled out something that glittered. This they tossed at James. "Add that to your discussions, Doctor."

James caught it, and held it up to the light.

It was a familiar ring of woven silver and gold.

James' breath caught in his chest. It was the very ring the King had offered him.

"And this, Barty," Fabian produced the envelope the King had tempted Barty with, handing it to the young doctor, "might be useful, if you decide to accept a position as royal physician."

James closed his hand around the ring, glad Fabian had distracted Barty so that he would have a moment to get his emotions under control. He wanted to dance, to sing! Part of him wished to put the ring on right now to see if it worked, but part of him also wanted it to be an experience he shared with his wife.

He placed the ring in his pocket for the time being, took a steadying breath, and watched Barty open the letter.

Barty unfolded the bit of paper and scanned it, a frown creasing his brow. "There's only a first and last name written here," he said, and then "wait- James?" He sat up, staring at the paper. "James! Rivers was the last name of the doctor from Whiston, wasn't it?" He looked up at James, his eyes shining.

James, eyebrows raised, nodded.

Barty stood up, pacing back and forth with the strength of his passion. "Then this must be the Raven's name! I can give him his memories back! And that means-" He stopped, a hand going briefly to his mouth. When he spoke next, his words trembled with excitement. "I wonder - does this mean his missing memories hold his father's cure for plague? My goodness." He sank back into his chair, pressing the letter to his chest. He took a deep breath, and let it out. "I almost can't believe it. So long we've looked for a true cure, and all along, it was within our own borders. I guess...I guess this means his father really did get the spell to work, before he died."

"Make sure you warn him, before you tell him," Fabian said softly. "Let him understand that getting his name back will bring with it knowledge of all he is, and was." They looked into the flames. "The truth can be a heavy burden."

Barty nodded. "I hadn't thought of that," he said. "Thank you." He folded the paper and tucked it into his vest, then perched anxiously on the couch once more. "He and Jeremiah have been gone all evening."

"Who knows how many shapes and lives that monster had stored away," Fabian said, shaking their head. "It may take them quite some time to catch up."

Barty nodded gravely, picking up his teacup, staring into the depths of the brown liquid with worried eyes. "I hope they're alright," he said in a small voice. "I know they are strong and capable, but..." he shivered. "The king doesn't fight fair."

"Former king," Fabian corrected, wearing their new title in their smile. They didn't seem at all worried. "Re-capturing him will doubtless be a challenge... but I think, as a team, they can rise to the occasion."

James sipped his broth, the ring heavy in his pocket. He could barely spare a thought for the hunt - his mind was so full of Jessica, and possibilities for the future.

"Tomorrow, Fabian," he asked, "can we take a trip back to the Living Waters? I would like to acquire a large supply of them, if possible."

Fabian smiled, and licked chocolate from their lower lip. "I have no doubt we can manage that. Feel free to raid the kitchen for as many jars as you can find."

James stood, feeling strangely breathless. "I think I'll do that now."

"Do you want any help, James?" Barty offered, setting aside his teacup.

James shook his head. "No, you stay here and sleep, Wayman. And…" he cast a sharp look at Fabian. "See to it that he doesn't get up to anything excitable. He needs rest and recovery only."

Fabian fluttered their eyelashes innocently. "You can, of course, count on me to keep his best interests at heart, Doctor."

James scowled at them.

Fabian pointedly ignored his glare. "Come, Dr. Wayman," they said, offering Barty their arm. "You can sleep in the room beyond. I will be here, simply a call away if you need any assistance."

Barty hesitated, looking from James to Fabian, but at last he gave a nod, accepting Fabian's arm and pulling himself up. "Thank you, um, Majesty." He gave a small smile. "I'll sleep better, knowing you're here."

James, satisfied there would be no mischief, left the room, closing the door behind him.

He paused a moment, listening to the two sets of steps shuffle to one of the free bedrooms.

He walked a few paces down the hall. Then, once he was sure no one was watching or listening, he performed a little hop-skip-jump dance, an enormous smile on his face.

Ring. Waters of life. Barty safe. A way home. His waiting wife.

It had been a hellish journey to get this far, but by heaven, it was almost over.

He really couldn't wait to see Jessica.

CHAPTER 28: ONE MORE HUNT

Jeremiah followed Shilling through the night-shrouded forest.

The rain had lessened some since the first outburst, but it continued to fall, pattering down over leaf and branch, soaking the hunters to the skin and quenching the parched earth until every tree stood in a thick layer of mud.

It was quite a marvel, how much the trees had changed in the few short hours since the king had fallen. Leaves of all shapes burst forth in response to the rain, cloaking earth that had lain exposed for centuries in a shroud of vibrant green. Living vines twined over the skeletons of dead ones. Mosses, ferns and lichens woke from their slumbers, soaking in the moisture. True, there was no wildlife yet, but Jeremiah had no doubt that would come in time. Already he saw small lights winking here and there; the tiny folk of the wilds realizing what was happening and uncurling from deep hibernation.

The lack of other creatures did, however, make tracking the fallen king all the easier for the large silver wolf ahead of Jeremiah.

The steady rain might have proved their task impossible if not for Shilling's nose. He'd had a little trouble at first, for whatever power the king had left still allowed him to change his shape enough to keep ahead of their hunting party. Rabbit paw prints in the mud became squirrel tracks up a tree became the flight of a dove through the air. Always, however, blood marked his trail. Always Shilling pursued him, ears pricked and tail wagging, paying no heed to the mud that splattered up his legs and belly. He had no need to change his own form; his wolf's nose more than enough to keep him on the scent. "This way, this way," he kept whining back to Jeremiah. "We are so close."

'I am surprised you are this eager,' Jeremiah commented at one point, pulling his hood down further over his face. He had to go more slowly, both for his own sake and that of their companion tailing not far behind. 'I thought the king terrified you.'

"Oh, he did!" the wolf snickered. "But now he wears no crown. And I, I..." he panted, the thrill of the hunt shining in his eyes. Even Jeremiah's heart grew bolder, sharing that eagerness with his friend. "I owe him, yes, I do. I owe him, for daring to harm my master, for his lies and treachery. He cannot hurt me now. A debt must be paid."

He lifted his nose and howled, sending goosebumps down Jeremiah's arms.

"Let us go," Shilling cried, bounding ahead again. "Let us go!"

Onward they went, down a hillside, across a river roiling with mud and silt, deeper into the burgeoning forest. Always they drew closer to the flagging once-king, his hot blood pungent in the wet night. Always their silent companion followed, his gaze flashing green every now and then in the shadows.

Finally, the wounded king could run no more. They found him collapsed against a fallen tree, coughing, bedraggled, once more in human form; this time that of a fair young man with blue eyes and ivory skin, his golden curls pressed close from the rain.

Shilling stalked up to him, growling, hackles up and fangs exposed.

The king, however, only had eyes for Jeremiah. "Please," he begged, looking up at Jeremiah. "Please, have mercy. Let me go and I will never harm you or your friend again."

"He lies," the wolf growled, snapping at the air. "I can smell it! He holds hatred in his heart."

But Jeremiah held up a hand, and Shilling calmed, still willing to translate.

'Will you swear?' Jeremiah signed. 'Will you swear on your life, your power and your name that you will not attempt to harm myself or any of my companions that you have seen this day?'

The king hesitated. He looked from the wolf to Jeremiah, his blue eyes calculating.

Then he smiled.

"I would have sworn not to harm you or your pet," he said, and paused to cough blood. The front of his ragged tunic turned redder, and not from what came from his mouth. "But you ask too much, Huntsman. Is it not my right to take revenge upon those who cast me out? Is it not my right to seek my throne, and to drag into the abyss those who stole it from me?"

Jeremiah raised an eyebrow. 'Is it not my right to slay you where you lie, for what you did to me? Or did you already forgotten that you not only broke your promise of my freedom, but also bared my throat to one you thought to be my enemy?'

"I am the King of Faerie!" the king said, his eyes blazing. "All life here belongs to me!"

'You were never my king,' Jeremiah signed clearly. 'I am a free man from the human lands. We had a business relationship, *and you threw that away of your own accord.'* He drew his sword. *'So...you refuse to make a deal.'*

"I do," spat the king. "But, ah, human man from the human lands..." he wheezed, spreading his empty hands. "Where is your honor? I am unarmed, injured, defenseless before you. I cannot even stand on my own." He coughed further, clutching at his chest, blood oozing between his fingers. When he spoke next, it was with a gurgling rasp. "How can you, in any sense of justice, strike down a man who hasn't even a fighting chance? What will your precious friend Bartholomew Wayman think, when he knows what you have done?"

Jeremiah looked down at the king with disgust. The Changeling had thrown him, Jeremiah, to his greatest foe with his hands tied. Would his hypocrisy and lies never end?

But, it did not matter.

'I do not kill men,' Jeremiah signed. *'I kill monsters. And although you are the worst monster I have ever known....'* He kept his sword bare, but slid back a pace.

"What Barty doesn't know," said a voice from behind the king. "Won't hurt him." The Raven stepped out from the forest shadows, his eyes gleaming green. In his hand was the iron stake that had held him in the dungeon for all these weeks. "And I am going to make *sure* that stays true."

The king's eyes locked onto the spike, an expression of horror contorting his face. He instantly shifted into a great golden wildcat and launched himself at the Raven with a yowl of fury.

Shilling leapt half a second after the king did, bellowing with rage. Silver hit gold in mid air as the two shape-shifters fought, fur flying, blood splattering, rain pouring down and mud churning beneath them. The king tried to break free from Shilling, swiping at the Raven with terrible claws, but every time he did, the wolf's teeth sank into his flank, his tail, his leg. Finally, when the wildcat turned with a howl of rage, slashing at the wolf's face with both paws, the Raven leapt. He threw himself on the wildcat's back, reaching around and plunged the iron stake upward and back, sinking it up to the flat end in the creature's throat.

The wildcat's eyes snapped wide open, and his snarl trailed off into silence. He fell on his side, mud splattering over his golden fur. Even as the Raven picked himself up, the corpse flickered through half a dozen more shapes, wolf, donkey, dove, until it at last lay still, a twisted, deformed thing still bearing a wildcat's claws, a dragon's scales, and a dozen more features that did not match at all.

The Raven wiped blood off his face. "No form to call his own," he panted, a wide grin of victory on his handsome face. "He must have traded it away ages ago."

Shilling limped back to Jeremiah, and the Huntsman crouched immediately, taking the wolf's poor torn face in his hands.

"It hurts," the wolf whimpered, blinking through the rain and blood. "And everything is a blur - am I going blind, Master?" His voice rose in panic. "I'll never be able to see you talk again!"

Jeremiah examined the gashes covering Shilling's face and body. They were terrible to behold, but...he looked up at the Raven, who stood over the corpse, gazing upon it with dark satisfaction. Jeremiah snapped his fingers, getting the man's attention, and gestured at the wolf. *'Didn't you say you were a healer, once?'*

The Raven couldn't read his words, but the message was clear. "I beg your pardon, of course."

He came over, knelt in the mud at the wolf's side and examined the scratches closely. "Deep," he confirmed, squinting through the darkness and rain, "But though your eyelids are damaged, the eyes beneath appear to be whole, though scratched on the surface."

Shilling whined out a noise of worry. "Can you fix me?"

The Raven closed his eyes for a long moment. "I once knew the spell. I think..." He took a deep breath, mouthed something silently, and opened his eyes, expression determined. "I can," he said, "but most of my experience is with healing people, not animals. Are you able to shift into the form of a person? Every little bit helps, when it comes to magic."

Shilling turned his snout to Jeremiah, nudging his face with a wet nose. "Master...?"

Jeremiah sighed, but nodded, holding up a finger.

"I believe that means, 'just this once,' the Raven said.

So Shilling shifted, there on the ground. He became a near-perfect copy of Jeremiah, from his hair in ropes to the gems on his tunic, though his skin, clothing and even his armor remained silver. His smile, however, was one only Shilling could wear. "Alright," he said, looking blindly up at the sky. "Now what?'

The Raven dipped his finger in the blood running down Shilling's face. "Now I will ask your friend here to hold his cloak over us so the rain does not ruin the spell," he said. "This will take a few moments, and then, with any luck, all will be well."

Jeremiah obliged, removing his cloak and holding it over the Raven and Shilling. The Raven wrote with speed and care, then closed his eyes and, his voice slow and distant like one remembering from a great length of time, said a few lines in the language of magic. There was a flash of light, a tingle of energy in the air, and Shilling yelped. "Ouch!"

Jeremiah watched, stunned and impressed, as the brutal scratches on his friend's face closed themselves.

"Ow, ow, ow!" Shilling continued to complain. "It hurts, ow! Oh!" Shilling blinked, shook his head, and looked about in wonder. "Actually, that feels much better."

He staggered up, then immediately fell back down again. "Whoops! I am not used to having two legs-"

He cast a guilty look up at Jeremiah, cleared his throat, and shifted back to his silver fox form. "How do I look?"

Jeremiah crouched down once more, caught the little fox in his cloak, and scooped him up into his arms. 'You have *terrible bald patches where your fur was. It looks like you lost a battle with a housecat.'*

"You mean I WON the battle."

Jeremiah smiled, shook his head, and looked to the Raven. He gave a slight bow, and signed, with Shilling's sullen translation, *'Thank you. It seems I misjudged you, on my initial hunt. You are no monster.'*

The Raven tipped his soggy hat. "Time will tell, I suppose." He hesitated, then said, "I am hoping my new companions will help me find the truth of that matter."

Jeremiah snorted. *'Knowing Dr. Barty, he won't let you rest until he has done so.'*

The Raven grinned at that. "I certainly hope you are right."

Together they turned towards the castle, and began the long trek back to light, safety and comfort.

EPILOGUE: 1728, FAERIE

Fabian the Necromancer King of Faerie stood at their desk and considered their options.

A dozen daggers of varying lengths, hues, curves and ornamentation lay on the surface before them. Several had been gifts from the boroughs: Fabian considered it a good sign that they had been King for barely two days and were already receiving tribute from the communal leaders of their subjects. Perhaps it had been Theli's idea - she had certainly been spreading the word that Fabian intended a new, better era for all. Amusing, how she had communicated Fabian's fondness for sharp objects along with her endorsement.

Each dagger reflected the personality of the community it represented: a dagger with a mahogany handle and worked all over in gold and copper filigree from the Decided; a dagger whose rivets resembled the phases of the moon from the Lycans; a dagger of pure silver engraved with the image of a deer on one side, a fox on the other, from the Shifters. The Mageborn had sent a dagger as well, but Fabian was still not sure why it glowed when unsheathed. They thought it best to leave it locked in the treasury until they found a mage trustworthy enough to ask. Perhaps Jack's new friend would consent to take a look, what was her name…

A knock on Fabian's door interrupted their thoughts. They twitched a finger, and their current corpse assistant, one of the skeletons from their army dressed in a faerie-style coat and trousers, clacked its way over to the door and opened it. The bony butler didn't do a very good job, the door jammed on its dry toes and Fabian, sighing, had to compel it to step aside to open the door fully. Flesh servants, although not as trustworthy, were so much less work

"I beg your pardon," a familiar anxious voice said to the skeleton. "Are your toes okay? Oh dear."

"Come in, Barty," Fabian said, unable to repress the smile curving across their face. "And don't worry. As you should know from your studies, skeletons have no nervous system, and cannot feel pain."

"Well, a nervous system has nothing to do with *emotional* pain," Barty said, giving the skeleton one last apologetic look before slipping past. "Perhaps it doesn't *like* having its toes jammed."

"I can assure you," Fabian said dryly, "it does not have an opinion on the state of its toes."

"Well, that's good to know." Barty gave the skeleton a hesitant pat on the shoulder. "Keep up the good work, sir."

Fabian shook their head. "I assume you are here to deliver some kind of message, Doctor? Or do you just want a little…" they drew out the pause, smiling just enough to make Barty uncomfortable, "…social time?"

It worked, even after all these days. Barty flushed and immediately averted his eyes, clearing his throat. "I mean - um, of course I am always pleased to spend time with you, sir, er-m…" He huffed out a flustered sigh. "What am I even supposed to call you now? Majesty? Highness?"

"I'd enjoy any of those," Fabian purred, "but you can also use my name."

"Fine then." Barty fixed his hat, re-settling the new, feather-accented topper over his brown curls. "Fabian. If, indeed, you do want to share a cup of tea or something similar, I, of course, would be more than happy to. As you well know."

He gave Fabian a look of such injured pride that the necromancer couldn't help but chuckle. "And?"

"...And, um, yes. Er. Between Grimley and 'Ven's magical efforts, the door is open. We can go back any time we like. I thought I should let you know." He hesitated a moment, tapping his fingertips together. "I thought - well. Usually you like to be involved in anything like this, yet you've been in your room all morning, so..." Tap, tap, tap went those leather-gloved fingers. The young doctor had found more than enough clothing to substitute for his lost professional attire, and now, in addition to the new hat, wore beautifully crafted boots, a snow-white shirt, new gloves and a truly glorious overcoat complete with shoulder-cape and many deep pockets. Regardless of his finery, though, he seemed not to have gained an inch of confidence, wearing his worry more brightly than any shade of color. "I thought I'd check on you."

Fabian gave him a long look. Despite everything - the danger, the betrayal, the hardship and the difficult truths faced, Barty still worried about Fabian as a person. It did not matter to him that Fabian was now Necromancer King of Faerie, Barty still cared.

Or perhaps *especially* because they were now Necromancer King of Faerie. That boy was sharper than anyone gave him credit for, including himself.

Fabian shook their head, giving him a dry smile. "I wonder if life will ever toughen up that soft heart of yours."

Barty straightened, a fond little smile on his face that Fabian had never seen before. "Well. 'Ven says my soft heart is the best thing about me."

'Ven: Barty's new nickname for the Raven. Fabian was not surprised that Barty had been drawn to the young man with a past full of twisted darkness. What surprised them, however, was how the Raven had blossomed under Barty's attention and friendship. Any lingering shadows from his captivity and loss were chased away when Barty entered the room, and he was all smiles. One almost didn't notice the lingering black patches on his skin.

"Still 'Ven I see…" Fabian said, watching Barty closely. "He did not choose to learn his name?"

Barty's smile vanished, and he nodded solemnly. "He… well. He says he's been getting flashes, memories slipping through. Things that are not easy for him to see." He sighed. "He jumps at shadows sometimes, Fabian. And he watches things move that only he can see. I heard him talking to someone once, but when I went into the room, he was alone. I worry about him." Barty shook his head. "He told me he isn't ready yet. I will respect his wishes of course, and I will try and help him feel more confident so eventually he will be able to face it all. In the meantime, I'll tuck his name away somewhere safe where he won't stumble across it by accident, and let him just *live* for a while." His worried brown eyes watched Fabian's face, looking for any trace of judgment. "Do you think it is the right thing to do?"

"You're asking the Necromancer King if being gentle with your murderous friend is a good choice?" Fabian gave a dramatically wicked laugh.

"No," Barty said, unflinching. "I am asking my wise friend Fabian, who has lived many lives and loved many people, if I am doing the right thing to help a man who has been very hurt and is still recovering."

Laugher evaporating, Fabian sighed, and shook their head. Barty never failed to surprise them, somehow. "I myself have never lived without my name," they said. "I do not know how much of a man's mind it hides. While the impulse is to say, yes, shield your friend from his own past so he can live in comfort, I think his symptoms are warning enough." They gave Barty a serious look. "He will need to face it eventually. His mind is already strained, if these flashes are anything to judge by, and you know what he is capable of if things go wrong. Not to mention, Doctor, he may need his name if you are to draw the cure for plague from his memory."

"I know." Barty looked troubled. "I'll watch over him, Fabian. I'll see to it that he doesn't get hurt, and neither will anyone else. I'm sure he'll see reason about the cure..." Barty hesitated. "I was hoping that, perhaps, he might come with me on my rounds, once I start working for you. Maybe being in an environment of healing others would help him heal himself as well, and see how much his knowledge is needed..."

Fabian gave a sharp grin at that. "If he truly is as skilled in magical healing as he claims, I don't see how I could possibly say no."

Barty beamed at them. "Thank you, Fabian! I mean, I figured you would be fine with it, but I still thought I should ask."

"Is that where you are going now? Back to Whiston to gather his things?" Fabian returned to their desk, Barty trailing after them like an eager duckling.

"Well, we are making a few stops actually! We will go to Whiston first, as you say, both to get his things and to collect all the notes about the plague spell so they can be hidden away and never cast again. Then we are going to check Plymouth just to be sure there isn't actually any plague there, and then we are going back to London to tell Director Peete we are working in Faerie instead of London. James will talk to Jessica about all that has happened, and I can tell Avram where I'm going and meet Rabbi Szalwiski and learn more about my heritage and my name and-" Barty paused in his growing list of commitments, blinking at the row of shining blades. "Um. Are you, um, bringing all of these?" He gave them a worried look. "Aren't you coming with us, to fetch Ruphys?"

"I am indeed going to Ruphys to give him an update on

the situation," Fabian said, carefully straightening one of the knives so it was in line with the others. "He will decide if he wants to follow me into another rulership position or not. The last one ended rather painfully for him." They gestured to the blades. "Choose one for me, I am having trouble making up my mind."

Barty's gaze was on Fabian, though, not the blades. "Are you seriously worried he won't want to come with you?"

Fabian gave Barty a grin so cutting it belonged on the table with the rest of the daggers. "I," they said, "do not worry. I simply plan for possibilities."

"Fabian," Barty said, putting a hand on their arm, "please believe me when I say this: Ruphys refusing to follow you, after how long he waited for you and how deeply he loves you, is not a possibility."

Fabian let out a soft snort, looking down at the knives that were somehow not nearly as sharp as Barty's sweetness. "Keep talking that way, Dr. Wayman, and I'll try to collect you right along with him."

They expected Barty to jerk his hand away as if he'd touched a hot poker, but he only patted their arm. "I think," he said bracingly, "that all of these are very impressive, Fabian, but I am fond of the classics."

He picked up their own, original knife from among the lot, not even glancing at the fancy gifts from other boroughs. He offered it to Fabian, his gaze steady.

Fabian accepted the blade from his hand, admiring the shine a moment before slipping it into their robes. They wondered what it must be like for Barty, going through life loving people so honestly, communicating with such subtle clarity, and yet never speaking the words aloud. All heart, that boy, but a heart neatly contained by respect and politeness. "I suppose we can allow for a sentimental choice, this time."

"As a treat," Barty agreed, his smile as warm as sunlight. "Are you ready to go?"

Fabian glanced in their mirror. The crown on their head

shone in the lamplight, glittering silver and red against their waves of silky black hair.

They took a deep breath and let it out. "I'm ready."

***

They stepped out of the floor length mirror in the bedroom they'd shared with Ruphys for a year. Night lay over the house like a burial shroud. The room was cold, dark and empty, the bed unmade, empty bottles crowding Ruphy's bedside table.

For a moment all Fabain could do was stand in silence, staring at the wine-stained glass. Why was the room so cold? Had something happened? Their connection to the spies in the house had been severed when they entered Faerie, they did not actually know anything about Ruphys' time without them.

They closed their eyes, forcing calm, forcing themselves to listen.

Soft noises from the next room. Ruphy's voice, not at all slurred, speaking gently to Willamina with the subtle Irish croon that only ever emerged when he thought he was truly alone. "Such a good wee lass, look at you. Did you have a long day? Did you get through it like a proper hero? Atta girl. Atta girl."

Fabian stepped over to the door, staring at the warm yellow light shining through the crack. Mina made fussy baby noises, but Fabian could tell it was the kind of fussing that meant sleep was not far away.

Ruphys continued, his voice even softer. "Now don't worry, little lady. It's alright. You can sleep safe, and maybe tomorrow, we can check the post, aye? Find a letter to read together? Wouldn't that be lovely? Here you go, safe in your crib…safe and warm. I'm right here, Mina, I'm right here."

Fabian closed their eyes. They pushed down the sudden pang of affection, deep inside, that pierced them worse than knives or fear or illness.

441

They knocked on the door.

Stillness and silence instantly fell on the other side.

Fabian swallowed hard, and then said in barely more than a whisper, "It's me."

They heard Ruphys' intake of breath. Two steps, sharp and quick, and the door jerked open, flooding their bedroom with warmth and light.

Fabian squinted, momentarily dazzled. Ruphys stood still, no more than a dark silhouette against the brightness. Still, they managed a crooked smile, spreading their arms in a gesture somewhere between grand and apologetic. "A lot has happened," they said through the tightness in their throat. "I... may have accidentally toppled another monarchy-"

Ruphys let out a noise somewhere between a laugh and a sob, and before Fabian could get out so much as a word of explanation, he caught them, enfolding them in his arms, burying his face in their neck. His warmth and smell and love washed over them in cascades of familiarity.

Fabian's breath caught in their throat. They wrapped their arms around him, leaning their face against his cheek, stroking his hair. "All this," they said, trying a raspy chuckle and not succeeding very well. "One might wonder if you had any faith in my return at all, Ruphys."

Ruphys said nothing, his warm tears on their neck louder than any word could ever be, the shaking of his shoulders and pounding of his heart against theirs sending waves through the necromancer's very soul. It occurred to Fabian, in fact, he might have been justified in worrying that they might not come back. After all, he'd lost them once before.

So Fabian set aside their countless practiced, polished, perfect explanations. They left their questions unasked and their tales untold, instead speaking back to Ruphys in the same language he was using, with a lingering kiss on the cheek, one hand rubbing up and down his back while the other wrapped around his shoulders, and simply being there, allowing him as many moments as he needed to ease the ache in his heart.

Eventually he drew back, his tearstained face so full of honest affection it hurt to look at. He cupped their cheek with a rough palm and kissed their mouth, his lips sweeter than honey-drenched wine, and twice as warming. "I missed you," he whispered.

There weren't enough blinks in the world to keep the tears from slipping down Fabian's face. They laughed, breathless and rough, and raised both hands, sliding their fingers into his hair, resting their forehead against his. "I missed you, too," they admitted, the words raw, unrehearsed. "Ah, Ruphys. So much has happened."

"Is everything alright?" he whispered, nestling his cheek against theirs, sinking down to the floor, pulling them with him. "Do we have time?"

They let him drag them down, ending up in his lap, warm, safe, contained. They removed their crown, tossed it on the stones in front of the fireplace, and took a shuddering breath, all but melting in his warmth. "All is well," they said, resting against his chest. "We have time, Ruphys. We have all the time in the world, at least for tonight. Tomorrow may be a busy day, if...if you want it to be."

"Tell me," he whispered back. "Tell me everything. And tell me I get to come with you, this time. Please..."

Fabian closed their eyes, letting out the breath they'd been holding for what felt like weeks.

"Would you mind terribly," they asked, tracing his scruffy jaw with their fingers, "raising our child in a castle?"

He kissed their fingertips, and they opened their eyes to meet his soft gaze. "So long as you are there," he said, "I think I can manage."

Fabian gave him a watery smile. "What if," they said, "the castle is in fairyland?"

He chuckled, and they could feel it through his chest. "I would not expect anything less from you." He nuzzled their forehead, placed another kiss in their hair where their crown had laid, and rested his back against the bricks of the fireplace,

443

relaxing completely. "Tell me everything."

"Everything?" Fabian said, now tracing their finger down his neck and along his collar bones. "Everything starts a long time ago, Ruphys."

He smiled at them, the firelight making his face all shades of rose and gold. "As you yourself said, we have all the time in the world, tonight." His eyes flickered briefly to the cradle across from them, and Fabian turned to look as well, but Mina slept soundly, her small breaths content and unafraid. Ruphys looked back at Fabian. "I'll help you start, if you like. Once upon a time…"

Fabian chuckled, and rested their head on his chest again. "Once upon a time, in a fallen kingdom far, far away," they whispered, "there was a little girl named Fiia, who was very, very hungry…"

They spoke long into the night. The fire died down to coals, though the room stayed warm. Ruphys did not interrupt, only held them close, stroking their hair or back when their voice faltered, listening to their entire tale. When at last they finished, he shook his head. "I can't believe it…"

"You can't believe that those foolish doctors went through all that trouble and ended up handing the evil necromancer a crown?" Fabian snickered. It was dark now, the coals giving off only the faintest glow to illuminate the edges of Ruphy's skin.

"No," Ruphys said, and Fabian could feel the smile in his voice. "I can't believe you tried to turn them down. Would you really have been content, living in this house with me and Mina? Would that have been enough for you?"

Fabian sighed, thinking about it. "I don't know," they admitted at last. "It is not easy for me to settle, Ruphys, as you know. Even when I try to lie low I tend to get drawn into dreadfully exciting matters, but…"

They went silent for a moment, listening to his heart beat, watching Mina breathe in her cradle.

"It is just," they said, more softly, "that in moments like

this, I am satisfied."

Ruphys held them a little more tightly. "Well, then," he said, "we will have to be sure we have many moments like this, once we are all moved into your castle in fairyland."

Fabian closed their eyes, letting out a deep, happy sigh. "Yes," they said, "please."

ACKNOWLEDGEMENTS

To Mom, Uncle Seth, and Kris (Dr. Doot). Thank you all for helping me with the edits, and being patient with my prickly nature. I know I can be overly protective over my dear story, but I tried very hard to listen to all you had to tell me, and I hope this is a better book for it.

To Arma and Jazz for supporting me as I worked through this whole process, thank you for always being understanding when I was late to game time because I 'just need to finish revising this chapter!'

To Lance, who let me craft an alternate-universe version of his son. I hope he will be very happy here, with his newfound companions and purpose.

And, of course, to you, dear reader, for picking up this book, for reading the last one if you did that, and for taking the time to get this far. It means the world to me; especially those of you who take/took time to leave a review on Amazon. I go and read those whenever I feel down, and they cheer me considerably.

ABOUT THE AUTHOR

Sam Artisan

Sam is a Jewish writer, artist, and cosplayer. When not petting dogs, Sam will be working on a new book about robots in a futuristic fantasy world trying to solve a murder. Keep an eye out for 'In Defense of the Anarchist!'

If you are curious about those cyberpunk shenanigans, check out the Fanaticartisan youtube channel. There's gonna be robots there, baby!

PRAISE FOR "A PLAGUE ON NECROMANCY!"

Mirabai Knight:

"a tightly plotted, swift paced romp full of magic and trickery and a dash of ghoulish glee. More than that, though, its central character embodied everything that I've always found so compelling about plague doctors: Compassion, kindness, courage in the face of calamity, and the desire to make things better even to the smallest degree, despite insufficient tools and scant knowledge. "

Jonas P.

"The main character is so noble and genuine, it's impossible not to love him immediately. As he battles through the challenges of being a plague doctor, and some more, you are truly transported to his side and sometimes even into his head. This book is a must read for any lover of adventure and magic."

Rutsby:

"Highly recommended if you're into: twisty plots, unpredictable yet relatable characters, friendship sprouting in hopeless darkness, self-sacrifice for the greater good, stinky London streets, surrender not being an option... all generously coated in dark magic and a sprinkle of quirky humor. Reader beware! Your assumptions will be tested..."

Dapper:

"Story: fantastic
Characters: irresistibly charming
Fabian: please don't recruit me into your skeleton army for I am hopeless."

Mads G.H:

"Quite frankly, this is the most delightful impulse book purchase I've ever made. The world is close enough to ours to make the differences fascinating, the details are just the right shade of gruesome without being sickening — and the plot. Oh, the PLOT."

Made in the USA
Columbia, SC
22 November 2024

47360864R00254